A FATED QUEST

THE MIRAVELD CHRONICLES

A FATED QUEST

SELINA R. GONZALEZ

Also available from Selina R. Gonzalez:

Fairy Tale Retellings

THE MIRAVELD CHRONICLES
A Thieving Curse (1)
The Dragon Prince's Heart (1.5. Available for free to newsletter subscribers)
A Lonely Dance (2)

ONCE UPON A PRINCE MULTI-AUTHOR SERIES
The Crownless Prince (releases Dec 1, 2023)

Sword & Sorcery

THE MERCENARY AND THE MAGE
Servant, Mercenary, Brother: Dresden Jakobs Vignette Coll. Vol. I (0.5)
Prince of Shadow and Ash (1)
Staff of Nightfall (2)
Servant, Mercenary, Brother: Vignette Collection Vol. II (2.5)
Bells of Winter: A Mercenary and the Mage Story (2.75)

BONUS SHORT STORIES AND MORE FOR NEWSLETTER SUBSCRIBERS:

selinargonzalez.com/newsletter-subscription

Map of
Talland
Kilkreth
Ae
Rethalyon

Miraveld

Highrook Castle
Aedyllan
Lake Marsing
Raylor Estate
Ruins
Tremblay
Eynlae

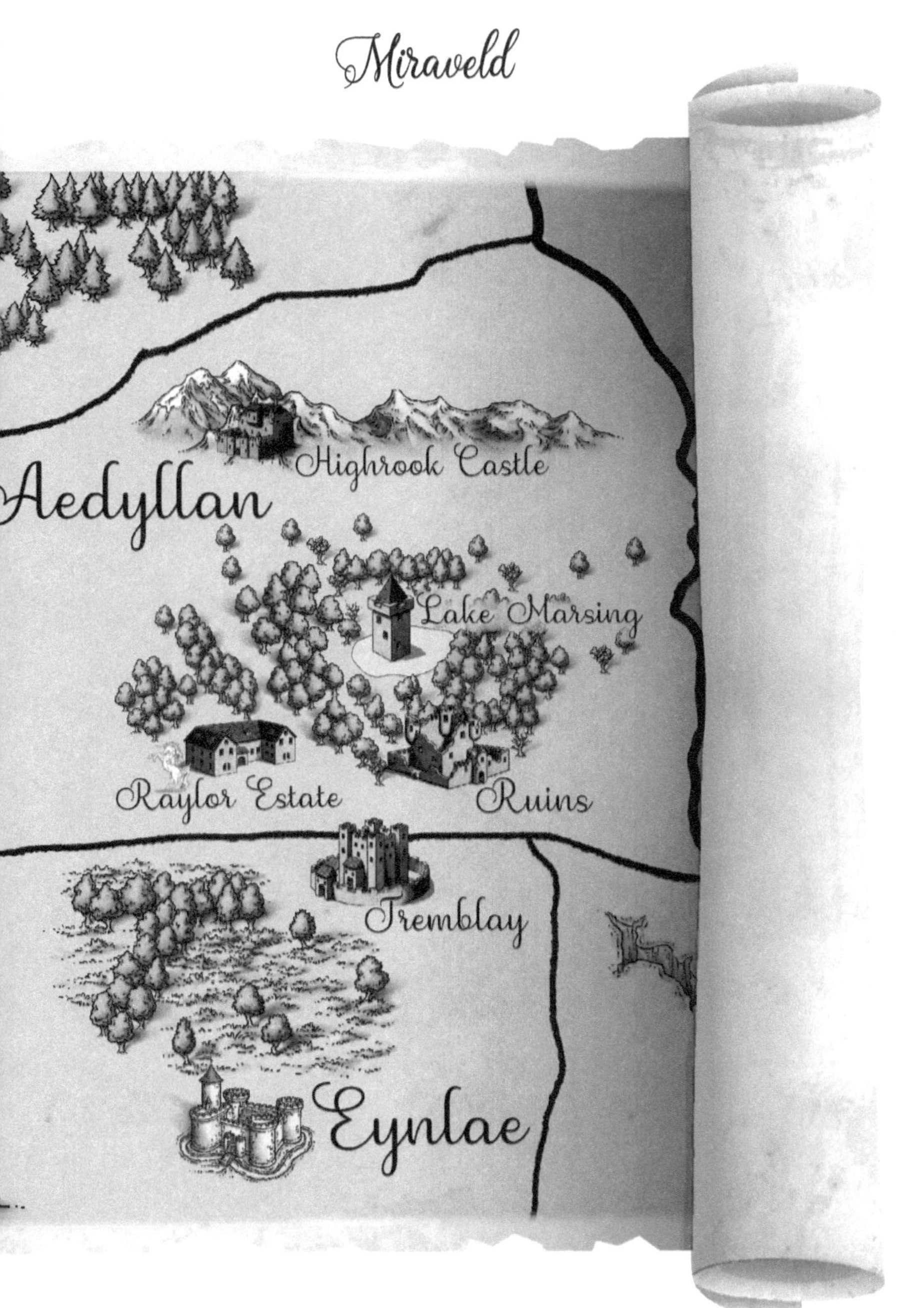

Prologue

othing lasts forever.

Once upon a time, the kingdom of Aedyllan was fractured, ruled by three rival princes. The three principalities vied for absolute power until one of the princes, Mortimer Faine, conquered the others and claimed the title of king. The history books say Mortimer's success was due to his leadership abilities and military prowess.

The fairy tales offer a different story: the legend of the Fae Blessing and Curse of Mortimer Faine.

One day, while he was still a regnant prince in a divided Aedyllan, Mortimer Faine saved a fae lady. In return, she offered the prince a boon. Mortimer wished to unite the kingdom under his rule and for his line to reign over Aedyllan for all time.

The lady warned that forever is not something within even a fae's power to grant, and powerful magic comes at a high price. But Prince Mortimer insisted, so the fae spoke a blessing, a curse, and a peculiar prophecy. The Faine house would reign over Aedyllan until the prophecy was fulfilled, at which time the king's line would be utterly destroyed, and a Faine would never wear the crown again.

She recorded her words on a scroll. Terrified of the curse, Mortimer denied the scroll's existence and shared the conditions of the dire prophecy with only his heir. Then he locked the scroll away.

After Mortimer united Aedyllan and became king, the Faine house prospered for generations. No assassination attempt against them was successful, no plot went undiscovered, no war against them was effective. While rumors spread of the existence of the Blessing and Curse, the Faine kings resolutely guarded the secret terms of the prophecy.

Officially, the royal family declared the story of Mortimer and the fae a myth, but the Aedyllanian royals grew cocky. The Faines believed their position was unassailable, protected by a prophecy with such improbable requirements it could never come true. Secure in their comfortable lives of power and pleasure, the kings were no longer good.

Until one night, the scroll was stolen, and the thief escaped.

For the first time in two hundred years, someone who was not a Faine knew what the fae had prophesied.

1

The halls of the Eynlaean royal castle were as dark as an underground tunnel. Feathery clouds obscured the dim glow of the stars and setting crescent moon. This early in the morning, most of the servants still slept, so none of the wall sconces or candelabras had been lit. Despite this, Prince Gareth carried no candle. A light could draw the attention of the guardsmen.

It wouldn't do if he were caught.

Unfortunately, he couldn't see anything. With every step, he risked misjudging the center of the hallway and crashing into a display of armor or a podium bearing the bust of some long-dead member of the royal family.

Gareth would be in enough trouble later without adding *broke Queen Ilsa's nose off* to the list.

Thankfully the carpet running down the middle of each hallway provided a guide. As for direction and knowing when to turn, he'd long ago memorized every hall, room, and passageway—including the secret ones—to better evade his caretakers as well as Raelyn's.

A pang of loneliness went through him. He'd left his sister in Rethalyon with her new husband a little over a month ago, and her absence was still an ache. If she'd actually died in the mountains as their parents had believed, Gareth feared he would have lost his mind with grief. Knowing she was alive, happy, and loved in Rethalyon brought him some comfort. And she was safe from Tristan, who had been sent to Talland.

He made a face in the dark. Alexander should have been harsher with Tristan, but Gareth wasn't the king and didn't get to make that call. Of course, Gareth had no intention of being a king. His current endeavor would land him in trouble after it was discovered, but it would be impossible if he were the king. His older brother, Frederick, had better not die until he was old and had a son to take the weight of the crown, because Gareth didn't want it. He didn't even want the crown of a prince because it came with expectations that caged him, demanding he be something he wasn't at the expense of all that he wanted, loved, and valued.

His father couldn't care less what Gareth wanted.

That was fine. Gareth had long ago stopped caring about what his father wanted as well.

At last, he made his way down to a servants' entrance and slipped outside. The waning moon tried to shine between a couple of clouds, casting a faint gray light over the leafy trees in the orchard. Pressed against the cold stone of the castle, Gareth cast a wary glance around before darting across the space to the fruit trees. From trunk to trunk, he glided through the orchard, silent as a spirit.

The orchardist's shed rose up out of the shadows ahead of him, a wood building with a thatched roof that was outlined by the first hints of dawn appearing in the pink-tinged sky. The latch raised at his gentle touch without protest, and Gareth slipped inside and guided the door shut behind him.

Inside the shed was dark, which was unexpected. As the building had no windows, a candle wasn't a danger inside. Maybe his conspirator was running late. That couldn't be good.

"Gibson?"

A scrape indicated the strike of flint, and a few sparks preceded a lantern catching. Gareth's momentary relief was doused in icy reality as orange light illuminated Sir Christopher's disapproving face.

"I'm sorry, Your Grace." Next to the knight, Daryl Gibson ducked his head, his shoulders bunching up. The squire was nearly eighteen, a couple of years younger than Gareth, and would be knighted soon. More importantly, he was close enough to Gareth's build and height and with similar enough light brown hair that they could pass for each other at first glance—a switch they'd pulled a few times over the last couple of years, usually for more harmless antics.

Today they'd planned to swap places so Gareth could accompany the hunting party leaving at dawn to slay a gryphon that had been harrying local farms. In the hustle and bustle of their departure in the dim morning light, none of the knights would have given Gareth a second glance. Meanwhile, Gibson would have snoozed in Gareth's bed to fool the servant that would bring him breakfast. No one in the palace or among the knights would have noticed the swap until it was too late to send Gareth back.

"Fortunately for everyone," Sir Christopher said, his scowl becoming more pronounced, "I had a suspicion you and Squire Gibson might be up to your tricks. When he snuck out of the squires' wing, I was waiting. Because he immediately admitted to this scheme, you haven't endangered his approaching tests for knighthood, Your Grace."

Gareth cast an apologetic look at Daryl before crossing his arms and staring back at Sir Christopher. He matched the older knight's scowl—or tried; he doubted he looked half as angry or intimidating. "There wouldn't need to be a scheme if you'd let me join the party."

"I'm not the one preventing it," Sir Christopher said. "But your father the king is right to—"

"He isn't right simply by virtue of being king!" Gareth threw his hands up and narrowly avoided whacking his fingers against the edge of a hoe hanging on the wall. "You *know* I'm capable!"

Sir Christopher shook his head with a sigh. "I'd say save it for your father, Your Grace, but if I may offer some advice—let it go. You are a prince, not a knight, and His Majesty has made up his mind. Your continued obstinacy is not helping you or your relationship with your father."

At that moment, Gareth wasn't certain he cared about salvaging his relationship with his father. He wasn't sure he'd cared since his father had refused to let him keep looking for Raelyn, even though Gareth had been right that she was alive all along. That situation had ended well, arguably better than if Gareth had found Raelyn, but that didn't make his anger with his father any less.

"Can't you let the ruse go through?" Gareth pleaded. "You can claim ignorance. If you didn't catch the deception in time, then it wouldn't be your fault."

"But I do know, Your Grace. Do you think I have so little honor as to willingly lie to my sovereign?" Sir Christopher fixed him with one of those chiding looks that made Gareth feel contrite in a way none of his other instructors ever could. He stepped forward and put a hand firmly on Gareth's shoulder. "Let's go."

After dismissing Gibson—to scrub the floors of the squires' dormitory, not to go on the monster hunting expedition as planned, and Gareth felt horrible about that—Sir Christopher escorted him back into the castle, gripping his shoulder all the way. The servants were up now, bustling about and lighting candles and pointedly not looking at the too-familiar sight of Sir Christopher guiding the middle prince through the hallways. Gareth turned toward his own room, but the knight pulled him in the other direction.

"He won't even be awake yet!" Gareth protested.

"His Majesty is an early riser, but more importantly, I have to leave, so this report has to be made now."

Gareth groaned, and Sir Christopher frowned at him. The grizzled knight was only slightly less frightening now that they were the same height than he had been when Gareth was younger and smaller.

Sir Christopher knocked loudly on the door to the king and queen's suite of rooms and waited. Gareth glared at a gryphon carved into the oak, mocking his failure. After a minute or two that felt like an eternity, the door opened inward. King Weston wore an embroidered crimson robe, and the candle in his hand cast flickering light over a trace of stubble along his jaw.

"Morning, Father," Gareth said, as cheerfully as he could muster.

"Please tell me he didn't try to sneak out and join you," Father said, leaning against the open door.

"He'd planned to switch places with Squire Gibson, but the squire was less successful than the prince at sneaking out." Sir Christopher's tone was apologetic. "The squire's punishment has been set, but I leave the prince's correction in your hands, Your Majesty."

Father nodded tiredly and opened the door further. "Gareth, inside. Sir Christopher, I thank you and dismiss you to your duties."

Sir Christopher bowed and left, but Gareth lingered in the hallway.

"You're probably hungry and you're not even dressed." Gareth rubbed the back of his neck, then pointed his thumb down the hallway. "And I'd hate to wake Mother. I'll just come by later—"

"In. Now." Father didn't wait for him to comply—he grabbed Gareth's wrist and tugged him inside, slamming the door behind him with an ominous bang.

2

As Father turned from the closed door, his face impassive, Gareth lowered his head and backed into the blue-and-gold-themed sitting room. Best to appear contrite and cooperative.

The door to the bedroom was shut, although his mother was unlikely to come to his defense, anyway. If he were fourteen-year-old Nathaniel, she would. And if he were Frederick, he'd get off with a stern lecture. But he wasn't the heir or the baby or either parent's favorite, so there'd be a punishment.

He didn't fear his father, not in the sense of worrying his father would ever harm him, but the limitations on his freedom that often constituted his punishments were torture.

"What were you *thinking*?" Father didn't shout, but for the intensity of his voice, he might as well have.

"That I could do some good."

"You killed a monster *once*. That's no guarantee you could manage it again. And you got hurt last time!" Father crossed his arms, his forefinger tapping against the sleeve of his robe. "I'd hoped your moment of glory and taste of hardship in Rethalyon would quell your rebelliousness and thirst for adventure, but no. It's gone to your head."

Gareth glowered down at his boots, fighting the urge to argue.

"And you drag Squire Gibson into your delusions. His knight-hood testing is in three weeks, Gareth! What if you had escaped and been injured or killed? Not only might your friend have carried guilt, it might have barred him from testing! Do you think of nothing but yourself?"

Gareth thought of his uselessness in the castle, of the gryphon terrorizing innocent people, of how he had failed to protect Raelyn the way he should have and how he wanted to protect others, but the king wouldn't understand any of that. He never listened.

"You are a prince, Gareth, and you're not a child. You need to start acting your age and station."

"And do what, exactly?" He looked up, unable to curb his tongue any longer. "What exactly is a prince meant to do? I can do so much more good and help so many more people out there with a sword in my hand than trapped inside these stupid walls!"

Father's brows drew together, his mouth pinching into a frown. "If I had any doubt that you don't pay *any* attention to your lessons…"

"Yes, lessons." Gareth folded his own arms, matching Father's stance. "Is that what a prince does? Attends lessons until he dies?"

"Those lessons teach you about your responsibility to the kingdom! How to interact with nobles, understand other kingdoms, and how to one day rule if necessary!"

"I'm not going to rule, and I'd be terrible at it. Frederick is in excellent health, as are you, and if Frederick and Angela don't have a son, well, I'll abdicate to Nathaniel."

Father's mouth dropped open. Even Gareth's shoulders hunched as shock registered over his careless words. He'd never spoken that aloud to his parents before—only once to Raelyn, in one of their conversations in a secret room while they were hiding from their tutors. His sister had understood. She always understood, unlike their parents and brothers. Her absence speared through him again, adding to his growing irritation.

At last, the king spoke softly. "You truly view your duty with such cheap regard?"

"What duty?" Gareth's fingers tightened around his upper arm. "The duty to sit in a castle all day, mediating meaningless disputes between petty nobles? Going over mind-numbing figures with the treasurer? Bartering away my future children for trade rights?"

Father reddened. "You're right; you would be terrible at ruling. You still understand *nothing*."

The words cut more than they should have. "Good, then we agree! I'm meant to be a knight! So let me be a knight!"

They stared at each other, Gareth's chest tight and his skin burning.

"Very well." His posture sagging, the king shuffled over to the nearest armchair, which faced away from Gareth toward the empty fireplace. He sank onto the sapphire fabric with an audible sigh. "You get your wish. You can be someone else's problem until next spring."

Gareth blinked, then hurried around the armchair so he could see his father as he struggled to keep his hopes and fears in check. "What does that mean?"

"You want to be a knight so badly?" Father rubbed his forehead. "Fine. Baron Tremblay needs knights at his castle near the Eynlaean-Aedyllanian border. Two knights have recently retired, and their positions need to be filled." He didn't make eye contact as he continued. "I'm sending you to take one of those positions. While you're there, you'll be treated like a knight in every way and will answer to Baron Tremblay and the captain of his guard. You will receive no special privileges as a prince or as the baron's cousin while you reside there."

Gareth tilted his head, torn between excitement, curiosity, and hurt. "You were already considering this."

"You've left me little choice, Gareth!" The king leaned forward in his chair, and he was definitely yelling now. "You nearly cost us peace with Rethalyon twice, a third if we count your assault on Tristan Carbrey after King Alexander named him as an ambassador! You've been insubordinate and caused trouble at every turn since we returned, and you won't listen to a word I say! I don't know what to do with you! So yes, your mother and Frederick and I have already discussed this—"

"Frederick?" Gareth tensed. "You discussed 'what to do with Gareth' with *Fred?*"

"He wanted to arrange a marriage for you. Force you to settle down somewhere out of the way."

"I wonder where he learned to marry family members off against their will." Gareth didn't bother to disguise the vehement disgust in his voice as his hands clenched and unclenched at his sides. "What right does Fred have to—"

"He'll be king one day," Father thundered. "That will make him not only ruler of Eynlae, but head of the royal family. Not that you've ever appreciated what it means to respect your king, as evidenced by your current behavior!"

He took a deep breath, as if trying to control his own temper. "Which is why I decided what you need is to learn some respect. Your mother and I had hoped we wouldn't have to go this far, but perhaps forcing you into a subordinate role will teach you some humility and force you to see reason. You'll have the rest of the summer through the winter to consider your choices and future."

That caught Gareth's concern, his anger at his older brother forgotten. "What happens when I return in the spring?"

Sinking back in the chair, Father turned his head away. "Depending on what you've learned, how you fare as a knight, and your cousin's report of you, perhaps you return to your position as prince and second in line to the throne and start actually playing the role of a prince and courtier. Maybe I'll confine you to the palace under guard for the rest of my life or arrange a marriage for you. Perhaps I'll try Alexander's unconventional method and see how you'd fare as an ambassador. Or…" Father's throat worked, and when he spoke again, his voice was brittle. "Perhaps I'll strike you from the line of succession."

Gareth's breath caught as initial delight gave way to darker fears. "You'd…disown me?" Despite their differences, something hollow opened inside him.

"No!" Father looked back at him, his expression strained. "You're my son, no matter how you test me. Regardless of what you think of me." He laced his fingers and stared down at them. "You'd still be a prince, but with no succession rights, less political power, and less wealth to your name, and your children would not be royalty or legally included in the line of succession. It's unusual, and many would see it as a mark of distrust and disdain. It's only ever been done once before in the history of Eynlae, in the case of…of a bastard."

Which meant that as ridiculous as it would be, some might wonder what that made Gareth. That he reckoned he could deal with, though, because he saw no other downsides. He was tempted to ask why not just do it and be done with it? It would allow him greater freedom to live the life he actually wanted, and it wasn't as if the king would miss their frequent clashing of wills, but some emotion in Father's eyes stopped him. It was like…

Heartbreak.

Gareth had stopped believing his father truly cared a long time ago. If he was honest, he hadn't believed his father possessed a heart ever since he'd learned of Raelyn's arranged marriage. Abandoning the search for Raelyn because she was presumed dead had convinced Gareth the king only cared about his crown and kingdom, not his children.

Maybe he was wrong.

That was an uncomfortable possibility because it would mean Gareth hadn't been fair to his father. So he closed the door on that thought, but he also didn't voice his desire to be promptly removed from the line of succession. For now, he would focus on the fact his so-called punishment was the ability to live out his knighthood dreams for the next several months. The rest could be figured out later.

"When do I leave?"

Father's chest rose and fell with a deep breath. He gave a small shake of his head and looked away again. "Tomorrow, if you're so eager. Even though we haven't had any problems with Aedyllan, Tremblay Barony comprises too much of our border to leave it without a full garrison, so it's best if you depart quickly, anyway."

"I suppose I should prepare, then." Gareth bowed, but his father spoke again.

"Pack lightly. You won't have need of court finery, and you'll be taking no servants."

"It's not unusual for knights to have servants," Gareth protested without thinking. Although he made less use of the palace servants than his brothers and some nobles did, he wasn't accustomed to having *none*, even on hunting excursions. But he could make do; he wasn't so helpless he couldn't function without a servant.

"If you want a manservant," Father said, his voice level, "you can hire one with your earnings from Baron Tremblay. I said you'll be treated as a knight. That means you'll be paid for your services—and you won't get a royal allowance."

Hm. Also an unforeseen wrinkle, but he'd be fed by the Tremblay estate, so he wouldn't have much need to spend. He never used his full allowance, anyway.

Just then, the door to the bedroom clicked, and Mother

stepped out. She was dressed, unlike Father, but her hair still fell loose and unbrushed around her shoulders. Gareth couldn't recall ever seeing her without her hair firmly coifed before.

She folded her hands in front of her and looked over Gareth and Father, the slight shadows under her eyes and the downward cast of her mouth making her look older. "I couldn't hear clearly through the door, but the raised voices and your expressions indicate the Tremblay plan has had to be implemented?"

Father rubbed his hand over one side of his face, an uncharacteristically undignified gesture. "Yes. He leaves tomorrow."

"Tomorrow?" Mother's eyes widened a fraction. "So soon? I…suppose that makes sense. How long did you decide, in the end?"

"Until spring."

"Oh." Mother nodded, her expression pinching. "You'll write, Gareth?"

Gareth resisted the urge to scoff. After years of mostly ignoring him other than to berate him or tell him to stop distracting Raelyn, his mother didn't get to stand there and act sad about him leaving home for a while.

"Of course, Mother." He smiled, hoping it was enough to be reassuring but not so genuine his parents would realize how excited he was and reconsider whether this qualified as a punishment. "But Tremblay Barony is very important to our defense, and I might not have much leisure time."

Father's eyes glanced to the side in what was almost an eyeroll. "Unfortunately, even knights are allowed free time. Although perhaps I should instruct the baron to have his men keep you busy and out of trouble."

Now it was Gareth's turn to fight an eyeroll. He only got in trouble at the palace because he was bored out of his mind with studies, meetings, or socially expected periods of rest and relaxation. Life as a knight would be far too exciting to give him occasion to cause trouble.

3

$\mathcal{G}$areth had to share a pack mule with the other knight being sent to Tremblay, Sir Walter Henty. The dour-faced man had strands of silver running through the black hair he wore tied back in a short tail. Henty's travel bag was smaller than Gareth's, which made Gareth self-conscious. He'd attempted to pack light, and his bulging sack still contained fewer items of clothing and other miscellany than he'd previously brought on mere two-day trips.

The problem was he was going away for far longer than two days, and there were a few things he didn't normally bring on a journey that he couldn't leave behind. He didn't know if Baron Tremblay had a library or what sort of books would be in it, and he couldn't *not* bring any of his favorite books of legends.

The trip to Tremblay Barony proved excruciatingly uneventful, not least because Sir Henty was a man of as few words as his grumpy countenance suggested. Gareth suspected the knight felt like he was on babysitting duty for an obnoxious prince, so he did everything he could to prove otherwise. He took care of his own horse, packs, and small shelter and made certain he remembered to replenish his water canteens. If he finished before his companion, he offered to help—although Sir Henty never accepted. Long days of horseback riding and nights sleeping on the hard ground left him aching and bruised, but he restrained himself from grumbling. If Sir Henty could bear it without complaint, so could he.

When they finally arrived at Tremblay Castle on a bright summer afternoon, Gareth was dirt-covered, sweaty, in need of a shave, and all around decidedly unprincely. He couldn't decide whether it felt humiliating or like freedom.

The castle itself was a testament to its foundation as a protector of the border. It was built on an expansive, grassy hill, doubtless at least partly man-made, giving it added height over the surrounding fields. A wide moat covered in wilting lily pads surrounded the base of the hill, while the imposing, crenelated outer walls topped the motte like a stony crown.

They presented themselves to the guard at the wood bridge over the moat. The knights on duty didn't seem to think anything of "Sir Walter and Sir Gareth, new members of the guard" and waved them in without a second glance. A well-worn path led up to the castle gate in a series of switchbacks.

They introduced themselves again, and the guard stationed at the gate nodded. "Captain Plinworth will want to see you. This way. You can dismount and lead your horses and mule. Our stables are next to the guardhouse."

Gareth blinked in surprise as the man left his post, but a glance up at the walls confirmed at least one other guard was on watch. Not to mention that the idea of anyone who wasn't supposed to be at Tremblay Castle attempting to enter was preposterous. Still, with a border castle as important as Tremblay, it was best to be cautious.

The guard led them through an open courtyard in front of the manor-like castle built of limestone. Gravel crunched beneath their boots; servants and guards called out greetings to each other as they ambled toward their destinations. Somewhere in the distance, chickens clucked, and a horse whinnied. Gareth's horse,

Fury, a massive buckskin destrier, whinnied in response. As they passed a tall wood enclosure covered in tangled ivy, the scent of flowers wafted on the air.

A knight stood in front of a door set into the enclosure, looking stern but bored. What could warrant a guard inside the castle? The height of the fence didn't permit even a glimpse inside. The guard escorting them must have noticed his curiosity, because he slowed down and pointed.

"That's Baron Tremblay's private garden. He keeps his pet firebird there, so it's strictly no entry."

Gareth whipped his head around toward their escort. "Wait, he truly owns a rare magical creature? He refuses to transport it, so I thought he was fabricating the firebird's existence every time he mentioned it at court."

The only thing more impressive would be a unicorn, but in all of Miraveld, only two families owned unicorns. Disappointingly, the Argents were not one of them.

"Court?" The guard raised an eyebrow. "You've been serving at the royal court before now?"

"I…er…"

Father had stated he'd be treated as a normal knight while in Tremblay, but…had no one even *told* the knights who he was? What if someone asked for his surname? Was he meant to lie?

The man chuckled. "Who did you insult to get sent out here?"

"You think it's a punishment?" Technically it was, but that didn't explain why this knight had jumped to that conclusion.

"It's a step down from the royal castle." The guard shrugged. "You tell me."

Sir Henty cleared his throat. Whether that was to draw their attention or because his voice was so disused, Gareth couldn't guess.

"Sir Gareth Argent is here looking for more practical experience."

When the guard went wide-eyed and nearly tripped over his own boots, Gareth sent Sir Henty an annoyed glare.

"I—you—I didn't—I wasn't aware…" He spun around and bowed. "Captain Plinworth said two knights would be coming to join the guard. He didn't say one was…was… Apologies, Your Grace."

"He's not Your Grace here," a deep voice boomed from ahead of them.

The guard whirled to face the newcomer and straightened like a scolded schoolboy. "Captain! They…we were—that is, I was just—"

"Escorting the new arrivals to me, I presume." Captain Plinworth strode over to them, his sword bouncing at his side and his black leather armor creaking softly.

His shoulder-length white hair was half tied back, but he hardly looked old enough for it. He was built like an ox, and his blue eyes were sharp in his weather-worn face. A layer of salt-and-pepper stubble covered his cheeks and jaw.

He crossed his arms as he looked Gareth and Henty up and down, his expression calculating. "Thank you, Sir Robert. You're dismissed. But know that while he's here, the prince is Sir Gareth, and he is not your prince. Only your brother-in-arms." He jerked his head dismissively, and the guard nodded before hurrying away.

Unsure what else to do, Gareth inclined his head in a gesture of respect. "An honor to meet you, Captain Plinworth."

The captain grunted. "I'm told you're to receive no special treatment or recognition. I'd argue that if that truly were the case, we should keep your true identity a secret. Apparently His Majesty worried you might be recognized, and that if you'd lied about your identity, that would cause more problems. Other than right now and when I introduce you to most of the men at supper, you won't hear me acknowledge who you are again."

"Good." Gareth nodded. Being a prince got tiring and made making friends more complicated. The question remained—would the other knights be able to truly treat him like a fellow knight, knowing who he was?

Plinworth leaned forward, his muscular arms still crossed over his chest and his mouth pinched in obvious distaste. "You'll sleep in the same rooms and on the same cots, eat the same food, work the same amount, do the same tasks, and accept the same punishments if you break the rules as every other knight here. Is that clear?"

"As expected," Gareth replied calmly.

"He's not a useless, spoiled child," Henty interjected to Gareth's shock. "Saw to his own needs and helped with camp and food and slept on the ground with nary a complaint."

Plinworth turned his attention to Henty. "That so? I've seen your service history, Sir Walter." He nodded. "If you vouch for the boy, I suppose I can give him a fair chance."

Gareth wanted to protest that with only a few months until his twentieth birthday, he wasn't a boy, but he decided that would probably have the opposite of the desired effect, so he kept his mouth shut.

"Come along." Plinworth turned away, and Gareth and Henty had to hurry to keep up. "We'll get your horses and mule taken care of, show you your new lodgings, and I'll give you a tour. You'll have the rest of today to acclimate and will begin your duties tomorrow."

4

*A*nika stabbed her sword at another gap in the crumbling walls, and an invisible force knocked her blade away. She huffed a strand of red hair out of her face. Hours of testing the perimeter hadn't revealed any weaknesses in her prison. Her own magic had no effect on the warding spell keeping her within the abandoned castle's walls, and no brute strength made an impact. Her stoic captor's magic remained powerful, even with her peculiar extended absence.

"Fae take you, Callista," Anika muttered. She slammed her sword back into its scabbard and scowled at the moss and ivy covering the stone.

She hated not knowing why the witch was holding her prisoner, loathed that there was so little she could do about it, and was ashamed that she'd been captured at all. It grated on her pride that she was more a distressed damsel than the knight she'd worked so hard to become. True, her instructors had trained her to combat swords and claws, not spells. She'd passed her trials with honor, and a lost fight didn't negate her knighthood. That didn't make her feel like any less of a failure.

Anika raised her hand and called up her magic, letting orange light flicker around her fingertips. If she'd trained instead to become the enchantress her father had hoped for, or if her magic were stronger, perhaps her situation wouldn't be so bleak. Her family might not be in danger. Her useless magic extinguished as she clenched her fist.

She turned her back on the wall.

Deep down, part of her was relieved the warding spell was impenetrable. In truth, if she had found an opening, she might not have used it. Her desperation to protect those she loved might have trumped her commitment to her duty to oppose the witch. Did that make her a terrible knight?

The excuse that escape was impossible didn't assuage her guilt. Her inaction meant Callista wouldn't hurt her family, but that didn't stifle the desire to do *something*. Hence the futile prodding at the barrier all morning.

Her mounting irritation demanded an outlet. She stomped through the tall grass in the bailey to the overgrown orchard, where she'd cleared an area to use as a training ring. As she moved through her sword forms and practiced controlled attacks and defensive moves, her mind calmed and her agitation lessened.

The late summer heat forced her to stop sooner than she'd have liked. With no way to bathe and no change of clothes, she didn't want to perspire too much. Hunger gnawed at her, so she made her way inside.

The castle hadn't been occupied in nearly half a century. Vines clung to the outside of the soot-blackened walls, and flowers sprouted from windowsills. At least Callista kept the main hallways free of spiderwebs and detritus, although Anika had had to clean her own room.

She paused before Callista's closed door—the only one in the castle—and reached toward the handle. Her magic could handle a lock. Perhaps on the other side of that door she could find the answers to what the witch wanted with her and what she was planning…

Callista's voice echoed in her memory. *"You may roam the castle grounds and have your sword back, but you will follow three rules. One, follow any command I give without argument. Two, do not interfere with me or anything I do. Three, do not attempt to harm me. If you break any of these rules, after I chain you in your room, I will use your sword against your family."*

Her stomach churned. Breaking in would almost certainly count as interfering.

Anika had never been much of a rule-follower, as her atypical status as a female knight of Aedyllan attested, but these rules she would follow. The consequences of breaking them weren't something she could live with.

A few more steps brought Anika to her own bedroom, which lacked even a curtain in the empty doorframe. Dust floated in the sunlight piercing through the boarded-up window. A bag of food Callista had given her before she left hung from the ceiling to deter rodents. The mess bucket and thin, straw-stuffed mattress on the floor did nothing to make the soot-stained stone feel less like a prison.

She chose a small, wrinkled apple from the sack. Something fresher would be nice. She could set another trap and see if this time she could catch a rabbit instead of a squirrel. That'd fill a few of the interminable hours.

If—no, *when*—she returned home, her best friend Scarlett would be positively appalled to hear the conditions in which Anika had been living. The thought brought a momentary smile to her lips, followed by a pang of loneliness.

What she wouldn't give for a book, some stitching, or someone to talk to.

5

$\mathcal{G}$areth was bored.

Actually, no, he reflected as he watched a lesser gryphon circling in the blue sky. He had passed bored two hours into this rotation. He was about to die from the monotony.

With an exaggerated sigh, he turned from the small hawk-cat gryphon to scan the surrounding wheat fields. Beneath his steel armor and the incessant summer sun, sweat slid down his back. He stood atop a large wood tower about a day's ride from the castle. This farmland ran all along the border with Aedyllan, making the barony a prime target for resource stealing should the Aedyllanians take such a notion into their heads.

Which, of course, they hadn't in well over a hundred years. Judging by the quiet, today would be no different.

As it turned out, the life of the average knight was *not* glamorous or filled with adventure, and this posting was, in fact, a punishment.

In the three weeks he had been at Tremblay Barony, opportunities for heroism had been in such short supply it was like trying to find flowers in the dead of winter. Guard duty at the castle or at any of the nearby watchtowers was about as dull as muddy slush. Patrols were a little better because he got to ride and move more, but they held no danger. No miscreants or monsters appeared. No Aedyllanian enchanters visited, either. Even the animals kept to themselves. A momentary glimpse of a chipmunk had been the highlight of his last patrol.

Tremblay Barony was well populated and had a steady stream of travelers because the Aedyllanian trade route ran through it. Accordingly, the more dangerous creatures had been driven from the area long ago. The worst pests the inhabitants usually had to deal with were raccoons, foxes, and lesser gryphons.

At least the lesser gryphons were entertaining. They grew about as long as a man's forearm, and instead of being part lion and part eagle, they were part cat and part smaller bird of prey, with many combinations. They rarely caused problems, and in fact were useful for keeping mice out of the fields. Some of the bolder ones sometimes approached humans, preening their feathers and rubbing against people's legs to beg for scratches or scraps of food.

Perhaps during his free time he could get out of the castle and attempt to catch a lesser gryphon fledgling. Domesticating a lesser gryphon sounded fun, and it'd be far more interesting to write to Raelyn about. He'd written her once in the last three weeks, explaining where he was and why—and complaining about how awkward it was.

Most of the other knights were nice enough. However, many clearly had mixed feelings on how to behave around the man they'd been ordered to treat as one of their own, but who technically still had a slim possibility of one day being their king. A few of them simply avoided interacting with him to skirt the issue entirely. That stung, but at least they hadn't decided to bully him as a prince with no power.

If he didn't catch a fledgling, his only fodder for letter writing would be the weather, and if he did that, Raelyn would know he wasn't happy—but if he didn't write her, she'd also be suspicious. The sooner he could get enough free time to hunt, the better.

Gareth marched around the perimeter of the watchtower's turret. At a slow pace that allowed him to examine the surrounding fields and distant trees, the small circuit took only a few minutes. The tower wasn't much wider than his bedroom back at the palace. Raelyn probably would have liked it. It wasn't as tall as the southeast tower at home, but he could still see a long way, and it was a peaceful location.

Too peaceful.

No, peace was good. Peace meant no one was getting hurt and no one's livelihood was in danger. Which also meant Gareth felt useless.

The trap door banged open, and a head of dark curly hair poked up. Sir Florian climbed up, squinting at the bright sunlight. His skin had bronzed under the sun in a way that made Gareth's light tan look pale. The main impact of all the extra sunshine Gareth was getting seemed to be nudging his golden-brown hair closer to blond.

"Anything out of the ordinary?" Florian asked as he closed the trap door. "Other than you."

"Ha-ha. Clearly, no. I don't care how irritable you get when you're hungry; if something exciting or concerning happened, I would interrupt your dinner break."

"There had better be a dragon or horde of invading Aedyllanians if you interrupt my meal," Florian said with mock seriousness.

Of the three knights Gareth shared a room with—a harder adjustment than he'd guessed it would be—Florian was Gareth's favorite. He was only a year Gareth's senior and one of the friendliest knights, with a ready sense of humor. He also genuinely didn't care who Gareth was. If Gareth had any friends at Tremblay, he liked to think Florian was one of them.

"Do you think if I interrupted your meal and tossed it to the invading horde, you'd be angry enough to take them all on by yourself?"

Florian guffawed and leaned his elbows on the wall of the tower. "Have you been reading those legends you brought with you again? Is there a tale in there of a knight single-handedly taking out an entire army?"

"No." Gareth adjusted his cuirass. "But it would be an incredible tale, wouldn't it?"

"I think I like the fields quiet, and you're going to end up brokenhearted if you keep filling your head with ideas of knightly heroism." The other knight straightened. "Speaking of quiet watches, you haven't had firebird duty yet, have you?"

Gareth shook his head as he moved to lean against the edge of the tower next to Florian.

"Want to take mine tonight? We can switch. I'm supposed to watch the firebird tonight and have all day tomorrow off, but I can take your duties tomorrow, because, um..." Florian reddened. "It'd work better for me to, uh, have tonight off."

"Mmm, would it?" Gareth snickered. "I take it Juliana and her parents have returned?"

"And there's a wedding in town and she invited me...you know, as her escort. All official-like."

"You are courting, after all."

The knight sighed, a dreamy smile on his face. "Yeah..."

Gareth nudged him as he moved to the other side of the tower. "All right; I agree to switch, as long as you stop your mooning."

"You'll probably fall for a girl someday, and then you'll understand."

That made Gareth snort. He glared out at the golden heads of wheat far below the tower as they swayed under a gentle breeze.

Nothing but wheat stretching on and on until it blended into grassy hills. A landscape as uneventful as his current future prospects.

"Not interested in romance?" Florian asked, obvious curiosity in his voice.

Gareth shrugged and moved to another vantage point with more views of peaceful fields. "If I'm allowed to make my own destiny, I'll travel the world as a knight, offering aid to strangers, slaying monsters, fighting evil-doers, and pursuing justice. Hardly a lifestyle any woman would want to marry into."

Florian's disbelieving chuckle grated on his nerves, and he glared over his shoulder. With an apologetic look, Florian held up his hands. "Just saying, that sounds impractical and idealized."

Maybe he was right, but Gareth still wanted to try.

"And if you aren't allowed to do what you want?"

Gareth returned his attention to the fields to hide the heat covering his face. "I'll probably be married off for political reasons. Spare princes and princesses are little better than high-pedigree studs and broodmares, apparently."

Wolf's teeth, how had Raelyn faced her arranged marriage so calmly? Knowing her marriage held the ability to protect her people from war doubtless helped, but Gareth could never decide if her acceptance of her fate was weakness or a bravery that awed him.

Only the soft rustle of wheat in the distance and the quiet whistle of the breeze around the tower sounded in response to his bitter admission. He squared his shoulders and searched the landscape for anything out of the ordinary, but a part of him was holding his breath, waiting to see what Florian thought of his words.

Just when he couldn't bear the silence any longer, Florian spoke. "I'll admit that's an advantage of being the son of a common-born knight I've never given much thought. I don't have enough significance for anyone to arrange my marriage without my consent.

If…" He took a deep breath. "If you don't mind my asking, is that why you're here? Did you refuse an arranged marriage?"

Gareth turned around and folded his arms. "No. Although I protested my sister's one too many times, and that was a factor."

"Oh." Florian's nose scrunched. "To be honest, I'd probably steal my sister away if my father tried to marry her to someone she didn't want to marry."

"At least you wouldn't almost cause a war defending your sister." With a wave of his hand, Gareth strode back across the tower. "And she's happy now. Somewhat nauseatingly in love with her husband and out of reach of her previous betrothed."

Quick footsteps announced Florian hurrying to Gareth's side. "I've heard bits and pieces of that. What happened, exactly?"

Gareth blinked. How had he not realized until that very moment how like his favorite legends this story was? He grinned at Florian.

"To understand that, I should start at the beginning—with the death of Rethalyon's King Philip and the story of a monster prince."

By one hour into his seven-hour shift guarding the firebird's garden, Gareth regretted agreeing to switch schedules with Florian. The only thing duller than standing on a tower and squinting across sun-bathed fields was remaining within two strides of a garden gate inside a fortified, well-guarded castle in the dark.

All right, it wasn't completely dark. There were stars and a sliver of the moon. The small lantern hung from a nearby pole cast a circle of soft golden light in front of the gate. His surroundings were mostly vague shapes of trees and bushes under the shadowy outline of the castle and outer wall. Combined with the darkness, the silence, unbroken except for the grating chirping of crickets, might have been unsettling if he hadn't been well aware he was in the safest place in the entirety of Tremblay Barony.

With a sigh, he leaned back against the locked gate. Were knights ever permitted to go inside and see the firebird? As prince, he could probably ask and be ushered in at once, but he was meant to be a common knight. Maybe by the end of his stay he could dare to ask Baron Tremblay to let him see the near-extinct bird...

Yelling and someone grabbing his tunic and dragging him upright startled Gareth out of a deep slumber. It took his bleary eyes a moment to focus, a man's bearded face appearing in triplicate before coalescing into a single image. The white of the man's wide eyes stood out starkly against his amber skin, and as he kept shouting, spittle landed on Gareth's face.

"What, were you drinking? Too spoiled to even stay awake for one night? You're damned lucky the lock is still in place, or...well I don't know what Tremblay is allowed to do to you, but I wouldn't want to find out! Now, answer me!"

Gareth shoved the knight away and looked around in confusion. He was sitting on the ground in front of the gate to the firebird's garden, and the pale, pinkish light of early dawn tinged the sky.

That couldn't be right.

He scrambled to his feet, checking that his sword was still at his side and confirming Sir Nevin was correct—the lock was fastened.

"How long were you asleep, Sir Gareth?" Nevin barked.

Gareth jumped and turned back to face the older knight. "I... I don't understand... I don't even remember feeling sleepy—"

Nevin made a sound of disgust in his throat. "Go wait in the mess hall until the captain is up and then confess your mistake." He sniffed. "It'll be worse for you if I have to tell him. Now get out of here." He shouldered Gareth aside with a muttered imprecation as he took up the post in front of the gate.

Gareth hurried away, his mouth dry and hands clammy.

How could he have failed only a few weeks into his posting? He'd never live this down. Father would never take his desire to be a knight seriously if he couldn't complete such a simple task as staying awake. But more importantly—

Why had he fallen asleep?

The last thing he remembered, he was leaning against the gate. And then…nothing. Waking up had felt like coming out of an abyss.

He had no proof, and he likely would sound like he was telling wild stories if he said anything, but Gareth had a gut feeling that something was amiss.

"We'll have to report this to Baron Tremblay." Captain Plinworth rubbed his temple. "And hope that the firebird is still there."

The rational part of Gareth's mind said it had to be—the garden was covered by a net so the bird couldn't escape, and the lock was still in place.

Another, more instinctual voice argued that if someone were to steal the firebird, especially if that someone were capable of knocking him unconscious with no memory of it, they'd cover their tracks and relock the gate. That didn't mean he bore no fault.

He was about to accept full responsibility if the bird had been stolen, but another knight approached.

"Captain." The knight shuffled his feet, glancing about as if searching for an escape, then bowed. "I need…to confess something." He glanced at Gareth and cleared his throat, his shoulders scrunching. "Alone, if that's acceptable."

Plinworth frowned, his sharp gaze raking over the knight, looking to Gareth and then back. "Sir Thomas. You were on watch last night in the southwest turret near the firebird's enclosure, correct?"

Thomas's throat bobbed. "Yes, sir."

A muscle in Plinworth's jaw ticked. "Did you fall asleep?"

"Yes, sir." The knight hung his head. "I swear I don't know what happened, Captain! I was—"

"Wide awake one minute and the next being awoken by your replacement?" Plinworth asked, his lips pinching as he glanced at Gareth.

"How…did you know, sir?"

That feeling deep in Gareth's gut that something was wrong grew.

The captain scrubbed a hand over his face. "Both of you, come with me. This can't wait any longer." He stood. "We need the baron to unlock the garden."

6

The firebird stared at Callista with reproach through the bars of its cage, which she had tied to her borrowed horse's saddle. The bird was beautiful, like a cross between a pheasant and a falcon. Red, orange, and gold feathers covered its body and formed its long tail, and a crown of slender feathers on its head flickered like flames. It let out a mournful cry, and the horse nervously sidestepped. She tossed the bird a piece of apple, hoping it was just hungry. The firebird gave a little shake that sent magical sparks flying, which landed harmlessly on the horse's side, then it ate the bit of fruit. Too quickly, it returned to staring into her soul.

What was left of her soul.

Callista slammed the thought away and finished the apple. Enough rest. She was starving and lightheaded, had barely slept the night before, and had used a lot of magical energy to cast two temporary sleeping curses, but she didn't have time to waste. She remounted, ignoring the firebird's depressed sigh, and headed off again down the forest path.

The horse needed to be returned to the farmer who had unknowingly lent it to her, and more dark spells needed to be cast. The next stage of the plan was in motion. Fate would do its part. She would need to be ready.

7

*G*areth dropped to one knee in the dirt before Baron Tremblay. Sunlight filtered through the leaves of empty trees in the firebird's deserted garden.

The net was intact.

Yet the firebird was gone.

"I have failed you." The words tasted sour, and Gareth rushed on, staring at the baron's muddied boots, too ashamed to look him in the eye. "My negligence has cost you dearly and brought shame upon me. Please allow me to regain my honor and seek the firebird for you."

He'd be lying if he said his heart didn't beat faster in excitement at the thought.

Yes, he'd failed spectacularly, and there was a very real chance his furious and distraught distant cousin might send him home in disgrace. Nathaniel would tease him relentlessly, Frederick would act superior, Mother would tell him he should let go of childish folly, and Father might lock him up for the rest of his life. True, Tremblay would be well within his rights to have Gareth strung up in the stocks on the battlements as punishment for the firebird going missing on his watch. But if the baron agreed…

It would mean a real quest.

A chance for adventure and to prove himself as a capable hero.

He held his breath, waiting for Tremblay's answer.

"How will you track a firebird?"

"I won't have to," Gareth said in a rush. "The gate was locked, and the net unbroken. Someone stole the firebird. I have to find the thief. I'm an excellent tracker, my lord. Please let me set this right and bring the bird back to you."

Baron Tremblay's boots scuffed the ground. "If you were any other knight, I'd give you a choice between bringing it back and a harsher punishment." His tight tone suggested his anger was barely controlled. "But I cannot ignore who you are—"

"Baron Tremblay," Gareth interrupted. "What exactly were the king's orders concerning me?"

His cousin sighed. "His Majesty's exact words were to treat you like a common-born knight with no family and no connections, with no preferential treatment or coddling."

Gareth tamped down a smirk and looked up. "Then send me to retrieve the bird as you would any other knight."

After a long pause, Tremblay nodded. "Very well, Sir Argent. I charge you with the task of retrieving my firebird or returning within one month should you fail. Whether you are successful or not will determine your punishment."

Gareth briefly bowed his head in acknowledgment. "Thank you, my lord."

"And if some*one* did actually steal my prize"—anger burned in the baron's eyes—"bring them to me. Unless they're a noble, then bring me evidence. And if they're Aedyllanian, either steal back my firebird without being seen or return empty-handed. I won't have you starting a conflict with Aedyllan."

"Yes, my lord."

There was a scuffling sound, then Sir Thomas knelt beside Gareth. "My lord, I would also—"

"Ten hits of the switch and a day without food or water,"

Baron Tremblay ordered. "The usual punishment for sleeping on guard duty, as you were not directly assigned to the firebird. And Captain, remind the men to be more vigilant."

With that, Baron Tremblay stomped away, leaving Gareth, Thomas, and Plinworth in the quiet garden.

Plinworth huffed. "I think I've determined why your father sent you here, Sir Gareth. You're an idiot."

Clamping down his irritation, Gareth stood. With a glare at the captain, he brushed off his trousers. "I'd best go pack some supplies."

"You'd have been better off accepting a punishment now," Plinworth said, undeterred. "If you don't find the firebird, you'll look like more of a failure. And if you're right that someone took it, anyone who can get inside Tremblay Castle and out with a firebird and without a trace is not a foe you want to face alone."

"I'm not a coward."

Plinworth tilted his head, studying Gareth. "You think this is an opportunity to prove yourself. It's an opportunity to get yourself killed."

"Well maybe I have a sense of honor and want to make things right!" Gareth's fists clenched. "Maybe I'm not content doing the minimum, living a boring life, standing guard in peaceful fields, or placating self-important nobles. Maybe I refuse to just do what I'm told by people who are convinced they know better than me and don't actually *see* me or care about me or what I want to do with my life!"

Thomas stood, dusting off his knees. "I wish I could help you. I, too, would rather at least attempt to make right the consequences of my failure."

"And if you came back without the bird, Sir Thomas, you'd be lucky to keep your title." Plinworth shook his head. "Sir Gareth, you can't force people to value your contributions or believe in your abilities by being reckless. There's wisdom in knowing when to take risks and when to cut your losses and accept that a situation is beyond your control or capabilities."

Ignoring the first part of Plinworth's advice, Gareth laughed bitterly. "Good to know you also would have given up on my missing sister. Some of us still believe in doing the right thing."

"I don't know much about what happened with your sister." Plinworth's hard expression softened into something akin to sympathy. "But some of us also know the right thing isn't always a simple, black-and-white answer and sometimes there's no perfect solution—and sometimes people make the wrong calls for the right reasons. Even because they do care and don't wish to see someone hurt for stupid reasons."

"Sure." Gareth turned away. "If that's what you want to call cowardice, go ahead."

Plinworth grabbed his arm. "At the least…if your hunt leads you toward Aedyllan, I advise you to admit defeat and return. Nothing good will come of a prince crossing the border alone, and I've heard rumors Aedyllan has seen a rise in banditry."

"I tire of repeating myself." Gareth yanked out of Plinworth's grasp. "*I* am not a coward. And currently, I'm not a useless prince, either." He stomped away without waiting for a reply.

By the time Gareth finished donning a shiny steel cuirass, greaves, and vambraces, packing his saddlebags with a blanket and extra garments, an assortment of food, and other items that might prove useful, and attaching a small birdcage to the outside of his bags, his anger at Captain Plinworth had cooled. Maybe the man wasn't a coward, just a pessimist. It didn't matter.

Gareth would prove him wrong. He'd find the bird and show that being honorable was the right thing to do, even when it was difficult, and he'd prove his worth as a man and a knight at the same time.

Retrieving a stolen firebird wasn't the most heroic quest he'd ever heard of, but as a first quest, he supposed it would do.

After he had proven himself, he'd have the rest of his life to go on adventures worthy of the story books—and in the future, he wouldn't spend most of the tale in a dungeon, like he had in Raelyn and Alexander's story.

As he rode down to the moat, morning sunlight glaring off his armor, Gareth smiled to himself.

He was a knight, and this time, no one was going to stop him.

8

There were two things Gareth knew for certain about the thief. First, he—or she—couldn't fly, at least not for long enough to remove the net and take the firebird that way, or he wouldn't have knocked Gareth and Sir Thomas unconscious. Second, he must not have come over the bridge, or those knights would have been asleep as well.

So he tied Fury to a shady tree and began his quest with the boring task of inspecting the ground around the moat. He walked along the outside, looking for a trail or other clue as to how the thief had infiltrated the castle.

He almost missed the trace evidence of an intruder. The grass was flattened in a section a foot wide at the edge of the moat, as if something had pressed it down. After planting a stick in the ground to mark the spot, Gareth hurried across the drawbridge and around the walls until he stood directly across from the stick. The grass in front of his boots had been flattened in a similar fashion—as if someone had placed a plank across the moat. He let out a low whistle. That was a daring way to cross a moat.

Although, given that the other guards reported it had been foggy, also a good way of getting across without being seen. Whoever the thief was, they had incredible balance.

After Gareth ascertained where the intruder crossed the moat, it was only a matter of time before he found a trail. The thief had attempted to leave no tracks near the castle, but there were enough hints of broken blades of grass and faint indentations in soft dirt for Gareth to follow. He mounted Fury and the pursuit began.

At least hunting being an acceptable leisure activity for princes was paying off yet again. Hopefully this time there were no flying dragon-men involved to make the trail disappear.

To his relief, the thief most likely did not shapeshift or get picked up by a winged man, dragon, or other creature, as the faint trail led into a sparse forest, where he found evidence of a small campsite and hoofprints. The trail left by the thief's horse was easy to follow, but that was where Gareth's luck ran out—because the tracks led to a road.

"Wolf's teeth," Gareth muttered.

He reined in Fury and looked up and down the wide dirt thoroughfare. A peasant pulling a cart of vegetables nodded at him as he passed, and a group of women carrying covered baskets pointedly avoided his gaze.

The thief must have gone this way at night, otherwise someone would have noticed a person traveling with a firebird. There had already been much traffic that morning, and even if there hadn't been, the road was rutted and well-worn. It wasn't a main route but was still one of many roads connecting Aedyllan and Eynlae. There would be no picking up the thief's trail on the road.

The question was…which way had the thief gone? Further into Eynlae? Or toward Aedyllan?

When the sun had risen, the thief would have had to leave the thoroughfare again, so eventually, there would be a trail diverging from the road. It might be difficult to find, though, as many travelers might have entered or exited the road at any convenient location. He would waste precious time if he looked in the wrong direction first.

Gareth steered Fury into the shade of a towering oak to weigh his options. For all of Father's complaining that Gareth never thought things through, if he'd learned one thing from Sir Christopher over the years, it was to be strategic. It was counter-intuitive, but slowing down first could help you be faster later. It was true of practicing new sword forms or drawing arrows from different quivers, it was true of assessing a new opponent, and it was true of forming a plan.

Whoever it was had broken in specifically to steal the firebird, which meant they knew of its existence. So many people served in the castle, though, that most of the inhabitants of Tremblay Barony probably had heard about it. Someone might have stolen the bird in order to "return" it for a reward, but that seemed improbable. They'd risk being caught and punished instead, not to mention many people would be nervous about handling a magical bird. Gareth had read enough about them to know they were mostly harmless, but magic was so uncommon in Eynlae it was unlikely a peasant would know that.

Beyond the borders of the barony, Tremblay often boasted about his pet. Even though Gareth hadn't believed it to be real, most nobles knew Tremblay claimed to have a rare firebird. Might a noble have stolen it to bolster their own name?

Even more ridiculous. No one would believe Baron Tremblay's pet went missing and then someone else suddenly had their own firebird. No noble would risk their reputation and wealth over such an obvious ploy.

That left the border…

Someone near the border might have heard from their neighbors about the bird. Further, an Aedyllanian might assume they'd be beyond the reach of Eynlae's justice.

Most significantly, while Eynlae had no known magic users of any strength, Aedyllan had enchanters—and their evil counterparts, witches. Alexander, Raelyn's husband, had speculated Henry Carbrey had obtained his curses in Aedyllan, but Henry was gone, and Tristan didn't know, so it was only speculation. Still, an enchanter or witch seemed a more likely culprit for the firebird's theft.

The problem was, despite Father declaring Gareth to be a mere knight while he served at Tremblay, he *was* still an Eynlaean prince. If a prince of Eynlae covertly entered Aedyllan and then had any confrontations with Aedyllanian nobility… Things could get complicated, and to say Father would be furious if Gareth caused a second diplomatic incident would be an understatement.

Gareth tapped gloved fingers against his thigh. He'd never visited Aedyllan, so it was unlikely anyone would recognize him. He wasn't planning on getting arrested or causing any problems, just retrieving a stolen bird. He probably wouldn't even be in Aedyllan long. Maybe he would catch up to the thief before they entered Aedyllan if he hurried.

With a decisive nod, Gareth turned Fury down the road toward Aedyllan.

Luck must have been on Gareth's side. Few of the travelers on this road had horses, so Gareth kept an eye on the sides of the road, and anytime there was evidence of a track leading off the road, he dismissed it if he didn't find hoofprints. The occasional horse dropping also assured him he was on the right track. He pushed through the day without stopping, eating some bread and raw carrots while riding.

It was midafternoon when he found it.

The thief was smart—they'd left the road on an area with dry dirt and little growth, so there wasn't much of a trail near the road. But he had been trained to look beyond what was just in front of his nose. Several paces from the thoroughfare, a ditch where rain runoff would collect had softer ground, tall grass, and brambles, which had been broken by the passage of something. Hoofprints confirmed a horse had ridden into the forest.

Gareth followed the tracks into the woods, eventually finding himself on an old trail. Perhaps it had once been used by villagers or a woodcutter, but it appeared to have been disused for some time. Undergrowth crowded on both sides of the narrow trail, starting to overtake it. While that helped hide the trail unless one knew to look for it, it also meant there were more opportunities for his quarry to leave evidence behind—smashed grass, snapped twigs, leaves crushed into the soil.

As the trail continued, the tracks became easier to follow. The thief had kept to a slow pace when they first found the trail—perhaps it hadn't been light enough yet to rush through the forest—but he'd clearly then picked up speed as he approached the Aedyllanian border. Although, Gareth reflected, he might actually be in Aedyllan already. The border was only marked on the roads.

Whoever he was following would be too far ahead for him to overtake easily, Gareth realized with displeasure. While he'd had to search for the trail at the castle and then ride slowly while searching for evidence, the culprit had likely ridden the road at a canter and had resumed at least a trot through the forest. Not to mention the hours Gareth had lost to sleep and the time talking to his superiors before packing and setting out.

Maybe Plinworth had a point that this task was more difficult than it appeared on the surface.

However, that didn't mean it wasn't worth trying. They couldn't let some Aedyllanian get away with robbing an Eynlaean baron's castle. Or let anyone get away with theft, for that matter. He'd also told the truth—it felt dishonorable not to find the firebird when it had been stolen on his watch, even if it wasn't his fault that he may have been magically sent to sleep.

Something orange-red flashed through the underbrush far ahead of him. Fury laid back his ears and tossed his head. Gareth reined the stallion in, his entire body on high alert.

Leaves whispered together and bushes shook to the right of the trail. It could be anything, even a squirrel or a friendly ginger tabby-cat lesser gryphon, but only a fool would assume something unseen moving in the forest wasn't a threat.

Gareth drew his sword, watching the quivering shrubs as he tried to track the quick movements of the creature. For a fleeting moment he hoped it was the firebird, but it was doubtful the bird would be running along the forest floor.

In a loud rustle, a fox leapt out of the bushes, directly in front of his horse.

Fury screamed and took a step back. Gareth eased his grip on Fury's sides and held the reins firmly yet not forcefully as he commanded, "Hold!"

After a small back kick, Fury obeyed. All that practice to train Fury to be a worthy war steed hadn't been wasted.

Gareth peeked around Fury's head and blinked. Not only was the fox still there, it had sat down in the middle of the path. Its fluffy tail curled over its black-socked paws, and it peered up at Gareth with intent golden eyes.

The fox tilted its head to one side, like an inquisitive dog.

"Shoo." Gareth waved his sword toward the fox. "Shoo!"

Its nose wrinkled as it straightened its head. "And here I was going to offer my help, and you start waving a sword at me."

Gareth yelped and nearly dropped the sword, but then pointed it more firmly in the fox's direction.

The fox that had just spoken, in an unnervingly normal-sounding male voice.

No, he was simply losing his mind.

The fox sighed. "Yes, I am a talking fox. And you're from

Tremblay Barony in Eynlae, I suppose, hunting a stolen firebird."

"Did you see the thief?" The words burst from Gareth before it occurred to him that talking to a fox when he was hunting a possible enchanter wasn't his wisest idea. "Never mind." He waved the tip of his sword toward the forest. "Get out of the way and leave me alone."

"I did see her." The fox made no move to leave.

Gareth's sword lowered a fraction. "Her?"

"Yes. Hooded woman on a bay stallion with a firebird in a cage." The fox tilted its head again. "If you ask me very nicely, I'll help you find her. Now why is the sword still out?"

"Because I don't know if I trust you, fox." Gareth frowned, thinking aloud, "In stories, when something talks that shouldn't, it's either a trick designed to lead the hero astray, or fate, and it will guide and aid the hero on their journey. But either way, the trickster or the guide claims they're going to help. How do I know if you're a guide or a distraction?"

The fox blinked slowly. "You have a very high opinion of yourself."

"Excuse me?"

"You just declared yourself a hero on some kind of grand quest that is so important either fate has sent you aid, or some powerful malevolent force has sent a trick. How do you know you're a hero?"

Gareth gaped at the fox before slamming his sword into its sheath. "You're wasting my time, so I've decided you're a spirit of chaos with no aim other than to delay travelers. Goodbye."

He backed Fury up, looking for a good place to leave the trail and go around the fox. Why had he told the fox creature "goodbye" as if it deserved such polite consideration? Irritating animal.

"My mother would probably agree with my being a spirit of chaos." Humor wove through the fox's tone as he padded after Fury.

"Go away."

"No. I've decided to help you, even if you're too stubborn to listen to me."

"Wise," Gareth corrected as he turned off the trail.

"What?"

"I'm too wise to listen to a talking fox. Foxes are not trustworthy."

With a huff, the fox stopped and held a black paw against its chest. "Untrustworthy? What a hurtful stereotype. No, you're definitely not a hero." It sprang forward, leaping onto Fury's withers directly in front of Gareth.

His destrier neighed and sidestepped, and Gareth transferred one of the reins to his empty hand so he could better control the horse with small, gentle directions. "Easy, boy." He'd trained the horse to hunt, so dogs and foxes didn't usually spook him, but the foxes also never jumped on him. Once Fury had settled, he turned his attention to the fox perched in front of him.

"What do you think you're doing?"

"Helping you, against my better judgment. Mostly because I don't like people who keep innocent animals in tiny cages." The fox's nose twitched. "It's not right."

Gareth nudged the fox's side, not quite able to bring himself to be more forceful and risk hurting the animal. "Get down, fox."

"Leo. And you're rude."

"What?"

"You're rude. Terrible manners, truly. Who raised you?"

"Not that." Gareth waved a hand, thinking with some amusement how offended his mother would be—even though he'd been raised more by nurses and tutors than his parents. "Before that."

"My name is Leo."

Gareth stared down at the fox. "Leo." One chuckle escaped,

then two, and when the fox gave him the most affronted expression he had ever seen on an animal, he broke down laughing. "You—are a fox—named…" He wheezed. "Lion?"

Leo's ears pinned back against his head. "And what of it? Judging me for my name and my species. I didn't have a say in either. What if I make fun of your hair for being such a light shade of brown it appears it's attempting and failing to be blond? Or mock *your* name, whatever it is. Since your manners are so terrible you can't even introduce yourself to me." The fox gave a delicate sniff, sticking its nose in the air like an affronted noble, and Gareth rolled his eyes.

"I'm Sir Gareth."

"Nice to meet you." Leo frowned. "Not truly, honestly. You've not been nice at all."

Gareth shook his head and focused on steering Fury back onto the trail. "Fine, you can tag along, but only because I'm wasting precious time arguing with you."

"Agreed. Are you always this stubborn?"

"Are you always this bluntly critical?"

"Only when the best candidate the Eynlaeans can send to retrieve their stolen endangered firebird is a lone, uncouth knight who looks like he hasn't been shaving long."

Gareth harrumphed. "First of all, I'm almost twenty and have been shaving since sixteen. Second, I thought by undertaking this quest, I'd finally get a reprieve from lecturing and scolding, but no, the entirety of Miraveld seems intent on making me miserable."

"Everywhere you go you end up getting lectured?" Leo hummed. "No, the problem couldn't possibly be you."

"Whoa." Gareth reined in Fury. "That's it, Lion-Fox. Get off my horse."

But Leo simply squirmed his way underneath Gareth's arm, then curled up behind him on top of the saddlebags. "My parents named me Leo, so that's what I answer to."

Gareth twisted to look at the fox, which was uncomfortable in his armor. "Off my horse then, Leo."

"No." Leo closed his eyes and rested his chin on his black paws. "There is a poor, captive firebird locked in an entirely too-small cage, and if you're the idiot tasked with saving her, then I am stuck with helping you."

Snorting in irritation, Gareth prodded Fury onward again. "I don't see why it matters so much to you."

"It just does. Go left."

Gareth scowled. "What is that supposed to mean? The trail—" But as he pushed a low-hanging branch out of his way, the trail ahead split into two. To the right, the trail continued with the same level of wear. To the left, the trail was fainter, nearly hidden in the undergrowth.

"You can waste time looking for evidence of which way the enchantress went," Leo said, "or you can trust me and go left."

"How do you know she's an enchantress?" He eyed the two paths, debating whether the fox's directions were a trick.

"Enchantment on the cage. I could smell it."

Wishing he could see his unwanted companion, Gareth exclaimed, "You can *smell* enchantments?"

"Does that make you trust me more or less?"

Gareth considered. If true, it would make the magical fox more useful…but only if he was trustworthy, which was still up for debate.

Leo sighed. "You don't trust easily, do you?"

"I don't find most people worthy of my trust. Or animals."

"Hm." Leo jumped up, placing his forepaws on the back of Gareth's shoulder to peer at his face. "You must trust someone."

"My sister," Gareth said without hesitation, then winced. "And even she's broken my trust."

Leo seemed to consider this, then sat down. "I'm sorry. I love my sister more than anything in this world, and I don't know what I'd do if she ever betrayed my trust. I think it'd crush me." He hopped to the forest floor and darted ahead, making Fury prance back in confusion. "Come on. It's safe. Follow me."

After a moment of hesitation, Gareth followed.

Maybe the strange fox was manipulating him by mentioning a sister, but his intuition said Leo wasn't lying about caring about his sibling. And somehow, that connection made him trust the fox.

He wouldn't let his guard down, not completely. At least Leo the talking fox, whether friend or foe, would make for a very interesting letter to Raelyn.

9

"We should stop here for the night." Leo looked around the small, grassy meadow and gave a sharp nod. "It'll be dark soon. You should have a fire built before that."

"Afraid of the dark?" Gareth teased as he dismounted.

Leo bristled. "No. Afraid of wolves. Lynxes and great bears, too, although I'm not sure if there are any around here. But there could be wolves."

"I suppose wolves, lynxes, and great bears do kill foxes."

"Don't remind me." The fox shuddered. "Sometimes they kill people too, you know."

Gareth tied Fury to a nearby birch. "I thought great bears were rarely seen anymore."

"Rarely isn't never." Leo stretched out and yawned, his rows of sharp teeth flashing in the pinkish light of the setting sun. "So a fire is good."

"Well then. I suppose I'll gather up the firewood and make the fire—"

"And bring out the food!" Leo's bushy tail wagged as he sat down and watched Gareth with those golden eyes.

"And you'll just…sit there," Gareth said flatly.

"I'm the guide." Leo licked a forepaw. "That's my contribution."

Either he was going to strangle this fox, or he was starting to like him. It did help Leo's case that he was very cute and looked incredibly soft. If he were not a talking fox, Gareth would be highly tempted to capture him and attempt to domesticate him. A fox who got offended over poor manners already was domesticated, though, Gareth supposed.

After he got a fire going and set up his blanket over a low branch as a makeshift tent, Gareth pulled out some food. He reluctantly shared with Leo, who seemed oddly excited about bread and affronted by Gareth's suggestion he go hunt a mouse.

"So how do you know where we're going?" Gareth asked. "Are you following the scent of the firebird or its enchanted cage?"

Leo licked his chops. "No. I know where the thieving enchantress lives."

All of the distrust Gareth had set aside snapped back into place. He pointed his breadcrust at the fox as if it were a weapon. "Is this a trap? Did this Aedyllanian witch send you to lead me to her lair? A scheme to capture an Eynlaean man for some wicked purpose?"

Or could this be a plot to ensnare Gareth specifically? Stealing the bird while he was on watch could have been planned. A gamble that he would take responsibility and go after the firebird himself.

"Yes," Leo said drily. "Aedyllanian witches eat young Eynlaean knights. They send foxes to lure young men with overinflated egos to their deaths." The fox lay down with a huff and a flick of his tail. "One would think you're a highborn noble with all of your self-importance."

He wasn't self-important. Frederick was self-important and had an out-of-control ego.

Not wanting to think about Fred and realizing the fox wouldn't tell him if this was a trap, Gareth changed the subject.

"How did you come to talk, anyway?"

"Same way you did, I suspect."

Gareth tore a bite off his bread. "Doubtful. No magic was involved in my learning to speak."

"Nor in mine."

Gareth considered this while he chewed. "Wait. Are you cursed?"

"I have questions if you think the ability to talk is a curse. And I just said no magic was involved—"

"In you *learning* to speak, right." He leaned forward. "I know someone who was cursed and sometimes was a dragon. He could still talk as a dragon. You're not a cursed human, are you?"

"Cursed to be a dragon? That's fascinating. Why? Where… actually, never mind. I'm too tired for stories you probably read in some book—"

"I'm not lying." Gareth narrowed his eyes. "And you're dodging the question."

"Because it's stupid. You really are egotistical to think you're special enough to have the statistically improbable experience of meeting two transmogrified humans in one lifetime." Leo curled into a ball and closed his eyes. "Now, if you'll excuse me, I've had a very long day of walking about on short legs and of dealing with an arrogant nuisance who keeps accusing me without warrant, but who was born with thumbs and the ability to wield a sword and so, unfortunately, is better suited for freeing stolen firebirds than I am."

"I never would have thought a cute talking animal would be so exasperating!"

Leo snorted but didn't move or open his eyes. "Don't call me cute. I have claws."

"Threat noted," Gareth muttered. Still, the fox seemed unworried, so either Leo was more trusting than Gareth or he was up to something.

Half afraid the fox would kill him, Gareth couldn't settle down enough to sleep for a while. He didn't remember falling asleep, but he awoke to something smacking his face.

"Wake up, hero. We've a trapped firebird to rescue and you're wasting daylight."

Leo's paw batted Gareth's forehead again, and he shoved the fox away with a groan. Rubbing his eyes, he peered out of his makeshift tent. "It's barely past dawn, you vulpine menace."

"And I've been awake and waiting for you since first light." Leo sprang away. "I helped myself to breakfast while you snored."

"I don't—you what?" Gareth charged out of his shelter, making for his saddlebags and supply of food.

The flap of the bag was still fastened shut by the loop and bone clasp, but that had been insufficient to stop his furry companion. One side of the bag was shoved open as far as it would go, and crumbs were scattered over the ground and inside of the bag. The thick leather had scratches, some venison jerky was missing, and only crumbs of bread remained.

Gareth glared at the fox. "What kind of worthless fox are you, stealing my food when you're in a forest full of perfectly good game?"

Leo fluffed his tail and gave Gareth a look of deep disdain. "Hurry up and eat or I'll leave without you."

"I thought you needed my thumbs and sword," Gareth mumbled. He glowered at the remaining jerky, trying to determine whether it was tainted with dirt and fox drool. It seemed clean enough, so he grumpily tore off a piece of the tough meat with his teeth.

"And you need my help to find the firebird, so it seems we're stuck with each other." Leo's whiskers twitched. "I'm going to relieve myself. Perhaps you can be ready by the time I'm back."

Gareth stuck his tongue out at the fox's retreating tail.

For claiming he wanted to join forces, Leo certainly wasn't worried about ingratiating himself. Which, perhaps illogically, helped Gareth trust him more. If Leo had been flattering and obliging, that would have appeared manipulative. Instead, Leo seemed to wish he didn't need help but couldn't avoid that he did—a sentiment Gareth shared. That felt genuine. Unwilling allies was a better situation than smooth-talking enemies.

Leo wasn't gone for long, so Gareth was still fastening the bags and saddle on Fury's back when he returned. Thankfully, though, Leo didn't grumble this time, just watched until Gareth had put his armor back on and mounted.

"Off we go." Leo bent down and wriggled his butt for a moment before leaping onto Fury's back behind Gareth. This time, Fury only spooked briefly. "Head southeast. We're leaving the trail."

With a roll of his eyes, Gareth directed Fury toward the southeast.

"A little less south and a touch more east."

"Maybe you should lead the way, then."

"Too tiring."

Gareth huffed. "Can you even see where we're going back there?"

In response, Leo propped his forepaws on Gareth's back and peered over his shoulder. "When I need to. This is perfect."

The woods were quiet as they continued on, filled with the peaceful ambiance of nature that Gareth much preferred to the echoing stone corridors of castles. Trees creaked and birds called, insects provided a low humming background, and squirrels chittered at each other or at Leo—who seemed unbothered by the rodents' antics.

In fact, as the day wore on, Gareth felt more and more that Leo acted decidedly un-fox-like. Sure, he looked like a normal fox. He fluffed his tail and walked and pounced and groomed himself like a fox. When they took a short break and Gareth turned around without looking and stepped on the fluffy white tip of Leo's tail, he certainly yowled like a fox. But he showed no interest in hunting nor any animal-like instincts.

That could just mean the fox had been raised by humans. Gareth had known an old noblewoman who had a tiny dog that she kept with her at all times and fed table scraps and rarely allowed outside. The spoiled thing had once watched a rabbit hop right past it with only mild curiosity.

Maybe the enchantress had raised Leo and then grown tired of him and tossed him aside, and that was why Leo wanted to help Gareth. Or perhaps the enchantress had stolen Leo away from the humans who raised him, and he couldn't find his way home. Alternatively, Gareth still wasn't convinced Leo wasn't a cursed man, but if that were the case, he'd have expected Leo to have had a stronger reaction to being asked if he was a human.

There were too many possibilities for his strange companion.

Late in the afternoon, as the lowering sunlight streaked through the forest in mesmerizing slashes between tree branches, Gareth cleared his throat.

"What exactly is the nature of your previous encounter with this enchantress?"

"Who said I'd encountered her before?" Leo snapped.

Gareth shrugged. "You know where she lives. You seem to have a personal interest in taking the firebird back from her. You don't like me but want my help anyway. You're telling me that's all a coincidence?"

Leo shifted behind him. "Maybe that's personal, and I don't know you well enough to talk about it."

The pained undertone in Leo's voice gave Gareth pause. "Sorry."

Whatever the enchantress had done, it must have been awful.

A curse seemed less likely if it was something personal that Leo simply wasn't comfortable discussing. The firebird thief might have hurt a friend or family member of Leo's. That could explain why Leo was alone. Maybe all of his bravado was a cover for whatever past pain or future fears he didn't want a stranger to see.

Gareth respected that. No one should be forced to bare their heart or their hurts to someone. Such trust had to be earned, and only Raelyn had ever held Gareth's confidence enough to allow complete honesty about his hopes and fears, his pain and joy.

"Do you know much about her magic?" he asked instead.

"Hm. She's powerful and uses dark magic." Leo's voice turned thoughtful. "Which I suppose makes her a witch, not an enchantress."

Gareth nodded. "I've read about that. In Aedyllan, you call those with the gift of magic enchanters, but if they learn the forbidden ways of curse-casting, you call them witches and they're shunned."

"*Sometimes* they're shunned. Not all witches are evil."

A disbelieving laugh escaped Gareth. "How does curse-casting not make one evil?"

"Plenty of people make mistakes or do wrong things but aren't *evil*," Leo said, his tone implying this should be obvious.

At least Gareth could rule out that Leo was cursed. If he'd suffered the way Alexander had, he wouldn't say something so inane. The fox's hint of condescension was bad enough, but his words reminded Gareth that Raelyn and Alexander had said something similar about the cad known as Tristan Carbrey—a sentiment with which Gareth disagreed. Still, even Alexander would never say the man who had cursed him wasn't evil.

"If you knowingly do something cruel or hurt others, then you're wicked. I don't see how there's room for any argument there."

The fox, however, pounced on the argument.

"That's ridiculous. Life has more nuance than that, not to mention it would be a sad world without any room for redemption or forgiveness." Leo shifted behind Gareth. "Some people might learn the forbidden magics and later repent. Some start to learn and turn back. There's actually some debate in magical philosophy over whether repentant witches are still witches or revert to being enchanters—"

"Magical philosophy?" Gareth interrupted, incredulous.

A note of defensiveness crept into Leo's tone. "It's a personal interest of mine."

"You're interested in…magical philosophy?"

"Are foxes not allowed to study philosophy?"

Gareth grew increasingly bewildered. "Can you read?"

"Humph." Leo hopped to the ground, and Fury shied to the side in response. "See, this is your problem. Too quick to judge and certain you're always correct. I'm a fox, so I'm untrustworthy and shouldn't talk or read or be interested in philosophy and eth-ics. Someone does something wrong and you condemn them. I'll have you know there are also stories of witches who used curses only to punish wrongdoers who had escaped the law, or witches who both cast curses and helped innocent people. Are they evil?"

"If they hurt—"

"If you come upon a man viciously attacking someone else and you fight him and end up killing him, haven't you hurt and killed? Are you evil? Maybe there can be good reasons for doing something that causes harm."

Gareth opened and closed his mouth. No words would come. He wanted to say that it wasn't the same, that Leo was making things complicated for no reason, that he couldn't use hypotheti-cals to make such a sweeping claim as "not all people who cast curses are evil." How could Gareth believe such a thing, when his sister and brother-in-law had both been hurt by a man who bought curses from a witch? But he couldn't find a good counterargument.

"So what?" he snapped. "Now you're defending this woman who stole the firebird?"

Leo's tail puffed. "I never said that. I don't know. Maybe she does have a good reason for being so cruel. That won't stop me from being angry about her actions or trying to thwart her, but I might have sympathy for her if she has a good reason. If she is wicked through and through, I also won't use that as proof that all witches are the same."

"If ignoring evil actions because someone had good reasons is supposed to make me trust or like you more, fox, it's having the opposite effect."

Leo sent Gareth a slit-eyed glare before trotting ahead, his nose in the air. "Maybe I don't care if some haughty, narrow-minded Eynlaean trusts me or not, knight."

Haughty? Growing up in the royal court, Gareth knew plenty of proud individuals. Fred always thought he was better than everyone. His baby brother, Nathaniel, had an air of intellectual superiority and thought tattling on Gareth and Raelyn proved he was more respectable. Father, of course, because he was the king and his word was expected to be accepted without question, even when he was wrong. Mother loved to lecture, although usually only Raelyn had been subjected to Mother's scolding. And plenty of the nobles who frequented the court were haughty, too.

Gareth had never thought of himself as proud.

Although, he reflected with a growing discomfort in the pit of his stomach, Sir Christopher would probably say it was pride that had motivated him to switch places with Squire Gibson. Maybe it had even been pride more than the desire for adventure or to do the right thing that had spurred him to undertake this quest.

No, that couldn't be.

Besides, the fox thought that believing he was correct was the same as being haughty. It couldn't be prideful to have strong beliefs or trust his intuition or know right from wrong.

What did a stupid fox know, anyway? Even if the bizarre creature did somehow get his paws on philosophy books and read them.

They didn't speak much for the rest of the day. Most of that talking was Leo giving one-word directions after he grew fatigued and demanded Gareth dismount, pick him up, and place him back on Fury's back.

As the sun drew close to the horizon, Leo broke the silence. "We're nearly there. Should be just on the other side of this copse."

They wound between the birch trees, Fury's hooves stirring up fallen leaves and making a dull thud on the soft dirt. Gareth gripped the hilt of his sword.

"Should we stop? Perhaps it would be better to approach the witch's hut on foot and scout it out?"

"Who said anything about a hut?"

10

efore Gareth could demand Leo explain what he meant, he saw for himself. The trees thinned, and ahead of them rose a towering wall of ivy. He reined in Fury, looking back and forth at the curving wall stretching to his left and right. Dark stone peeked through the tangled vines.

"As you can see," Leo drawled, "she lives in a castle, not a hut."

"She's a *noble?*" Gareth ground out. That complicated things.

"I don't think so. They're ruins. She hides in them, like an opossum moving into another animal's abandoned den."

"Oh. Good." A castle was more ground to search for the firebird than he'd anticipated, but at least he wouldn't have to worry about guards.

The fox leapt down, tumbling a little as he landed. Fury shifted his weight on his back legs, and Gareth soothed the horse to ensure he didn't kick Leo.

"This is the back," Leo said. "We should rest and eat, and I'll give you instructions so you can sneak in as soon as it's dark."

"Sneak in? I'm not a coward." Gareth dismounted and scowled at Leo. "I'm a knight, not a burglar."

Leo sat with a sigh. "Your task is to retrieve the firebird, not fight a witch whose powers you know nothing about. Trust me.

Just sneak in."

"And how"—Gareth waved at the castle wall—"am I meant to sneak *into a castle*?"

Leo's ears twitched. "Castle ruins. Let's eat, and then I'll explain."

"All you do is eat and talk."

"Heh. You sound like my sister."

Shaking his head, Gareth drew his sword and used it to prod at the vines. At first, this just revealed another layer of thick, dead vines. A little further, and the point of his sword scraped against black stone—leaving a light-gray line behind. Frowning, he held the vines aside with his sword and leaned closer.

"It was burned," Leo said, padding over to Gareth's side. "Fifty or so years ago, the lord of this castle attempted to rebel, and his entire family was wiped out, down to the babe in its cradle, and the castle was set aflame. Since it was mostly stone, it's still standing, for the most part. But it's blackened and weakened and has some holes, which you will use to get inside."

"No wonder it's so overgrown." Gareth let the vines fall back into place and looked around. Not only was the wall and much of the ground surrounding it covered in vines, but the grass was wild and unkempt, and the forest had crept nearly to the walls, as if the woods were trying to swallow the castle and its memory.

Leo nodded. "The castle and surrounding lands were left to rot as a warning to others not to challenge the king. At some point, this witch took up residence there."

"How large is it inside?" Gareth craned his neck, trying to see the top of the wall.

The fox made a humming noise. "It was a moderately sized castle. I expect the firebird will be in the garden. First, though, supper."

"Hm." Gareth returned to Fury and withdrew a sack of nuts from his bags, then sat in a shorter patch of grass.

Leo trotted over and sat down, sniffing the air. "I don't smell food."

"Thanks to you, several days' worth of rations have already been consumed." Gareth pushed down the grass in front of Leo and dumped a handful of nuts in the spot. "So this is all I have. But tell me, how does a fox come to know so much history?"

The look Leo fixed on him could only be described as scathing. "You already know I read." He batted at the nuts with a black paw. "You should have packed more food."

"I didn't plan on feeding a fox with a pit for a stomach," Gareth groused. "I'll have to hunt something on my way back to Eynlae. I could try to trap something tonight, but that does not seem to fit into your master plan, Protector of Firebirds." He straightened. "Wait. Foxes eat birds. Is this entire thing a scheme to get me to steal the firebird for you so you can eat it and, I don't know, absorb its magical powers or something?"

Leo barked a laugh that sounded decidedly more fox-like than human. "I don't think it works that way. Fire powers sound like a nightmare, anyway. No, Sir Doubt, simply one magical creature not wanting to see another suffer."

"Hm." Gareth munched on his nuts, watching with open amusement as Leo ate his portion—an endeavor that included much disgruntled frowning and lots of theatrical crunching.

Once the nuts were consumed, Leo licked his lips, then turned to Gareth. "I'll show you a place in the wall where you can sneak in—"

"Wouldn't the gate be open? I presume it would have been wood and burned down."

Leo's tail flicked with clear irritation. "There are magical wards on the entrances. Don't be daft."

"And you didn't think to mention this before now?" Gareth demanded.

Leo flattened his ears. "What difference would it make knowing before now? It's not like you could have learned to counteract the magic if I'd told you previously. You'll sneak in so you don't have to face the witch or her magical wards, as long as you don't get caught."

"Sneaking isn't very heroic," Gareth grumbled as he brushed crumbs off his hands and stood.

"How do you feel about staying alive, hm?"

"It's insulting you think I don't have a chance against this witch. Although I suppose all the best stories have a villain throwing magic at the ill-prepared hero."

Leo snorted. "Again with painting yourself as some legendary figure. You've never fought someone with magic. I'm being practical, unlike you with your head in the clouds."

If Leo kept up this infuriating stream of criticism, Gareth was going to be tempted to wonder what he'd look like in a red-fur-trimmed coat. "Practical, is that what you call it? I think you're a fox who has spent all his time studying philosophy and doesn't have the first clue how to apply it practically and has no idea what humans are capable of."

"Spoken like someone who would rather hit things with a sword than open a book." Leo stood, his back arching as he lowered his head, and his whiskers twitched.

"First, I've read a lot, thank you." Mostly legends and tales, but Gareth suspected the fox wouldn't appreciate that as much. "Second, which of our skills is better suited to undertaking this quest?"

"I only need your thumbs," Leo protested. But then his posture eased, and he sat down, his ears drooping to the sides. "I apologize. I didn't need to denigrate your strengths and interests to elevate my own. People do that to me all the time because they don't value the same things I do, so I should know better. I just…"

He sighed. "Why do people always think fighting with brawn is so much more important than having a capable mind? Can't they both be important?"

Gareth hesitated, unsure how to respond. Genuine apologies directed at him weren't something with which he had much experience, but he was well acquainted with feeling frustrated that people only saw what he *wasn't* good at while ignoring what he was good at. "I…shouldn't have insulted you, either. That was…petty. It's not your fault you're just a fox—"

"I'm not *just* a fox!" Leo's ears swiveled back against his head.

"I didn't mean that as an insult! You *are* a fox without thumbs—"

"I'm aware," Leo snarled. He stood and shook himself. "It's getting dark. I'll show you where you can get inside." He started off to the right.

Gareth followed, leading Fury and trying to think of some way to explain himself and fix the insult he'd accidentally given. Maybe there was no good way to say he thought that as a human, he should be better than a fox. Yes, if he thought about it like that, it did sound terrible.

Ahead of him, Leo paused with one paw raised and peered back.

"One other thing—once you're inside, don't approach anyone you see, and don't touch anything made of gold."

Gareth rolled his eyes. "I already said I'm not a burglar. I'm here for the firebird; I'm not trying to steal other things this witch probably stole anyway."

Leo shook his head as he padded on ahead. "I didn't say don't take. I said don't *touch*. Gold is a pure metal with exceptional longevity and is a good balance of soft and sturdy. Those qualities make it exceptionally well-suited to harmonize with magic. For this reason, gold is one of the easiest substances to enchant, but obviously the hardest to obtain."

The fox's voice took on a familiar cadence—a tutor giving a lecture. Maybe princes were bound by fate to spend their lives in endless lessons. The thought almost made Gareth laugh, but he'd already insulted his vulpine companion enough.

"Things that decay," Leo continued as he moved through the tall grass, "such as wood, will leach the magic too quickly. Iron is too brittle and prone to rust, which can make the spell unstable. Stone takes more magical energy to fill and has to be forcefully sealed to prevent the spell breaking the stone, which means spells stored in stones usually have to be activated by an incantation that works like a key. There are other methods, but incantations for spelled stones have the least room for error, which is important. Once activated, the enchantment takes effect immediately."

"I've seen stones like that," Gareth said.

Anger and fear flooded his mind at the memory of Tristan Carbrey pressing a cursed stone over Raelyn's heart while Henry Carbrey held a knife to her throat. Maybe Tristan had redeemed himself a little by cutting off the incantation and attacking his father instead, but Gareth would never forget the terror in Raelyn's eyes or his own horror as he was powerless to protect her.

Lost in thought, he nearly stepped on Leo's tail, as the fox had come to an abrupt stop. "Where did you see enchanted stones?"

"A blackguard tried to use a love spell on my sister." The words came out in a low growl. "So if you wonder why I don't believe it's possible for someone who casts curses not to be evil, it's because a twisted witch sold terrible curses to a wicked man, and he used them to torment an innocent child and a young woman, all in pursuit of power."

Leo's head tilted as he took a long look at Gareth, his gaze traveling from Gareth's head down to his boots and back. "So you're not just a random Eynlaean knight," he said slowly.

Gareth stiffened. "What are you talking about?"

The fox glanced around and lowered his voice. "How could casting a love spell on a mere knight's sister help someone in their pursuit of power? If a union with your sister could grant a man more power, she must be important—a high-ranking noble. Which means you must be, too. You're not…the baron's son, are you? Or Baron Tremblay himself?"

Some of Gareth's tension eased. "No, neither of those."

"Then who are you?"

"Maybe after I have the firebird in hand and this castle behind me and know that this wasn't a trap, I'll tell you, fox."

Leo watched him a moment more, then started forward again. "At least now I know why you have such grandiose ideas about yourself. You're probably really *Lord* Gareth or *Duke* Gareth or something, not *Sir* Gareth."

Following behind, Gareth suppressed a snort. What would Leo think if he knew he'd been sassing a prince of Eynlae for the last two days?

But better to keep his secret. Alone in Aedyllan with a fox of questionable trustworthiness outside of a witch's lair was *not* the time or place to proclaim his true identity.

Leo sat and inclined his head toward a spot in the wall. "Here."

Gareth bent down and peered at where Leo had indicated. A hole less than half his height was partly filled with grass and vines that he'd have to cut away to get through. He turned back to Leo. "You expect me to crawl through?"

"Is that too difficult or insulting for such a grand hero?" Leo rolled his eyes. Gareth hadn't known foxes could do that. "Crawl in through here and head to your right. When you come to a half-collapsed arch, turn left, and go straight. That will bring you to the garden. I'll wager that's where she's keeping the firebird."

"You're not coming with me?"

"And frighten the bird?" Leo shook his head. "If it starts squawking because of me, that would ruin the point of sneaking in."

That was difficult to argue with, but something about Leo remaining behind unsettled Gareth.

Unfortunately, there was no good alternative. He tied Fury to a birch tree. In the pinkish glow of dusk, he hacked his way through the vegetation and then retrieved the cage from his saddlebags. As he got down on his hands and knees, Leo snickered.

Gareth shot him a glare. "If this is a trap, I'm going to make you into a fur coat."

The fox wrinkled his snout. "Cruel. Now remember. Be quiet, be quick, avoid the witch, and whatever you do, don't touch anything made of gold. In fact, probably best to touch nothing other than the bird."

"Yes, yes. And you—don't let anyone steal my horse while I'm gone."

11

*I*nside the ruined castle wall, Gareth scrambled to his feet. A half-collapsed building jutted up nearby, jagged against the darkening sky. Chaotic overgrowth covered the ground and clung to the stone. He turned to his right, his eyes straining in the fading light.

As he made his way through knee-high grass, he drew his sword. The plan was to avoid the witch, and he didn't have any idea how a sword would fare against whatever form a witch's magic might take, but he wouldn't be taken down without a fight.

He crept through the dark, sword in one hand and birdcage in the other, listening intently. The main castle still stood, although in places the walls had crumbled. Gaping holes filled with ominous blackness marked what had once been doors and windows. Deep shadows gathered in every corner and behind every moss-covered chunk of stone. Gareth grasped the hilt of his sword. There were too many hiding places for some beast that had taken up residence in the ruins—or for a witch hoping to catch a young man for some nefarious purpose.

Ahead of him, the looming remnants of an archway reared up into a half of a point before breaking into uneven edges. Beyond the arch, a torch flared.

What if it wasn't a torch, but the firebird? Gareth crept up to the pillar forming the still-standing half of the arch. Peering around the soot-blackened stone, he squinted at the brightness of the flames.

In the orange glow, a woman with coppery-red hair in a long braid moved through a series of familiar attack forms, the sword in her grasp flashing in the torchlight. Her movements flowed with the precise surety of someone who had practiced long and hard, and her weapon never wavered. Over an undershirt with dark sleeves, a sleeveless blue tunic fell past her knees in long panels that parted over snug trousers. The fabric stretched across broad shoulders as she moved, and a hint of muscle pressed against her sleeves. Gareth gaped, captivated by her precision and strength.

She turned, and he inhaled sharply.

The young woman was gorgeous—and scarred.

Three raised, pinkish lines marked the right side of her face, running vertically over her eye. Her expression was focused and fierce as she completed her movements.

Was this the witch? Did witches often practice swordplay? But who else would be exercising in the dark in the witch's lair?

Gareth turned to follow the fox's directions and knocked his boot against a small piece of rubble, sending it flying. The pebble clattered against a pile of stones under the collapsed arch.

The woman spun toward the sound, her sword snapping up into a guard position. Gareth cursed himself and pressed back against the remaining column, hoping it was wide enough to hide him.

The whisper of boots through grass drew nearer, and flickering torchlight spilled around the pillar concealing him.

"If that's you, witch, you needn't skulk about in the shadows to spy on me." The woman's voice was clear and strong, with an undercurrent of irritation. Gareth's breath caught.

Unless that was a trick to get him to reveal himself, this *wasn't* the witch.

"Is someone there?" she called.

Maybe the woman would turn away. Or maybe she was a prisoner as much as the firebird and needed his help. But if someone with the fighting skill of that woman couldn't escape the witch, Gareth might not fare any better in a fight. The thought settled like an icy stone in his stomach.

The *whoosh* of a blade warned him, and Gareth dropped to a crouch, right as the woman whirled around the side of the archway and swung her sword through the air where his neck had been. He leapt aside and raised his own sword, just in time to parry her next attack. She dropped the torch onto a stone so she could wield her sword two-handed.

Up close, she obviously couldn't be any older than his own nineteen years. Her height matched his own, to his surprise. Since this girl wasn't the witch, they might be on the same side, but she kept up her skilled assault, so it was all Gareth could do to focus on defending himself and not tripping in the tall grass, forget attempting a conversation.

He didn't want to die, but he also didn't want to seriously hurt her before he knew who she was. He swung the birdcage in his left hand and rammed it into her side.

With a grunt, the woman flinched backward, her attack broken. As quickly as any knight, though, she adjusted her stance to defend, and if he didn't act quickly, she'd begin attacking again.

Acting on an intuition he didn't fully understand, Gareth lowered his weapon. "I never thought I'd say this, but I'd rather talk than fight for a moment, if you don't mind."

The girl lunged, and unable to get his sword up in time to block, Gareth scurried backward. His back slammed into the outer wall as the tip of her blade scraped against his breastplate. Without pause, she closed the distance between them and held the edge of her sword against his exposed neck.

Oh, she was *good*. Although he'd feel freer to admire her skill—and those intense eyes—if he wasn't also very worried he was moments from death.

"I yield, my lady!" Gareth dropped his sword to prove his point, but the girl didn't remove her blade.

"What are you doing here?" she hissed, her face inches from his. "Why were you trying to sneak up on me?"

Gareth gulped, oddly tongue-tied. "I'm here for a firebird. It was stolen from Baron Tremblay of Eynlae." He awkwardly lifted the birdcage in his other hand. "I didn't mean to sneak up on you. I thought you might be the witch, and then I…" His face burned. "I was impressed and watched you. Sorry."

"Oh." The woman eased back a little.

"Do you always attack first and ask questions later?" Gareth was glad Sir Christopher or Father weren't there to point out the irony of his query.

"When I'm a woman imprisoned in a ruined castle in the middle of nowhere, and someone sneaks up on me in the dark, hides and doesn't respond to my call, and generally acts suspicious, yes." Her gaze bored into him, and she still held the sword against his throat. "It wouldn't be the first time a man tried to take me by surprise."

Either whoever had tried to attack her was a fool or she hadn't started training yet at the time, because surely no one who'd observed her skills would attempt such a thing.

"Ah, sorry," he said. "I only wasn't sure if we were on the same side—but I think we are. The witch is both of our enemy."

Finally, the redhead took a couple of steps back and lowered her sword. Her lips pursed as she glanced around. "I don't know how you got in, but you should leave before she catches you."

"The witch?"

She nodded.

His gaze returned to her scars, three lines cutting through her eyebrow and over her cheekbone, although her eye itself was intact. Once, when he was fifteen and Raelyn was fourteen, he'd bloodied a squire's nose for making a crass comment about Raelyn becoming a young woman. At the time, Father had said Gareth had been born a protector. He didn't know if that was true, but the sight of those scars stirred a fiery, protective instinct in his chest.

"Did the witch do that to you?" he blurted.

The sword-maiden's brow wrinkled, then understanding flashed over her features. "Oh, that. No. But she is dangerous. I can't leave this place, but you might still have a chance."

A sinking feeling crept through Gareth. "Did a talking fox lead you here to be trapped?"

"A talking fox led you here?" Eagerness laced through her voice, decidedly not the reaction Gareth had expected.

"Yes…a rather opinionated fox named, of all things, Leo."

An amused chuckle accompanied a slight smile, and Gareth had the incongruous thought that he'd love to say something that could earn a full smile from her.

"So he's—" She bit her lower lip. "Never mind. You should go. Now." She turned and headed back toward the arch, pausing to retrieve her dropped torch.

"Wait!" Gareth reached after her, as if somehow that would stop her. "Why don't you come with me?"

She slowed and shook her head. "I can't get past the walls. I hope whatever magic allowed you inside allows you to leave again. Go, now."

"But—" He searched for something, anything to say to convince this mysterious young woman to let him help her. "I'm Gareth. What's your name?"

Her steps faltered. "Anika," she said, so quietly he almost didn't catch it. "Leave, Sir Gareth. And don't return."

With that, Anika took off at a run, her torch disappearing around the castle.

Gareth took a halting step forward, then froze. Go after her? Heed her warning and run? Or retrieve the firebird and escape?

He couldn't run. He didn't have that in him.

Anika didn't want his help. Perhaps she didn't need it, which presented Gareth with a confusing mix of emotions from uselessness to…a warm, jittery feeling he couldn't name. If he went after her now, though, he'd risk losing his way or getting caught by the witch.

It might take more than one knight to help Anika escape, or she would have done so already. He would need assistance. There was also the fact he couldn't leave with nothing to show for it and return to Eynlae in complete defeat.

"I'll come back for you," he whispered.

Gareth turned to his left and rushed through the night, seeking the garden and the firebird.

Before long, he located what must have once been a garden. Like everything else, it was overgrown with moss, vines, wildflowers, and saplings, but the area was wide open, and Gareth's boots clicked on cobblestones between the wild grass.

He stole through the garden, searching the trees for any sign of the firebird. Illustrations depicted the creature as a red and yellow bird rather like a cross between a hawk and a pheasant, with long tail feathers and a plume. According to what he'd read, firebirds more glowed than burned—while the flickering light of their wings mimicked fire and could shine brighter when the bird was agitated or excited, its magical flame was heatless and didn't burn—usually. They could erupt in real flames, but that typically killed them.

He rounded a tree, and a dim, pulsating glow caught his attention. A relieved sigh escaped him. As he crept closer, though, his relief soured to frustration.

The firebird was asleep…

In a large cage made of polished gold.

❧81❧

12

*H*ow to retrieve the firebird without touching its gold cage?

There was always the possibility that Leo had lied about the gold. Perhaps it was a clever misdirection, and gold was the only thing that *couldn't* be enchanted, and thus the only thing safe to touch.

Gareth walked around the cage, evaluating his options. The gate was secured with only a simple hook-and-eye latch. If he used his sword, he could lift the hook without touching the cage—assuming a blade didn't count as "touching." But the gate wasn't terribly wide, and he'd have to scoop the firebird out of the cage without touching the gold bars. Then he'd have to get it into his cage without it flying off or squawking. It seemed a shame to take it from the larger cage where it was slumbering peacefully to shove it into the smaller cage he'd brought.

"Don't touch anything made of gold."

"You should go, now."

Unease grew in his core. Trust the philosophical talking fox of questionable motivation and do everything in his power not to touch the gold? Simply take the entire gold cage? Or retreat and form a new plan?

Grumbling under his breath, Gareth used the tip of his sword to lift the latch and open the cage. The firebird raised its head and blinked at him with red eyes burning like embers, the gold-tipped crimson feathers lifting on the crown of its head.

"Shhh." He sheathed his sword, opened the gate on his smaller cage, and inched closer. "I'm here to help you."

The bird stood and shook its wings.

"Stay calm, birdie." He reached into the cage and gripped the firebird by its back, pinning its wings to its sides. "I'm taking you home."

As he drew the bird out of the cage, he held his breath. Just as he approached the opening, the firebird wriggled and attempted to free itself from his grasp. The back of his gloved hand brushed against the cage—

Pulsating lines of glittering lavender light burst from the top of the cage and arched overhead before crashing into the ground, enclosing Gareth and the firebird inside a cage of light.

With a curse, Gareth shoved the firebird back inside the golden cage and slammed the gate closed. No point in avoiding touching it now. Unfortunately, closing the firebird back in its cage changed nothing. The bars of light remained in place, keeping him trapped. The bird released a plaintive, hawk-like cry. Experimentally, Gareth knocked his small birdcage against the purple light. The magical prison crackled and vibrated, emitting sizzling sparks. Steam curled off his brass birdcage, accompanied by the scent of burnt metal.

Another curse that would have horrified Mother escaped through his gritted teeth. The fox *had* told the truth. And Anika probably had been right that he should have run.

He threw down the brass cage with a clang, eliciting a frightened squawk from the firebird in its gold enclosure. Now all he could do was stand there, a deer caught in a hunter's trap with no hope of escape or options other than waiting for his death.

Assuming the witch killed him and didn't curse him.

In the distance, a lantern appeared, vanishing between trees and reemerging closer. A tall woman wearing a hooded cloak strode forward, her pale, angular face cast in sharp contrast by the flame of her lantern. Her faded green dress hung loosely on her lanky frame. A braid of black hair was pinned in place over the crown of her head.

She came to a stop just outside Gareth's prison and lowered the lantern, peering down at him through the shining bars.

"Witch," Gareth spat.

A frown pulled at her thin lips. "Knight. Or should I say, thief?"

"I'm only retrieving what *you* stole." Gareth crossed his arms, irritated at having to look up at the witch's face. She was only a few inches taller than him and thin as a reed, but her cold expression gave her an aura of power.

"You came all the way from Eynlae for a bird?"

"Don't act like it's a random pheasant," he snapped. "Or that you didn't take it for the purpose of luring an Eynlaean here." He gestured at the magical cage surrounding him.

The woman sighed. She was young, probably only a few years older than Gareth. Subconsciously, he'd been expecting an old hag, not a young woman.

"I didn't force anyone to pursue the firebird. I needed it. The entrapment spell was merely a precaution." She tilted her head thoughtfully. "But since you're here, I have a task for you, knight."

Gareth instinctively grabbed the hilt of his sheathed sword. "I'm not doing *anything* for you, witch."

"You're really not in a position to argue." The bars of the magical cage quivered and shrank, inching closer to him. "I could kill you, or perhaps turn you into a quail and eat you for breakfast. But I'm willing to bargain with you."

He eased his hand off his sword. "What do you want?" With

a choice between certain death and hearing her out, he might as well stall for time.

"I'm concocting an intricate spell. It requires freshly plucked feathers from a firebird"—she motioned toward the caged firebird—"and water purified by a living unicorn's horn. Bring me a unicorn, and I'll give you the firebird, and you can return to your Eynlaean lord."

He huffed a disbelieving snort. "A unicorn? Is that all? Shall I pick up some dragon scales on my way?"

The witch pursed her lips. "I didn't ask you to hunt down a wild one."

Understanding hit Gareth like a charging bull. "You want me to steal one from the Aedyllanian royal stables."

Wild unicorns had been hunted nearly to extinction in Miraveld a few hundred years ago—their horns were useful for purifying water, restoring blighted fields, and as an ingredient in many concoctions. Only two places boasted small herds of domesticated unicorns: the queen's stables on the Isle of Darviat and the stables of the royal family of Aedyllan.

The Aedyllanian kings regarded their unicorns as one of their most valuable treasures. Although the noble family that cared for the unicorns had a lowly title, they were treated with great respect—but if harm befell any of the creatures, the stablemasters would be held responsible. Stealing, injuring, or killing a unicorn carried the penalty of death.

"Even if I believed I possessed the ability to steal a unicorn from the royal stables without getting caught," Gareth said, "I can't."

"Too moral?" The witch raised an imperious eyebrow.

It might start a war if an Eynlaean prince were caught stealing a unicorn from the king of Aedyllan, but he couldn't say that.

"I wouldn't succeed," he said instead. "What difference does it make if I die at the hands of the Aedyllanian stablemasters or at yours?"

"I see." The witch nodded, then held her empty hand forward. Her eyes closed, and her forehead scrunched. A faint violet light gradually grew brighter, then with a flash like lightning, a familiar red fox appeared, dangling from her fist by the scruff of his neck. "Perhaps I kill this friend of yours, then?"

Leo wriggled, his paws helplessly swinging through the air as he growled and snapped his teeth. He turned angry golden eyes on Gareth. "You bumbling suit of armor! I—"

"Hush." The witch shook Leo. "Otherwise, I'll take your voice."

Leo's jaws snapped closed.

Gareth gritted his teeth and watched the fox for any sign this was a trap. The witch had summoned Leo far too easily—but did that mean they were partners? Or simply that the witch had been observing Gareth?

"Here are your options, knight." The witch watched him, her marble-esque face devoid of emotion. "One, I skin this fox and make myself a nice fur-trimmed cloak, and then I shrink this cage until it crushes you. Two, we make an oath. You retrieve a unicorn for me; I don't care how you do it. We will exchange the bird for the horse, and then I'll let you leave. I'll even let the fox accompany you on your mission. What is your choice?"

His fists clenched so tightly his fingers ached. He hated the very idea of helping some witch make a spell that could potentially do great harm, but Leo had helped him. Leo could be annoying, but if he wasn't working with the witch and she killed him, Gareth would carry that guilt for as long as he lived…as short as that might be.

Of course, Gareth didn't want to die, either, but he wasn't a coward. So it wasn't fear that made up his mind. He'd make this compromise—temporarily—for Leo and to give himself a chance to stop the witch and help Anika. That was what he told himself, anyway. And if it turned out Leo had deceived him, at least his conscience would be clear.

"Fine," he ground out.

A smile twisted the witch's mouth, although it somehow looked more weary than triumphant. "Then I swear to release you and this talking fox to go on this errand. Return within ten days with a unicorn, and I will exchange the firebird for the unicorn and allow you to go free. Your turn."

"I swear…" Gareth worked his jaw. He'd never broken an oath or promise before, and he didn't want to start now, but there was no other way out of this. "I swear to leave here in peace, obtain a unicorn from the Aedyllanian royal stables, and then return here, where I will exchange the unicorn for the living firebird."

A line of shimmering lavender sped from the witch's chest and crashed into Gareth. He gasped as an icy-hot sensation speared through his heart. Even the witch grunted as if in pain. Then the thread of purple light vanished as if it had never been there.

"It is done, and the oath is sealed." The woman waved her hand, and the lavender cage of light flickered and then vanished. "If either of us reneges on our side of the deal, the oath-breaker's heart will be crushed by the binding spell, and they will perish."

"What?" The word came out embarrassingly panicked and loud, and Gareth cleared his throat. Wolf's teeth, he should have known better than to make a promise to a witch. It seemed they were as cruel and cunning as the fae themselves—or at least the stories of the fae.

In response, the witch only nodded. She dropped Leo and lifted her lantern to illuminate Gareth's face. "Good luck, knight."

"Wait," he blurted. "Why are you holding a young woman captive?"

Some fleeting emotion pinched the witch's expression for the blink of an eye. "She's none of your concern right now. Your only concern is the unicorn, assuming you don't want to die a painful death."

With that, she turned and strode away into the shadows.

"Let's go," Leo snapped. "Before I give in to my base desires and bite your ankles."

13

$\mathcal{B}$ack outside the castle walls, Gareth led Fury well away from the ruins before stopping to make camp. Leo didn't speak a word, although his lips pulled back in a slight snarl every time Gareth looked his way. From opposite sides of the small campfire, prince and fox stared at each other for a long moment. Too many thoughts swam through Gareth's head for him to know where to begin or what to say. Leo's whiskers trembled, the look in his eyes murderous.

"I told you not to touch anything gold!" the fox burst out. "I even said 'best not to touch anything other than the bird.' Those were my exact words!"

"Well, you're a fox," Gareth muttered, his pride still sore from his being so easily captured and forced into a magical oath. "What do you know?"

"I'm a *talking* fox." Leo's tail bristled. "How many talking foxes have you met, you walking ignoramus?"

"Right now, I'm wishing none!"

He'd failed in his quest—just like Captain Plinworth had predicted—and proven he wasn't a hero of legend, just like Father and Frederick always said. After everything that had gone wrong, he was *not* going to be scolded by a haughty canine who would have made an excellent royal tutor in another life. He wasn't in the mood.

Leo growled. "Oooooh, yes. It must be my fault because the knight is so much wiser than me, the humble fox. I'm not the one who took a magically binding oath! I'm not the one who thought he knew better and didn't listen to advice and mucked everything up!"

"Oh, shut up, Frederick!" Gareth froze, his ears burning as he lowered his gaze to his boots.

After a long moment, Leo asked, his tone gentler, "Who in all of Miraveld is Frederick?"

"My older brother." Gareth shook himself and looked up. "I did *try* not to touch the gold cage. At this point, it doesn't matter. The point is that what happened, happened, and now we have to deal with it."

"We?" Leo barked a laugh. "This is your mess. Your oath and your heart at risk of being crushed."

"Don't pretend like I didn't give in partly to save your furry hide," Gareth snapped, even though that wasn't entirely fair. "The least you can do is help me."

"I already tried, and you didn't listen." Leo stuck his nose in the air.

"You try getting a bird out of a cage without touching said cage!"

"Perhaps you should have tried coaxing it out instead of reaching inside."

The fact that option hadn't occurred to him felt like a slap in the face. Not that Gareth had any idea how to coax a firebird. Maybe Father did have a point about him rushing into things. But thinking about Father only soured his stomach, so Gareth pushed that thought aside.

"Anyway," he said, "it's not only about me. That witch has a young woman trapped in that castle, and I think she needs help. If I can get the unicorn and trade it for the firebird, then I can go back to Tremblay Barony and ask for help—"

"Because an Eynlaean baron is going to send a contingent of knights into Aedyllan?" Leo interrupted. "Why would he do that?"

"Ah…" Gareth floundered, unsure if he actually could convince Tremblay to do that. "Well…maybe not. But if I can get inside the witch's castle again, maybe I can help Anika."

Leo stood, his entire body stiff. "Why'd you say her name like that?"

"Like what?" An inexplicable blush rose to his cheeks.

"Like…like you were savoring it. Stop it."

"All I said was 'Anika.'"

"Well, just don't say it, then! You don't need to say her name."

Gareth raised a brow. "Why do you care? How do you know her?"

"None of your business," Leo snarled. He padded around in an agitated circle before sitting again. "But…was…did she seem all right? Not hurt?"

"She has scars on her face, but she said they weren't from the witch. Otherwise she seemed fine. I came across her practicing sword fighting, and she attacked me." He smiled, gazing into the flames. "She's good—really good. I'd love a rematch. In the daylight, on more even footing. Get my honor back from her pinning me against a wall." He shook his head. "I wish she would have come with me. I don't know if she didn't trust me enough or was too afraid of the witch…but maybe telling me her name means she does trust me."

Leo stalked over to Gareth. "You know what I think?" He batted Gareth's cheek with a forepaw, more of a punch than a slap.

"Hey, ow!"

"I think you should stop thinking about Anika!" Leo trotted back to the opposite side of the fire, where he sat down, glowering over the flames. "Or I won't help you."

Gareth couldn't help a slight smirk. "I don't know how to explain to you that a fox and a human is never going to work out."

"That's not—" Leo sighed. "Whatever. Lucky for you, I've been to the royal unicorn stables before. I grew up around there, in fact. So I'm going to be more helpful than you'd have guessed, and certainly more than you deserve."

"I still saved your life."

"You endangered it by getting caught in the first place."

"But here's what I don't understand." Gareth leaned forward, resting his arms on his knees. "How did the witch know you were helping me or that you were there? She caught you even easier than she caught me. I had to activate a trap, but she just…summoned you, somehow, and already knew we were working together. Care to explain that?"

Leo's ears lay back as he ducked his head. "No."

That answer was worse than if the fox had claimed not to know. "So you do know, you just won't tell me?"

"No."

"To which part?"

"Listen, I didn't have to warn you about the gold. Trust me or don't, I don't care, but know that I hate that witch even more than you do." Leo curled into a ball and covered his face with his bushy tail.

Taking the hint, Gareth crawled under his blanket shelter and lay down. Despite Leo's warning, a strong, redheaded girl whose blade sang through the air haunted his dreams.

14

*A*s Leo and Gareth left the ruins of the castle, Anika collapsed against a tree trunk and let herself breathe again. It had taken all of her self-control not to attack the witch the moment Leo had appeared in her grasp, dangling helplessly, but she knew better. It wouldn't have ended well for either of them, and she had to believe the witch would keep her word—so long as both Leo and Anika did as they were told, neither of them would be harmed.

Unfortunately, though, the Eynlaean knight had mentioned Anika to the witch. She didn't want to be chained up in her room, especially not when she still hadn't figured out how to get into the witch's room without breaking any rules. Whatever Callista was planning, the answers had to be hidden in there—and probably the answer to how Anika could escape as well. She'd gotten a glimpse inside the witch's bedroom when she returned with the firebird, and there had been massive tomes and several scrolls scattered over a desk and the floor. One of them had to contain something useful.

She turned to head back inside and swallowed a scream when she nearly bumped into the witch.

"I didn't leave the castle," Anika said quickly as she backed away. Her fingers itched to grab the hilt of her sword. "I was practicing my swordplay and that knight found me—"

"I don't care that he saw you." Callista crossed her slender arms. "I want to know why you didn't tell me someone was here."

"Why in Miraveld would I tell you? I want to know *how* he got inside. I thought you warded the castle?"

Callista shrugged. "Technically, no. Maintaining a constant ward to block anything and everything from entering or exiting would take a ridiculous amount of magical energy, and the barrier would be worn down by every animal or large insect that tried to pass through it. The spell isn't on the castle walls; it's on you."

Of course. Because just as Callista leveraged Leo's life to keep Anika in check, she'd secured Leo's compliance by keeping Anika trapped in the castle. Anika suspected there was more to her own imprisonment than controlling Leo. Nothing Callista did was logical, but she seemed stressed about things proceeding according to some master plan. A plan which apparently involved Leo helping this knight and Anika rotting away inside this decrepit castle while her parents anxiously waited for news.

"You're allowed to wander the castle on my goodwill," Callista said. "So I'll ask you again—why didn't you tell me of the intruder?"

If only the witch weren't so tall. Anika was used to being slightly taller than most Aedyllanian women, and looking up at Callista made her feel much less confident. She mustered her courage and focused on keeping her tone level and challenging.

"You never ordered me to tell you of intruders, so I disobeyed no orders. I also didn't want you to hurt or imprison anyone else." She frowned. "He's likely to get himself killed if he attempts to steal a unicorn. And why even send him? You have me."

As usual, her captor's antics made no sense.

Callista turned away. "He'll be fine."

Anika snorted. "You must not understand how serious unicorn theft is. And you had an opportunity to demand one when you visited my father."

Callista stared off into the distance. At last, she sighed, and when she looked back at Anika, there was a lifeless quality to her eyes. "What do you know about the magical theory of prophecies?"

Anika shrugged. "Not much. Prophecies take an enormous amount of magical energy and ability, far more than most humans possess, so I never paid them any heed."

"True enough. Prophecies are a very particular, powerful kind of magic with an interesting relationship with fate and destiny that no one entirely understands. Because they are such large uses of magic, prophecies also tend to have unpredictable and dangerous side effects. More importantly, prophecies want to come true—some would argue they *need* to, like a bowstring drawn taut that must be released. This one has been aching to be released for a very long time. That is why I couldn't use you to get a unicorn. It's also why the boy won't die breaking into the royal stables." Something like pain or regret flashed across her face before she turned away. "Fate won't let him, and neither will I."

Anika's lips parted. This was what the witch was up to—watching a prophecy unfold? No...it sounded more like... "Are you trying to force a prophecy to come true?"

In the dim moonlight, Callista's profile looked as unfeeling as stone. "Trying implies I might not succeed. And I can't fail."

"What will happen if you succeed in bending fate to your twisted will?" Horror bled into her voice. After everything Callista had already done, this prophecy had to be something terrible.

Taking a deep breath, Callista met Anika's eyes. Although her expression was more exhausted than angry, steel underlaid her words. "All you need to know is that you had best play your part and not test me. Leo doesn't need to be hurt, but I will do whatever it takes to achieve my goal. Am I clear?"

Fear arrested Anika's voice, so she nodded.

"Good." Callista departed, leaving Anika alone in the dark garden with one glaring question.

What prophecy was Callista forcing to come true?

Prophecies were uncommon, but there could still be any number of prophecies she'd never heard of with small or large stakes. Yet Anika knew of only one that had yet to be fulfilled.

A mixed blessing, prophecy, and curse from legend, one that no one could say definitively was real or just a story, but most Aedyllanians believed must exist.

If it *was* real…

And if the witch had gotten her hands on it…

Anika needed to get into Callista's room, no matter how dangerous it might be. If her suspicion was correct, this no longer affected only her and her family and friends.

The fate of the royal family and the entire kingdom of Aedyllan might hang in the balance.

15

$\mathcal{L}$eo resumed his role as navigator the next morning. Gareth was back to wondering if he should trust the fox. What were the odds that the witch would send him to steal a unicorn and Leo would just happen to have grown up near there and know the way? Certainly, Gareth would have struggled to get there on his own with only a murky knowledge of Aedyllanian geography, so he should be grateful. The witch and Leo didn't seem to be on friendly terms, which was reassuring. Still, he couldn't shake the feeling there was more going on than a witch deciding to send him on an errand because it was convenient.

"I don't suppose you could steal a unicorn by yourself," Gareth mused as they rode down a dusty, empty road late that afternoon. He'd been relieved when Leo said they could take the road for a while—dodging branches got tiring.

"How would a fox steal a horse? They'd either trample me or run away rather than follow me. Although your horse has been mostly fine."

"That's because the stablemaster and horse trainers and I all spent more hours than I can count training and slowly desensitizing him so that he'll be steady in hunts and battles," Gareth said flatly.

"Hm, not true for the unicorns. You'll have to go in alone. We don't need the unicorns spooking and causing a ruckus."

"Great. I get to do the hard part again."

"I thought knights like a challenge?" Leo hummed. "I don't blame you for wanting to avoid this one, though. You don't want to get caught."

"More than you know," Gareth muttered.

A shove against his back, and then Leo's whiskers tickled his cheek as he leaned over Gareth's shoulder. "Because you're... Duke Gareth?"

"I'm a knight."

"Sure. And a duke."

"Not a duke."

"A baron."

"No."

"A duke or baron's son."

Gareth sighed. "I'm a knight, all right? That's all." It wasn't a lie. That was all he was supposed to be at the moment...still, if he were caught stealing from the king of Aedyllan, he might be stuck between "instant death" and "admit who you are and potentially start a war."

Father might lock him in his room for eternity if he nearly caused *another* war.

"Hmmm, I don't believe you." Leo rested his chin on Gareth's shoulder. "Oh, I've got it. You're a baron or duke's bastard."

"No!" Gareth shrugged hard to dislodge his furry companion.

"Humph." Undeterred, Leo continued to rest his paws on the back of Gareth's cuirass. "You're someone. Your attitude, your bearing, your high-quality armor and sword, your story about your sister, and your paranoia about stealing from the king of Aedyllan all point to you being a high-ranking Eynlaean noble or related to one."

"Why would it matter to you if I am?"

Leo finally sat back down. "I suppose it wouldn't change much. I just hate not knowing things. And I like being right."

Gareth snorted. "No, really?"

"Trouble is, I didn't pay proper attention when learning about the noble families of Eynlae. I don't even recall your royals' names. Well…King Winston, I think?"

"Weston," Gareth corrected.

"Oh, right! King Weston, Queen…hmm. Janice. No. Gillian? Oh! Giselle! And then Crown Prince…Theodore?"

"Ha, not even close." Although Gareth would *love* to see the look on Frederick's face if someone called him Theodore.

Leo made an irritated tittering sound. "This is going to bother me now."

"Frederick," Gareth said without thinking, and immediately bit his tongue.

"Oh, easy for you to remember," Leo grumbled. "Your brother is also named Fr…wait." He gasped. "*Prince* Gareth?"

Gareth's entire face went red. "Of course not. Don't be ridiculous."

Leo squirmed under Gareth's arm and popped up in front of him, his black-tipped ears fully perked as he searched Gareth's face. "Fates and blessings, you're a *prince*? What in Miraveld is an Eynlaean prince doing hunting down a baron's stolen firebird by himself in Aedyllan?"

"You have your secrets, fox. I have mine."

Based on the way Leo's eyes narrowed and he tilted his head, that answer didn't satisfy him, but he went quiet. Just as Gareth was about to ask if he was going to keep sitting basically in his lap and staring at him, Leo spoke again.

"At least you've never been to Aedyllan, right?"

Gareth nodded.

"And the Raylors—the noble family that cares for the unicorns—haven't been to Eynlae, so they shouldn't recognize you. Obviously the ideal situation is not to get caught, but if that does happen…" Leo hesitated. "Maybe don't mention being Eynlaean. No, you just can't get caught."

Abruptly, he jumped up, resting his paws on Gareth's chest so they were eye to eye—and Leo's head was completely blocking the road. "One of the ways the Raylors have protected against thieves is they use gold that has been infused with alarming charms. They won't capture you the way the witch's spell did, but they're magically linked to an alarm bell. The harnesses, saddles, bridles, reins, the latches on the stalls—they're all gold or stitched with gold thread, and you have to say a secret password so they won't set off the alarm."

"Which is?"

"I don't know." Leo's ears fell as he sat back down. "So this time, *listen* to me. Do whatever it takes to avoid touching anything gold. You'll need to bring in your own rope and get creative with the latches."

Gareth sighed. "Wonderful. How do the Raylors have enchanted objects?"

"Oh, most of them are ancient." Leo turned around and rested his forepaws on Fury's withers so he could peer forward at the road. "The first Raylor who caught and tamed the unicorns was an enchanter. Sometimes a Raylor is born with a little magical ability, and they can place new enchantments or strengthen old ones. Occasionally they've had to hire an enchanter."

"Is one of the Raylors an enchanter now?" Gareth asked, a bit apprehensive.

For a moment, Leo was silent, and Gareth wondered if the fox hadn't heard him. "There isn't a magic-wielder at Raylor Estate anymore, no."

There was a note of sadness in Leo's tone that made Gareth decide not to press the issue. After all, he had just chided Leo about not pressuring him for secrets. He did wonder, however, if an enchanter or enchantress who used to live at the Raylor Estate had given the fox the ability to speak.

Leo stiffened, the hair on his shoulders rising as his alert ears swiveled. He lifted his twitching nose to sniff the air.

"Is something—"

"Get off the road, now." The fox laid back his ears. "Someone is coming toward us. I hear hoofbeats and men's voices and smell a lot of horses and people."

"So? Having a pet fox is unusual, but if you keep your yapper shut—"

"It's not that! They could be bandits." Leo spun around, bit one of the reins, and pulled, making Fury angle toward the side of the road.

"All right, all right." Gareth nudged Leo's muzzle and took over steering Fury into the forest, continuing until they didn't have a good view of the road and would be unlikely to be seen. "I'll have you know I don't enjoy running from a fight, but if you're right, it sounds like I'm outnumbered."

After a couple of minutes, the sound of hoofbeats preceded a large group riding in the opposite direction they'd been traveling. He couldn't get a good look at them through the trees, but he caught glimpses of sunlight flashing on what appeared to be armor and weapons. After they disappeared down the road, Gareth waited a couple more minutes in silence before he directed Fury back onto the road.

Leo wormed back under Gareth's arm to settle into his usual spot atop the saddlebags. "Bandits have become more of an issue in the last few years," he said grimly. "Big bands like that are becoming more common."

Gareth shook his head in disbelief. "I didn't know bandits were a problem in Aedyllan. Sure, few places are entirely free of banditry, but criminals aren't usually so…blatant. Bandits in Eynlae favor areas where it's easy to hide, because my father sends knights out if reports of anyone harassing our people make it to the palace."

Leo growled. "According to King Silas, we don't have a bandit problem. But that's what happens when you get rid of all road patrols and guard posts. It saved the crown money, but some of the very men that used to protect Aedyllan now terrorize it. They went from a stable occupation to being jobless and penniless, and there were too many former guards looking for work all at once."

"That's ridiculous," Gareth declared. "What is the point of the crown if not to protect the kingdom—the whole kingdom, not just the palace?"

"I suppose when all attempts to kill you or overthrow your ancestors have failed, you decide you can do whatever you like, the kingdom be hanged." Leo stood and spun around, bumping into Gareth's back before he lay down again. "This is making me agitated. Let's talk about something else. What's the Eynlaean palace like?"

As that seemed a harmless enough topic, Gareth described the palace—Leo was exceedingly disappointed he didn't have more to say about the royal library—until the fox dozed off. When Gareth elbowed him, Leo would wake up just long enough to confirm directions.

As the sun edged toward the horizon, Gareth halted Fury and dismounted. Leo pried open one eye before lifting his head.

"Why are we stopping?"

"Because *someone* ate all our food. I want to hunt while it's still light out." He scooped up Leo, prompting an annoyed yowl, and set him on the ground. "And by *I*, I mean you."

16

"N o." Leo stretched out, sticking his rear in the air as he yawned and revealed all of his pointy teeth.

"You're a predator," Gareth protested.

"I'm a scholar."

"Well, right now, you're going to be both, or we won't have anything to eat, because I didn't bring my bow."

"Fine," Leo grumbled.

The fox might not have wanted to hunt, but he was good at it. Watching Leo tilt his head back and forth before springing into the air and diving into a rabbit hole was at once the most impressive and funniest thing Gareth had ever observed.

He was ready to take the rabbit and call it a day, but Leo's nose twitched. He licked his lips.

"I smell quail. Wait here so you don't scare them."

When Leo reappeared several minutes later, Gareth changed his mind. The most amusing thing he'd ever seen was Leo's self-satisfied prance as he returned with a mess of feathers sticking out of his mouth.

When they returned to Fury, Gareth built a fire. "Do you prefer one of those? You can help yourself to one and I'll take the other."

"Beg your pardon?" Leo looked from the rabbit and quail to Gareth and back in confusion. "You… Fae take me; you expect me to eat this *raw?*"

"Isn't that what foxes do?"

"Not this fox." Leo nudged the rabbit toward Gareth with his paw.

Too baffled to argue, Gareth took the rabbit. "Well, at least help, then."

He set about dressing the rabbit while Leo plucked the quail—with a lot of spitting and complaining about how dry the feathers made his mouth. Eventually, though, they had both kills cooking over the fire.

"Don't set your expectations too high." Gareth rubbed the back of his neck. "I've skinned a kill before, but…I, uh…"

"You've never cooked before," the fox said flatly.

"No."

"Unsurprising, prince."

"Don't call me that." Gareth turned the stick holding the rabbit and quail over the fire. "And clearly, I packed no salt or seasoning."

Leo heaved a dramatic sigh. "Alas. My trials never end. Oh well. At least it's not a handful of nuts."

"For which you were very ungrateful."

"We're trading. Food for help. It's an even exchange."

Gareth snorted. "Sure, if you say so."

While the meat cooked, Leo explained the rotation of the guards at the Raylor Estate, a subject with which the fox was suspiciously familiar, as well as the best ways to sneak into the stable. After a filling but not impressive meal, they continued on their way. A couple of hours after sunset, they reached their destination.

The Raylor Estate was a sprawling expanse of wheat, open fields, and several buildings scattered along one side of a long lake that glittered in the moonlight. Lush forest surrounded the estate, granting it a secluded, peaceful ambiance. The entire property was enclosed in a dry-stone wall which only came up to Gareth's chest. Leo said it was more for keeping the unicorn herd in when they were at pasture than to keep people out.

In the distance, moonlight reflected faintly off the limestone walls of an impressive manor with several turrets spearing into the sky. The long, squat building of dark brick near the manor was the unicorn stables.

Hidden in the forest, Gareth tied Fury to a tree—loosely enough that the horse could break free if needed—and untacked him, then removed his armor and sword. The heavy steel would only hinder his stealth mission. He wrapped his rope around his waist.

Standing in front of the wall, Gareth rolled his shoulders. "How painful do you think death by crushed heart would be?"

Leo batted at his calf. "Defying the witch would be an agonizing and pointless death. Don't even consider it. Hurry up."

"Will the stablemasters be punished? I don't want—"

"They'll report it as a death and be fine. Unicorns do die, you know. Go already."

With a deep inhale, Gareth climbed over the wall.

This infiltration was worse than sneaking into the witch's castle. That had almost felt right. He'd been sneaking through a villain's dilapidated lair to reclaim stolen property for his liege. As he crept through stalks of wheat, he was filled with a stomach-churning sense of wrongness.

There was nothing noble about stealing from innocent people. To do so at the behest of a witch made it worse. He had every intention of doing his best to return the unicorn to the Raylors— after he secured the firebird and helped Anika—but that only assuaged his guilt a little.

How to accomplish all of that was a problem for tomorrow. As he paused at the edge of a wheat field, watching for the patrolling guards, he hoped that stealing a unicorn wouldn't bring him ill fortune. Some legends claimed killing a unicorn was bad luck. Although considering how close the unicorns had gotten to extinction, that was probably a baseless myth.

After a pair of guards passed around the corner of the stables, Gareth made a dash across the wide cobblestone path that wound around the buildings. Pressing his back against the brick, he didn't dare breathe. No shouts sounded; no footsteps came pounding in his direction. Slowly, he released his breath.

Keeping to shadows along the wall as much as possible, he edged around the stable toward one of the side doors. As Leo had predicted, it was bolted shut from the inside.

Gareth pulled out his dagger and, following the fox's suspicious directions, felt down the narrow space between the door and the doorframe until he found a slightly wider notch. The dagger easily slipped into the notch, and he worked it up the narrowing space until, just as he thought the dagger would become stuck, it struck against something metal. After a bit of maneuvering and jiggling that sounded far too loud, the latch flipped up.

This time when he tried the door, it swung out, its well-oiled hinges near silent. He eased the door closed behind him and returned the dagger to its sheath.

Inside the stables there was an odd, dull glow. The light was faint and irregular, and unless his eyes were tricking him, it was inconsistent in color. Gareth tiptoed into an aisle that ran the length of the stable between the two rows of stalls. As he caught sight of a unicorn for the first time, he understood the soft light.

A unicorn stood in its stall, looking out a small, high window. It was built like a destrier, tall and muscled with an awe-inspiring presence. The horse had a silky, pale-amber coat and a long, shiny mane and tail that looked like spun gold. A twisting gold horn protruded from the center of its forehead, and from the horn emanated a gentle, yellow-tinged glow.

It was the most beautiful thing Gareth had ever seen. Apologies to Fury, but he had the intense desire to ride a unicorn. How did anyone ever hunt and kill these magnificent beasts?

He peered into another stall. A slender gray unicorn that was built like a swift riding horse and had a silver mane and tail, with a more delicate beauty than the gold unicorn, slept on a layer of straw, its silver horn glowing faintly. In the next stall a sturdy black unicorn slept standing, its blue-black horn emitting a subtle blue light. Gareth had heard that unicorns came in as wide a variety as non-magical horses, but still, seeing the differences amazed him.

A snort drew his attention. The massive gold unicorn had turned toward him and was sticking its head over the wood gate of its stall. Its coppery eyes watched him, and then the unicorn gave a little toss of its head, its mane shining in the moonlight filtering in through the small windows.

"Easy there, boy. Or girl." Gareth crept closer, mesmerized. The unicorn didn't shy away, just waited. On the narrow end of the wooden wall separating its stall from the next one, a bridle and set of reins sparkled with golden thread. They were alluring, as they seemed the only tack worthy of placing on the unicorn, but Gareth forced himself to ignore them.

"Hello," Gareth whispered. Gently, he offered his hand, letting the unicorn snuffle at his palm until it pressed its velvety nose against him. He grinned. "Good unicorn."

A flash of metal on the top of the stall gate caught his attention, and he crouched slightly to squint at it. Etched into a small bronze plate was *Tempest*. That didn't provide any clarity on the unicorn's gender, but at least he knew its name.

"Hi, Tempest." As he scratched under the unicorn's jaw and

the horse leaned its massive head into his hand, he removed the rope from his waist. "Just going to slide this over your head, all right?"

He loosened the loop he'd previously prepared in the rope and guided it over the unicorn's face. Its height combined with the extra length of its horn made getting the rope onto its neck a challenge. Even balanced precariously on his toes, he kept catching the rope on the horn. Thankfully, the unicorn lowered its head with a gentle snort, as if taking pity on him. As soon as the loop was around the top of its neck, Gareth rocked back off his tiptoes and slid the rope down.

But as he dropped his left hand to the gate, more focused on the gorgeous unicorn in front of him than anything else, he misjudged the distance.

His hand didn't land on wood.

Instead, cold, unforgiving metal met his skin as his palm slapped against the stall's latch.

Somewhere nearby, the high-pitched clang of a bell pealed through the night air.

17

"olf's teeth!" Abandoning caution, Gareth slammed open the latch and threw the stall gate wide. "Come on, Tempest."

He tugged on the rope, but Tempest stood there, unmoving. Shouts sounded outside, and whinnies traveled up and down the stable.

"No, no…come on. We don't have time to delay!" Gareth clicked his tongue and applied gentle pressure to the rope.

Tempest took a leisurely step forward.

"Good…" Gareth leaned over to peek. "Ah, girl. Good girl. Come on—"

A door further down in the stable banged open, and three guards rushed in, the light of their torches so bright that spots danced in Gareth's eyes.

With a muttered curse, he looked to Tempest. "Either you can help me get out of here and we can both make a grand escape, or I leave you behind in this little stall."

To his shock, Tempest dipped her head and walked out of the stall. They were close to the unlocked door where he had entered…but the unicorn wouldn't fit through there. He jogged away from the guards toward the set of double doors at the far end of the stable, picking up speed as Tempest matched his pace.

"Stop right there!"

The three guards charged after them, swords drawn. Somehow Gareth would have to lift the crossbar that secured the double doors before the guards caught up to him—

A resounding *slam* made him jump as another side door was thrown open, and two more guards raced into the stable, blocking his exit. One brandished a sword, and the other drew his bow.

Gareth skidded to a stop, and Tempest halted as well, tossing her head. Dropping the rope, he held up his hands and dropped to his knees.

According to Leo, the guards wouldn't hesitate to carry out the punishment for stealing a unicorn immediately. The fox had stressed the importance of not getting caught. While Gareth agreed, he'd also thought it prudent to have a backup plan.

"I surrender and, as a noble, demand an audience with Lord Raylor at once."

All right, it wasn't a great plan, but he was gambling that the guards would err on the side of caution and take him captive until they could speak with their liege rather than kill him on the spot.

"Luckily for you," a gruff voice said behind him, "we're already under orders to take anyone caught breaking in tonight to Lord Raylor at once."

Rough hands seized his wrists and wrenched his hands behind his back. Cold metal cuffs clicked into place, and then the guard yanked up on the manacles, straining Gareth's shoulders and forcing him to his feet.

At least he wasn't dead.

But there was something foreboding about the guard's words. Anyone caught breaking in *tonight*. As if they'd been expecting a thief.

If that accursed fox had betrayed him, Gareth would put a dagger through his eye.

Assuming he survived this.

The archer returned his arrow to his quiver and then led Tempest back to her stall. Other unicorns poked their heads over their gates—lithe horses and big pulling horses, sorrels and roans and more, all with dimly glowing horns the color of unpolished gems or metals.

The guards shoved Gareth out of the stables too quickly for him to get a proper look at any of them. Still, at least if he were to die, he'd do so having touched a living unicorn.

The thought brought no comfort. His family would never know what had happened to him or why. He'd never see Raelyn again or meet any children she had with Alexander. There were so many things he wanted to do and places he wanted to see, monsters he wanted to slay and people he wanted to help.

Stealing a unicorn was such a stupid way to die.

If only he had his brother-in-law's charm. Or even Frederick's irritating but effective oratorical capabilities. Truthfulness was one of the few qualities he possessed, which got him into trouble more often than not, but maybe, this time, the truth would help him.

Although Lord Raylor probably wouldn't be sympathetic to his story of being forced to commit a crime by a witch.

The guards led him through an unobtrusive servants' entrance and through narrow, undecorated passages. Even those gave a sense of the manor's grandeur—the ceilings were high, the floor covered with rugs, and the hallways long.

When they left the servants' passages and entered a wide hallway, the Raylors' wealth became more obvious. Statues, tapestries, and weapons decorated the walls and alcoves, and a plusher pine-green carpet ran down the center of the hall. The manor was decorated nearly as well as the royal castle in Eynlae.

The guards pushed him into a sitting room with padded armchairs and a chaise covered in a fur blanket. As one of the guards went around lighting candles on small end tables, Gareth's hopes rose. Such a cozy room was hardly a place to be sentenced to death.

The guard holding his arm tugged him over to stand in front of an empty fireplace. "Stay there and don't move," he snapped.

Both guards left the room, further bewildering Gareth. Sure, he only had a dagger on him—which the guards hadn't even bothered to take—and his hands were locked behind his back, and he had surrendered quickly. Still, being left alone as a prisoner in a sitting room was a tiny bit insulting. He was beginning to think the tales of instant death were greatly exaggerated.

How bad would it look if he took a seat? Might not be comfortable with his wrists shackled, anyway.

Wolf's teeth. Being a prisoner was not enjoyable, and he was too young to have been someone's captive three times already.

The door opened with a soft click, and a middle-aged man walked in, a lantern in hand. He wore wool slippers and a satin robe over a long nightgown. His short, auburn hair was a mess, and his wide eyes swept over Gareth with confusion.

"She said you'd be a knight." The man—Lord Raylor, most likely—closed the door behind him. "You look more like a vagabond."

"Who said?" Apprehension rose, and he shifted his arms, making the manacles' links clink.

Lord Raylor moved to stand in front of Gareth, their heights near enough equal Gareth was unsure who was taller. "The witch that has my daughter." Raylor spat out *witch* like a curse.

Gareth's jaw fell open as he looked again at the lord's red hair. "Anika?"

The light in the lantern fluttered as Raylor nearly dropped it. He grabbed Gareth's shirt and yanked him in so close spittle landed on his cheeks. "How do you know her?"

"I—I was trying to steal—retrieve, get back, that is—something else the witch stole," Gareth stammered. "I saw a sword-maiden named Anika who said she couldn't leave."

"Was she all right?" Raylor shouted, giving Gareth a small shake. "Was she hurt?"

"She seemed fine," Gareth reassured him. "No injuries other than some old facial scars."

Raylor slumped, his grip on Gareth's shirt loosening. "You did see her. She was alive and all right." He shook his head and took a step back. "Why are you trying to steal a unicorn?"

The witch warning the Raylors that he was coming and Lord Raylor being Anika's father had thrown him off balance, but finally, his senses snapped back. He rolled back his shoulders and attempted to put on an air of confidence and grace.

"First, I want to say I'm not a thief or vagabond. I am a knight, and I hated committing such a crime, but the witch left me no choice."

"She threatened you?"

"Me and a friend of mine, a talking fox named Leo… Anyway, she made me swear to bring her the unicorn or she'd kill us, then cast a binding spell. If I break my promise, her spell will crush my heart."

Lord Raylor paced back and forth. "She sent me a message by hawk today, saying a knight would attempt to steal a unicorn to-night. Then she instructed me to send the knight to the old tower in Lake Marsing." A muscle in his jaw ticked. "You're to go alone if I want to see Anika again, and to do your best to rescue her from the tower."

Gareth blinked. That didn't make sense. What game was the witch playing at?

Raylor stopped pacing and turned back to Gareth. "Please. I don't know why this witch is targeting us, but Anika is innocent. Rescue my daughter. If you bring her back…" He gulped. "I'll give you a unicorn, so the witch's curse won't kill you. I swear it on my honor. Return my daughter to me, and I'll give you any unicorn you want."

"Can you do that?"

Raylor glanced away. "I can claim one died unexpectedly. It's unlikely, but not impossible."

So Leo had been right about that. He felt guilty for putting the man in this position, but it wasn't really Gareth's doing. The witch was the cause of all of this.

"I promise on my life, I will do everything I can to bring your daughter home unharmed."

Raylor looked unconvinced.

"My sister was taken once," Gareth said quietly. "I would have torn the mountains down, fought every monster in Miraveld, and sacrificed myself to find her and bring her back safely. And my father…he left her. He gave up." His throat caught, and it took him a moment to continue.

But Raylor must have taken his pause as judgment. "Please understand, I'm not relaxing in my manor by choice. I was riding through Aedyllan searching for her myself, but that witch told me to go home and call off the search or my daughter would never come home. I'd never abandon my child, not by choice. Please, help her."

Gareth nodded. "I understand. I don't want to see anyone suffer, either. I'm glad to see a father who clearly will do anything to get his daughter back. But…I'm afraid I am…not well-traveled. Could you tell me how to get to Lake Marsing?"

18

Leo was pacing along the top of the stone wall when Gareth returned. He bared his teeth, his ears going flat against his head. "What happened? The alarm bell went off! I thought you were dead!"

"Aw, I didn't know you cared so much."

Leo's whiskers twitched. He turned around, his tail sticking straight up as he pointed his posterior in Gareth's direction to leap onto a tree stump and then to the ground—which Gareth suspected was on purpose.

"Making me worried for no reason. Although I see you failed." The fox sniffed the air. "But somehow stole food? How did you escape? What happened?"

Following Leo, Gareth climbed over the wall, then paused to adjust his clothing. "Lord Raylor let me go." He held up the large sack full of provisions and a rough map of Aedyllan. "And gave me food."

Leo froze. "I beg your pardon?"

As succinctly as possible, Gareth explained what had transpired.

"This fae-cursed witch gets stranger by the day," Leo muttered.

"She told me she needs the firebird's feathers and the unicorn's horn for some spell, but if that was true, why warn the

Raylors I was coming? Why doesn't she trade Anika for a unicorn directly? Why involve me at all?"

Leo lay down, his ears drooping and pointing out on either side of his head like a comical hat as he rested his snout on his paws. "Maybe she takes pleasure in playing with people and making them dance to her whims."

"Whatever she's up to," Gareth said while ignoring how cute Leo looked and the urge to scratch his ears, "she needs to be stopped."

The fox snorted. "How do you plan to do that, then?"

Not being in the mood to admit he had no plan, he instead said, "First things first, I have to help Anika."

"I'll come with you."

"You…will?"

Leo made a motion almost like a shrug. "You can use all the help you can get."

That felt uncomfortably like an insult to Gareth's capabilities, but then, given his performance so far on this quest, maybe that was warranted. With a sigh, Gareth pulled his blanket out of his saddlebags.

It took a little effort to get the words out of his mouth, but he managed a quiet "Thank you. For your help."

"To be honest, I mostly just want to help Anika."

"Because you know her from living…inside Raylor Estate? Near it?" Gareth prodded.

When Leo didn't answer, Gareth wrapped himself in his blanket and lay down. He was terribly curious, but he wouldn't pressure the fox for answers. If Leo decided to trust him, he'd have to earn the right to know.

"Lord Raylor…" Leo's voice was so soft, Gareth wasn't entirely sure if he was supposed to hear him. "He really said he'd never abandon his child? His daughter?"

It seemed a strange question, but Gareth rolled over toward Leo. "Yes."

"That's…that's good." Leo curled into a ball with his back to Gareth.

Whatever had happened to Leo's family? Did he have parents somewhere out there to look for him? He'd mentioned his parents had named him, so they must have talked, too. Would it show he cared or be rude if he asked Leo about his family? The fox at least had a sister, although Gareth wasn't entirely sure if she was still alive.

A few minutes later, what sounded like muffled crying came from the fox's direction. Gareth pretended he was asleep and couldn't hear. He wouldn't intrude on a friend's private grief. But he made a mental note to let Leo eat as much of the leftover quail and rabbit for breakfast as he wanted.

The journey the following day was uneventful, which was both a blessing and a curse. A blessing because they made excellent time. A curse because, when bored, Leo turned into a consummate professor, prattling on about magical philosophy and ethics and the history of the study of those subjects at Aedyllan's university. Gareth stopped listening, making noncommittal grunting noises whenever Leo paused for a response.

As dusk approached and Gareth turned his mind to finding somewhere to sleep for the night, he realized Leo had ceased talking at some point.

"Sorry, did you ask me something?"

Leo sighed. "You're worse than my sister. I know you haven't been listening for hours."

"How do you even talk for hours? And that's the third time you've mentioned a sister." Gareth's curiosity got the better of him. "Where is she?"

"You must have *something* you're passionate about and could talk about for hours. You can't only be a walking suit of armor."

Gareth scowled, half at the insult and half because Leo had completely ignored the question about his sister. Why mention her if he didn't want to talk about her?

"Maybe Sir Roderick," he admitted as he turned Fury off the road into a small clearing in the forest. "I've read every version of the stories of his life and adventures and could retell most of the legends from memory. I have some theories and musings about the differences in some of the stories or why there are a few stories that only have one extant version."

"Sir Roderick. Really?" Leo jumped down from Fury's back. "You could talk for hours about the legends of Sir Roderick."

"Wait, now; I didn't insult philosophy as an interest."

"Other than saying a fox couldn't study magical philosophy."

Gareth dismounted. "I was surprised, that's all. Admit it, a knight being intrigued by a legendary knight is less strange than a fox being obsessed with magical philosophy and ethics. Besides, if it hadn't been for legends and tales, I'm unsure my tutors ever would have convinced me to read anything."

Leo sat down, his bushy tail swaying. "You're not a knight, though. You're a prince."

"I'm both, in a way, but I'd rather be a knight only." He tethered Fury and began unpacking. "I'm just a spare prince, anyway."

"Oh." Leo nodded thoughtfully. "Is that why you're here? Is hunting down this firebird a test to become a knight?"

"Sort of. If I fail, I certainly won't live it down, and Father might confine me to the castle out of embarrassment."

He didn't want to think about going back. He'd been gone for days already. Had Baron Tremblay told his father what had happened? If he didn't make it back, he hoped Tremblay wouldn't be in trouble for letting him go. Particularly after being gone for so long, though, he couldn't return empty-handed. He wouldn't be able to face Frederick's gloating or Sir Christopher's weary disappointment or the court's snide judgment.

"If you do succeed, then what?"

Gareth frowned. "Are all talking foxes so nosy, or is it just you?"

Leo's entire body drooped. "Sorry."

The fox looked so dejected that regret pricked at Gareth. "I don't feel like being judged more, that's all. I get enough of that already."

The look Leo gave him seemed almost knowing. "Your family doesn't approve of you wanting to be a knight."

He said it like an observation, as if he already knew. Gareth nodded.

"My family didn't always approve of my interests, either." Leo's tail curled around his paws as he dropped his gaze to the ground. "I suppose I was treating you the same as they treated me." He chuckled softly. "They'd probably prefer you, honestly."

Gareth snorted. "If you were human, I'm sure my father would be *thrilled* to have such a studious young man as his son in my place." He paused in fishing some food and water flasks out of the sack Raylor had given him. "How old are you, anyway?"

"I lose count." He gave a squeaking, fox-like giggle as his gaze darted around. "What's for supper? I'm starved."

"Is talking your version of working up an appetite?" Gareth teased as he sat down next to the fox. "Vegetable pies with beef gravy. Raylor seemed confused when I asked for a second, but I told him I have a big appetite."

Leo licked his muzzle, his eyes going wide as Gareth set one of the cloth-covered bundles in front of him and unwrapped it to reveal a small pie. "Maybe we can be friends, even if you weren't listening to me all day."

"Maybe tomorrow I'll talk your ears off all day with theories of combat."

The fox barely lifted his snout from where it was buried in his pie, but his nose wrinkled. "Ugh. It's like you have all of Anika's bad traits and none of her good ones."

Gareth hurriedly chewed and swallowed the bite in his mouth. "All right, hold on. How exactly do you know Anika? Did she find you as a kit and raise you or something? Although Lord Raylor didn't react to my mention of you."

"No, he wouldn't. He…he doesn't know me." Leo returned to his pie, but with noticeably less enthusiasm.

After a brief hesitation, Gareth set down his own pie. There were things the fox wasn't telling him, things about how he was connected to the Raylors and the witch. Secrets that might affect his mission to rescue Anika, which was worrisome. But why should Leo trust him with his secrets when Gareth wouldn't share his own?

The words stuck in his throat, and he had to take a swig of water.

"I…if we're going to be friends…" Gareth rubbed the scruff on his jawline. "You might as well know I'm here because of a punishment more than a test."

19

Leo slowly lifted his head from his food to meet Gareth's eyes. "Punishment?"

Gareth nodded, fidgeting with the linen wrapper of his pie. "My father and I have never seen eye to eye. I don't think he likes me. I don't respect him much, either. At this point, I'm unsure which of us started disliking the other first. He cares more about his crown and power than us—his children, I mean. I've always argued with him, but…this spring, when we were taking my sister to her horrible arranged marriage, her horse bolted in the mountains, and she went missing. Father forced me to stop searching for her."

He took another drink, avoiding looking at Leo. "I hated him for that." His grip tightened on the flask. Maybe he still did. "And then I tried to convince her betrothed to look for her, and he dismissed her as dead and not worth trying to find. He didn't even care." An edge crept into his voice. "So I punched him."

Leo made a sound somewhere between a squeak and a cough. "I, um, can presume your sister was betrothed to a foreign prince?"

"Crown prince." Gareth broke a piece off the edge of his pie crust and crumbled it between his fingers. "An insufferable churl, but still a crown prince. I nearly started a war and spent a few weeks in a dungeon, until my sister miraculously appeared at the Rethali palace."

"So your father sent you away?" Leo whispered.

"No. Not then. It's a long story and complicated, but we also disagreed about how to deal with some new developments related to Raelyn's arranged marriage. That tension didn't disappear after we returned home."

"Is…your sister all right? I've heard some snippets of news here and there, but I admittedly don't pay much heed to Eynlaean or Rethali affairs."

"Oh, yes. Happily married to the rightful king of Rethalyon now. He's a good man, at least." Gareth shrugged. "But my father and I have argued more ever since. Then I got caught switching places with a squire to sneak off and join a gryphon hunt, and Father sent me to serve as a knight at Tremblay Barony. Thought it would cool me off, I suppose."

Silence descended over them for several long moments, interrupted only by Fury quietly snacking on grass.

Gareth sighed. "There isn't a definite plan for me when I go home. I'm honestly unsure if in my father's mind this was a threat or bribe, but he said after I return, he might strike me from the line of succession. I'd be free to be a knight and roam as I please."

In the heartbeats that followed, he waited for judgment or derision from the fox.

"Did he seem happy about that idea?"

That wasn't a response Gareth had expected. "No. He seemed sad, like he didn't want to do it, which I don't understand. It would be perfect, and it isn't as if he likes having me around, anyway."

"Somehow I doubt that," Leo said softly. "Are you really running from a role as prince that you don't want, or are you running from a complicated relationship because that's easier?"

"Of course it's easier!" Gareth snatched up his pie, regretting telling the fox anything. "This entire quest has been a mess and hasn't gone as planned, but it still has clear objectives and a villain and a way to know if I've won or not!"

Leo blinked at him. "You don't win or lose in relationships. You're on the same side."

"Whatever." He tore into his pie.

Leo returned to eating as well, and they didn't talk any more that night.

The next day, Leo asked—more like demanded—that Gareth tell him Raelyn's story. It still irked Gareth how small a role he'd played. It was a thrilling tale nonetheless, and he felt closer to Raelyn in the telling, so he secretly relished the opportunity. Or maybe not so secretly, as Leo at one point tittered and told him he should consider becoming a bard instead of a knight.

After he finished the story, Leo was quiet for a while. That was fine with Gareth, as his thoughts had drifted to wondering how Rae and Alexander were doing…and whether Tristan might have actually frozen to death in Talland. It was still summer, so that seemed unlikely, disappointingly.

"You know, I think you got something wrong in your story," Leo said tentatively.

Gareth recoiled. "That doesn't make sense. You weren't there. What could I have gotten wrong?"

"I think it hurt your father terribly to give up the search for Raelyn. I don't think he had any good choices."

Every muscle in Gareth's body tensed. "The right choice would have been to keep looking for her, even if it was hard."

"So you believe your father thinking about peace and ensuring the security and prosperity of his people, an entire kingdom, was morally wrong?"

"Well…" He hesitated. "At the expense of my sister, yes."

Leo wiggled under his arm to come around in front of him and sit on Fury's withers, his golden eyes intense. "Is it that simple? Was Raelyn wrong to be willing to go through with marrying Tristan if Alexander had been denied his crown?"

"Yes!" Tightening his grip on the reins, Gareth glared over Fury's ears at the empty road ahead of them. "That villain didn't deserve her—"

"So she was evil for choosing kindness and wanting to protect people at the cost of her own happiness and safety? Isn't that what a hero does?"

"I never said she was evil—"

"Just wrong."

"Not like that! Foolish, maybe. I wish she hadn't needed to choose to be kind! I wish she had stood up for herself more and not let Father push her around—"

"Maybe she thought it was more important to stand up for her people and ensure peace than to stand up for herself. It must have been difficult for her."

Gareth glared at the fox. "She loves Alexander! Father demanded too much of her. Agreeing to stay in the betrothal unless and until Alexander was recognized as the rightful king was killing her."

Not that Raelyn had admitted that, but Gareth knew her well enough to tell. Risking Henry's wrath by testifying in Alex's favor and revealing the cursed love spell stone had also been a good indication of what she really wanted.

"What is your point, fox?" It was taking all of his self-control not to throw Leo off his horse.

"You can accept Raelyn was doing her best in a difficult situation with no easy choices. You can rationalize stealing a unicorn for a witch—"

"Yes, because otherwise we *both* would have died, fluff brains. And no one would have known about Anika being held prisoner! Or so I thought; I didn't expect the witch to tell her father where she is. I—"

"You chose the option that seemed wiser to you. You chose saving me and staying alive to have a chance to help Anika over what might, at face value, seem the more moral choice to refuse to aid a witch or commit a theft." Leo tilted his head. "Why can you not accept that maybe your father made decisions for similar reasons? You even said he mentioned not wanting to lose another child, but I don't think it was cowardice, like you claimed. It was love. Your father believed that by preventing you from searching for Raelyn, he wasn't sacrificing a child he already lost. He was saving you."

A confusing mixture of indignation and guilt flamed over Gareth's skin. "What do you know? You've never met him!"

"You're correct," Leo said, his tone gentle yet chiding and completely annoying. "I can't know for certain. But I believe that he loved you and didn't want to lose you, too. Just like I believe that when you punched that crown prince, your father couldn't bear the thought of you being hurt or killed, so he rushed back to Eynlae to bring another bride to free you."

"He did that for the treaty, not me."

Leo rested a black paw on Gareth's breastplate and sat up straighter. "If it was only for the treaty, why did he take you home afterward? You argued with him and yelled at him and nearly caused a war, and he didn't punish you."

"Probably thought time in the dungeon was enough."

"He didn't even restrict your movements or put a guard on you after you returned to Eynlae." Leo's voice took on an exasperated quality as he returned his paw back to the front edge of the saddle. "He seems reluctant to strike you from the succession.

He sent you to be a knight, yes, probably thinking you'd be bored and wouldn't like it, but he still gave you what you wanted, and—"

"Shut up or you can get off my horse and go your own way." As soon as the angry words were out, Gareth regretted them, but shame tied his apology behind his teeth.

After a moment, Leo turned to sit facing forward on Fury's withers. Fury's hooves clomped over the dirt, and Gareth wondered with agitation how much further it was to Lake Marsing.

Then, so quietly Gareth barely heard him, Leo spoke again. "My father and I argued a lot, too. Sometimes I felt he'd never understand me, but eventually, he did. Now he doesn't remember me, and I…suddenly I remember the good memories more, and they feel a lot more important than the arguments. Not that the arguments didn't sting. Some of them still do. You're right. Relationships are much harder than quests. They're messy and sometimes they hurt more than a monster's claws, and I won't pretend that some relationships aren't better abandoned or that some hurts won't leave scars. I don't think that makes fighting for relationships in general any less worthwhile than facing down a manticore or completing a quest.

"I don't know your father. Maybe I'm wrong. But he's not like Henry Carbrey, cursing his own son. I won't tell you what to do. But perhaps…when you get home…you could try to respect and understand your father, too, if you expect him to respect and understand you. Perhaps you'll find you've misunderstood him as much as he's misunderstood you. That might not fix it; relationships take effort on both sides—but that goes for you as much as for your father."

Gareth's grip tightened on the reins until his palms ached. Hadn't he wondered the same thing when his father told him, *"You'll always be my son"*? Was it possible he'd been misreading his father all this time?

Or maybe it was a bit of both misunderstandings and Father being harsh, and that was why he'd rather be angry and blame his father for everything. That was easier than sorting through that sometimes his father was wrong, sometimes he tried but made imperfect decisions, and sometimes he was right.

But wasn't that how everyone was? Gareth and Raelyn and their brothers and his acquaintances…they all did hurtful things at times. Even Raelyn had lied to Gareth, despite the fact they'd always trusted each other, to protect Alexander. It had hurt—it still did—but he'd forgiven her. Yet examining if he was being too proudly stubborn to extend the same courtesy to Father felt like trying to force himself to touch fire.

"I imagine it's hard being a prince or princess," Leo mused, looking over his shoulder at Gareth. "Your parents have so many responsibilities and difficult decisions to make all the time, so many times they have to choose what to prioritize, and only a bad king would choose his own feelings over what would benefit his kingdom. I'd know, my father and his friends complain about our king often enough."

Gareth snorted. "I would not have guessed talking woodland creatures get together to critique a human king."

With an unamused glare, Leo circled back around to face him, shaking his head. "Still, that had to make you feel lonely and less important. Maybe your father just didn't love you the way you needed. I think that's all right to admit while still acknowledging the ways he did love you. It can be difficult to hold both of those, though. My father can never undo the ways he hurt and discouraged me when I so desperately wanted him to value the things that I was good at. But over the last couple of years, he has tried to make up for it, to be more supportive, understanding, and encouraging."

Now the blasted fox was making Gareth's throat all thick and his eyes sting. "I suppose he wanted you to be better at catching prey," he tried to joke in an attempt to get the conversation off of himself.

"Close enough, I suppose." Leo turned back to face forward and fell silent.

A riot of thoughts swirled around Gareth's mind as they kept riding along the deserted road that was starting to be reclaimed by grass. Leaves fluttered in the branches of the trees lining either side of the old road, rustling in the light breeze and tossing up a scent of dust and forest musk. Fury's hooves clopped against the dirt as the sun arced high overhead.

In the muddle of his thoughts, he snagged on a few strange things Leo had said.

The fox had a sister, one he deeply loved but had also hinted would stop listening to him when he droned on about philosophy.

He knew Anika…and thought her flaws were similar to Gareth's.

Flaws like not listening?

Leo had dodged the question about his age.

He had a father who for some reason didn't remember him, which Gareth had assumed was due to an affliction of old age…but he'd also said that Lord Raylor didn't know him, even though Anika did. And Leo's father discussed the shortcomings of his king, something that wouldn't seem to affect a fox…

That was what Leo had been hiding.

"Wolf's teeth." Gareth almost dropped the reins.

"What is it?" Leo stretched up to brace his forepaws on Fury's neck as he sniffed the air. "What's wrong?"

"You're not a talking fox!"

Leo looked over his shoulder, his head tilting to the side. "Trust me, you have not hallucinated these conversations."

"No, I was right! You *are* a cursed human. You're Leo Raylor!"

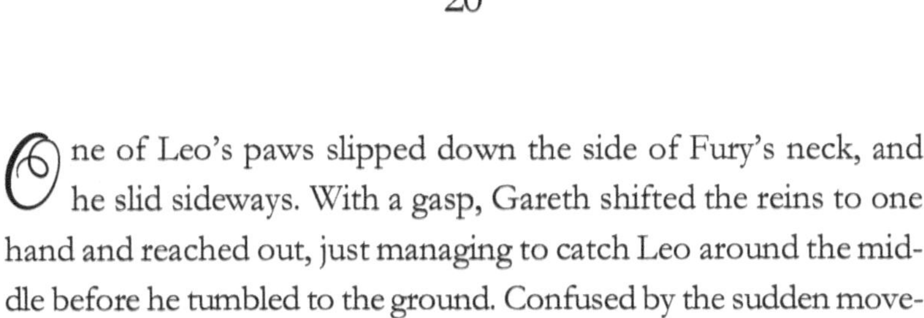

ne of Leo's paws slipped down the side of Fury's neck, and he slid sideways. With a gasp, Gareth shifted the reins to one hand and reached out, just managing to catch Leo around the middle before he tumbled to the ground. Confused by the sudden movement along his shoulder, Fury reared, and for a brief moment Gareth was desperately trying to hold on to both animals.

Once Fury had calmed, Gareth settled Leo back in front of him and gaped at his companion. "Why did you deny…ohhhh." While he was a dragon-man, Alexander hadn't been able to say he was cursed or who had cursed him, either. "You couldn't admit it, could you? And your curse made your father forget about you?"

That was a horrifyingly cruel addition to Leo's vulpine curse.

"Oh." Visibly trembling, Leo ducked down, making himself smaller. "I don't know if you're allowed to know that… I can't tell anyone. Please don't say that; I don't know what the witch will do. I'm just a fox." His wide eyes darted back and forth. "A talking fox who says nonsensical things—"

"Leo." Unsure what else to do, Gareth eased his palm onto Leo's head and stroked down his back. A more violent tremble went through Leo.

"I know I betrayed you and lied. Don't be angry, please; I need to go with you. The witch said she'd hurt Anika if I didn't accompany and help you—"

"It's all right." Gareth swallowed a lump in his throat as he kept gently stroking Leo's soft fur. "I knew you had secrets. Although you had me convinced you weren't cursed."

A high-pitched whimper escaped from Leo. "I'm sorry—"

"Really, it's all right," Gareth insisted. "You didn't willingly deceive me. Right?"

Leo shook his head emphatically.

Shifting in his saddle and unable to make eye contact, Gareth admitted, "You were protecting your sister by lying. I…probably would do the same thing."

Blast it all, Leo might have a point. His entire life, Gareth had viewed the world as if it were black and white, and wrong was always wrong and the right thing to do was always clear. He still believed in pursuing what was just and right, but…maybe in a complicated world with wicked people, sometimes there were shades of gray.

Sometimes deception protected someone.

Still, that didn't mean he was ready to accept that forcing a daughter into a marriage to a murderer's son or preventing a brother from searching for his missing sister was forgivable.

Gareth forced his attention back to Leo, who had started to relax as Gareth stroked his fur, but anxiety still showed in his eyes.

"Will you be stuck like this if you don't do what the witch says?"

The only response was a keening whimper as Leo squeezed his eyes shut.

"Sorry. I won't talk about it anymore. Unless you want to, however much you can." Pushing his luck, Gareth gave in to the urge to scratch behind Leo's ears. "I'm sorry for all the teasing when I thought you were a fox."

Leo opened one eye. "I will accept your apology if you keep doing that because it feels really good, but never mention me allowing you to do something so undignified. I may look like a fox, but that's not all I am."

Grimacing, Gareth almost withdrew his hand. It was weird to think about scratching behind the ears of an adult human, so he focused on how soft Leo's fox ears were. "Deal. Because you are very soft, but only, I imagine, as a fox."

Leo barked a series of high-pitched fox laughs. "The girl I courted for a while might disagree. She really liked my hair."

"Oh, see, now you made it awkward!" Gareth snatched his hand away. "Why did you stop courting?"

Looking disappointed to no longer be having his ears scratched, Leo sat back up, swaying slightly as he readjusted to Fury's gait. "Oh, it was never exactly official. We were both too young. Then she met some dashing young lord with muscles and a bigger inheritance, and she decided that suited her better than the prospect of being married to a university professor."

Gareth blinked. "You're a professor?"

"Well…not yet. I want to be, but I have to attend university as a student first." Leo ducked his head. "That's what most of my arguments with my father were about. I'm not his heir, but he thought I could do better than becoming an academic. But it's all I've ever wanted." His entire body drooped. "I shouldn't even be telling you this. Foxes aren't professors. Forget I said anything."

It was more difficult than sitting through a lecture on kingdom finances, but Gareth managed not to ask all of the questions running through his mind—about how Leo and Anika had been caught and what Leo knew and how he'd gotten his father to understand his studious nature and how in all of Miraveld Leo the Philosopher was Anika the Sword-Maiden's *brother*.

"Well." Gareth shifted one of the reins to his free hand. "At least now I understand why you didn't want me thinking about Anika."

Leo yowled, prompting Fury to sidestep. "And I still don't!"

"Is she courting anyone?" Gareth asked with a smirk.

"None of your business!" Leo squirmed around Gareth, returning to his place on Fury's hindquarters. "Anika is off-limits. I don't care if you're a prince. I will not answer questions about her. You're not even supposed to know…you know."

"Aw, come on. You won't even tell me how she got to be so good at swordplay?"

Leo harrumphed. "The same way all you walking suits of armor do. Training and practice."

Gareth would have pressed to find out who had trained a girl and if that was common in Aedyllan, but Leo's forbidding tone dissuaded him. He didn't want to be attacked by a fox.

Besides, if he was right, based on the directions and rudimentary map Lord Raylor had given him, they would reach the lake that evening. As soon as he had helped Anika escape the tower, he could ask her all the questions he wanted to.

21

The tower was in better condition than Anika would have guessed given its history, but it was still a death trap.

Early the morning after the Eynlaean knight had failed to steal back the firebird, Callista woke Anika and told her they were moving to Lake Marsing. Anika hadn't yet had a chance to attempt to search Callista's room for the prophecy, but she couldn't come up with any reason to stall.

Then the witch played her game-winning move: "I don't want to have to harm your brother."

So Anika gritted her teeth and went with Callista. The witch cast an impressive spell that gave them the swiftness of a galloping horse and endurance to maintain the speed. When they arrived at the lake, Anika rowed them out to the tower in a tiny boat while Callista scarfed down an entire meal without offering Anika a bite.

They passed through an empty doorway and crossed the grass-covered floor of the tower to a worn spiral staircase in the back corner. Slick, damp moss coated the stone steps, and their ascent disrupted birds, lizards, and a snake that slithered directly in front of Callista, brushing against her shoe. It was one of the few times any real emotion showed on the witch's face, as her eyes and mouth widened in horror and a squeak caught in her throat.

They walked right past the barren second level with its crumbling wooden floor and climbed to the third story. Callista chained both of Anika's wrists to the wall and gave her a bag of food and an empty bucket. The floor was sturdy enough to hold a moldy bed covered in bird droppings and a warped desk and chair, but Anika still thought the witch insane for traversing the rotting wood to access the square opening in the stone ceiling.

An enchanted vine pulled Callista up onto the roof—yet again igniting Anika's jealousy—where she called a gryphon with a spelled whistle. Dust showered from the ceiling when the hulking gryphon landed. After shackling the poor beast to the roof, the infuriating woman ordered Anika to hand over her sword belt. She took the weapon and left, with only the instruction not to attempt to leave on her own.

Three days later, Anika stood at the end of her chains' length, looking out one of the three barred, glassless windows at the sunset reflecting on the lake. Above her, the gryphon's claws and talons scratched against the roof as it shifted. It had tried to attack her the first day, but one eagle forefoot barely fit through the access hole in the roof, so it had quickly given up. Its leash was significantly longer than hers, allowing it to dive into the lake to fish. That meant the gryphon could attack anyone who approached the tower.

Of course, no one would come. No one knew she was there.

She turned away from the window and slumped against the wall. Warm, orange-tinged sunlight streaked in through the windows, the opening to the roof, and a thin arrowslit in the rounded wall of the stairwell. It didn't make her surroundings any less depressing.

Moss sprouted out of every crevice, and bindweed grew between the floorboards. She'd seen more insects crawling in and out of the disintegrating mattress than she'd have wished to see in her entire life. It was for the best that her restraints left her little range of movement.

Callista had magically soldered the chains to the wall above the stone landing at the top of the spiral staircase. Thankfully Anika could still walk to the window in one direction and down a few steps in the other, as well as lie down, but the iron manacles chafed her wrists. The window at her back provided a decent view, and she could empty her waste bucket out of it with varying degrees of success. Standing there involved trusting the edge of the floor, but the monotony had long ago surpassed her fear of falling through the wood.

At least she had the ability to make her prison marginally more comfortable. Shortly after Callista's departure, Anika had used her meager enchanting skill to grow herself a bed of moss and enough bindweed to weave the vines into a living blanket. It wasn't exactly comfortable, but it provided some warmth, especially when the wind off the lake whistled through the windows at night. Making the bed also consumed most of a day and then left her with a pounding headache for several hours.

Anika heaved a sigh and moved back to the stone landing. With nothing else to do, she dropped to the floor and did push-ups for the third time that day. Moss caught between the links of her chains, but at least it muffled the clattering.

When her arms were aching, she collapsed to the floor and rolled onto her back. The end of the gryphon's lion tail had fallen through the hole in the ceiling, and she lay there, watching it twitch back and forth.

"What are we doing here, big fellow?" Only the quiet sound of the beast's breathing answered her. "I wish I knew. At the very least, I'd like to know if Callista's coming back for us before I run out of food."

Or perhaps sending someone. That seemed illogical, but so

did most of what the witch did. What strange plot was she following in her quest to make a prophecy come true?

If I knew what the prophecy entailed, I could foil it. Anika frowned. Unless it was a good prophecy? Surely no desirable prophecy would involve kidnappings and curses. And yet…

She tore a leaf off of some bindweed and rubbed it between her fingers. If the witch was attempting to activate *the* most famous Aedyllanian prophecy…

In a way, it might be difficult to blame Callista. Anika paid less attention to court talk than she probably should, but even she knew that many people were unhappy with King Silas Faine. Those who believed the Fae Blessing and Curse of Mortimer Faine existed claimed that the royal family knew they were protected from any consequences, so they abused their power. Those who dismissed the legend as a tall tale said the royals were complacent, not because they were magically protected, but because they foolishly trusted that people were too afraid of the prophecy to attempt anything. Those people rarely had a good answer for all the failed coups, assassinations, and attacks against the Faines over the last several decades.

Anika had never had the patience or interest to scrutinize the finer points of those arguments or what was so bad about the royal family. There was nothing she could do about it either way, so it hadn't seemed worth forcing herself to pay attention. She regretted that now, because if she knew, she could have discussed it with Callista and possibly gained her trust. If she'd won the witch's confidence, stopping her would be easier.

Because even if King Silas was a tyrant, that prophecy couldn't come true—in the legends, it was said the fae lady's curse predicted the entire royal line would perish. That would plunge Aedyllan into chaos and, with no preparation, likely a civil war. Things might be worse than two centuries ago, when Mortimer Faine united the kingdom through war and the brutal annihilation of his rivals. Anika wanted to be a knight, but she didn't want to raise her blade against her fellow Aedyllanians as they fought over who would rule.

She tossed aside the bindweed leaf and moved to sit with her back against the wall. Above her, a whoosh of air and shifting shadows announced that the gryphon had taken flight. They were both prisoners, but she envied its ability to leave the tower.

Then the gryphon screeched, an earsplitting sound of fury. Anika grimaced and pressed her palms over her ears.

The gryphon landed again, and Anika frowned at the ceiling. "What's gotten into you?"

She hurried to her west-facing window, the clinking of her chains mocking her captivity. The sun was dipping below the horizon, and she squinted against the glare. For a moment, she didn't see anything, but then movement on the shore caught her attention.

Were there figures on the beach? Someone with a horse if her eyes weren't deceiving her.

Was someone coming for her after all?

"Don't be ridiculous," she muttered.

Who would know to look for her? Even if Leo knew she'd been moved, Callista had cursed Leo not only to be a fox, but to be forgotten by everyone except for Anika and the witch. They wouldn't trust a random talking fox who claimed to be a son they didn't have, especially not when a witch held their daughter captive.

Sighing, Anika settled back onto her mossy cushion.

Where was Leo? Was he still helping that cute knight? Or had Callista given him a new task? Wherever Leo was, whatever he was doing, hopefully he was safe. She thought he was. They had something of a connection—whenever one of them was hurt or in serious danger, the other somehow just knew.

She hadn't had that sense recently, which must mean he was fine. Unless his fox curse interfered with their connection, but she wouldn't dwell on that possibility. Trapped alone in the tower with no indication of how long she would be there—other than that the food Callista had given her was starting to run low—she was on the verge of going mad as it was. If she added anxiety about whether Leo was safe, she would break.

22

The tower really was *in* the lake, right in the middle of it—and it wasn't a small lake, either.

The setting sun cast the sky in vibrant reds and oranges, and the vast lake reflected the colors, making it look more like a lake of fire than water. Nearly a third of a league out from the pebble-covered shore, a lone tower of dark, weathered stone jabbed into the air, listing a little to one side. Sunlight glinted on metal, possibly bars blocking the windows. Half of the crenellations along the top of the square tower had crumbled. Something shifted on the tower's roof, something large, but Gareth couldn't make out what it was.

"Fae take that witch," Leo muttered. "This tower has been abandoned for over twenty years. It used to be a prison for high-ranking nobles who were troublesome enough to need to be put away somewhere but not enough to be executed. Legend has it that's where Prince Marcus Alimer was imprisoned by his father, back before Mortimer Faine became king and united Aedyllan under one banner again."

Mention of the legend of the romance of Marcus and Adriana almost distracted Gareth from the quest at hand. It was far from his favorite legend, but it was one of Raelyn's favorites. She'd have stars in her eyes when he told her that he'd visited *the* tower of Marcus Alimer. He shook his head and focused on the present.

"Then around a hundred years ago," Leo continued, "a flood turned this valley into a lake. Since it was on a large motte, the tower was mostly untouched. The king at the time shored up the hill and dammed the lake to make a more secure prison, but the tower has been slowly tilting. King Silas finally left it to rot." He growled. "It's dangerous without whatever creature is on top of it, and that witch trapped Anika in there!"

Gareth peered up and down the shoreline and squinted into the distance. "Yes, but first problems first—how do we get there? Even if I was confident I could swim there and back, which I'm not, I'd have to leave my armor behind to do so, then potentially face that creature. Not to mention I don't know if Anika can swim."

"Assuming the witch hasn't harmed her, she can swim—but I don't know about that distance." Leo's whiskers twitched. "Let's keep that as a last resort."

Nodding, Gareth frowned at the lengthening shadows of the trees behind them. "I hate to make her wait another night, but I don't think we have a choice."

Leo slumped. "Agreed. We can look for a boat in the morning. Maybe there's one along the shore somewhere."

"The woods do look closer to the water on the other side, and it looks like there are rushes down at that end." Gareth pointed to their right and the far end of the lake. "Worth checking—"

A high-pitched screech pierced the air, similar to a golden eagle's cry and far louder. Fury neighed and backed up a few steps, tugging on the reins. Gareth leapt back, drawing his sword as his eyes turned to the sky, and prepared to release his horse.

"Wolf's *teeth*! Leo, hide!" But as he turned in a circle, he couldn't spot the source—until his gaze went to the tower. The creature had risen into the sky. It beat its wings and landed on the tower again. With that sound, he didn't need to see it clearly to know what it was.

"Gryphon," Gareth muttered. He slammed his sword back into its scabbard. "How did the witch convince a gryphon to guard the tower for her?" He frowned. "Or it's claimed the tower as its nest and the witch got Anika inside while it was away."

"Aren't gryphons…extremely territorial?" Leo asked, a slight wobble to his voice.

Unable to do anything about the creature right then, Gareth turned away from the lake and led Fury back to the tree line. "Yes. Territorial and often aggressive."

They also had massive talons that could pierce plate armor and sharp beaks designed to tear flesh from bone, to say nothing of the claws on their rear lion legs. However, given how Leo slunk along the ground next to Gareth with his tail tucked, he kept those thoughts to himself.

"I know that you care about Anika," Gareth said as he tied up Fury and worked on removing the saddle. "But perhaps you should stay on the shore."

"You're worried about me getting underfoot and being another person—well, fox—to worry about." Leo lay down, resting his chin on his paws in a forlorn manner. "I have teeth and claws…but they are very small. Anika is the fighter, not me." A quiet whimper shook his small frame. "If we find a boat, I can't even row. It's the wiser thing, to leave me behind."

Leo stared out at the lake, sorrow glimmering in his eyes.

Gareth shifted uncomfortably before setting down Fury's saddle. "We can decide tomorrow. For now, we should eat and rest."

"Do you think Anika has food?"

"If the witch wanted her alive to be rescued, yes."

Although why the witch would *want* her own captive rescued, Gareth couldn't comprehend. This entire thing might be an elaborate way to kill him, although she'd had the chance at the castle ruins. Either the witch took demented pleasure in toying with people, or she was out of her mind. He had yet to decide which option might be preferable.

Either way, while the gryphon was the most pressing concern, if he survived the coming fight, he'd still have a whole slew of other problems.

Gareth awoke to dew clinging to his hair and blanket and a fox snuggled against his side.

Pale, early-morning sunlight peeked over the woods on the other side of the lake, making the water look like scattered diamonds. The air held more of a chill than previous mornings, probably affected by the cold lake, and their small fire had burned out.

If it had been a little odd to interact with a talking fox—as his natural instinct to cuddle a small, furry animal felt wrong when said animal was discussing philosophy—knowing Leo was actually a human made it more awkward. Leo likely would not appreciate Gareth rubbing his belly.

With a squeaky yawn, Leo stretched out and bumped into Gareth's shoulder. Blinking, he lifted his head, the confusion of sleep clouding his eyes.

"Morning, fox."

Leo sat up and rubbed a paw over his face. "At least you're warm, so you're good for something."

Gareth also sat up, rolling his eyes. "Keep insulting me and I'll throw you in the lake."

"Hmmm, some regal prince you are."

"That's why I don't want to be one." Gareth grinned, then got up and stretched.

After a rushed breakfast of dried fruits and nuts—which Leo

complained about endlessly —they mounted Fury and set off around the edge of the lake, searching for a boat.

At the south end, they found a small rowboat, just big enough for two people, mostly hidden in the rushes. Gareth tied up Fury, pulled on his helm, and got the boat into the water, but he paused before rowing out.

"Any words of warning or wisdom?"

Leo huffed. "As if you've ever heeded my advice."

"Accidents, both times."

"Suuuuure. This time, watch out for gold traps. Bring Anika back in one piece and alive. Don't fall into the lake; you'll drown in that armor."

Gareth cast the fox a deadpan look of exasperation.

Leo laughed, the *keeek, keeek, keeek* giggle sounding more fox-like than ever.

"And you," Gareth said. "Stay out of trouble and don't let—"

"Anyone steal your horse; yes, yes." Leo waved a black fore-paw. "Get going already."

Gareth settled the oars into place and rowed away from the shore.

"And Gareth?" Leo called.

He stopped rowing so the splashing wouldn't cover Leo's voice. "Don't die."

Nerves tightened in Gareth's chest, but he plastered on a smile. "Don't worry. I haven't done anything to warrant a legend about me, so I can't die yet!"

Leo shook his head and turned, trotting back to the forest and Fury.

The water splashed from the oars as Gareth rowed. Beneath his armor, he quickly began to sweat, but he didn't slow. Anika had been stuck in that tower and the Raylor siblings had been separated long enough.

He was halfway to the tower when the gryphon spotted him and let out an earsplitting shriek. Gareth rowed faster, his heart pounding. He'd ended up here because he'd wanted to fight a gryphon, but that was with the aid of more experienced knights and, more importantly, on the ground. Not in a rowboat. Falling into the lake and drowning was a bigger possibility than he cared to admit.

Another cry echoed over the lake, and Gareth looked over his shoulder at the tower.

The gryphon had risen into the air and was moving in his direction, but something trailed from one of its back paws…a chain. The line went taut, and the gryphon strained against it. The gryphon couldn't reach Gareth yet, but it'd be able to long before he reached the small hill at the base of the tower.

If only he'd brought a bow. The bow wasn't his best weapon usually, but the gryphon was stuck beating its wings in one place.

With no better options, Gareth drew his sword and placed it on the bench across from him. Swallowing back his trepidation, he returned to rowing, each push of the oars bringing him closer to the gryphon. It went against everything his mind screamed at him, but he focused on going faster and faster.

Then, as a moving shadow out of his periphery warned him of the gryphon's dive, he pulled the oars into the boat, letting it continue on its own momentum, and snatched up his sword. As he stood and turned to face the beast, the boat wobbled. His jaw clenched, and he eased his feet into a wider, more balanced position. Now that he was closer, the gryphon was even larger than he'd expected. Every breath heaved in his chest, but he kept his sword low. The gryphon opened its beak, its talons reaching for him as its shadow swallowed up the rowboat.

At the last moment, Gareth ducked and swung his sword in an upward arc. An eagle foot swiped at him, but he dodged, and only one talon caught on the front of his shoulder with a sound of rending metal. At the same time, his blade met the gryphon's chest, raining down bloodied feathers as long as his arm. The gryphon screamed and lurched back up toward the sky. Gareth staggered back a step. The boat swayed, and he clamped his teeth around a curse.

Overhead, the gryphon flew in a tight circle, kicking its back paw at the chain. A short gash had been torn in the front of Gareth's breastplate near his right collarbone, and his shoulder stung. But a rivulet of gryphon blood trailed down Gareth's sword, and a small smile tugged at his lips.

23

$\mathcal{S}$omething had angered the gryphon.

Anika rubbed her eyes and pushed off her bed of moss. She'd never been much of a morning person, but the gryphon's screeching had ruined any chance of sleeping away more of another day stuck in the tower. The gryphon cried out again, but that time, it sounded pained.

She shuffled over to the window, gingerly rubbing at the sores developing on her wrists from the manacles. Her rougher imprisonment in the tower had grown her hatred toward Callista, which she hadn't thought possible after watching Leo scream as he transfigured into a fox. Shoving her tangled red hair out of her face, she looked out the window. A gasp rushed out of her, and she gripped the bars, pushing her face against the cold metal to gape at the scene on the lake.

A poor knight in a rowboat was fighting for his life against the gryphon. The creature dove, but the knight held firm, stabbing his sword. Unfortunately, he moved a breath too soon, and the beast twisted sideways, receiving only a minor cut along its side, but it also made a grab for the knight's head. The man stumbled, sprawling across the length of the small boat, while the gryphon came away with his helm gripped between its talons.

The gryphon looked at its worthless prize and shrieked before dropping the piece of metal, which plunged into the lake with a splash.

In the precipitously swaying rowboat, the knight scrambled back to his feet. His shaggy light-brown hair took on a golden tint in the sunlight. He lifted his sword, a look of grim determination hardening his face as he prepared to face the gryphon again.

"Sir Gareth?" The knight's name escaped her lips in a whisper.

Had the Eynlaean knight come for her? He *had* been reluctant to leave her in Callista's lair, but why would he risk himself for her after meeting her once—and after she'd held a sword to his neck at that? How could he even know she was there? Yet for what other reason would he row out to an abandoned tower and face a gryphon?

The gryphon attacked again. Anika bit her knuckle. If only she could help him. But she was chained, weaponless other than the magic she wasn't adept at using, and separated from Gareth by water.

This time, Gareth ducked and didn't swing his sword. Instead, as the gryphon dove at him, the knight sprung up, thrusting his sword straight upward. The massive form of the gryphon blocked her view, but its wings sagged as it threw its head back in a scream that warbled into silence. A twinge of pity went through Anika. The gryphon had been trapped, forced to play a part in Callista's twisted game just like Anika and perhaps this knight. It hadn't needed to die.

But her sorrow at the unnecessary loss quickly turned to horror.

The gryphon fell, its eagle head splashing into the water, but part of its lion haunches landed on the side of the rowboat. Trailing behind it, the chain crashed down across the bow. The boat tilted until a third of the hull rose above the surface of the lake, the weight of the chain providing some counterbalance. Gareth pressed back against the rising side of the boat, but his sword-arm was trapped beneath one of the creature's legs, which was sprawled across the hull.

He was going to fall into the lake.

With his metal cuirass, greaves, and vambraces to weigh him down, he would almost certainly drown.

Anika's magic stirred inside of her, and yellow light tinged her fingertips. What spell would help? Frantically, she searched her memory and came up with nothing. Even if she knew a spell, she wasn't good enough at long-range enchanting to risk it. She might make things worse instead.

She slammed a palm into the metal bars. "Come on, Gareth!"

Gareth freed his arm, but the shift in weight tipped the rowboat further. He shoved and kicked at the gryphon's back end, bracing his upper body against the opposite side of the boat. Every beat of her heart pounded against her ribs. The gryphon slid off the boat and sank into the water. Metal links clattered against wood as the chain followed, but Gareth kicked it over the front edge of the bow. Her breath caught as for a terrifying moment, the boat looked like it would flip.

Gareth threw himself against the rising hull, and the boat crashed back in the opposite direction. He hit the bottom of the vessel, awkwardly braced against one of the benches. After a moment of perilous rocking, the boat steadied, and the Eynlaean sat up. His hair was dark with water and plastered to his forehead.

Anika released her breath in a rush and sagged against the stone wall.

Gareth looked at his sword in his hand, then let loose a whoop that brought a smile to her face. He set down his weapon and within moments returned to rowing toward the tower, avoiding the chain that still connected the tower and sinking gryphon.

A metallic groan preceded a loud metallic *crack* as one of the links snapped. As the bottom part of the broken chain plummeted into the water, she was glad the knight was moving so quickly.

When the tower blocked her view of his progress, Anika paced back and forth as much as her chains would allow while she waited.

"Don't try to leave by yourself. Behave, and maybe you'll see your brother again."

That was what Callista had said. Did that include not accepting a rescue? Technically she wouldn't be leaving *by herself*, and the witch hadn't said anything about refusing someone's aid. Besides, how could she insist Gareth leave her there after he'd nearly died fighting a gryphon to save her? Although, she still didn't know for certain that was his aim. Maybe he didn't know she was there.

She turned the wrong way and got twisted in her chains. With an irritated grunt, she spun back around and shook the infernal things, the clatter of metal echoing in the tower. How would Gareth free her from the chains? Would it violate Callista's orders if Anika broke them?

Although she had tried to train her magic under two different tutors, neither had the same flavor of magic that she did, and both had been impatient with her. Neither had lasted long. There were too few enchanters in Aedyllan anymore, and when they got an offer to train someone whose magic showed more potency, they abandoned her. She'd never been good at learning from books, either, needing to be shown, to see a technique and learn by doing, so she'd never taken to enchanting like she did to swordplay—to her parents' disappointment.

However, she had enough knowledge, skill, and magic that she could break the manacles herself. The problem was, she didn't know for certain whether that would put Leo at risk.

"Hello?" Gareth's voice echoed faintly up the tower. "Lady

Anika? Are you here? I know I didn't answer you last time, but if you're alive, please say something. I'm not here to harm you."

So Gareth *was* there for her. Her heart gave a little leap.

"I'm at the top of the stairs," she called.

At the least, she could find out how he'd known where she was, then decide if she risked leaving with him.

Bootsteps stomped up the stairs, steady and not rushed, as if the knight were on the alert for more beasts that might try to kill him. She almost called to let him know there weren't, but she wasn't positive that Callista hadn't left behind any magical traps.

After minutes that dragged on for a small eternity, Sir Gareth finally appeared around the bend of the stairs, his sword clutched in both hands. Water still dripped off the ends of his damp hair. There was a small tear in his plate armor at the front of his right shoulder that hadn't been there before. His bright eyes searched the top level, then he grinned at her as he jogged up the last few steps.

"Remember me?"

"Sir Gareth."

His smile widened, a little lopsided and cute, momentarily distracting her. This was not the time, Anika chided herself. "What are you doing here?"

"Um, rescuing you." Gareth's smile vanished, an angry look settling over his features as his gaze locked on her chains. "I don't understand." His hard blue eyes lifted to hers. "Why were you allowed to roam around freely with your sword at the castle ruins but are chained and without your sword here?" His face paled. "Is it my fault? Because I mentioned I saw you?"

"No," she said quickly, anxious to dispel the growing horror in his expression. "She didn't care that you saw me. How did you know I was here?"

"Somewhat long story, but basically, the witch told me where to find you." Gareth frowned at her wrists. "Maybe I can break open a link with my sword—"

"I don't know." Anika took a step back from him.

"Pardon?" Gareth's forehead creased. "You want to stay here? This place isn't safe, and your father wants you home."

"My father?" She disliked the way her voice cracked, how she leaned forward as if desperate. "You spoke to him?"

Dropping one hand from his sword to reach for one of the chains, Gareth nodded. "I'll tell you all about it after we get you out of—"

"You're more likely to break your sword than these chains."

He paused, his hand still outstretched. "Then I'll get a new sword. This is an excellent sword, but it's not irreplaceable. Even if it were a priceless heirloom, another sword would do the same job."

Anika gaped at him. "You're so careless with your weapons?"

He let his hand fall to his side, his mouth falling open with obvious affront. "Careless? With *weapons*? What kind of knight would I be if I didn't take good care of my blade? A sword is a warrior's life. A well-crafted sword is a necessity, and I'm fond of this one. I'm not willing to risk breaking my sword because I don't care about it; I'm willing to break it if it saves you." He huffed in exasperation. "Isn't that what swords are supposed to be for? Protecting and saving people? Wolf's teeth, what in Miraveld is the purpose of having a sword or being a knight if the sword itself matters more than that which it was forged to protect?"

A fiery passion burned through those words, and Gareth seemed to draw himself taller as he spoke. Those pale-blue eyes watched her with an intensity that stole her breath. The warmth that flared over her skin was a strange, foreign feeling, but not at all unpleasant. It took her a moment to get her tongue to work.

"You don't even know me. And you're Eynlaean. I don't think

any knighthood oaths you've taken would apply to me."

Confusion scrunched Gareth's face. "Helping someone shouldn't be contingent on where they're from. What's really going on? Do you not trust me?"

She did, Anika realized with surprise. She didn't usually trust that easily. But this Sir Gareth wore his heart all over his face and said things she had argued before herself. She *wanted* to go with him. Not just to get out of the tower, but because she wanted to get to know him better. However…

"I'm afraid if I leave, Callista will hurt Leo."

"Callista? Oh. The witch?" Gareth shook his head. "I don't think so. She sent me to rescue you, in a roundabout way. Leo is waiting near the shore for us. Probably getting more agitated by the minute."

"Leo is still with you?" Anika took a step closer to him. "Is he all right?"

"Still a fox, but otherwise he's unharmed and well."

Wait, how did Gareth know Leo had been cursed?

"He talks a lot," Gareth said with a small smile, as if guessing what she was thinking. "I figured it out."

He pointed his sword at her chains. "Now, are you going to let me rescue you or not? I think it's what the witch wants, for whatever reason. She told your father the only way he'd see you again is if I freed you from this tower."

If that was true, Callista wouldn't go after Leo if she left with Gareth. But if this was what Callista wanted, what unintended consequences might her escape cause?

"If she does try to stop us or hurt Leo, I'll do my best to stop her," Gareth said, as if reassuring her.

That was chivalrous and made her like him even more, but it didn't matter.

"I still can't." She crossed her arms over her stomach and

leaned back against the wall. "Callista is trying to make some prophecy come true. What if this is part of it? What if the prophecy causes something bad to happen?"

Gareth's lips pressed together. "I don't know anything about making prophecies come true. But rescuing an innocent young woman who is chained in a tower can't be the wrong thing to do, and your brother and father need you back."

Leo…she wanted so badly to see him. The rest of her family, too, but it was Leo she missed the most.

Anika gulped. "All right. I'll handle the chains."

A quick rending spell, which was more like *un*weaving the elements of the metal rather than how she usually pictured her magic as weaving together the essence of things as she saw them in her mind's eye, and the manacles cracked in half. With the spending of magical energy, a dull headache pressed between her eyes. She rubbed her forehead, then straightened to find that Gareth had taken a step back and was staring at her with his head cocked.

"You're an enchantress?" he demanded.

"Um, yes?" It was rare, sure, and she recalled hearing enchanters were almost never born within Eynlae, but it wasn't *that* unheard of. "I'm not very good. The magic in me is small—"

"But an enchantress, right?" Gareth gripped his sword, a tense readiness to his stance. "Not a witch?"

She glowered. "May I remind you: a witch chained me up in here! A witch who cursed my brother and threatened to harm him if I didn't do as she said. So don't you dare suggest I'm in league with her."

"Right. Sorry. I just…" Gareth's lips pinched into a tight frown. "I hate witches."

There was a vehemence to those words that couldn't be only from Callista's twisted games, but the top of a rotting tower didn't seem the place to ask about it.

Anika sighed. "I swear on my twin's life that I'm not a witch."

His jaw dropped. "*Twin?* Leo isn't just your brother; he's your *twin?* Oh, some things make even more sense now." He shook his head. "Let's go. I'm worried the longer we tarry here, the greater the chance that witch might send some other monster."

Without waiting for a response, he turned down the stairs, his sword coming up into a ready position. Oh, yes, despite his wariness of her magic, she trusted this Eynlaean knight.

She just hoped that he still trusted her.

24

$\mathscr{A}$nika Raylor was an enchantress.

Gareth felt rather foolish that he hadn't put it together. Leo had said there wasn't a magic-wielder at Raylor Estate *anymore*. He'd thought Leo meant since one died or left a long time ago, not since Anika was taken.

At least she wasn't a witch. After all the hurt a witch had caused by giving Henry cursed talismans, and after dealing with the vile antics of this Callista, a righteous fury burned in his heart against any and all witches. Leo might be right about some things, but he was wrong to suggest that witches could be good or redeemable.

He descended the spiraling stairs as fast as he dared. They were worn and slick in places and had patches of moss, and he didn't want to slip and fall.

There were no traps or additional monsters, much to his relief. His right shoulder had been wrenched badly when the gryphon's carcass had pinned down his sword, and trying to free the blade had strained his shoulder more. He'd pushed past the pain, focused on not falling into the lake and then getting to Anika. As the adrenaline wore off, however, the pain was more noticeable by the moment. He clenched his jaw, willing himself to keep his sword steady and his senses alert.

Sunlight streamed in through the doorless exit as they crossed the grassy ground floor. The edge of the rowboat peeked up outside, where he'd left it grounded on the muddy shore near the base of the tower. He grimaced, not looking forward to rowing with an injured shoulder.

It could be worse. There could be another gryphon.

Gareth paused in the entryway, checking the surrounding lake for any sign of an enemy or monster. Only clear blue skies, the calm surface of the lake, and the warming air of the late summer morning greeted him.

He stepped outside, more of his tension fading. "All clear."

Trusting Anika to follow, he went to the rowboat and crouched beside it to clean his blade in the lake. The pain in his shoulder grew in intensity as he wiped away the gore and then placed the sword in the boat, as he didn't want to sheathe it while wet and risk it rusting. He turned to Anika and motioned to the rowboat.

"After you."

She climbed in and sat on the closer bench that faced the far shore. Gareth shoved the rowboat off the mud, swallowing a curse as a stab went through his shoulder, then leapt in. The vessel rocked under the motion, but as he settled onto the opposite bench, it evened out.

With a relieved sigh, he retrieved the oars and rested them in the U-shaped oarlocks. But the moment he tried to pull the oars through the water, a fiery pain spread through his right shoulder. He bit his tongue, refusing to cry out, but he couldn't hide the way he stopped rowing and bent forward.

"What's wrong?"

Gritting his teeth, Gareth forced himself to straighten. "Strained my shoulder is all. Don't worry." He tried again, but this time, a muffled yelp escaped him.

"Let's switch sides. I'll row."

He looked up and his protest died on his tongue. She'd trained with a sword. A hint of lean muscle pressed against her fitted shirt and tunic along her shoulders and biceps, and any knight would have strong legs from training to fight on horseback. The growing ache in his shoulder had taken on a stinging pain in the front. While it felt like half failing at a rescue to have the damsel row them back to shore, Anika had offered and was more capable of the task than him at that moment, as much as it rankled his pride. He pulled the oars back into the boat and nodded.

"Thank you."

"You rescued me." Anika shrugged. "Rowing so you don't further injure yourself is the least I can do."

The way the boat rocked as they carefully switched seats made him nervous, but soon they were re-situated, and Anika began to row. Her physical strength became more obvious as she leaned back and forth, moving the oars through the water.

"You said you'd explain what you meant about Callista sending you to rescue me in a roundabout way," she said while she rowed. "I saw her force you to agree to steal a unicorn from my father, but I don't understand how that led you here."

"Frankly, I don't either." Gareth frowned. "She warned your father I was coming, so his guards were waiting to catch me. She also told him where you were and told him to send me. Your father will give me a unicorn for returning you, but to be honest, I'd do that anyway."

She smiled a little at that, and it made her look even more beautiful. Wisps of her red hair framed a symmetrical face with a strong jawline, full lips, and soft cheekbones. The rest of her hair fell about her long neck and across her muscled shoulders.

"It must have to do with whatever prophecy she's attempting

to force into effect." Anika shook her head.

Sunshine caught her eyes, and Gareth couldn't decide if her irises were more blue or green between the splashes of golden brown. Daylight revealed copious freckles on her nose and cheeks that he hadn't noticed in the dark. The three pinkish scars that cut down through her right eyebrow and over her cheekbone were slightly raised and uneven. Would it be rude to ask her about them? His staring probably was rude. As she rowed, her tunic pulled a little against her curves. With heat spreading over his face and a strange lump in his throat, Gareth found himself unsure where to look, so he turned his attention to his injured shoulder.

Any movement of his neck or right shoulder hurt now. Had he dislocated it? He'd never dislocated anything before. But part of his shoulder burned rather like his arm had when he'd been scratched by the manticore. The small rend in his armor was ugly and irritating, and also too narrow to see anything through.

Under the armor, he was soaked with sweat and lake water from the huge splash caused by the gryphon's carcass. As soon as they got to shore, he was taking the armor off. Possibly with help, as embarrassing as that might be, since the throbbing in his shoulder didn't seem promising for removing the cuirass on his own.

Gareth looked to Anika, trying not to focus on her scars. "I don't suppose you know any spells for a potentially dislocated shoulder?"

She shook her head, her expression apologetic. "I know a mending spell that is good for closing up cuts that aren't too serious. I know a little about splinting and binding wounds and making slings and such. But that's the extent of my healing knowledge."

"That's about all I know as well." Gareth tried to roll his shoulder and immediately regretted it.

"Basic knowledge for a knight, right?"

He managed to smile despite the concerning level of pain.

"Exactly. If you're heading out to fight something, you should at least be able to hold yourself or a fellow knight together long enough to get to a real healer."

Not that he'd been in a situation before where there wasn't someone with healing knowledge amid the throng of servants and knights that usually accompanied him. Both a perk and annoyance of being a prince.

As they neared the shore, an excited yapping sounded, then Leo called out, "Anika!"

Gareth leaned to the side, suppressing another wince from the movement. The fox raced back and forth along the shoreline. "I'm here, too, if you were wondering!"

Leo's tail wagged even as he wrinkled his snout. "Did you lose a hand to the gryphon? Why aren't you rowing? Unchivalrous."

Anika laughed, a boisterous, lively sound so different from the carefully restrained titters of most of the ladies at court. "All limbs attached, but he's hurt. And you know I'm perfectly capable."

Briefly, Leo sat down, only to hop back up. "Well, row faster, then!"

She shook her head but did speed up.

Within minutes, the hull bumped against the bottom of the lake. Before Gareth had a chance to, Anika leapt into the shallows and tugged the boat.

"Hold on, I'll help—"

"Nah, stay there. Your moving about will just make this more difficult." With a grunt, she dragged the rowboat onto the shore, then straightened.

The moment she turned around, Leo launched himself up at his sister, and she barely caught him in her arms. Whimpering, whining sounds of crying came from the fox as he wriggled against and sniffed at her.

"Are you all right? Did she hurt you? You reek. I missed you and was so worried."

Anika squeezed her cursed brother to her chest, burying her face in his fur.

Feeling very much like an unwanted observer, Gareth climbed out of the rowboat, biting his tongue at another, sharper twinge of pain. He turned his back on the reuniting siblings and slid his sword into its sheath.

"I was worried about and missed you, too." Anika released a strained chuckle that sounded like she was holding back tears. "You also smell like a dirty dog, just so you know."

A high-pitched *keeehh-eh-ehh* fox giggle burst from Leo. "I *am* basically a dog. What's your excuse?"

"The bathing facilities in ruins are, surprisingly, lacking." Her voice dropped lower. "Leo, are…you all right?"

"Fine. Better than fine, now that you're safe." There was a soft thud. "I appreciate the awkward attempt at privacy, but you can stop pretending you're fascinated by the lake."

Gareth snorted and turned around. Leo was back on the ground, looking at Gareth, but Anika was gazing down at her brother with a strained expression. It had to be difficult for her to see her brother like that. When Leo glanced back up at her, her countenance smoothed, a warm smile pulling at her pink lips. She faced Gareth.

"Thank you for your assistance, Sir Gareth. And for looking out for my brother."

He shrugged, immediately regretting the painful action as he sucked in a breath through his teeth. "Leo has looked out for me just as much, if not more. And other than defeating that gryphon and getting a rowboat to you, I'm unsure I did much for you."

It certainly was not half as valiant or impressive as Gareth had envisioned saving a captured damsel would be.

"I wouldn't have broken those chains without your convincing."

Leo snarled. "Chains? She chained you?"

"They were loose," Anika said. But one hand drifted to her opposite wrist, drawing attention to the bruises and welts left by the manacles. She quickly dropped her hands back to her sides. "Also, getting the boat there and slaying a gryphon aren't small matters." A frown twisted her lovely face as she motioned toward Gareth. "We should get that armor off you and take a look at your shoulder."

Leo hopped to his feet before Gareth could voice his agreement. "Come on. Camp is this way!"

Gareth lifted an eyebrow as he joined Anika in following Leo. "Camp? A horse tied to a tree hardly counts as a camp."

"Well, once you put up a shelter or whatever you want to do, it will be." Leo glanced over his shoulder. "And a fire makes a camp. I gathered wood while I waited so I wouldn't lose my mind."

"Aw, did you get lots of good sticks, boy?" Anika asked, her tone teasing.

Leo turned a glare on her, his muzzle wrinkling back to reveal his teeth. "You're just missing your favorite pointy metal stick."

With a sigh, Anika patted her left side. "Fae-cursed witch confiscated it and wouldn't tell me why."

Soon they were back in the dappled shade of the forest, at the spot where Gareth had left Fury. Leo had created a very messy, spread-out pile of sticks and branches, many of which had obvious teeth marks.

"Don't even say anything," Leo warned as he padded around the pile. "Those of you with fingers can make a more organized pile."

With a snicker, Anika turned to Gareth. "Let me help you with your armor."

"Thank you." It was a relief to not have to ask.

She helped him remove his baldric. Her deft fingers made

short work of the fastenings on the cuirass, for which he was thankful. It was difficult to function with her standing so close and her hands brushing against his forearms as she removed his vambraces and then his sides and left shoulder. As she helped him pull off the cuirass, Gareth clenched his teeth around a yelp and squeezed his eyes shut for a moment.

"Oh, blast." Anika hurriedly set aside the cuirass. "No wonder."

Before he even had a chance to look at his shoulder, she was reaching for him, her fingers grasping at the bottom hem of his shirt as she tugged up on it.

Heat flamed over Gareth's face. He forced a chuckle through his confusion and moved his arms to keep his shirt in place. "Erm, this feels a little fast..."

Anika glanced at his eyes with an unamused expression. "You're bleeding."

"I'm what?" Gareth exclaimed. He touched below his collarbone, where his arm met his torso, and his fingers came away slick with blood. "That talon didn't only mess up my armor. I'd felt some pain, but I assumed it was just the force of the gryphon hitting my shoulder."

"You were probably so focused on staying alive, you didn't notice until the rush of battle wore off. Not uncommon." She released his shirt with one hand to motion at her scars. "It stung at first, but after the fight was over, the pain fully set in. Now. Shirt. Off."

Gareth complied, doing his best to help get the soaked shirt off without jostling his right shoulder too much. He tossed it over a branch.

"I need more light." Anika gently shoved on his torso, moving him until sunlight fell over his wound. Gareth pointedly stared out into the forest, trying to ignore her hands against his chest and her breath on his skin as she leaned in closer. "Good. I don't see anything caught in the wound, but this is deep. Do you have any clean water?"

"I'll get it!" Leo jumped up onto Fury's back and stuck his head into a saddlebag, emerging a moment later with a water canteen clutched in his mouth.

Anika took it from him, and the places where her hands had left Gareth's chest suddenly felt cold. He drew in a couple of deep breaths—both to steady himself against the growing pain in his shoulder and because he'd nearly stopped breathing while she'd been touching him.

It wasn't as if he'd never been touched by a woman. He'd danced at many balls, and more than a few young noblewomen who were angling for a tiara had flirted with him. Dancing or flirtatious touches while clothed in layers of court finery were a decidedly different experience than bare skin to bare skin against his chest, though. And none of those girls had ever made his stomach twist the way Anika did.

"Sir Gareth?"

He blinked and looked over at Anika. "Sorry, did you say something?"

Her forehead furrowed. "Do you want to sit down while I rinse the wound and use a mending spell? You're looking pale and there's…kind of a lot of blood. Also magical healing can make people nauseous."

"Oh. All right." Gareth lowered himself to the forest floor.

No, this was decidedly not how he had seen his first time rescuing someone going. Second time, if he counted Raelyn, but he really didn't. He hadn't made it to his sister while she was still in need of rescuing, and when he had thought that he was going to confront a monstrous dragon-man and save her, she was actually the one trying to save Alexander.

Maybe he wasn't as cut out to be an adventuring, heroic knight as he'd thought.

"I'd warn you this will sting," Anika said as she knelt beside him, "but I see you probably know that." Her fingertips grazed the four faint white lines on his upper left arm before she returned her attention to his right shoulder. "Hold still."

Gareth mostly kept his moan behind his lips as she thoroughly rinsed the cut. The laceration couldn't be the only reason for his pain, but the stinging wound overpowered the ache of his muscles. He glanced down. Blood stained most of the right side of his torso and had gotten onto Anika's hands. More blood trickled out of the wound, but not at an alarming rate.

Setting aside the now-empty canteen, Anika nodded. "This is bad, but it seems to have missed any major veins and is starting to clot. That will make healing it easier." She pressed her palm against the wound, causing him to bite his tongue to keep from crying out, and a yellow-orange glow emanated from her fingers.

If Gareth had guessed what magical healing would feel like, he'd have thought it would be more, well, magical. Soft and dreamy and pleasant. Instead, he spat out the strongest curse he knew as it felt like he was stabbed by a hundred needles and burned at the same time. After his initial jerk of surprise, he managed to hold still.

Thankfully, about a minute later, Anika pulled her hand away, and the pain dulled to a light stinging and itching.

"Sorry," Gareth muttered.

Anika quirked a smile. "Nothing I haven't heard or said before." She quickly looked away, a bit of red creeping into her face. "And um, sorry. I'd have warned you, but then you might have said no. It'll sting for a while and then likely will be sore for a day or two. All I really did was force the cut to close itself and your muscles to realign properly, but your body will still have to finish the work.”

“Ah.” He experimentally moved his shoulder and grunted. The pain spread so much around his shoulder in the front and back, he wasn’t entirely sure what the root cause was. “Thank you. That’s still an improvement over normal healing, and faster than stitches.”

“You’re welcome.”

Leo nudged Anika’s arm with his head. “Are you all right?”

Her fingers rubbed her temple for a moment, but she smiled. “Fine.”

“It gives her headaches,” Leo said. “Enchanters can experience various side effects. Once Anika had such a bad headache, she had to spend hours in a dark, quiet room to recover.”

Gareth’s lips parted. “I didn’t realize—”

“And this is why I didn’t mention that.” She waved a hand. “You risked injury or death to help me. I’m not allowed to risk a headache?”

That silenced him. “Thank you, though. Again.”

She nodded. “Do you have another shirt?”

“Oh. Yes.” He was probably red as a tomato. “I packed extras. I’ll—”

“No rush.” Anika stood, his dirty shirt in her hand. “I just wanted to know if we could use this shirt to make a sling. I’ll go wash it off in the lake first.”

Gareth scrambled to his feet. He wasn’t an invalid, and this was getting to be a bit more than his pride or sense of chivalry would allow. “You’ve been chained up for…I don’t know how long. And separated from Leo longer. You should relax. My shoulder isn’t so bad that I can’t wash a shirt. And besides”—he motioned with his left hand at the blood staining his torso—“I need to clean up myself, anyway.”

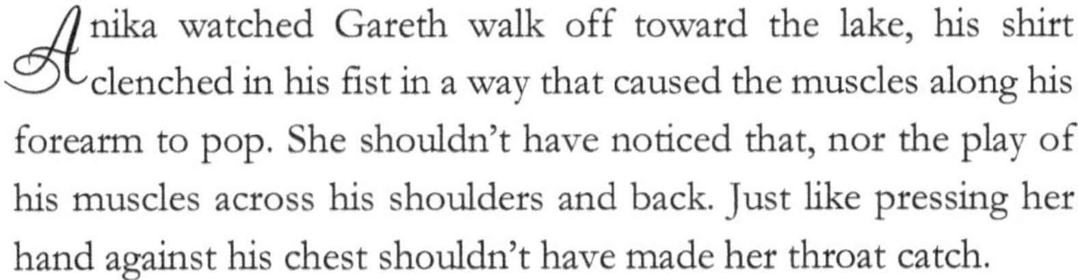

nika watched Gareth walk off toward the lake, his shirt clenched in his fist in a way that caused the muscles along his forearm to pop. She shouldn't have noticed that, nor the play of his muscles across his shoulders and back. Just like pressing her hand against his chest shouldn't have made her throat catch.

She'd heard other girls talking about the physical features or personality traits they found instantly alluring in a man. At the time, Anika had thought there weren't any traits or features she would be immediately attracted to.

It seemed perhaps her weakness was muscular knights with disheveled golden-brown hair, a quick smile, untrimmed stubble, and icy blue eyes that roiled with a storm of strong emotions. A knight who at least appeared to embody the ideal of self-sacrificial bravery, dedication, and virtue that she sometimes wondered if only knights in stories actually possessed.

Or maybe she'd been stuck with Callista or by herself for too long, and any young man who'd come with an offer of rescue might have looked attractive to her.

Leo poked her leg with his nose. "If you've stopped gawking at the Eynlaean, can we talk?"

A bit of heat crept into her cheeks, but Anika tossed her hair over her shoulder as if she were unfazed. She sat next to her brother. "How are you doing?"

He leaned against her side. "Better with you here."

Words tangled in her mind as she tried to sort through what to say. Things had been difficult, and she'd often worried the boredom and worry would drive her to madness.

But Leo'd had it worse. Cursed to become a fox, cursed to have his family forget about him so they wouldn't look for him. And the way he'd acted since she escaped the tower with Gareth… His laugh didn't sound human anymore. He'd snarled like an animal and whimpered as he squirmed in her arms in his excitement.

"Leo…are you sure you're all right?"

His ears pinned back. "Of course!" At her questioning look, his entire body sagged, and a soft whine escaped him. "You noticed?"

"Did Callista say you might become…" Anika couldn't get the words past her throat.

"Just a fox?" He shook his head. "It's probably nothing to worry about." His vulpine smile did not ease her fears. "Are *you* sure you're all right? The witch really didn't hurt you?"

"No." Tentatively, she reached out and stroked Leo's back. His fur was surprisingly soft, and some tension she hadn't even realized she was carrying eased out of her. Leo relaxed more, too.

"Why did she put you in the tower?"

"Didn't say. I suspect it has to do with her plan."

"She has a plan?" Leo looked up at her. "I find that doubtful."

"She admitted she's trying to force a prophecy to come true."

His whiskers twitched. It was adorable, but it also reminded her of the way Leo would wrinkle his nose as a human, and it sent a pang through her. "A prophecy? What prophecy?"

"I don't know." Anika rubbed the silky fur between his ears. "I thought I'd break into her room and see if I could find whatever prophecy she so desperately wants to come to pass she would try to meddle with destiny, but before I got a chance, she took me to that infernal tower."

Leo was quiet, probably thinking, putting pieces together faster than she ever would. While Anika's strength and speed were in her body, Leo's had always been in his mind.

"That could explain things. Why she's done so many things that on their own and together otherwise are illogical. How she hasn't seemed surprised by anything that has happened. It makes no sense…unless she's following a script."

Leo sighed. "But prophecies are messy. They don't always work the way you expect them to, and often lines are vague with many interpretations."

"She seemed to think prophecies want to come true; that she's just nudging it. She also implied this one is powerful." Still rubbing Leo's head, Anika frowned out at the forest. "Maybe it's because it's the only one I know about, but I'd wondered—"

"If it's the Fae Blessing and Curse for the Faines," Leo finished.

Her hand froze with her fingers buried in his red fur. "Do you think it's real?"

"Of course it's real. The royal family wouldn't have wasted so much breath and ink over the centuries denying it if it weren't real."

"Ha, that's what I told my tutor as a boy," Gareth said. He approached the campsite. "Also my opinion that, as the story had no clear lesson or ending, it couldn't be a fable, or someone would have given it a nice, neat moral by now."

He held his still-damp shirt at his side, and the red line of his wound stood out starkly against his bare chest. Anika forced her gaze up to his face as he sat down beside his saddlebags a mere pace away.

"But why are you talking about the fae prophecy about the Aedyllanian throne?"

Anika opened her mouth to answer, but Leo cut her off.

"None of your concern."

She withdrew her hand from Leo's head. Did he not trust Gareth? What could Gareth possibly do with that information, anyway?

Gareth looked between them, his mouth pressed into a line.

"We're wondering if—"

"Anika!" Leo snapped with a bit of a vulpine snarl at the end of her name. "The *foreign prince* doesn't need to know."

"The *what?*" Her attention shot back to Gareth, who pulled a white shirt out of his saddlebags and pointedly avoided her gaze as red crept into his cheeks. "You're a prince?"

"I'm not officially a prince at the moment, in a way…" Gareth tugged on his left ear, still avoiding looking at her. "I'm serving as a knight under Baron Tremblay, which is why I went after his firebird, but…well, yes." He cleared his throat.

Good thing she hadn't flirted with him. A prince was unlikely to deign to court the daughter of a low-ranking foreign lord.

"The…crown prince?"

Gareth scoffed and shook out a wrinkled blue garment. "No, thank goodness. Just a spare."

Just a spare. As if being an extra prince made him any less royalty. Although he looked more like a knight than a prince. Those muscles and the scars on his arm didn't speak of a life of lounging about on cushions. But then, what was a prince supposed to look like? Why would a prince spend all his time lazing about if even she, as a lady, didn't do so? Still, she was struggling to get her mind around the fact she was sitting across from a foreign prince—and that a prince had risked his own neck to rescue her.

"Isn't it dangerous for you to be wandering around Aedyllan alone? Both for you personally and, well…politically?"

"Exactly why I've been trying to keep that particular secret."

He scowled at Leo.

Leo snorted, apparently unbothered by a muscular, sword-wielding prince glaring at him. Her twin had never had the greatest sense of self-preservation. Of course, Anika hadn't helped him learn to. She'd always been there to finish any battles that he started with words if the other party decided to end the argument with fists.

"Yes, well, you weren't supposed to realize I'm human, and I wasn't supposed to realize you're a prince. Turns out we're both bad at secrets and good at reading between the lines."

"You're certainly bad at secrets." A bit of teasing humor came through, and Gareth smirked at Leo before attempting to pull on his undershirt, which involved a lot of grimacing.

"Here." Anika stepped up to his side. "Let me help."

"I can get it." Gareth didn't look at her as he struggled to get the shirt over his head without raising his shoulder. "It's just a little more difficult than I thought it'd be."

"You should be moving that shoulder as little as possible. If I—"

"You don't need to coddle me because I'm a prince." He kept his furrowed gaze on his garment.

She frowned. "I'm not offering because you're a prince. I'm offering because you're hurt and need help. There's no shame in that."

Gareth finally lifted his eyes to her face, studying her for a moment before he nodded. "All right. Thank you."

She helped him maneuver into the shirt and tried to focus on the soft fabric and not the strange feeling in her stomach every time her fingers brushed against his skin. Then she helped him pull on a short-sleeved blue tunic and fasten the multitude of buttoned closures down the front. Once his tunic was on, he held up his damp shirt.

"Could…you also help me turn this into a sling, please?"

"Of course." It took a few moments to get the shirt wrapped around his arm and body and tied in such a way it held his arm across his torso. When she finished, she returned to sit next to Leo.

"Returning to the prophecy conversation," Gareth said, "if I'm piecing this together correctly, this witch is causing all of this trouble in an attempt to create more chaos and make the Faine line end by activating the fae curse."

Ignoring Leo's warning shake of his head, Anika nodded. "That's my suspicion."

"So we stop it," Gareth said.

"I won't let—" Leo choked. "Hold on. Wait. What did you say?"

What in Miraveld had her brother assumed the prince was going to say?

His eyebrows pinching, Gareth repeated himself. "We have to stop the prophecy from coming true. Assuming it hasn't already."

"You want it…stopped?" Leo asked, clearly suspicious. "Why?"

Anika nudged her twin. "What's the matter with you?"

Leo ducked his head and flattened his ears. "If the prophecy comes true, there will be no king, no heir, no clarity about what happens next. Aedyllan would be weakened." He bared his teeth at Gareth. "Eynlae could take advantage of that, especially if they knew it was coming. *That* is why we shouldn't have told him."

Gareth's eyebrows shoved upward. "Eynlae has no desire to conquer Aedyllan or anywhere else. My father is far from perfect, but he's the furthest thing from a warmonger."

"Also irrelevant, since Gareth wants to prevent the prophecy," Anika pointed out.

"Should we, though?" Leo turned to her. "The Faines' blessing was always meant to end. It's not right for a family to hold that much power, magically protected from any challengers or consequences. It's made them cruel and selfish, careless and callous."

Shifting under her brother's regard, Anika plucked a blade of grass and twisted it around her finger. "It could cause another war, though. You know I want to be a knight, Leo, but I'm reluctant to kill my fellow Aedyllanians in service to a noble who may not care how many bodies it takes for him to claim the crown. Stopping the prophecy seems safest."

"Even if power isn't in the right hands now, and a change could benefit Aedyllan in the long term?"

She should have known Leo would be more aware of whatever issues people had with the crown than she was.

Gareth grunted. "First you argue curse-casters aren't evil, and now this? And I was actually starting to like you, fox."

Leo's tail bristled. "I mentioned the discussion of whether repentant witches are still witches or are enchanters, which is an interesting question of taxonomy as much as morality, but also not relevant—"

"Knowingly and willingly causing the death of an entire family and plunging a kingdom into war isn't moral, Leo." Gareth shoved to his feet, gripping his right shoulder. Fierce emotion shone through his eyes again as his face settled into hard lines like he was preparing for battle. "That shouldn't be up for debate."

Leo stood as well, his back arching. "And yet you would rather have had war with Rethalyon than see your sister wed to Tristan Carbrey. You expressed disappointment that the Carbreys were not executed for their crimes. You can't stand there and claim there is *never* reason for bloodshed when evildoers exist who may not be able to be stopped any other way."

Gareth opened his mouth before closing it again with a loud click.

Meanwhile, Anika looked between the two, feeling lost. They'd spent days together, talking about things that she had no basis of reference for, although she was unsurprised that arguments over philosophy had occurred. Leo needed philosophical conversations like she needed the rush of pushing herself in a practice duel.

But this wasn't the rhetorical back and forth that Leo enjoyed. This was life and death, and not only for the monarchy.

"I confess that I haven't kept up with criticisms of the Faines," Anika said slowly, "but is whatever they've done really worth the violence that a succession crisis would instigate? What about the young Faine children? What about the innocent lives that would be lost or changed forever in the aftermath?"

Gareth thrust his left hand toward Anika. "See, listen to your sister."

"Yes, Leo. Listen to your elders." She tried and failed to hide her smile, a full grin breaking out when Leo gave her a flat stare.

"Ten minutes still doesn't count."

"Does too."

Leo shook his head, but his combative posture eased, and he sat back down. "Look, I don't know. We should ask Father for his insight. Either way, I *don't* think an Eynlaean prince should have any say in an Aedyllanian problem."

Gareth knelt beside the messy pile of sticks and began arranging them into something more structured. "Like it or not, I'm involved now." He tapped the end of a stick against his chin. "Although, we have a bigger problem."

Leo's narrow, sidelong look at Gareth made him appear every inch the stereotype of a cunning fox. Anika had to force herself to stay serious and not laugh, while simultaneously feeling a pang of sorrow and fear. How much longer did her brother have before he lost his humanity entirely?

"What problem, nosy prince?"

Gareth pulled a face, indicating he'd taken the barb as more friendly teasing than sincere. He motioned at the three of them with a stick. "We don't know what the prophecy entails. Only Catrina does."

"Callista," Anika corrected, although she wasn't sure why. It just felt wrong to call someone by the incorrect name.

"Whatever." Still working at building a pile of firewood with his left hand, Gareth continued speaking. "We have no way of knowing what will further the prophecy or foil it. In the story of Sir Roderick and the Prophecy of Elinford, a sorcerer was attempting to prevent a prophecy that predicted his doom, but he didn't have the full text. In trying to stop Sir Roderick, he ultimately caused his own downfall. Regardless of whether we want the prophecy to occur or not, what if anything we do might have the opposite effect of what we intended?"

Leo sighed. "I hate to agree with a point predicated on an unproven legend, but you're right. As the saying goes, fighting your destiny may only serve to make it arrive faster."

Well that was disheartening. Anika drew her knees up to her chest. "So what do we do?"

She hated this feeling of helplessness and lack of direction.

Gareth's mouth curled down. "I've decided I hate prophecies. They're as bad as diplomacy. Tell me to fight and point me in the right direction, that I can do. Usually I'd say give me a clear villain and at least I know what to do next. But for all I know, if we go fight Callista, that is what the prophecy wants. It's unfair." He placed another stick and half of his carefully constructed pile fell over. "Wolf's teeth," he muttered.

"Here." Anika got up and went over to his side. "Let me help. I imagine you aren't used to doing this one-handed."

"And with the wrong hand at that," Gareth moaned.

They worked together to arrange the sticks into a pile that would burn cleanly. Gareth sat back on his heels and smiled. "I appreciate it, Anika."

Her mind failed her as she stared at him, leaving her awkwardly tongue-tied. Gareth wasn't at all what she would have assumed a prince to be like—he was both kinder and more rugged. He seemed self-confident but not superior, humble enough he didn't expect her to serve him, and secure enough in his manhood her strength didn't intimidate him.

If only he weren't a foreign prince who would eventually go home and never think about her again.

26

The thoughtful, searching look in Anika's eyes brought a lump to Gareth's throat.

He'd never thought much about romance before. Other things had occupied his mind and time. Things like building his strength and skill to be a better fighter or spending time with Raelyn when he wasn't stuck in lessons that were both tedious and unproductive for his goal of becoming a traveling knight. A wife had never featured in his daydreams.

But he'd never met a woman like Anika.

A woman who could fight, who was strong, and who also wanted to be a knight. It was stupid, but he hadn't thought those women existed outside of his books. For the first time, a relationship didn't seem like something that would have to wait until after he'd pursued the life he wanted. Or he'd assumed he'd have to balance going off on adventures and coming home so he didn't constantly leave a wife alone. A woman like Anika could go with him.

Gareth forced his gaze away from her and stood, pretending to stretch his legs after crouching on the ground. What was he thinking? He barely knew her. So she was attractive and could swing a sword—that hardly made her a good option for a wife. But Anika was also warm and relaxed, with a sense of humor…

No, he wasn't going down this path. They had a witch to stop, a prophecy to prevent, and he still didn't know what his future held. Besides, Anika might turn out to be the most selfish person he'd ever met.

Although she'd rather have remained chained in a rotting tower than risk any harm befalling her brother…

He shook his head, as if that would dislodge these ridiculous thoughts. "We should decide what we're doing next. Or maybe I should go hunt something down for us to eat."

Leo snorted. "By that I assume you mean *I* will hunt. No thanks."

"I'll carry it back," Gareth said with a wink. "We have some dried meat and fruit, but I thought we might as well make use of this firewood and have something fresh."

Anika stood and brushed dirt off her fitted trousers. "I'll go. You two stay here. I know a trapping spell, and you should rest, Gareth. Since we don't know what Callista has planned, it's possible you'll need to be in fighting condition again soon."

She turned to head deeper into the woods, and Gareth hesitated. Should he offer to go with her? He'd been taught not to leave a woman undefended. Anika probably didn't really need him, though, especially while he was injured. Still, she was unarmed, and letting her wander off alone without any protection went against his sense of honor. Should he offer her his weapon? He rubbed the pommel of his sword with his thumb. It had been drilled into him to guard his sword closely and not lose sight of it when out on his own.

Although, if he'd been willing to risk breaking his sword to free her, why was he debating letting her borrow it?

"Anika, wait." He picked up his baldric with the sheathed sword still attached. "Here." Gripping its scabbard in his left hand, he held out the weapon. "Just in case."

"Are you sure?" Anika's wide eyes went from his face to his sword and back again.

He lifted his good shoulder. "If anybody attacks us, I'll have Leo bite their ankles."

That drew a laugh from her, and it wasn't a sweet, gentle laugh, but he loved it. She took the sword and buckled the belt around her own waist with practiced familiarity. Something in the set of her shoulders relaxed. That was a feeling Gareth recognized.

"You aren't often without a sword, are you?"

Anika shook her head. "It's felt like part of me was missing." She patted the hilt of the sword and inclined her head in a small bow. "Thank you, Prince Gareth."

Hopefully she couldn't tell he was blushing again. "Er, Gareth is fine."

She nodded, then turned and strode into the forest.

Something knocked against his leg, almost pushing him off-balance. "Stop it." Leo headbutted him again. "No thinking about Anika."

"It's going to be difficult not to think about her at all," Gareth said drily. "It'd also be very rude and ungentlemanly to ignore her."

Leo batted at Gareth's knee above his greaves with a paw. "Just…stop looking at her all…all…however it is you keep looking at her. And keep your hands off of her. No touching. Or the only ankles I'll be biting will be yours."

Working to keep his expression serious, Gareth raised an eyebrow. "I'm afraid that's not possible. Some touching is going to occur whether you like it or not."

The look in Leo's eyes turned murderous as his back arched. "Why you—"

"We only have one horse, fur for brains. I'm not walking all the way back to Raylor Estate."

"Ah…oh." His pinned-back ears still conveyed displeasure,

but at least Leo no longer looked like he was considering clawing Gareth to death. "Fine. But still: Hands. Stay. Off."

Shaking his head, Gareth gave an exasperated grunt. "What exactly have I done to make you think I'm so dishonorable?"

"Well…nothing, I suppose—"

"And I'm pretty certain Anika can defend herself."

Leo's head lowered. "That doesn't mean I'm not going to look out for my sister. You'll go back to your castle and your crown in Eynlae, and I don't want to see her hurt because you played games with her heart while you were off on your little adventure."

Nodding, Gareth sat down next to Leo. "Don't worry. I was just as defensive of Raelyn and as prickly toward Tristan before he'd even done anything, despite the fact he was her betrothed. I understand wanting—needing—to protect your sister. I wouldn't have intentionally hurt Anika before, but after watching Raelyn flinch away from Tristan's kisses…" His fingers curled into the grass and dirt of the forest floor. "I'll *never* be like that."

After a moment, Leo gave one slow nod and sat down as well. "However…"

Leo side-eyed him with a soft growl.

Despite the smile that kept trying to come through, Gareth maintained a serious expression as he raised his hands. "I'm just saying, what if she flirts with me first? Maybe I'll take her with me when I go back to my crown and make her a princess." At Leo's affronted gape, his smirk finally escaped. "Or, you already know that I don't even want to be a prince. Maybe I'll move to Aedyllan and become your brother-in-law."

Leo stood and made a strange and frankly terrifying half yap, half scream as he bared his teeth.

Laughing, Gareth lightly shoved him aside. "All right, all right, calm down. I'm joking! I barely know her!"

Leo gave a little growl, but he eased back to sitting.

He should stop teasing, but it was too amusing to watch Leo get riled. Holding back more laughter, Gareth said, "Which is why I'd have to court her first—"

With an earsplitting screech, Leo launched himself at Gareth in a blur of red, white, and black fur. The fluffy impact was surprisingly hard, knocking Gareth onto his back and drawing a pained yelp from him. Sitting on Gareth's chest right above his arm in its sling, Leo started swatting his paws at Gareth's face as if he were trying to punch him. The rapid slaps to his cheeks were a little terrifying, but they didn't hurt, and Leo was clearly holding back and being careful with his claws.

"Leo!" Gareth shook with laughter as he tried to block Leo's paws with one arm. "All right—Leo! Your paws are not made for punching, and you look more adorable than—ow!"

Although Leo had landed a minorly painful blow on his nose, Leo's fur tickled his neck, drawing more laughter from Gareth. He tried to explain that Leo sitting on his chest was not helping the pain in his shoulder, but he couldn't speak beyond wheezing out *Leo* as he defended himself and laughed. With one arm trapped in a sling, he couldn't push the fox off, either.

Leo's ridiculous vulpine chortling of a high-pitched *eh, eh, eh* added to Gareth's laughter. Between his arm and Leo's batting paws, Gareth caught glimpses of Leo with his eyes squeezed half shut and his mouth thrown open in mirth.

There was a loud stomping sound, then Anika shouted, "Leo! Are you—what is going on?"

Leo half rolled, half fell off Gareth's chest, still fighting fox giggles. Gareth pushed himself upright, also struggling to bring his laughter under control despite the stabbing pain from his injury.

Anika stood nearby, his sword gripped in her hands as she stared, her entire face pinched in confusion. "I thought I heard someone scream, and then there was that strange sound…what happened? Were you fighting or playing?"

"Both," Gareth and Leo said at the same time before they broke down in another fit of mirth.

A sharp twinge went through Gareth's shoulder, and he groaned and gripped it. After taking a few deep breaths, he finally suppressed his laughter. "Sorry. Didn't mean to alarm you. I was teasing Leo and he tried to get back at me, but foxes are not good at fist-fighting."

Anika raised an eyebrow as she turned an unimpressed frown on her brother. "Human Leo isn't good at that, either."

Leo licked a paw, somehow making the action look dignified. "We were just sorting out a minor disagreement."

"About what? If it's about the prophecy, we should discuss that together."

"Erm…" Leo shared a guilty look with Gareth.

"You know…" Gareth waved a hand. "Philosophy and…ethics…and things…"

"Right…" She rolled her eyes. "Behave, you two. And no screaming, whichever one of you that was."

Gareth quickly pointed at Leo. "That was all him."

"Not my fault foxes make such stupid noises." Leo sniffed.

A bit of worry crossed Anika's face, but she smothered it. "And no attacking Gareth. He needs to relax." With that, she went back into the forest.

27

$\mathcal{C}$allista chewed on her thumbnail and paced in her room in the abandoned castle. A grungy rug that was heavier than it looked muffled her footsteps. She'd had to use magic to drag it and the desk in, and to nail a thick curtain over the glassless window. Then she'd cleaned the rubble out of the chimney and mounted a door, which unfortunately did little to prevent rodents from finding their way in. A down-stuffed mattress on a small cot covered with warm blankets completed the space, making it as comfortable as possible.

It was still bleak and drafty and miserable.

And lonely.

Oh so lonely.

If only she hadn't had to sell her flute to afford the gold leaf to gild the firebird's cage. Music might have alleviated the crushing silence.

She missed Anika, despite the fact they'd barely spoken. Having another human around, even one who hated her, had been a relief from the oppressive emptiness of the ruins.

But Anika's absence proved that the plan was progressing. Soon Callista would be able to stop hiding.

Hopefully.

By now, the Eynlaean knight should have made it to Lake Marsing. He would face the gryphon to rescue Anika—assuming the girl didn't free herself first. Considering how much she loved her twin, though, she wouldn't risk it. If anything, Anika might not let the knight rescue her, but Callista couldn't say, "Stay put until that Eynlaean man comes to save you." She'd already said more than she should have in mentioning the prophecy to Anika. But it was so hard to carry everything alone.

Her grief.

Her anger.

The growing numbness in her chest.

The weight of securing vengeance.

And the knowledge of what else she'd have to do, the lines she'd have to cross, before it was done.

That was if things kept going to plan. If Callista had arranged the pieces correctly and the prophecy worked.

She'd spent two years planning this. Learning the spells and curses she would need, finding all the people and animals the prophecy required. At first, she'd been too afraid to hope destiny would be on her side—after all, nothing had been on her side for years—but it had to be.

Why else would she have stumbled into the twins and decided to use them for the roles of the captive girl and talking fox, only to discover they were the children of the lord that kept the royal unicorns? Why else would she have found a firebird conveniently in an Eynlaean lord's possession? Who surely, as he'd in fact done, would send an Eynlaean to recover it, providing her with a foreign hero?

Her professors had been right. Prophecies wanted to come true.

Yet there was still too much left to chance. She couldn't force everyone to follow the steps of the dance she had orchestrated.

They could step out of line, and she had no idea if that would foil the prophecy and undo all her efforts.

And then there was the last piece.

The step she most dreaded.

She went to the desk and yanked open a drawer. The scroll inside slid with the motion, and she snatched it up. As she unrolled it and read the lines written in a strong, thick hand in ominous black ink, she held her breath, as if, somehow, in her hundredth time reading it, it might have changed.

It hadn't.

Mortimer Faine and his descendants shall prosper and flourish and rule the kingdom of Aedyllan. None shall prevail against their line or their rule so long as this prophecy goes unfulfilled. But nothing lasts forever, and such great magic demands a steep price. Beware, for should your line no longer be of noble heart—

A time will come when a fox will speak and seek to offer aid,
A warrior will risk his life to save a girl in chains,
A girl traded for a unicorn, a unicorn for a fiery bird,
And a foreign hero's life will end to save a crying maid.
Then at last shall death and ruin have the final word,
And on the throne of Aedyllan shall never again sit a Faine.

Fae were twisted, Callista had decided the first time she'd read the prophecy, and she hoped she'd never have the misfortune of meeting one. She'd never wanted this, not any of it, but she had no choice if she wanted to see justice done.

The curses she'd cast didn't really change her, not in any physical way. Much like lying or extortion or violence didn't leave any obvious mark on the perpetrator, but the guilt was corrosive. She could either hate herself or become numb to conviction.

Or she could stop, but she hated the idea of letting Silas Faine and his sons continue unchecked even more than she hated what she had become. The blood of her mother and father and both of her brothers cried out to her for vengeance. There was no justice in the halls of Highrook Castle, so she would see it fall.

Should she visit Raylor Estate to ensure things were progressing according to plan? No, she couldn't waste magic rushing to beat the knight back to the ruins to exchange the unicorn for the infernal firebird.

Hopefully the twins would accompany him, otherwise recapturing them to leverage against him would be more complicated. A gut feeling told her they would, if only to beg her to break the curses on Leo.

And then…

Her stomach twisted.

She'd kill the Eynlaean and keep her promise to her brother. Perhaps when the Faines breathed their last, her family and friends and everyone the Faines had ever harmed, directly or indirectly, would know peace. Perhaps then the icy rage clawing at her heart would finally leave her alone.

When Anika returned, she cast a suspicious glance at Leo and Gareth as if not quite trusting that they had been peacefully lying on the grass on opposite sides of the unlit stack of firewood the entire time she was gone. She'd caught a hare, and she set to skinning it, adamantly refusing Gareth's offers to help. She did hesitantly agree to let him set up a makeshift spit to roast the hare over the fire, which didn't take long. So while she worked on preparing their dinner, Gareth decided they might as well return to discussing the prophecy problem.

"I was thinking, there's a way we can find out for certain if Callista is trying to make the prophecy about the Faines come true without asking her."

Leo stood and stretched, his pointy teeth flashing in a big yawn. "Oh?"

"You could visit your king." Gareth could go, too, but selfishly, he wanted to make the unicorn for firebird trade and be free of the binding spell. He'd have to figure out another way to get a unicorn since he wouldn't be returning with Anika, but he could solve that later.

Nodding, Anika kept dressing the hare. "I suppose if anyone would know if it's even possible for her to know the contents of the prophecy, it would be the king, right?"

"Exactly." Gareth lightly rolled his aching shoulder, trying to prevent it from getting too stiff. "He'd also know if the things she's orchestrated so far are what is in the prophecy and what comes next. At least, if I knew there was a prophecy that if it came true could result in my death and the deaths of my entire family, I'd definitely know what it says."

"Hm." Leo tilted his head. "But if I were the king and someone came around asking about it, I'd be suspicious that *they* are the ones trying to make the prophecy come true and are confirming they've got it right."

Leave it up to Leo to assume the worst. Gareth picked up a leaf and spun the stem between his fingers, watching it flash in the sunlight streaming through the branches overhead. "All you have to do is explain where to find the real culprit. He'd be incredibly stupid if his subjects came to him trying to save his life and he assumed they were the villains without even checking their story."

A sound that was half snort, half sneeze came from Leo. "Naively optimistic. I already told you the Faines are greedy and cruel. I don't trust King Silas. Which brings us back to if we *should* stop the prophecy. I maintain that we should go home. To our home, that is." He motioned with a paw between himself and Anika. "Father can help us make an informed decision."

Right, as if there could be any information that made "wipe out a family and cause a civil war" acceptable. Gareth scoffed as he tossed aside the leaf.

Anika's lips pursed. "Leo has a point. Besides, I don't feel right about running off to the palace when my family is worried sick. I should go home and let them know I'm all right."

"Also that," Leo agreed.

Gareth didn't want to keep Anika from her family, but he also didn't want to play right into the witch's hands. At the same time, he didn't particularly want to die. Perhaps Callista had lied, though. Could the binding spell truly crush his heart if he didn't obey? Given what he knew about curses, that seemed likely.

As Anika was almost done dressing the hare, Gareth fished his flint out of his pack. Frowning, he set about starting the fire. "Well I can't go to King Silas. I'm not one of his subjects, but you're both Aedyllanian nobility and might have a chance at an audience."

He shrugged his good shoulder. "I could probably get an audience as a prince, but I don't have proof with me. Not to mention if Leo was suspicious of my motives as a foreign prince, I can only imagine what your king would think."

Either Callista's binding spell or King Silas would likely kill him. It might just be a matter of which got him first.

"Exactly!" Leo gave a sharp nod. "All the more reason we should talk to my father. We have to take Anika back anyway, so—"

"That's Callista's plan, though." The fire caught, and Gareth rocked back on his heels. "She wanted your father to send me here and bring Anika home, likely because she knew your father would reward me with a unicorn. But she didn't trade you directly because she needs me *specifically* to bring her the unicorn."

She wants it badly enough she'll kill me if I don't. Did he really want to die to *maybe* stop a prophecy? His stomach twisted.

"You're correct," Anika said, a grim set to her mouth as she placed the hare on the spit over the fire. "I even asked Callista why she didn't just leverage me against my father to acquire a unicorn. That was when she mentioned a prophecy."

His attention locked on the roasting meat, Leo smacked his lips. "Unless she told you about the prophecy to raise your suspicions, hoping we would warn the king, because *that* is what she actually wants. Seems suspicious she told you, doesn't it? We wouldn't be having this conversation if she hadn't. Remember, we don't know what the prophecy says—or if it's the one we're guessing, or even if there truly is one at all."

This was all so convoluted it was giving Gareth a headache. If Sir Roderick were here, what choice would he make? In the legends, he always knew what to do. Even when he didn't, it worked out all right in the end, and the books never spoke of Sir Roderick being plagued by doubt or confusion. Maybe the storytellers took liberties to make Eynlae's favorite hero appear more heroic.

If only he could know the outcomes before committing.

The thought rammed into him like a charging destrier.

Was that how Father had felt in the mountains? Had he wished he could know for certain whether they would find Raelyn alive if they kept looking or find her dead, or search for months and never find her? Gareth had been convinced they would find her if they looked long enough, denying the alternatives, but even though he'd argued he *knew*…he hadn't, not truthfully.

If Gareth had been wrong…perhaps eventually he would have accepted that calling off the search was the right thing to do.

He'd been right, though. His gut, as it usually did, had steered him in the right direction. So what were his instincts telling him this time?

Pressing his eyes closed, Gareth tried to ignore the scent of smoke and cooking meat, the pop and crackle of burning wood and the rustle of leaves overhead, the prickle of grass against his palms. His personal interest in staying alive aside, should they take Anika home?

Send the twins to warn the king and ask for his help in stopping Callista?

Or reunite a girl who had been held captive with her family?

As he opened his eyes, he knew the answer his heart gave.

If Anika were Raelyn, he would take her home. Some potential prophecy wouldn't stop him.

Was his heart right this time? For once he wasn't sure.

But Anika should get to go home. Leo, too.

Wait…Leo.

On the other side of the fire, Leo was still intent on the roasting hare, his grin a little feral as his bushy tail lazily swept back and forth behind him.

"I haven't thought…" Gareth gulped. "What about Leo?"

Anika's expression was strained as she glanced toward her brother. "I don't know. I don't know how to break a transmogrification, or even if it's possible for someone other than the witch who cast the curse to undo it. All I ever got out of Callista was a vague implication that Leo would be returned to normal if we did as she said."

Leo dragged his gaze away from their dinner to look at her. "That could mean the curse is primed to break once she's done with us, or that she'll undo the spell once she no longer needs us."

"Either way," Anika said, "that means we have to do what she wants."

Was that the real reason Leo wanted the prophecy to happen? He hoped when it did, he would return to being human? Somewhat guiltily, Gareth realized he couldn't blame Leo for that. He didn't relish the idea of his heart being crushed if he defied Callista, either.

"Or she lied." Leo looked back to the food, but this time, it looked less like he was interested in the sizzling meat and more like he was avoiding their stares. "It doesn't matter. We shouldn't make decisions based on me. Every curse has a way to break it. It's an immutable law of magic. It's actually related to why the fae prophecy exists, just in reverse. A curse is an unnatural way of forcing nature to change, and that's like pulling back on a harp string but never letting go. It seeks release, to return to equilibrium, so the curse leaves an outlet—a way to be ended.

"Likewise, the fae blessing unnaturally changed the fate of the

Faines and Aedyllan. It needs an end, and maybe trying to stop the prophecy from occurring is like trying to stop an inevitable death. But I digress. The point is, no one can create a curse that can't be broken. It's just a matter of finding the right curse-breaker."

Leo glanced at Anika. "So don't worry about me. But you…" He turned his attention to Gareth. "I'm surprised you're so against doing Callista's bidding. Aren't you forgetting something important?"

"No." Gareth rubbed at some dirt on his trousers, avoiding the twins' eyes. "I don't want to choose what to do on the basis of what's best for myself alone."

Anika looked between them. "What do you…oh." Her face paled. "The binding spell. I can't believe I forgot. And I—I'm sorry I didn't intervene. I couldn't risk Leo."

"I understand." Although it was embarrassing that she'd watched him be totally at the witch's mercy. "Since you have magic…do you know if she told the truth? About my heart being crushed if I don't bring her a unicorn?"

"It's dark magic, which I don't know much about," she murmured, "but yes. I think she did."

Gareth gave a small nod. The roasting hare no longer smelled appetizing. "I'd thought, maybe, if I didn't bring you home and instead stole a unicorn like I originally was going to, perhaps it would be enough to ruin the prophecy."

"That's a terrible plan!" Anika slammed a hand to the ground. "If you returned without me and attempted to steal a unicorn a second time, my father would kill you. Or Callista might if you wrecked her plans."

"Your life or death isn't a small matter, Gareth," Leo said quietly.

"And it's more than I want to risk over mere speculation," Anika declared. "Let's return to my father's estate. Please."

Gareth swallowed against the tightness in his throat. Truthfully, he didn't want to argue. "It seems I don't have a choice," he conceded.

The twins nodded, and relief showed on Anika's face.

They lapsed into silence, Anika turning the hare every so often. Leo lay down, his chin resting on a forepaw. It was an uncomfortable sort of silence, the kind of uncertainty and things left unsaid. The quiet itched along Gareth's skin, making him antsy.

They needed a new topic, and fast, or this awkwardness would never disappear.

"I'd like a rematch, by the way." Gareth grinned across the fire at Anika. "This time on equal footing. When we get to your father's estate, do you think he'll let me stay around long enough to grab some practice swords and get a couple rounds in?"

Anika lifted an eyebrow. "If either of us had an advantage last time, it was you. You were wearing armor, and I wasn't."

"Mm, true, but I was hiding, so you got to take the offensive first. Plus it was dark, you had that blinding torch behind you, and I was trying not to seriously hurt you."

Leo lifted his head. "So what, now you want to actually attempt to hurt her?"

"*Practice* swords, Leo." Gareth scoffed. "The whole point is I can't do worse than bruise her. Well, chance of broken bones, but I think she's good enough that won't happen."

Across from him, Anika beamed at him. The flickering glow of the fire made her look wilder and more dangerous in a way that did something odd to Gareth's heart.

"I'm sure we can work something out. It'd be fun to fight you again." She sighed. "Callista was heartless for taking my sword. I'd say we try again right now if I had a weapon. Well, and if you weren't injured. You better be healed enough by the time we get there."

"You'd...*now?*" Gareth stared at her. "With sharpened swords?"

She shrugged. "Surely you don't always practice with blunt blades?"

"Um…yes?" He leaned forward, both fascinated and horrified. "You practice spar with sharp weapons?"

Her expression conveyed just as much confusion as he felt, and a little judgment. "Of course. Only occasionally because it does cause you to hold back. But it's better to get your first sword wound in a controlled environment from a friend than in battle. And better to get your first taste of what it's like to draw blood with your own weapon in a practice match than in a life-or-death situation." She glanced away. "I vomited the first time. It wasn't even a serious wound. It impressed on me how serious it is when I draw my sword. It's designed to harm and kill and isn't to be unsheathed lightly."

Gareth nodded. He could see the wisdom in that, although it sounded a bit cruel and reckless to knowingly hurt an ally.

Leo stretched out on his side. "His Highness probably doesn't have much choice in practicing with blunted weapons. Who is going to risk wounding their prince?"

In response, Gareth snatched up a pinecone and chucked it at the fox. It bounced harmlessly off Leo's furry side, prompting a flat, unamused glare.

"I'm thinking after we eat, we should start out," Gareth said, changing the subject from his title. "There's no reason to stay here."

Anika and Leo agreed, and then Anika declared the hare looked cooked through, so they ate quickly. Once the fire was extinguished and covered with dirt, Gareth stored his vambraces in his saddlebags, as putting them on sounded too troublesome, then he picked up the cuirass.

"Ah-ah, no." Anika snatched the cuirass away from him. "No extra weight on that shoulder. Keep it in the sling and rest it."

He frowned. It didn't matter that she was right. "I'm not leaving it behind, and it will be in the way tied to my saddlebags with both of us riding."

"True." Anika looked down at the shining steel in her hands, then back at Gareth. "Help me get it on, then."

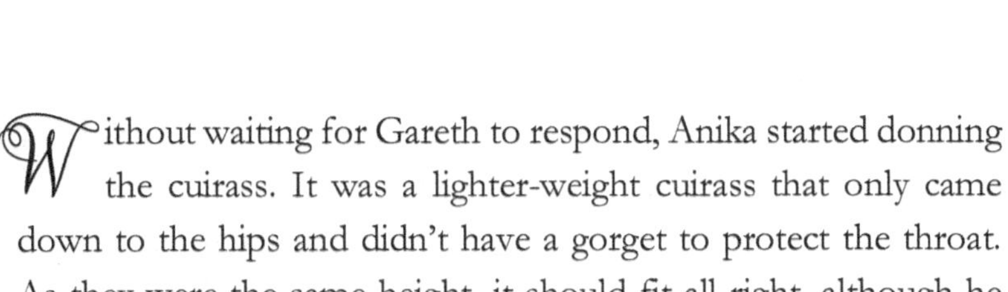

29

Without waiting for Gareth to respond, Anika started donning the cuirass. It was a lighter-weight cuirass that only came down to the hips and didn't have a gorget to protect the throat. As they were the same height, it should fit all right, although he was broader and slightly more muscular—a thought she quickly shoved aside.

Abruptly, Gareth gave a little start, then hurried forward to help. With one hand, the only assistance he could really offer was holding the backplate up while she did the buckles. The armor was a touch loose, shifting back and forth in a way that would be terrible in a fight, but at least the bottom edge wouldn't dig into her thighs while on horseback.

The only issue was the jagged teeth of metal poking outward from the rend left by the gryphon's talon. She still had a dull headache and didn't have the strength or skill to fix it properly, but something had to be done. She held her hand over the gash and used her magic to flatten the protruding pieces and smooth the sharp edges. Pain stabbed into the base of her skull, but it was bearable.

"There, that's better." Anika looked up from the breastplate. "And it fits almost perfect, right?"

Gareth made a choked sound. "Yeah." His voice came out squeaky, and he cleared his throat. "That…that will work. Good, uh, good thinking. And good magic. That is, the fixing." His entire face turned red. "What I mean is, thank you."

For some reason, a blush rose to her cheeks as well. Had the closeness of assisting with the cuirass flustered him? Or…surely it wasn't that he liked how she looked in armor, right? Drawing attention when she wore armor wasn't unusual, but it was typically curiosity, condescension, or disapproval. Not the wide-eyed, almost yearning look the prince was giving her.

Leo trotted up and headbutted Gareth's leg. "Ankles."

That random declaration, for reasons Anika couldn't fathom, only made Gareth more flustered. He focused on buckling his sword belt about his waist, as he'd opted not to use the baldric, which would put pressure on his injured shoulder.

"We should go up." Gareth quickly shook his head. "Get mounting. *Mount up* and get going." His entire face was red now, and Anika was fighting a losing battle not to laugh. "Uh. I'll go in front."

He turned away as Anika stifled her chuckles. Leo gave her an annoyed look, his ears swiveling downward.

Gareth mounted his buckskin destrier with ease, despite his injury. Reaching down, he offered her his left hand. They clasped each other's forearms, and he helped her swing up behind him, where she squeezed into the space between his back and the saddlebags. As she settled into place, her thighs touching his, he stiffened. Her face heated. They'd just have to get used to it. There wasn't enough room on the saddle for her not to be pressed up against him.

Leo crouched down before springing up behind her and curling into a ball on the saddlebags.

Gareth clicked his tongue, and they started off.

"This is Fury, by the way." He patted the warhorse's thick neck.

"Fury." She grinned. "Very…forceful name."

"Heh, yes, well. I picked him out as a foal four years ago. I thought Fury was a good name for a horse to ride into battle."

"Mmm, I had similar thoughts when I named my mare."

After a pause, Gareth said, "Not going to tell me her name?"

"Graedyr," she admitted hesitantly. "It means *swift death* in the Old Tongue."

"That's fantastic." He sounded like he genuinely meant it, too, not like he was mocking her.

They fell into easy conversation as they rode, with Leo occasionally cutting in, and thankfully, Gareth's stiffness eased. They'd been on the road for a couple of hours when Leo scrambled to his feet. He leaned his forepaws on Anika's back, stretching up as he sniffed the air.

"Someone is coming toward us. I hear hoofbeats and smell horses and people, but I think only a few."

Gareth nodded. "More bandits? Or just travelers?"

"I'm not a fortune teller," Leo grumbled.

Anika glanced up and down the road. "This route isn't used much. It's less direct, unless you're going to Lake Marsing, which isn't a popular destination."

With a heavy sigh, Gareth turned off the road. "If it's only a few, normally I'd rather take my chances, but we only have one sword and one cuirass between the two of us. No offense to your ankle-biting skills, fur-butt."

"And you're injured, hollow-helm," Leo rejoined.

Boys. Anika rolled her eyes.

They'd barely entered the forest off the side of the road when a couple of men appeared around a bend. They wore simple clothing in dark, neutral colors of rough, common materials, but a gold pendant bounced against one man's chest and sunlight gleamed on precious stones in rings on the other man's fingers. Chainmail sleeves stuck out from under the one with the pendant's tunic, and the other wore a steel breastplate. Both bristled with a variety of weapons and had a hard, cruel edge to their faces.

One of the men said something to his companion, too low for Anika to hear. She held her breath as they rode nearer, and Gareth pulled Fury to a halt. She'd also prefer to avoid a fight when she was wearing ill-fitting armor, had no sword, and had an injured man and her brother in talking fox form to worry about.

Just as the men came parallel to them on the road, they turned their horses toward the forest. The man with the rings rapidly unslung his bow and nocked an arrow, and the other drew a sword.

"We saw you running away," the one with the sword crooned. "Come out and play."

"If you do, we'll be friendly," the archer added as he drew his bow. The sharp arrowhead eased sideways as he scanned the forest. "I spy a bit of a horse. Come out and I won't need to turn horsey into a pin cushion."

The reins creaked as Gareth's hand tightened around them.

"We only want your valuables," the swordsman said with a mocking lilt. "Play nice and we'll be nice in return and not hurt you."

"Leo," Gareth said in a low voice. "You might actually need to bite some ankles."

Her brother jumped down. "I'll try for a surprise side attack."

Anika started to protest, but Gareth was already turning Fury back toward the road. "When there's an opportunity, use my sword," he whispered. Then he shouted, "We're coming out, and we're cooperating!"

As they cleared some leafy branches, the bandit with the sword sneered. "Smart lad."

Anika ground her teeth together. "What's the plan?" she hissed near Gareth's ear.

He didn't acknowledge her. "I'm afraid we have no valuables, though, good sirs."

The archer snickered. "We'll be the judge of that. Come out onto the road."

Gareth obliged, stopping Fury between the two men. Leo had vanished entirely.

"The cuirass the boy is wearing looks valuable to me," the archer said. "But…wait, now. What's this?" He leaned forward. "A *woman?*"

"Probably eloping and on the run from her parents." The swordsman tsked. "Seems you've already had a bit of trouble." He waved his weapon in the general direction of Gareth's right arm in its sling. "That's what you earn for stealing away a bride. Seeing as you can't use that fine sword of yours, how about we take it off your hands? And we'll relieve you of the weight of that cuirass, miss."

"So generous of you," Anika muttered.

"Should have stayed safe at home with your parents, little lady."

Gareth lifted his hand. "Let us dismount, and I'll help her take the cuirass off."

"Nah." The archer jumped off his horse and slipped his bow over his shoulder. "She comes down and I'll help her out." The leering smile he sent her way made her skin crawl.

"All right," Gareth said, his voice quavering. "We'll give you what you want, just don't hurt us."

She gaped at the back of his head. This man was nothing like the one who had slain a gryphon and been so determined to rescue her he hadn't realized how badly he was injured.

"Hurry up, girlie," the archer said.

"My love, do as he says."

The confusion of Gareth calling her *my love* almost overcame her ability to think, but Anika stammered out her agreement and dismounted to the left, on the same side as the archer. Ugh, why did Gareth have such a big horse? The hilt of Gareth's sword was level with her shoulders, which wasn't ideal for drawing it.

A blood-curdling woman's scream sounded from the other side of the archer's horse, making Anika jump. The swordsman cursed as his horse shied, and Fury laid back his ears and danced backward a couple of steps, but the archer's horse bolted. As the archer shouted and turned to chase after his mount, Anika grabbed Gareth's sword.

"The swordsman!" Gareth drew a dagger from his boot and kicked Fury into motion, chasing after the archer. She'd leave that bandit to him and focus on her own opponent.

The rush of battle spread through Anika's veins as she sprinted forward, running in the opposite direction toward the still-mounted swordsman. He'd steadied his mount, thankfully a riding horse that wasn't as tall as Fury. The bandit snickered at her charge.

"We both know you don't know what to do with that."

"Sure about that?" Anika swung toward his unprotected back, and he brought his sword around to block.

But he had twisted to meet her attack and held his weapon at an awkward angle, and with the force of her blow, the sword wrenched from his grip and clattered against the road. Cursing, he wheeled his horse around and drew a short sword and a long dagger.

"One of us doesn't know what to do with a sword." Anika smirked. "But it isn't me."

With a shouted insult, the bandit leapt off his horse. His boots had barely hit the ground when Anika's borrowed sword arced toward his head. He got his short sword up just in time to block, and then stabbed toward her right arm with his dagger. She dodged the blade, already moving the sword into another slice toward his legs.

The bandit jumped back, his face red with rage. "Oh, you'd better hope I kill you. Because—"

He cut off as he focused his energy on the duel. Talking while fighting never went well, and his weapon choice had been ill-conceived. Gareth's broadsword had a longer reach than the bandit's short sword, and she gave him no opening to get close enough to make effective use of his dagger. The edge of her blade cut across his right shoulder, and he dropped the short sword with a yelp. She whipped the tip of her sword up to his throat.

"Yield."

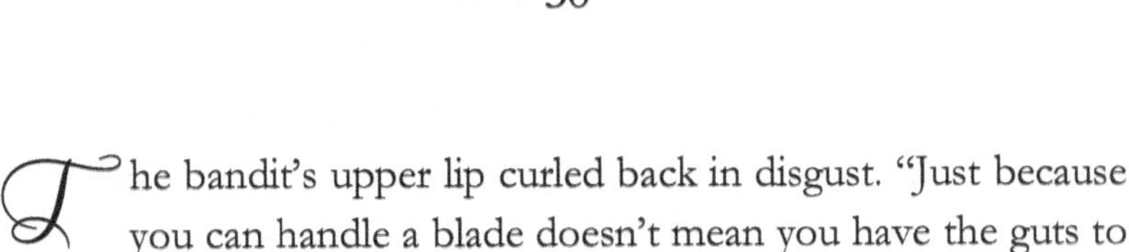

30

The bandit's upper lip curled back in disgust. "Just because you can handle a blade doesn't mean you have the guts to finish it." He added an insult to Anika's gender and spat as he backed away.

It wasn't the first time she'd heard it, but her fingers still tightened around the sword's grip as she moved the weapon into an attack position.

"Pretty sure she does," Gareth said mildly as he strode up on her left. She glanced over at him, pleased to see he'd apparently subdued the archer without further injury.

"The question is," Gareth drawled, "do you?"

The bandit laughed as he freed a spiked mace from a holder on his belt. "I've killed men and women for causing less trouble than you two. I'll gladly add you to the count."

She didn't want to kill anyone, but she wouldn't turn her back on an angry, dangerous opponent, either.

"Why you!" A blur of red fur shot between Gareth and Anika, snarling as it ran straight for the bandit. The man jumped back and brandished the mace, preparing to strike the fox.

"Leo!" Anika screamed as she lunged forward.

Something glinted through the air past her, and then the hilt of a dagger protruded from the bandit's left shoulder. He cried out as Leo darted between his legs, passing him. The swordsman faltered between the threat behind him and the one in front, leaving himself wide open to Anika's attack. Her sword cut across his throat, and he crumpled to the ground.

Leo scampered around the body, whining. "Anika! Are you all right?"

She dropped to her knees and set down the sword, and Leo jumped into her arms. "I'm fine! Are you all right?"

"I helped!" Leo wriggled in her arms and licked her face, then abruptly went still. He squirmed backwards and slipped free. "Erm. Hm. Sorry. Got overexcited that everyone was all right."

"And that you helped," she teased as she ruffled the fur on his head. He batted her hand away.

"So everyone is all right?" Gareth asked. "No injuries?"

"Yes, fine," Anika said, electing to omit the way her hands quivered as the moment she killed the bandit replayed in her mind.

"Good, good."

Turning toward Gareth, her gaze fell on the archer's body sprawled in the road beyond him. She released a slow breath to steady herself and looked up at her companion. "Are you all right?"

"Oh, yes." But Gareth's face had gone pale, and he swayed slightly as his throat bobbed. "I see now why your instructor had you practice with sharpened blades—" He cut off abruptly and spun on his heel, making it a couple of steps away before he vomited.

Leo tilted his head. "He carried himself in the fight better than that looks. His horse knocked the archer down, but the man drew a knife and stabbed toward Fury, so Gareth jumped down to fight him. I bit the bandit's leg." His nose wrinkled. "Kind of gross. But that helped Gareth get the advantage, even with his right arm in a sling. Stabbed him in the throat. It was a lot of blood, and I'm pretty sure the prince hasn't killed a man before."

"No," Gareth said quietly. "I hadn't."

Anika dug her fingers deeper into Leo's fur. "Me neither."

Gareth cleared his throat and turned toward her, a bit more color in his cheeks. "Honestly, I wasn't planning to do it, but he wasn't holding back, and…training took over. The movement is the same as a straw dummy, but it doesn't feel the same." He rubbed the side of his neck, avoiding her gaze. "Sir Christopher once told me not to pull a blade on a man I wasn't prepared to kill. I'm not sure I took him seriously at the time."

She lifted a hand from Leo to wipe some blood off her cheek. "I'm trying not to think too much about it." Now that the adrenaline was wearing off, that was getting harder.

"At least you kept your dinner," Gareth said wryly.

"Like I said, I vomited the first time I drew blood, and that wasn't even a kill." She picked up his sword and stood, relieved that her hand didn't wobble. "No judgment."

He gave her a faint smile. "They were robbers, murderers, and who knows what other crimes they've committed, and they'd have killed us. Maybe I should, but I don't regret it. Still, I think I prefer slaying monsters. This…feels different."

"Agreed." She shuffled her feet and glanced at the nearby corpse. "How wrong would it be to…well…"

"Loot the bodies?" Leo interjected. "It'd be practical."

Anika gaped at her brother. "I was going to say, 'drag the bodies off the road and not bury them.'"

"Oh." Leo stood and shook himself. "I see no problem with that. We don't have shovels, anyway. While we're at it, might as well take their supplies. They probably stole everything, you know. At least take this dead idiot's sword. Then you'll both be armed."

Gareth released a short laugh. "If we don't, someone else will. Besides, I'm unsure respect for the dead extends to their ilk."

"Why, that was almost philosophical of you," Leo remarked.

"Yeah, yeah." Gareth waved a hand dismissively. "How are you so unaffected, anyway, fur-butt?"

Leo tilted his head all the way to one side. "Maybe it'll affect me later. Right now, I'm happy we're all safe. And…I think foxes care less about death," he added quietly.

Yet another indication that Leo was becoming more fox-like troubled Anika worse than the dead bandits. They needed to get home and decide on next steps. Maybe going along with the witch's plan would be worth it if it restored Leo. Could she really doom an entire family to save her brother, though? She didn't want to examine that too closely.

"We should get moving," she said. "I'll check the bodies if you get their horses…" She looked around. "Or horse. The other one made a run for it, it seems."

"Yeah, thanks to that accursed sound Leo made." Gareth adjusted his sling and cast an exaggeratedly horrified look at her brother. "What in Miraveld was that?"

"As I have said before," Leo said primly, "it isn't my fault foxes make such stupid noises. I didn't know that's what was going to come out. I was going for more of a roar. Apparently foxes don't roar. They yowl."

"It sounded like a woman screaming." Anika shuddered. "Like a banshee from a story or something."

Leo flicked his tail. "Don't you have a sword to clean and return to Gareth instead of picking on me?"

"I can do both." She winked.

Gareth retrieved a cloth from Fury's saddlebags and wiped down his dagger, then gave the rag to Anika to use while he found water and rinsed his mouth. After wiping down the blade, she returned the sword to its scabbard for him, insisting that he not move his right arm. It was more awkward and tricky than she'd thought to sheathe a sword in a scabbard someone else was wearing, and once it was done, she scurried off to claim the bandit's sword, belt, and long dagger for herself.

The bandit's horse kept shying away from Gareth, despite his calm attempts to approach it. "Oh, come on, boy," he coaxed. "We'll be nicer than the bad men. Promise. Anika will ride you and she's very nice, even though she killed your previous owner in front of you."

She finished buckling the sword belt around her hips and crossed her arms. "Really, Gareth?"

"What? I said you're nice." He grinned at her over his shoulder before looking back at the horse. "Here, boy. It's all right..." He took a step forward, and the horse tossed its head and bolted several more steps aside. Fury gave an unimpressed snort.

"Do we really want to waste time on this?" Leo asked.

The horse neighed and kicked its hooves as it skittered further from Gareth's approach.

He flung up his hands. "I give up."

"Let me try." Anika approached the horse from a slightly different angle, and this time, the poor beast had apparently had enough. It turned tail and galloped down the road.

Leo snickered. "Maybe he really didn't like that you killed his owner."

She made a face at him.

Gareth fiddled with his sling again. "I suppose we'll have to continue with one horse."

"It's not so bad," Anika blurted before she thought better of it. Both Leo and Gareth stared at her, Gareth's expression softening into something pleased, while Leo's ears pinned back against his head.

Gareth slapped his thigh. "Right. Let's get these corpses off the road so they aren't in other travelers' way, and then we should get going."

31

They'd been riding in silence for a few minutes when Leo spoke. "Bandits wouldn't be nearly as big of a problem if the king hadn't withdrawn all the guards and rangers. Since bandits drove us into the woods near the witch's hideout, I probably wouldn't be a fox if not for the king."

A spike of anger at the king went through Anika. In the past, she'd paid little heed to the grumblings about the king disbanding the highway guards and had assumed the rumors of increased banditry were exaggerated, as gossip often was. After two run-ins with bandits, the evidence otherwise stared her in the face.

What kind of knight was she that it took experiencing the danger herself to force her to pay attention to things that affected the safety of people she'd sworn to protect?

"I still don't understand why any king would do that," Gareth said. "It sounds unbelievable."

"King Silas insists the guards and knights employed by townships and lords are enough, and if they aren't, then those townships and nobles aren't managing their holdings properly."

Anika could imagine the pinched, judgmental look Leo would have had on his face if he were still human, his eyes narrowed, one eyebrow slightly raised, and a tight frown.

"Clearly, he's wrong," Leo continued. "So maybe now you can see why some people would be more than happy if the Faines' rule ended."

Anika found herself agreeing. Why *should* a king who didn't care about his people be allowed to rule unchallenged, just because his ancestor had saved a fae?

But Gareth snorted. "You know, banditry and worse proliferate during wars and periods of civil unrest, such as the aftermath of a royal line being exterminated and everyone arguing over who should rule. If it's such a problem, why don't people petition the king to reinstate the guards?"

Leo shifted against her back. "Other than the fact the king doesn't care? It's nearly impossible to get an audience if you have a complaint."

Gareth started. "Doesn't your king have public grievance days?"

It took Anika a moment to recognize the squeaking, yapping sound Leo made as he shook behind her as fox laughter. "Ha. No. His grandfather was the last Aedyllanian king to have grievance days. If King Silas had them, he'd have to make them a grievance week."

She slouched—well, as much as she could while wearing a metal cuirass and sitting behind Gareth. Her policy of ignoring things she believed she had no power to change had proved faulty. Sure, it was difficult enough to attempt to make her way as a female knight, forget meddling in the affairs of men far above her status. But as a knight, she had not only sworn to protect Aedyllanians, she had sworn fealty to King Silas. It grated on her that she had taken that oath so lightly, without any consideration for whether the king deserved her loyalty.

"I still don't think that warrants invoking the prophecy," Gareth said. "King Silas Faine alone won't bear the consequences. If the stories about the prophecy are right, so will his children and grandchildren and probably anyone else bearing the Faine name."

They fell silent, the steady clop of Fury's hoofbeats replacing conversation. An occasional call of birds in the surrounding woods provided a counterpoint to the buzz of insects and the intermittent rustle of a breeze brushing through the leaves and grasses.

Anika kept thinking about both Leo's and Gareth's arguments. She'd always considered her first duty as a knight to be protecting those who could not defend themselves; a shield for the helpless and a sword for the downtrodden. Never had she stopped to consider what she would do if she found that duty at odds with her oaths of fealty.

Of course, she hadn't made those oaths directly to the king, and he didn't even know she existed. Her father had performed the ceremony in his capacity as a lord. As he'd told her many times, it was possible that the royal family wouldn't recognize her as a knight. While Aedyllan had no laws against a woman being a knight of the realm, it simply wasn't done. In that case, maybe it mattered less if she wasn't as unflinchingly loyal to the crown as she had sworn to be.

Leo would probably argue something about how the oaths of fealty operated under the assumption that the lord was deserving of accepting the oath, and that the liege had a duty to his vassals. By not taking that duty seriously, the king had already broken their contract. Easy for Leo. By not becoming a knight, he'd avoided taking such oaths in the first place.

As evening approached, storm clouds gathered, turning the sky a roiling, menacing shade of dark gray. Soon, it started to drizzle, the raindrops gradually getting larger and falling faster, plinking against the cuirass Anika wore.

"Perhaps we should shelter in the forest," Gareth said, shouting a little to be heard over the thrum of rain.

"No," Leo shouted back. "We're nearly to where this road

meets the thoroughfare that connects the townships of Brecklure and Scrivendon. There's an abandoned guard post there where we might be able to shelter."

Gareth nodded and urged Fury into a trot.

Soon the old post arose in front of them, through the gray haze of the escalating storm. It was a small structure of lichen-covered stone and about the size of a bedroom, with an empty hole for a doorway.

Gareth halted Fury in front of the building and dismounted, then reached for the saddlebags. "I have a torch in here. I'll go in first, make sure it's safe—"

"The chivalric instinct is appreciated," Anika said, "but may I remind you that you're injured, and I also have a sword." A sword with rust spots, a balance she didn't like, and chips in the edges speaking to poor maintenance, but it was functional.

"Right. Sorry." Gareth reddened.

By the time Anika had dismounted, he'd fished a small torch and flint out of his saddlebags. He struggled to light it, sheltering it between his body and Fury's.

Thunder cracked, and the flash of lightning was nearly blinding. The wind was picking up, too, driving the rain against Anika's back in undulating torrents.

The torch finally caught. "Together, then?"

Anika drew her sword, and they barged through the doorway together, Leo on their heels.

The sputtering torch illuminated a large, mostly empty room—doubtless any furniture had been scavenged, much like the door. She sheathed her sword, wrinkling her nose at the mess.

Someone had left the charred remnants of their fire in the middle of the room. There was a fireplace set into the wall to the right, but it was overflowing with ashes. A faint stench of urine persisted despite the scent of falling rain, and some broken items had simply been abandoned.

Leo shook like a dog, sending droplets of water flying. She stepped away from him with a disapproving grunt. He just looked up at her with his tongue lolling out one side of his mouth, completely unrepentant.

Gareth scraped his boot back and forth across the dirt on the far side of the room, then nodded. "No debris here, so best place to sit." He shoved the torch into the ground. "I'd ask if there's any objections to me bringing Fury in, but I'm bringing him in regardless."

Anika laughed. "Might as well. We already brought the dog in."

Leo's fur bristled. "Rude!"

"Don't shake like a dog then," Gareth said with a wink. He slipped outside and returned momentarily leading Fury. The destrier had to lower his head under the doorway and was almost too wide, but he made it inside.

"I'll search for some firewood that isn't soaked through," Gareth said. "Can you untack Fury? I'll help with the cuirass when I get back."

He was gone again before she could reply.

Unlike Gareth, Anika wasn't injured, so she took the cuirass off by herself. A pity it had done very little to keep her tunic dry. Then she untacked Fury, who seemed relieved to lose the damp saddle. Gareth hadn't returned yet, so she used one of the charred pieces of wood to scrape some of the ashes out of the fireplace.

By the time Gareth arrived with an armful of kindling and water dripping off his nose and soaked overtunic, the torch had burned down to a faint flicker.

"Don't know if this is dry enough to catch," he said as he dumped wood, grasses, and leaves onto the ground.

"That's fine." Anika gave him a reassuring smile. "You left too quickly for me to say anything, but it doesn't need to be dry. I can dry the wood."

"Really?" Gareth motioned to the pile and stepped back. "I'll leave this to you, then."

Unfortunately, he watched her as she crouched by the wood, but she wasn't about to admit to a handsome foreign prince that being observed while performing enchantments made her self-conscious. Even her best friend, Scarlett, was rarely allowed to observe her attempts at spellcasting, and Scarlett never judged her feeble abilities. Holding her hands over the kindling, Anika let her magic unspool from within her and out her fingertips in a warm yellow glow.

The energy of her magic called to the energy—or perhaps, more so, the *thing*-ness—of her surroundings. She focused on the firewood and pulled the water out of it, like spinning thread from a tangled mass of wool and neatly pulling it together. The water coalesced into a large, floating drop, which she shucked off to the side. The golden light of her magic vanished as she cut off the flow, and she looked up to Gareth, who was watching her with wonder.

"I can start the fire, too," she found herself saying, despite the dull headache coming on. "After we get this arranged better."

"That's amazing."

Together they arranged the wood and foliage into a more orderly pile at the edge of the space she'd cleared in the fireplace. Not all of the smoke would drift into the chimney, but between the chimney and the open door, the air wouldn't get too smoky.

The torch snuffed out right as they were finishing, but that was all right. The shimmer of her magic cast an ethereal glow as she wove the magic into flame and set the kindling alight. Within moments, the wood caught, and she withdrew her magic. A pounding started up behind her left eye, but it was worth it for the warmth of the fire and the delight on Gareth's face.

Gareth sunk to the ground with a sigh, holding out his hands toward the flames. Anika took a seat next to him, and Leo plopped down beside her. Wind whistled around the building, sometimes blowing in a spray of rain through the open door opposite them. Thankfully the rain didn't reach far enough to threaten their fire, and soon it was burning merrily and driving out the chill.

"Can you do that drying thing to our clothes?" Gareth asked eagerly.

Her growing sense of pride immediately snapped. "Um…I—"

"No," Leo snapped. "She cannot."

Gareth glanced between them with a frown. "I wasn't trying to be demanding. Or would you see through my clothing or something?" Red bloomed on his cheeks.

Anika laughed. "No. It would just take a lot of energy. It's not really an accurate analogy, but if you think of my magic as a bowl of water that refills itself, my bowl is small and refills slowly. And, um, well, like I mentioned earlier, if I empty the bowl too much—"

"You get headaches." Gareth nodded. "Sorry. I forgot. Being magically dry isn't worth making you feel awful." He started unbuttoning all of the fastenings on his overtunic. "This is so much easier with two hands," he muttered.

"I happen to have two hands." *Why in Miraveld did I say that like that?* Stifling her embarrassment, she simply nudged his hand out of the way and finished unbuttoning his tunic.

"Thank you." He maneuvered his left arm free, then removed his sling and frowned at his right arm.

Anika laughed. "Are you always this reluctant to ask for help?"

He ducked his head. "According to Sir Christopher, that is a fault of mine, yes. Can you please help me?"

She pulled off the tunic—a little more difficult than she'd expected as the wet fabric clung to his undershirt—and Gareth moved so he wasn't sitting on the long back of the garment. He picked it up and laid it against the stone near the fireplace to dry. His soaked white undershirt was nearly transparent and clung to every line and curve of his torso. Heat rose in her cheeks, and she quickly turned her attention to the fire.

"I'm not going to offer to help, because even if that wasn't strange, I think I'd be more of a hindrance than help," Gareth said as he sat by the fire. "But if you want to remove your outer tunic, I promise I won't look. I have another shirt in my bags you could put on, if that'd be more comfortable."

"Oh." She had to look red as a strawberry now. Taking off a soaked layer did sound nice and would speed up drying…

"I'll bite him if he looks," Leo said solemnly.

Anika laughed. "Thank you. I appreciate it." A few minutes later, she'd peeled off her tunic and slipped Gareth's spare gray undershirt over her black one for an extra layer of modesty. Gareth's eyes widened for a moment when she sat down, but the look passed swiftly.

"So," Leo said, raising his voice to carry over the wind lashing the building and the crackle of the fire. "Is there food left in your pack, or…?"

"I see being a fox hasn't affected your appetite," she teased.

"Oh, so he's this food-obsessed even when he's human?" Gareth snickered. "Yes, there's more dried meat and nuts—"

"Oh, joy." Leo's ears flattened.

Shaking her head at Leo's dramatics, Anika stood. "I'll get the food."

By the time they finished eating, the rain had lessened to a gentle patter. The warmth of the fire built within the guardhouse. While they were all still damp, they weren't soaked anymore. Gareth's hair still hung in darker waves around his face, though. It was oddly alluring, so she tried not to pay attention to it. He leaned toward the fire, resting his left elbow on his bent knee, and motioned to her face.

"Can I ask what happened?" He gave an awkward laugh. "I suppose that is asking, but you don't have to tell me."

"My scars?" At his nod, she exchanged a quick look with Leo, who was already smirking, as much as a fox could. Feigning nonchalance, she leaned back on her elbows. "Bobcat."

Leo yawned. "Oh, come on. Don't be humble." He moved onto her lap, crawling into a warm, cozy, and smelly ball. She blinked down at him, then shrugged, accepting that Leo was a lap fox now. "She's started giving fake answers to avoid all the disbelieving replies. It was a dragon."

Oh, they were jumping all the way up to dragon? Either Leo thought Gareth particularly gullible or he wanted to see Gareth squirm as he tried not to be one of the doubters.

"A *dragon*?" Gareth's elbow slid off his knee, and he almost toppled toward the flames. He straightened, admiration in his bright expression. "That's incredible. When? Where? What kind? What did it look like? What happened? Did you kill it?"

She stared at him, off-kilter. That wasn't how this conversation usually went. Gareth appeared fully ready to believe she had killed a dragon, and that sent an unexpectedly warm and fuzzy feeling through her chest.

Leo's high-pitched fit of giggles echoed against the stone walls as he tossed his head back over her leg. "Ha! Dragon." Another couple of yapping laughs, then Leo took a deep breath and repositioned himself on her lap.

Gareth turned his head away, his blush evident even in the firelight.

"Sorry," Anika said, taking pity on him. "People are often

demeaning about the scars and my story, so Leo and I came up with this game. I say something believable and not too dangerous. Leo argues with me not to be humble, then says something wild and improbable. Usually the person struggles to believe it and gets any disbelief or judgment worked out on the theatrical lie, while Leo berates them for being rude. Then they're relieved when I admit it was a bear and let it drop instead of asking more questions and saying anything condescending."

"Oh. I'm sorry." Gareth focused on something on the ground. "You really don't have to talk about it—"

"I'll tell you my story if you tell me yours."

He looked over at her, his forehead scrunching.

"The scars on your left arm."

"Oh. Manticore. We were on the pass through the mountains into Rethalyon when it attacked. I landed the killing blow, but it got in a hit of its own first." He rubbed the spot on his arm through his sleeve and winced.

Now it was Anika's turn to gawp in admiration. "A manticore? I've never seen one." His expression was still pinched, so she curbed her excitement. "Does it hurt when you think about it?"

"Hm? Oh, no. The manticore also spooked my sister's horse, but that's a longer story, and more my sister's than mine."

"A story that's the reason I knew he would believe *dragon*," Leo said.

That must be a much longer story to go from a spooked horse to a dragon.

"I can tell you that one tomorrow, if you're interested," Gareth said casually. "We'll have time on the ride."

"I'd like that." She brushed her fingertips over the scars where they crossed over her cheekbone. "Aedyllan has a tradition for becoming a knight. You must spend two days and two nights alone deep in the wilderness to meditate on your purpose as a knight.

You're only allowed to bring weapons and your armor, so you have to find your own shelter and provisions. Only after you return, having proven you are capable and dedicated, are you permitted to take the knight's oaths. My second night, a great bear found me."

"Hold on, wait. *Great* bear is hardly the same thing as *bear*."

That was painfully accurate. While a bear was bad enough with its bulk, strength, and sharp claws and teeth, great bears were worse. Fully grown, they topped eight feet when standing on their hind legs. Their teeth and claws were bigger than a bear's, and short tusks protruded forward from their bottom jaw. The curving horns that sprouted from their head could be used for battering like a goat, and their tail was long and furry, reminiscent of a wolf's. She shuddered and was thankful once again that the horrible things had been hunted nearly to extinction. But like any monsters, they were difficult to kill off and good at hiding their cubs.

"It was a young one, not quite full size—"

"Wolf's teeth, that's still impressive." Gareth gave a low whistle. "Don't minimize that. You survived a great bear! That's incredible."

"She *killed* a great bear," Leo amended.

Anika fiddled with her thumbnail, blushing under the warmth of their admiration and pride. "It was a close thing, despite it probably being no more than a year old. It was an exhausting and mentally taxing fight. I barely made it home alive."

"If you're trying to make yourself sound less impressive, not only am I confused why, but it isn't working. Please, brag to me." A genuine, encouraging laugh carried over the snapping fire as Gareth grinned. "When I got home, I told everyone who would listen that I'd killed a manticore. Drove my sword up into its heart, barely evading its venomous tail and fearsome jaws, and getting some scars as a souvenir to prove it."

"Great bears have an even longer reach than you'd guess." She hesitated, but he just nodded, listening with rapt attention. "I thought I was doing all right until its claws grazed my face, and blood in your eye…well, it stings, for one thing, and makes it harder to see. The beasts are also tough. It took so many blows but wouldn't go down. I was covered in its blood by the time it knocked me to the ground and stepped on my sword arm."

He winced, but it appeared a sympathetic look of imagining her pain and panic, not judgment for letting herself get pinned.

"My hunting knife saved me. Drew it from my thigh sheath and slammed it through its throat, barely managing to shove the bear over so it wouldn't fall right on top of me." Pride, terror, and the echo of the rush of adrenaline mixed in her chest at the memory. "It still cracked a rib, and I dislocated my shoulder getting my sword arm free, though."

"Quick thinking and strength to avoid being crushed," Gareth said in reply.

"Thanks." Anika glanced at Leo in her lap, wondering if he was proud of her for owning her story in a way she rarely did. Most people either implied she should have done better or were too frightened by the story to listen. Scarlett had tried, and she was very proud, but she'd also turned green when Anika had tried to tell her about the fight.

Leo was watching the prince with his head cocked. As if he felt her gaze, he sent her a smile full of sharp teeth and nodded.

"Is it too strange and dismissive if I say they suit you?" Gareth rubbed at the scruff on his jawline. "The scars. Not that I'm happy you experienced that pain and fear, or that I wouldn't still be impressed without them, but…they don't make you any less attractive. Maybe more, since they show that you're fierce and a survivor."

He…*liked* the scars? Sure, she swung between seeing them as striking and intimidating and fearing they ruined her looks, but he didn't merely find them interesting but…attractive? She didn't know how to respond to that, so she deflected.

"Fierce?" She disguised her awkwardness with a chuckle. "I was terrified."

"Sir Christopher would say fear keeps you smart, and that keeps you alive."

"I'll assume any wisdom you do possess came from this Sir Christopher," Leo intoned.

Gareth made a face at her brother. "Rude. Although probably accurate."

They shifted to discussing their favorite—and least favorite—tutors and mentors until the rain picked back up and their fire was burning low. Neither of them felt like braving the storm again in the hope of finding more firewood. So after they put their dried overtunics back on, Anika hesitantly suggested they huddle together under Gareth's blanket to sleep. Leo gave her a suspicious look and Gareth got a little tongue-tied, but they agreed.

She fell asleep with her back pressed against Gareth's back and Leo tucked against her stomach. And, although she wouldn't admit it out loud, it wasn't at all unpleasant.

32

A dove cooed somewhere nearby, the sound grating on Gareth's nerves and pulling him out of a deep sleep. As he was dragged to consciousness, sensations filtered back in. Warmth over him and along his front, but chill air against his back. A dull ache throbbed in his right shoulder. At some point during his slumber, he must have slipped his arm out of the sling and tucked it up under his head, while his left arm had curled around something warm—

Breath catching, Gareth opened his eyes to a head of red hair. They'd fallen asleep back-to-back, a logical way to combat the damp cold, but at some point, he'd rolled over and wrapped his left arm around Anika's torso. His entire body went stiff. Oh, this looked bad. He wasn't responsible for things his treacherous body did while he was sound asleep, but Leo wasn't likely to accept that. Better to remove his arm now.

Carefully, so as not to wake her, he lifted his arm, eased away from her, and sat up. A few twinges and pinches in his right shoulder accompanied the movement, but he was pleased that despite lying on the injury, the pain had greatly improved. Anika's magic must have sped his healing more than expected.

Now that he was sitting, the blanket only covered one of his legs. Part of him wanted to return to cuddling against her—strictly for warmth, of course—but his conscience wouldn't allow it. Ah, well, might as well get up. Being all-cold was better than being half warm and half cold and thinking about the girl asleep beside him.

He silently settled his arm back into his sling, strapped on his sword, and checked on Fury, then slipped outside to relieve himself. Tendrils of fog curled over the three diverging roads that spread out from the guard post, and early dawn light cast the grasses and trees in a soft, golden glow. Gareth stretched and drew in a deep breath.

There were definite advantages to waking up in a massive, soft bed with cushions and thick blankets, knowing a warm breakfast would be waiting for him and a hot bath could be drawn with no effort on his part. But even after a night on the hard ground, he felt rested. Standing there in the foggy morning, the crisp air carrying the scent of damp earth and thriving forests, a sense of peace and rightness settled into his soul.

When he returned, Anika and Leo were digging into the packs for breakfast. He crossed his arms in mock offense. "Couldn't possibly wait for me? Or even ascertain that I was alive?"

A bit of red crept into Anika's cheeks. "I saw you slip out, so I assumed you were fine and could take care of yourself. And Leo is a pest when he's hungry."

He huffed a laugh. "Don't I know it."

"A fox needs to eat," Leo said with a wave of his paw.

They ate quickly and remounted. As they rode, Gareth recounted the story of Raelyn and Alexander again. He thought he told it a bit more coherently and with more dramatic flair each time.

"And so Alexander and Raelyn were crowned king and queen of Rethalyon and lived happily ever after," he finished.

A snort sounded from Fury's rump. "It's been a few months. Happily ever after. Hm."

"Are you trying to wish ill upon my sister and brother-in-law?"

"Of course not," Leo said. "I just think you're overdramatic and read too many legends and tales."

"You're stuffy and read too many treatises or whatever it is you read."

Anika laughed, and her breath brushed past his ear. "You're both ridiculous. But what about Tristan Carbrey? What is he doing now?"

Gareth's upper lip curled. "He was sent to Talland as an ambassador. I have no idea how that's going for him." *Hopefully terribly.*

"Interesting. I hope that's a good fit for him."

"What?" He wished he could look at Anika, but she was sitting too close behind him. "Why? He *should* be rotting in a cell."

She didn't answer right away. "I understand why you don't like him. I feel sorry for him, though. It sounds like his father was awful and like Tristan was hurt and didn't know what to do. If he truly believed that Alexander was a wicked liar who had purposefully seduced Raelyn and his father was innocent, doesn't his anger make sense? His actions weren't right, yes, but we tend to do what we're taught. If Henry was vicious and cruel, that's probably how he raised Tristan. That doesn't excuse his cruelty, of course, but it says something about his heart that he overcame his upbringing to defy his father, admit he was wrong, and swear his fealty to his cousin. Maybe with his father gone, Tristan has a chance at bringing his true character to the surface."

Gareth hadn't thought about it like that. He especially hadn't considered what the situation would have been like had Alex *actually* been as wicked as Henry claimed. Before he knew the truth, he'd been ready to kill Alex, too. He'd accepted the truth much faster, but he was used to trusting Rae. Tristan would have been used to believing his father.

Begrudgingly, he muttered, "I suppose."

These Raylor twins seemed determined to force him to question all of his assumptions and deeply held resentments. It was exhausting and frustrating. Not to mention, if he wasn't sure he was ready to forgive his father, he *certainly* wasn't ready to forgive Tristan.

Did that make him as bull-headed as his parents claimed he was?

Damn it all.

He lapsed into grumpy silence.

As the day dragged on, not talking got awkward—and not talking made it harder not to think about Anika's thighs against his, her breath occasionally tickling the back of his neck, and her arms bumping him when she shifted.

"How did Calissa catch you two?" he asked to break the silence.

"Callista." Anika paused, then muttered under her breath, "Not sure why I care."

"Right…Callista, then."

Anika's sigh ruffled his hair. "Leo and I were returning home from visiting a party at—well, another noble's estate; I can't imagine you'd know them. We were chased into the forest by bandits. My father had sent three knights with us, and although I'd brought my sword, I wasn't wearing armor. It was a polite social function, and I hadn't thought anyone would be so bold as to attack a band of five." Her tone darkened. "I won't make that mistake again.

"The knights insisted we split up. They lured the bandits away, but while we were waiting for them to return, a lavender cage of magical light sprung up around Leo and me and our horses. My magic did nothing against the cage, and then…" She gulped. "Leo screamed."

"Turning into a fox is painful," Leo said, his tone defensive.

"Alex said his curse hurt, too," Gareth said so his friend would know he wasn't judging him.

"When the witch showed herself and removed the cage," Anika continued, "I leapt from my horse to fight her, but her magical capabilities and knowledge..." She faltered. "She overpowered me quickly. I should have grabbed Leo and ridden away."

"It wouldn't have helped," Leo said sourly. "She wouldn't have let us get far."

"What did she do once she had you?" Gareth asked.

Anika shifted behind him. "Threatened that if either of us didn't cooperate, she'd kill the other. She set up magical wards that kept me inside and him outside the castle so we couldn't see each other. A week later, she left and took Leo."

"That was when she stole the firebird," Leo supplied. "And told me to guide you and honestly do my best to help you steal the firebird back."

"Ah-ha!" Gareth said. "I was right to be suspicious of you. You were sent by evil forces."

Leo made a sound like an exaggerated yawn with a touch of a yowl. "But I was also sent to help you on your quest."

"By the villain," Anika noted.

"That still makes me the hero of the story," Gareth joked. "Since you *were* specifically sent to aid me."

Anika groaned. "That makes me the damsel in distress."

"A very capable damsel." Gareth's mouth pinched. "Besides, I was also caught and have this stupid binding curse that might kill me if I don't do as I promised. Maybe I'm the damsel in distress."

That made Leo laugh more than it had any right to, but his loud *heh heh heh* fox giggles soon had Gareth and Anika laughing as well.

As night approached, they finally reached Raylor Estate.

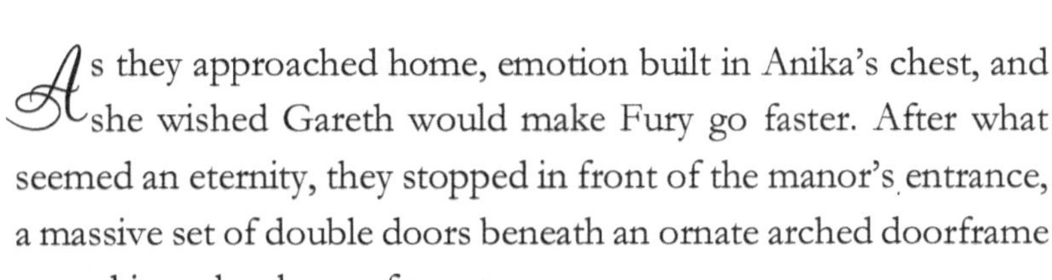

33

As they approached home, emotion built in Anika's chest, and she wished Gareth would make Fury go faster. After what seemed an eternity, they stopped in front of the manor's entrance, a massive set of double doors beneath an ornate arched doorframe carved into the shape of two trees.

Leo half slid, half jumped down, and she immediately followed, not waiting for Gareth as she hurried forward. One of the doors opened, and her parents ran out, her mother sobbing loudly and her father's eyes wide.

"Anika!" Father cried.

"My daughter!" Mother barreled into her with such force, Anika stumbled back a step. Father wrapped his arms around both of them and squeezed, seemingly unbothered by the unyielding edges of the cuirass she wore.

"I'm all right," Anika said as tears slipped down her cheeks. "I'm all right."

"We were so worried." Mother sniffled, still clinging to her.

Father rubbed her shoulder. "I'm sorry. I'm so sorry I didn't rescue you; that witch—"

"I know. It's all right." She smiled and swallowed back the flood of emotion that threatened to choke her. "I missed you so much."

Conrad, her older brother, appeared in the doorway, his expression crumpling into relief as he sagged against the door. "You're safe. You're home and you're safe." The light of the setting sun caught on his tears.

A quiet whimper caught her attention. Leo sat a few paces away, his ears drooping and head hanging low. His fluffy tail rested limp and lifeless on the dirt as he watched their reunion. For a moment, tears blurred her vision. She squirmed out of her parents' crushing embrace and wiped her eyes before picking up her twin.

Conrad drifted over to their parents as they all watched her curiously. "You…have a pet fox now?"

A keening cry escaped Leo as he buried his face against her arms. Anika trembled with a suppressed sob. "It's Leo."

Father's forehead wrinkled. "An…interesting choice of name for a fox."

"My twin," Anika said like a plea. "The witch cursed him to be a fox and to make you all forget him, but please, *try* to remember." Even as she said it, she knew it wouldn't work.

"Nothing we can say will make them remember," Leo said, a canine whine undercutting his words.

Mother yelped. "Did that animal just…speak?"

Someone cleared their throat. They all turned toward Gareth, who was standing by Fury and looking more than a little uncomfortable. "Lord and Lady Raylor, perhaps we could retire inside to speak? We have things we need to tell you, and we could all use a meal."

Leo's ears perked up. "Yes. Food, please."

At least he hadn't lost his appetite, Anika thought wryly.

"Hm." Father's mouth pinched downward. "I don't care if the fox speaks. Wild animals aren't allowed in my manor."

Leo's ears fell again.

"He's not a wild animal," Anika raged, her tears barely contained. "He's your son! Leo! My twin brother!"

"Leo?" Conrad echoed, and for a moment, hope sparked in her heart, but he only frowned. "I don't have a brother."

"Don't you have any family portraits?" Gareth asked as he strode over to stand at Anika's side. "A witch can erase your memories of him, but I doubt she erased all evidence of him."

Father reddened. "Er…" He cleared his throat. "We…simply haven't gotten around to commissioning one."

A lie. They hadn't been able to afford a family portrait. Once, the crown had rewarded the Raylors handsomely for caring for the unicorns. Before Anika was born, their stipend had been reduced to just enough to allow them to live comfortably and hadn't been increased since.

However, thinking about evidence of Leo's existence did spark an idea. Anika snapped her fingers. "His room! Surely his room still exists."

Mother's eyes widened. "That…that room…"

Father swallowed hard. "There is this room. The one next to Anika's…we can't recall why it's there and we keep avoiding it. We don't dare touch the door or even speak of it, but we don't know why."

"Good." Leo sniffed. "That means you didn't disturb my research."

Anika would have laughed if it weren't for the way Leo's voice quivered, his heartbreak barely concealed.

"And that horse," Father said slowly.

"Horse?" Anika perked up. "Did the knights find our horses after they ran away?"

Father nodded. "There's a horse stalled next to yours, but no one can remember who it belongs to."

"Anselm!" Leo wriggled and put his paws on her shoulder, peering over at the horse stable. "Anika, Anselm and Graedyr are all right!"

Anika nearly started crying. She'd assumed she'd never see her mare again.

"Your horse's name is Anselm?" Gareth asked.

"He's named after my favorite philosopher." Leo's tail wagged.

Gareth snorted. "Naturally."

Darkness was gathering faster as the sun hid below the horizon. Even the torrent of emotions could no longer distract Anika from the gnawing in her belly.

"I know you can't remember Leo," she said. "But we're tired and hungry. I want to eat and bathe for the first time in weeks, but I won't leave Leo outside. So he comes with us, or I stay out here in the dark."

"No, no, bring him." Mother bustled forward, tugging nervously on one of her long auburn braids before she hesitantly patted Leo's back. "Um. Welcome home, Leo?"

Leo made a sound uncomfortably like a canine yip of joy and squirmed in Anika's arms. "I missed you, Mother."

Mother's tight smile looked panicked and uncertain. "Come inside."

Father called for a servant to see to Gareth's horse and ordered others to prepare food or baths for them and a spare room for Gareth.

"I'll stay with Gareth," Leo announced as he jumped out of Anika's arms to the hallway carpet.

"Not that I mind," Gareth said, "but why?"

Leo tucked his tail. "I don't want to go into my room right now. Like this."

Anika bit her tongue, her heart shattering. Curse her stupid, useless drop of magic. If she were a better enchantress, even if she were a better knight, Leo wouldn't be cursed.

"Two baths in my room, then, if you don't mind," Gareth said with a grin. "One of them can be very small. Maybe a large bucket."

"You are *not* bathing me." Leo stuck his nose in the air.

Father coughed. "If you want to be inside, you will need to be cleaned." He motioned toward the floor, and all three of them took a step back—revealing dirty boot and paw marks on the plush carpet. "For now, just…attempt to minimize the mess, if you please?"

Anika and Leo exchanged a look as they followed their parents to the dining room. She often got in trouble for tracking in mud, but it was a first for Leo to be the culprit in dirtying the carpets.

As they sat at the table, Conrad motioned to Anika's torso. "I thought the knights said they led the bandits away because you weren't wearing armor?"

"It's mine," Gareth supplied as he sank back into his cushioned seat. He motioned to his sling. "Shoulder injury made wearing it inconvenient." He grinned at her. "But thanks to Anika's magic, I'm healing up quickly and should be able to handle it tomorrow."

The arrival of servants carrying a random assortment of food took priority over any further conversation. Anika, Leo, and Gareth devoured the leftover bread rolls, boiled vegetables, cold steak pies, and fruit. After Callista's rations, the array of food tasted decadent, and she abandoned any propriety to shovel down food until she could hardly move. Leo did likewise, and hopefully he was too busy eating to notice the grimaces their parents sent him as he stood with his front paws braced on the tabletop and splattered food around his plate. Gareth was the most dignified of all of them, somehow managing to not look like he was gorging himself, even though he consumed food almost as quickly as she did.

Prince indeed. He'd probably had table manners drilled into him since he was old enough to hold his own silver spoon.

Once she couldn't eat any more, Anika settled back in her

chair with a sigh. She wanted that bath now. And her bed…oh, how she'd missed her bed. Maybe the life of an itinerant knight wasn't what she wanted. Or maybe she just wanted the reassurance she'd have a bed to come back to when she needed it.

"Your baths and guest room should be prepared and ready," Father said.

Leo opened his eyes and lifted his head from the arm of his chair. "We have things we should discuss—"

Father held up his hand. "You all look exhausted. Whatever it is, I'm sure it can wait until tomorrow."

That sounded good to Anika. She really didn't want to discuss Callista and the Faine prophecy when she was mired in post-large-meal sluggishness. Thankfully, neither Gareth nor Leo argued. They probably were looking forward to a real bed as much as she was.

Back in her own room, nothing had changed. They'd left everything as it had been…or not quite. She was pretty sure she'd left her bed unmade and her nightclothes on the floor as she often did when she had to leave early, but her room was clean and tidy. A fire roared in the fireplace, and a wood tub filled with water had been placed before it.

The water was warm, although she wished she'd eaten faster so she could have gotten in when it was hotter. Still, the lavender and eucalyptus scented water eased the aches and pains of sleeping in less than comfortable places and long days of riding behind Gareth.

Slumped as far down into the tub as she could manage, Anika peered over the rim at the firelight reflecting off of Gareth's cuirass where she'd left it on the floor. Why did he have to be a prince? What a cruel twist of fate to meet a man who didn't judge or belittle her but still seemed to see her as a woman…and he would leave her.

He didn't belong to her kingdom and far, far outranked her.

If only Scarlett were here. Her friend was both a realistic anchor and a source of encouragement. What Anika wouldn't give for one of their talks. Maybe one of the kinds where Anika talked between taking out her frustrations on a straw dummy while Scarlett made new paintbrushes or snacked on sweets and offered sage—and often lightly teasing—insight or commiseration.

Ah, well.

After Gareth was gone, he'd be a fun story to tell Scarlett, and eventually, the sting of knowing she could have fallen for him if he were a knight and not a prince would fade.

34

$\mathcal{G}$areth was right to insist on bathing Leo first.

Although it took some cajoling, Leo sat in the small metal basin with his ears sticking out flat to both sides of his head as he stared Gareth down with murder in his eyes. But he behaved himself, letting Gareth work the soap through his fur and into his paws and then thoroughly rinse him.

The problem arose after he hopped out of the basin. Gareth picked up a towel, but before he had a chance to use it, Leo shook himself and sent water flying *everywhere.*

Droplets splashed against Gareth from head to toe and all over the rug, the side of the tub, and a nearby wardrobe. Water sizzled as it sprayed into the fireplace, but the fire scarcely flickered.

"Leo!" he groaned.

"Heh." Leo ducked his head. "Sorry. It was instinctual."

Gareth sighed and twisted around to check the bed a couple of paces behind him. "Good news; it looks like it didn't reach the bed." He frowned. "I think because I blocked it."

Leo gave that high-pitched, rasping, foxy chuckle. "At least you have your bath next."

"And I think it has fox water in it now." He wrinkled his nose as he peered at the large wood tub beside the fireplace, then shrugged. "Ah well. Come here."

With that, he captured Leo in the towel and thoroughly rubbed him down. When he'd finished, he stepped back, took one look at his handiwork, and broke down laughing.

Leo's fur stood out at all angles, making him a large ball of fluff with a very peeved expression.

"Laugh it up, steel for brains." Leo shook himself again. His fur settled a bit, but he still looked like a red ball with black paws sticking out of the bottom. He sulked his way over to the fireplace, where he stretched out and immediately closed his eyes as if settling down to sleep.

Gareth peeled off his damp clothes and tossed them into a pile before easing into the water. It was barely warm, but with the heat of the fire, it wasn't too bad, and he hadn't bathed in so long it felt wonderful to scrub the gunk off his body.

He was still bathing when someone knocked and said they'd come to collect his clothing to launder it, which was thoughtful, but also unfortunate timing. Gareth awkwardly hunkered down in the tub as an older man gathered his garments and said they'd be returned in the morning.

After Gareth dried off, he gratefully pulled on the clean undershirt and short, thin trousers the same servant had left on the bed and climbed under the blankets. *Glorious down-filled mattress and soft blankets.* He rolled on his side and closed his eyes, overcome with exhaustion.

A sudden weight and slight jiggling of the bed made his eyes snap open, and he propped himself up on his elbow. At the foot of the bed, Leo did a few spins in a tight circle before he plopped down into a ball.

"Try not to kick me," Leo mumbled. "Good night, princeling."

Gareth settled back onto his soft pillow. "Good night, fox."

Breakfast was awkward, although Gareth wasn't entirely sure why. Maybe it was because Leo was eating noisily, and his parents still looked uncomfortable with a fox eating off their dining table, even if he claimed to be their forgotten son.

Maybe it was the looming conversation they needed to have about the prophecy.

Or maybe it was that Anika was wearing a dress, and it was very distracting.

It seemed she didn't wear dresses often, because Leo had asked what had gotten into her, and Lady Raylor had been delighted. Anika had blushed at both family members' reactions, but she'd blushed even more when Gareth told her she looked nice.

And she did.

It wasn't a fancy dress, certainly far simpler than anything his mother or sister or the ladies of the Eynlaean court wore. The white underdress had billowing sleeves that gathered below Anika's shoulders and at her elbows, then flared out to drape off her forearms. An overdress laced up the front over her torso and was open down the front of the skirt. The forest green fabric was woven with a subtle leafy pattern that gave it an understated elegance despite the simplicity of the gown.

While not a dress that would have drawn admiration in a palace, it suited Anika. The loose, flowing skirt of the white underdress stopped just above her feet and wouldn't restrict her movement. Her athletic form and the strength in her shoulders were still apparent, it didn't hide her curves, and the rich green made the fiery copper of her hair brighter. She still moved with strength and surety, and paired with the feminine airiness of her dress, she was the most alluring, beautiful woman Gareth had ever seen. It was difficult not to stare at her.

After breakfast, Lord Raylor insisted they move to a sitting room to discuss everything that had happened. The comfortable chairs and the bright sunlight streaming through a gigantic lattice-work window felt at odds with their serious topic.

Anika explained everything that had happened to her since they'd separated from their guards. Then Leo explained his side of the story—which covered Gareth's story, mostly, for which he was relieved. It was embarrassing enough to hear someone else talk about him walking right into Callista's trap.

"So this prophecy the witch Callista is trying to enact," Anika said slowly. "We're wondering if it might be…*that* prophecy. The Fae Blessing and Curse of Mortimer Faine."

"And if it is," Leo added, "whether we try to help or stop it."

Their mother's eyes widened.

Lord Raylor made a humming sound. "If it is, and the Faines fall right now…the consequences could be dire. We have no way of knowing exactly what it would look like, since we don't know for sure what the fae woman said, assuming the prophecy is real. If we accept that it's real and that this witch can cause the blessing to end and with it the entire Faine family…" He shook his head.

"There are a few lords who might seize the throne, and they'd have very different goals after they secured the crown. Duke Alimer might have the military strength required, and he has been criticizing the Faines' inequity, ineptitude, and injustices for years. I suspect he would be a merciful victor. However, many others would follow King Mortimer's example from two centuries ago and eradicate their rivals. If the wrong lord secures the crown, Aedyllan might see bloodshed unlike any before. If we knew that the Faines would fall and when, we could prepare and avoid much violence. But…" Raylor spread his hands. "There is too much we do not know. With his distant ties to the Faines, would Alimer even survive the prophecy? If he gathers support in advance and we're wrong, King Silas would punish the insurgents. It would be equally disastrous."

"Which is why," Gareth said, speaking up for the first time since they'd entered the sitting room, "in my estimation, it is best to stop this prophecy. I have decided I won't bring a unicorn to—ah!"

He doubled over, clutching at his chest.

"Gareth?" Anika exclaimed, and a moment later her hand gripped his left shoulder.

A black paw landed on his knee, and Leo peered up at him. The fox's face wavered in and out of focus as Gareth's eyes watered from the pain.

"I'm overruling your inane decision." Leo spun around. "It's not up for debate. If Gareth wants to live, we have no choice for now but to keep following Callista's choreography."

"I've never been much of a dancer," Gareth wheezed. Another painful squeeze attacked his heart, and he moaned.

Anika's fingers dug into his shoulder. "If you don't bring Callista a unicorn, the binding spell will crush your heart!"

He was excruciatingly aware. But if he did, she'd be one step closer to her plan—whether that involved causing bloodshed through a two-hundred-year-old fae prophecy or something benign, he didn't know for sure. Yet if she was plotting something terrible, the moment he delivered that unicorn, he'd be complicit.

Was preventing that worth his life?

"We'll find a way that doesn't involve you dying," Anika begged.

"I agree," Lord Raylor said. "He'll have his unicorn, as I promised. As soon as we leave this room, I'll see to it, and he can leave at once."

"But—" Gareth ground his teeth as sweat beaded on his forehead.

Anika lightly shook him. "Say you'll accept it!"

"Don't throw your life away for hypotheticals we can't verify," Raylor said sternly.

"If you think the *potential* of innocent people being killed isn't worth bringing about the Faines' deaths, why do you think your death is worth only *potentially* preventing that?" Leo stood on his hind legs so his nose almost touched Gareth's face. "What about your family? Your sister? Don't you want to see them again?"

He did. He wanted to see Nathaniel grow up and tell Raelyn this whole unbelievable story. He wanted to meet Raelyn and Alexander's future children. Could he give all of that up to stop Callista because of a theory?

"All right. I'll take the unicorn to the witch."

Immediately the pain ceased. He straightened, and Anika released his shoulder. Even though her panicked grip had been slightly painful, he was disappointed.

"Good." Leo sat back down on the floor.

Gareth rubbed his temple. "But what if saving myself destroys Aedyllan's peace?"

Leo huffed. "You were willing to do anything to save your sister, even if it risked the peace of *two* kingdoms."

"That's…I…it's different," he muttered.

But was it?

"Young knight," Lord Raylor said, his tone grave, "it is not up to you to decide the fate of kingdoms."

Gareth nearly laughed. No, it wasn't, not really—that usually fell on his father or siblings—but, as evidenced by the consequences of his conduct in Rethalyon, the actions of even spare princes could have an alarming impact on the fate of kingdoms.

Prince or simple knight, the fact remained, Raylor was wrong. "By obeying the witch, I might be part of the deaths of an *entire family.*"

"Not by choice or intention," Lord Raylor pointed out.

That was true. Gareth had made the same argument to get Anika out of the tower. But that was before he understood the possible ramifications. Intent didn't negate harm. If their conjecture was correct, and he proceeded *knowing* his actions might indirectly cause bloodshed, even if it was against his will…

Was that morally acceptable?

His usually reliable instincts were muddled, and he hated it.

Lord Raylor frowned. "Frankly, King Silas doesn't deserve his throne, and for his injustices, hardly deserves his life, and his children are shaping up to be worse."

"I know the king hasn't taken recent petitions seriously and made some harmful edicts," Anika said as she returned to her chair, "but what have his sons done?"

Her father's expression pinched. "Crown Prince Lucius and Prince Justin are the main reason I have never and will never bring you with me when I visit the palace, Anika. There's a reason why I ensured you were not at the manor when Prince Justin visited the stable. They…have voracious appetites and a sense that they are entitled to satisfy their selfish hunger with whoever catches their eye. Willing or not."

Indignation roared through Gareth. Loath as he was to admit it, even Tristan hadn't been that bad.

"Aren't they both married?" Anika asked incredulously. "I thought the crown prince had children."

"Indeed." Raylor's expression darkened further. "They do not care, and their father the king turns a deaf ear to the complaints of his daughters-in-law. He won't even permit the other aggrieved women to state their accusations."

"But what about their children?" Gareth demanded. "The fae curse would kill them, and surely they've done nothing wrong."

"That is true," Lady Raylor admitted. "I understand your perspective, Sir Gareth, but you are old enough to be better informed about our kingdom than this. King Silas does not listen to his people, neither did his father, and his sons are following the same path. I have no hope their sons will be any better after growing up in that castle. If there were a way to spare the young Faines, perhaps that would be best—or perhaps it would only lead to more conflict and injustice in the future."

Gareth opened his mouth to protest that wasn't fair, but neither was allowing the Faines to continue ruling as they currently did. "I'm…actually Eynlaean," he said instead. "The firebird was stolen from my liege in Eynlae on my watch, so I was sent to retrieve it."

Lord Raylor lifted an eyebrow. "Interesting. I wouldn't have expected an Eynlaean to care so much about what happens in Aedyllan."

"Aedyllanians are people the same as Eynlaeans. Not to mention unrest in Aedyllan could spill into Eynlae."

"A valid concern." Raylor inclined his head. "What you don't understand is that the corruption and self-interest in Highrook Castle are old and deep, a sickness not easily removed. So much so that few people are even willing to work in the palace anymore, for any price."

"That's an understatement." Vehemence filled Lady Raylor's voice. "Serving in Highrook went from being an honor to a punishment. Many of the servants and guardsmen are little more than slaves, forced to work as recompense for some crime they may or may not have committed or as payment for any debt they owe anyone. Last week, Lord Bouchard's youngest son couldn't pay a gambling debt, and he was given a choice between imprisonment and taking a position as a palace guard."

Gareth could make no argument against such evidence of mistreatment. The widespread resentment against the Faine name alone would probably doom Silas's entire line. He couldn't fathom acting with so little regard for how his choices would affect his family—

Prodding shame made him wince. It wasn't the same, but how many times had he not cared how his actions hurt his parents or made Father's role as king more difficult?

"People don't refuse to work at Highrook on mere principle," Leo said with a twitch of his whiskers. "The servants are mistreated, and the guards keep dying. Whether one believes in the fae blessing or not, it can't be argued that when someone tries to harm the royal family, the only ones who die are the guards."

Lord Raylor nodded. "Perhaps an example would help. Several years ago, a man whose lands had been wrongfully seized by the crown was denied a hearing or any compensation, leaving him and his family homeless."

"I heard about that," Anika interjected, her tone sorrowful. "It was terrible. While the poor man was petitioning for a hearing, his wife and their unborn child perished. He heard King Silas was staying at an inn while traveling, and somehow he managed to drug the guards, barricade the king inside his room, and burn down the inn. The king escaped, but many lives were lost—the perpetrator, one of the guests at the inn, a porter who worked there, and four guardsmen. Everyone was talking about how King Silas did nothing for any of them or their families."

Gareth gripped the arms of his chair until his fingers ached. The injustice of it burned through him like fire. What had Leo said?

"Even if power isn't in the right hands now, and a change could benefit Aedyllan in the long term?"

"Still..." Anika said quietly. "If that curse is activated, more people than the Faines alone will suffer."

"People are suffering now," Leo said.

They all fell silent.

There was no perfect answer, Gareth realized with dismay. No way of predicting the outcomes, only a blind attempt to do the right thing with the information they had.

Had Raelyn felt this conflicted when she had to choose between staying with the man she loved or going to the palace to marry Tristan and save Gareth?

Was this exactly how his father had felt in Rethalyon?

Gareth hunched in his chair.

Did he owe Father an apology? Perhaps he at least owed Father a conversation where he didn't start with angry assumptions.

Wait. Do I…actually want to go home and talk to Father?

The thought wasn't as repulsive as it once had been.

To do that, he had to stay alive.

But could he stay alive if doing so meant helping a villain?

35

*A*nika looked over at Gareth, whose expression was troubled. The agony on his face as he'd clutched at his chest was burned into her mind. She didn't really care what Callista was doing or whether the Faines should be overthrown or not.

She didn't want to watch Prince Gareth die in her family's sitting room.

"We can consider this again if Callista wants us to do something else, but for now, we don't need to waste any more time deliberating. All of this is hypothetical, but we definitively know we can save one person." Anika seized Gareth's arm and dragged him out of his chair. "Let's get you a unicorn."

To her relief, Gareth didn't protest, and let her lead him to the unicorn stable. Anika turned to the first stall and reached for the gold-stitched bridle. It wouldn't alarm for her—the complex enchantment allowed any Raylor to touch the spelled metal, while anyone else would need to know the password.

Anika had tried to study the enchantment once. It had appeared to her mind's eye as a shining, complex tapestry of so many threads that she'd quickly realized she had no hope of ever understanding how it worked. Her tutor had understood more of it, although he'd described the spell as many shades of colors so expertly blended into a seamless gradient within a complex pattern that even he couldn't hope to comprehend or replicate it.

Hardly surprising. Her several times great-grandfather, who had created the enchantment and tamed the start of their unicorn herd, had been an enchanter of legendary power and ability.

As she lifted the bridle off the hook, a demanding neigh came from further down and across the aisle.

A golden unicorn, one of their large, draft-horse-sized variety, had stuck its head as far out as its stall door would permit. The unicorn tossed its head and gave an impatient whinny.

Gareth chuckled. "Hello again, Tempest."

Tempest whinnied again and lightly kicked at her stall door.

Anika tilted her head. "I…think she wants to go with you."

"Can you understand the unicorns?"

She couldn't help a little snort. "Of course not. But isn't that what it looks like to you?"

"She'd probably be less excited if she knew where we were going and why. I think she just wants out of the stable."

Still, he walked down to Tempest's stall, and Anika left the bridle and trailed after him. He held out his palm to the unicorn, murmuring something that sounded reassuring. Tempest pushed her velvety nose against Gareth's palm, leaning into him for a moment before stepping back, snorting, and stomping a forehoof.

"She's impatient," Gareth noted with a grin. He spun toward Anika. "I'll take her. After I trade her to Callista for the firebird, I'll steal her back again."

A good plan, except for the part where he was in this mess because he'd previously failed to steal something from Callista, but she decided to keep that thought to herself. Instead, she bridled Tempest and grabbed a saddle.

"Oh, we won't need that," Gareth said, although he sounded disappointed. "I'll ride Fury."

"Well, I don't want to ride Tempest bareback."

He stared at her. "Sorry?"

"I'm coming with you." She strode past him into Tempest's stall.

"You…no. You just got home, and Callista—"

"You may have stopped wearing the sling, but you're still hurt. Besides, you don't know your way around Aedyllan as well as I do. You might need help."

It was barely an argument. For some reason, though, letting him go face Callista alone made her panicky. Perhaps she wasn't ready to say goodbye to him yet and was grasping at any little reason to spend even a few more days with him…

No, it was only that she was worried about sending someone, anyone, to face the witch alone. That was all.

"You might as well come," Leo said. He was sitting just outside the side door Anika had left open, peering inside as if unsure whether he wanted to enter. "I think I'm supposed to go with him, anyway, and I'd rather know you're all right."

Of course. Callista had ordered him to help the Eynlaean retrieve the firebird, and Gareth didn't have the bird yet.

"Then I have to go," Anika said. "I want to be there if—when—she turns you back."

Gareth tapped his hand against his side, then shrugged. "All right. I wouldn't mind having you along." He reddened. "For reinforcements. You know. Another knight can't hurt." He coughed and looked anywhere other than at her, and she smothered a smirk.

Leo made a hissing sound. "Don't make me change my mind, princeling."

Anika shook her head. As if Leo got to decide for her what she was doing, where she was going, or who she spent time with.

After she led Tempest outside, she pointed Gareth in the right direction to find Fury, then headed inside to gather supplies. She nearly ran into her father on his way out of the manor.

He peered past her at Tempest and huffed a laugh. "Good choice. She won't be missed."

Anika glanced back at the unicorn. "What?"

"She bit Prince Justin last time he was here. I had to talk him down from ordering her to be killed." Father shrugged. "She's always been…hm. Spirited? Or perhaps opinionated."

"Ah, I can see that. She insisted we take her."

"Really?" Father made a thoughtful humming noise, then looked over at Anika. "Where are you headed in such a hurry, anyway?"

"To gather supplies. Actually, could you ask the kitchen to gather some food for three while I change and—"

"Wait!" He grabbed her arm. "You aren't going with him, are you?"

"Of course?" With a frown, she looked from his hand on her forearm up to his face. "He can use any help he can get, especially if he does try to steal Tempest back again. Besides, Leo has to go with him, and I'm not being separated from Leo again."

Frustration pinched Father's expression. "And I can't lose you to that witch again!"

"What about Leo? Don't you want to have your son and your memories of him back?"

He hesitated. "It's dangerous—"

"It's dangerous for Gareth, too." Anika yanked her arm out of his grasp. "I'm a knight as much as he is. Gareth is injured and my brother is a fox. I won't lounge around here when I know I could help them."

Father's shoulders slumped. "If you're killed—"

"You don't think I can help them," Anika said quietly. The words ripped through her heart, reopening old wounds and tearing new ones. "I don't care if you don't believe in me. I'm going."

"No!" Father winced. "I mean, no, I don't doubt your abilities. I know you're capable, which only proves how powerful that witch is. I just had the most hellish week of my life worrying about you. Can you blame me for not wanting to go through that again?"

The raw emotion in his voice chipped at her resolve but couldn't change what her heart knew was right. "Father, I'm a knight. That is going to involve danger sooner or later. You can't both let me be a knight and keep me safe at home."

He sighed. "I know. But must you run headfirst into *this* danger?"

She steeled her spine. "The lives of my brother and a man who risked his life to help me are at stake. I vowed to use my sword to protect and serve, and that's what I intend to do."

Father watched her for a long moment, then nodded. "A part of me wants to argue, or even forbid it and lock you in your room. But you're right. You're a grown woman who has always forged her own path, and I knew what I was agreeing to when I knighted you." His unhappy gaze drifted to her scars. "I'm trying to honor your choice, even when I wish your choice had been different— and safer and closer to home."

"Thank you." The fact that her father still sometimes wished she'd been a better enchantress and had honed those skills instead hurt, but she did appreciate that he was trying.

Anika headed to the kitchen and asked for as much food as they could gather quickly, especially anything that wouldn't spoil within a day or two, to be brought to the courtyard. Then she went to her room and changed from the dress into a more practical ensemble of a knee-length green tunic and trousers. She stuffed a change of clothes into a bag, as well as some odds and ends that might prove useful.

It was a shame the witch had taken her sword. She donned

her own cuirass and leather vambraces and belted her second-favorite sword and a dagger about her waist. After grabbing her bag and Gareth's steel cuirass, she hurried back outside.

In the courtyard, Gareth was already mounted on Fury. Leo paced back and forth while Father watched him with a small frown. At her approach, they all turned their attention to her.

"Did the kitchens deliver the food?"

Gareth jerked a thumb at his saddlebags. "Yes, and plenty of it—assuming Leo doesn't gorge himself."

Leo hissed, and Anika laughed.

"I'd ask you to be cautious and stay safe," Father said, "but I don't suppose you'd listen."

"I won't be reckless." Anika smiled as she strapped her bag and Gareth's cuirass to Tempest's saddle. "I doubt Leo will let me."

"I will not," Leo agreed. He crouched down and wiggled before leaping onto Fury's rump. To her surprise, Tempest watched the fox without reaction.

She paused at Tempest's side. "Not riding with me?"

"The unicorn is too tall. This jump is difficult enough." Leo curled into a ball behind Gareth.

"We'll watch each other's backs, Lord Raylor," Gareth said solemnly.

"Thank you," Father said. "Your mother and Conrad and I will be waiting impatiently for your return, Anika. And Leo."

"We'll try to end this quickly." Anika sent her father a reassuring smile and then turned Tempest away from the manor.

Logically, Gareth knew he should have joined Lord Raylor in asking Anika to remain behind. He hadn't overheard, but Leo had, and he had ranted about it to Gareth.

Confronting the witch would be dangerous—not that Anika couldn't deal with danger as a woman, but even two people might not be enough to defeat Callista. Anyone accompanying him was putting themselves in harm's way. Worse, Callista already knew she could threaten either Anika or Leo to control the other. He also had a grim certainty that the witch wouldn't hesitate to kill someone if it achieved her plans.

Not to mention, spending time with Anika might be a dangerous proposition to Gareth himself. Or, more accurately, to his heart. He couldn't deny his growing attraction to her, but what did he have to offer? She might not want to be a princess any more than he wanted to be a prince. If he renounced his title, he wasn't sure what that would look like. He couldn't ask her to marry some penniless, disgraced Eynlaean knight.

Of course, she might not be interested in him or in marriage at all. However he looked at it, there was a chance spending more time with Anika would lead to heartbreak.

Despite all of that, he was happy to have her by his side. Even if he was very jealous that she was riding Tempest.

They alternated between a walk and a quick trot to cover as much ground as possible. All of them wanted to get this over with, and Gareth was eager to have the binding spell removed. He didn't want to feel that pain again. When they finally stopped to eat, it was well past midday and Gareth was starving.

Anika dismounted with a groan and stretched. Tempest snorted and tossed her head, almost as if judging her rider for not having better saddle stamina.

Following suit, Gareth stretched out the tightness in his back and thighs, only to have Leo headbutt his calf.

"I'm famished! Stop dallying and get out the food!" He licked his lips. "Or I'll get it out myself—"

"And get slobber and fur all over everything," Gareth said with distaste. "Absolutely not. I'm getting it now."

At the top of the supplies from the Raylor Estate, he was surprised to find a squat clay box with a lid. Inside were three bundles wrapped in woolen fabric. Peeling off the layer of wool fabric revealed three still warm steak and vegetable hand pies that smelled delicious.

Leo sniffed. "Mmm. Hurry up!"

"You're not going to starve in the next minute, Leo." Gareth joined the twins where they sat in the shade of a weeping willow. He set one pie in front of Leo and handed another to Anika.

"So…your father."

She glanced up from her pie with confusion. "What about him?"

Gareth adjusted his baldric and sword to be more comfortable. "How did you change his mind? Leo said it sounded like he didn't want you to come."

Her expression turned sad and heavy, and he wished he'd kept his mouth shut.

"He didn't. At least this time it was out of fear for my safety, but in the past, he opposed me becoming a knight. If any of his children were going to become a knight, for a long time, Father thought it should be Leo." Anika frowned. "When he said he wanted me to stay home, I was afraid he'd changed his mind. Gone back to how things used to be, when he was cynical at best of my martial ability and angry my interests didn't align with his plans. When I was born, it had been three generations since there'd been an enchanter in the Raylor family. My father had high hopes for my magical ability, and he had difficulty letting them go. He's trying and we're much better now. His reluctance today came from a place of love rather than judgment, but it still hurt a little." She shook herself and bit into her pie.

Gareth nibbled at the flaky, buttery crust of his dinner. She hadn't really answered his question. "But he still respected your choice. How did you make him do that?"

She laughed softly. "Unfortunately, you can't force someone else to respect or accept you. Eventually Father realized he could either accept Leo and me as we are or lose any connection with us—and he didn't want that."

Gareth nodded slowly. That was both encouraging and frustrating, as he wished there were some simple thing he could say or do that would force his own father to accept his dreams.

They finished eating in silence—more or less. Leo chomped with much licking of his lips and whiskers, then turned big, pouty eyes on Anika and Gareth and whimpered while they finished their food.

"You don't even love me," Leo muttered as Anika pointedly licked her fingertips clean.

"You're acting like we didn't all eat the exact same portion," she said with a roll of her eyes.

"And like we aren't at least twice the size of you," Gareth added.

Leo stuck out his tongue. "Not if I were my usual size."

"His usual size is two inches shorter than me and twiggy," Anika said in an exaggerated whisper.

"One inch! At most!" Leo's fur puffed out, his tail looking remarkably like a feather duster, before he gave himself a shake and turned his backside toward them. "We should get going, any-way."

"Agreed." Gareth brushed off his hands and stood. He cast a longing look at Tempest before smothering his jealousy and turn-ing toward Fury. Behind him, Anika cleared her throat.

"Do you want to switch mounts for the next part of our jour-ney?"

Gareth whirled around. "Really?"

Tempest whinnied and pawed the ground before fixing one eye on him.

Anika laughed. "I think she likes you and would like to switch, too." She patted the unicorn's neck. "Rude, though. Father was right that you're opinionated."

In response, Tempest lipped at Anika's hair as if to say it wasn't personal.

Trying to contain his excitement, Gareth went to Tempest's side, but paused with his hands hovering over the gold-stitched sad-dle. "Wait, I won't set off those bells back at the stables, will I?"

"They have a limited radius," Leo said. He jumped onto Fury's rump and settled on the saddlebags. "And the magic somehow knows when someone has been given permission. If a Raylor pre-pares a unicorn, someone else can ride it without triggering the alarms."

Gareth nodded, and with one more admiring look, he mounted the unicorn. She pranced a little, almost as if she were also excited.

"You're spectacular," he breathed.

A pleased-sounding whinny answered him.

Anika and Fury pulled up beside him. Fury laid back his ears and tossed his head with a high-pitched neigh before abruptly turning toward Tempest.

"Easy!" Anika pulled back on the reins, and Fury's teeth clacked together before they reached Tempest's neck.

"Whoa!" Gareth tugged on the reins to separate the horses, but Tempest had other ideas. She reared up slightly, slammed both forehooves into the ground, and then released a long, squealing neigh. Fury shifted for a moment, then subsided, and his head lowered into a relaxed stance as his ears turned forward again.

"Wonder what she said," Gareth mused. He looked to Anika. "Sorry… I should have realized Fury would get jealous. He's had other riders but hasn't seen me on another horse."

"We usually keep the horses and unicorns separate, but when they do mingle, the horses always defer to the unicorns, so I also wasn't expecting that," Anika said with a chuckle. She pointed through the trees. "There's a meadow there that we can cut through. Race you across?"

Tempest leaned forward, as if ready. Gareth grinned. "Absolutely."

The moment they cleared the trees, Tempest broke into a gallop. They flew across the expansive meadow, reaching the other side far too quickly, with Fury and Anika and Leo on their heels. Exhilarated laughter ripped from Gareth as he stroked Tempest's neck.

"Oh, I love you, girl." He winced and glanced at his horse. "I love you too, Fury."

Fury's ears swiveled toward him, but he didn't seem to understand what Gareth meant. Tempest, however, snorted as if annoyed to share Gareth's affections.

He made a mental note to himself that unicorns were much smarter than regular horses and to watch what he said around Tempest.

"Let's not do that again," Leo complained. "If there are claw marks in your nice saddlebags, Gareth, it's not my fault."

They had to slow down anyway as they rode between trees again—a decision they'd made because the roads were less direct, and Leo had an uncanny sense of which way they needed to go. While silence wasn't uncomfortable, Gareth also wanted to talk to Anika while he had the chance. Even if defeating the witch went smoothly, he'd have to return home.

"So…how does magic work?" he asked as he leaned out of the way of a branch. "I've always wondered what it feels like and how an enchantment is cast. The stories don't explain."

"Probably because how an enchanter experiences magic varies wildly," Anika replied. "Vibrations, sounds, colors, threads. It's uncommon for two enchanters to explain their experience of magic in the exact same way. For me, it's sort of like weaving. I have to pull the right threads into the correct pattern."

Gareth considered this for a moment. "That sounds… complicated. How do you teach someone if you don't experience magic in the same way?"

"It's difficult and often theoretical. Part of why I didn't make much progress with either of the tutors my father hired. They tried, but they'd be talking about directing a stream or mixing colors into new shades while I'm weaving thread, and I'm better with things I can see and touch than abstract theories." She shrugged. "Knowing what magic is possible or sensing their spells did help, though. We perceive the elements of magic in unique ways, but the elements themselves remain constant, and magic is somewhat instinctual. Like once you've learned to pick up one object, you can grab other objects too, you know?"

"Then…can you just make up an enchantment for anything?"

"Ha, I wish." Anika steered Fury around a sapling in their path before continuing. "Most enchanters, including myself, need direction, and magic has limits. Powerful enchanters with time to experiment are usually the ones who discover those limits and find new ways to use magic in the process."

"And those who have the money to risk it," Leo added. "Magical experimentation can have horrible side effects. Usually only those with deep wells of magic, incredible control, and money to pay for any damages attempt to discover new enchantments. Hardly anyone experiments anymore."

Gareth switched the reins to his other hand. "That almost seems a shame."

"There are already endless tomes of spells and treatises on what is and is not possible, most of which are old," Anika said.

Leo sat up, and Gareth was unsurprised when his professor-sounding voice emerged. "Most of which were written during the reigns of King Mortimer Faine and his son, King Jairus. Jairus founded the Aedyllanian Royal University while he was crown prince, after his father built the new palace—"

"I don't think he wanted a history lesson," Anika teased.

"Someday I'll have willing students," Leo said with a sigh.

"Anyway." She stared straight ahead over Fury's ears as if purposefully avoiding looking at Gareth. "Unfortunately, my magic isn't strong. I'm not exactly bad at magic, but I'm not good, either. Sadly I took far more naturally to physical endeavors like sword fighting, and I feel more like myself with a sword in my hands."

Gareth had to drift away from Anika and Fury and focus on dodging branches for a moment as the trees grew closer together. Once they were close together again, he asked, "Why unfortunately and sadly?" There was something about the weight she put behind those words that bothered him.

"I have a gift not everyone has. My second tutor said even my negligible amount of magic was wasted on me when my true skill lies elsewhere. Magic is what helped my family originally tame the unicorns and make their fortune. My father used to say an enchantress is more useful than a knight—"

"That's stupid and unfair!" Gareth protested, his sense of justice roaring to life as her words pricked his own insecurities. "Everyone has stronger or weaker talents and things their personality and desires make them a better fit for, and no one can be everything. You also have eyesight and not everyone has that, but no one is telling you to take up manuscript illumination simply because illuminators need keen eyesight. Why should we be forced to abandon the things we love and excel at just because we have some other quality not everyone does?"

The stunned silence that greeted his outburst made him slouch in the saddle. He was always too opinionated and forceful—

"That sounded personal," Leo remarked gently.

Gareth worked his jaw, debating with himself. What did it matter if he trusted the twins with his deepest hurts and desires? They'd stay in Aedyllan while he went home, and they'd never see each other again.

"My parents would rather I put my energy elsewhere, too," he said heavily. "Into things they deem more appropriate for my station. I have a position and power that very few have."

"But you don't want it," Anika said, and it didn't sound like a question, but like she understood in a way no one but Raelyn ever had. It gave him the courage to keep talking.

"No. I've never wanted it. Being a prince is not all there is to me—it's the thing I have the least control over, too. I have other skills and passions. Why don't those matter? Why shouldn't passion and hard-earned skill and the things you want to do matter, just because you have another talent someone else prefers? If someone is a talented sculptor but their passion lies in painting, doesn't it seem cruel to tell them they can only sculpt? Why can't we appreciate both? Just because you're an enchantress doesn't mean that's the only facet of you that matters. All of you matters, not just the parts that are most useful to someone else."

Now it was Gareth's turn to focus resolutely on the forest in front of Tempest. He'd never put it in those exact words before, but that was what he wanted his father to realize. More than anything, he wanted his parents, especially Father, to see and value *all* of him.

A voice whispered Father didn't value the active, restless, adventure-seeking part of him because it was worthless. It was lesser, unneeded, and foolish.

Gareth's own voice echoed in his head. *All of you matters, not just the parts that are most useful to someone else.* He firmly believed that about Anika.

How desperately he hoped it was true of himself.

"I'm sorry your father doesn't understand you," Anika's soft voice interrupted his thoughts. "I know that pain. Before my father accepted my knighthood, I had to learn patience and a lot of resilience. There was a while where I was careful to stay calm when talking to him, because he took any emotion as a sign I couldn't handle being a knight. As if having a heart that could break made me less capable of wielding a sword." She snorted, and Leo made a sound of disapproval as well. "I didn't give up pursuing my dreams, though, and I strove to understand him, too. I think at times he wanted me to hear him as much as I wanted him to hear me."

Gareth hadn't considered it like that. Trust and respect needed to be mutual. Had he ever tried to truly appreciate Father instead of wishing his father weren't the king? If he tried to understand, would that help?

Leo yipped. "It took a while, and admittedly a lot of hurt happened first, but our parents came to appreciate that our strengths are, in fact, still strengths even if they aren't the strengths they would have preferred. I want to be a professor and Anika wants to be a knight, and we'd do those things with or without their approval. They finally chose to believe in us, and they've supported us a lot the last couple of years. If we could get through to our parents, there is hope for you and your father, Gareth."

"Thank you," he whispered.

Once again, Gareth felt curious about returning home, rather than dreading it. For the first time in a long time, he hoped he and his father could do better at valuing each other as they were instead of wanting someone different.

"But even if he never understands or appreciates your strengths," Anika said, "all of *you* matters, too, Gareth. Not only the parts that are most princely or what your father expects."

Gareth's throat was too tight to convey how much he appreciated her reassurance.

Maybe when he returned home nothing would change. But Gareth could try to adjust his narrow idea of the "right" thing to do and humbly strive to understand Father instead of believing the worst. And hopefully, Father would attempt the same in return.

Callista took the bulging sack of food from the market stall with a murmured thank you. That was the very last of her coin. She'd done her best to conserve it over the last couple of years, hunting and gathering food as often as possible and trading labor for supplies. Very rarely she would do something that required small spells, but she tried to avoid that—it drew unwanted attention. Made her too memorable.

As far as she knew, King Silas had never searched for her, at least not publicly. Perhaps unsurprising. A large-scale search might have revealed why he was hunting her, and the Faines would never admit the prophecy was real, let alone that it was stolen. Still, it was better not to risk leaving the king any clues to her location.

As Callista walked, she ate one of the fresh bread rolls. Too quickly, it was gone, leaving her with a gnawing in her stomach, a side effect of using her magic to sense the curse she'd placed on Leo Raylor. That was all she allowed herself to eat, though. She'd need the food far more later.

Leo was moving toward her hideaway, which meant the Eynlaean knight was too, and, if things proceeded as she hoped, Anika Raylor was with them. Callista would need food to recover when it was over.

The side effect of magic use that Callista experienced was hunger. It was like the enchantments fed on the nutrients she'd consumed, leaving her ravenous and parched. Being half-starved in turn made her weakened, fatigued, anxious, and irritable, and it sometimes muddled her thoughts. Often it gave her insomnia and made her look sickly pale. She'd become chilled or passed out after using a lot of power more than once. She'd learned to eat as large of a meal as she could afford if she expected to use a lot of power, and to have more food on hand to eat immediately afterward.

It had drawn some derision at the Enchanters College, where people should have known better. The other enchanters all had their own negative side effects. She'd had a tutor for whom using his magic made him narcoleptic. He'd cast an enchantment and simply fall asleep. One student would experience a mind-mouth disconnect and temporarily be unable to speak clearly. Another student would become so weak she could scarcely lift her hand until she'd had time to rest.

Yet many of the students—although, admittedly, mostly the students who didn't have magic themselves and attended the other, larger colleges at the Royal University—liked to laugh at her for her appetite and ask how she could eat like a warhorse but look like a skin-and-bones old nag. She'd suspected it was truthfully less about her appearance than because she was a poor guardsman's daughter without a drop of noble blood, while most of them had titled parents or were themselves titled and often wealthy.

She shoved the recollection of their taunting into the back of her mind. The girl who had studied at the Enchanters College in the Royal University was a different person.

A person who would have reacted in horror if someone had told her one day she'd use dark curses and earn the epithet *witch*.

Life was far crueler than schoolboys. Life took everything and left few choices.

The things she'd done so far she didn't like, but the things she had yet to do…

It made her want to break her promise. To abandon her pursuit of vengeance.

But any time she considered it, her brother's dying moments haunted her.

Royce, slumped on the floor in a hallway in Highrook Castle, his blood staining the polished, dark wood.

"Promise me," he'd pleaded. His pale blue eyes, glistening with pain, had locked with hers as he'd grabbed her wrist. "Callista, promise me you'll do whatever it takes. Make that prophecy come true. For our parents and Jacob. For Kay. For Anna and everyone else they've hurt. Promise me."

They hadn't even opened the prophecy yet. Neither of them knew what it said.

As guards had turned into the far end of the hallway, Royce's fingers had tightened on her wrist. "Promise, Calli! Don't let it be for nothing."

It'd taken her a moment to force her tongue to work. "I promise. I'll make it come true; no matter how long it takes. I'll see the Faines' cruelty ended. I promise."

"Go." He'd shoved her away with a hand slippery with blood. "I'll tell Mother and Father and Jacob…you're avenging us. Now, run."

With tears blurring her vision and the shouts of the guards and their arrows chasing after her, she had.

She'd left her only remaining family member to die alone in the palace and clung to the hope of justice. Of retribution for everything the royal family had taken from her.

Then she'd read the accursed Fae Blessing and Curse of Mortimer Faine, and she'd despaired. Would Royce have still asked her to make that promise if he'd known what that prophecy would turn her into?

She'd spent months in hiding, afraid she'd be found and executed, at the same time afraid she wouldn't, and she'd have to keep her promise when she didn't know how. The prophecy had sounded impossible.

Now the final two pieces were almost ready to click into place, like tumblers in a lock as elaborate as the one that had sealed the prophecy in the palace vault.

Soon the door would swing open, and long overdue retribution would rain on the Faines. For every life they'd taken or destroyed, every heart broken and hope crushed, every injustice swept under a rug and plea for help ignored, the Faines would pay in blood.

The remaining two lines of the prophecy echoed in her head, like the deep clang of cemetery bells.

A girl traded for a unicorn, a unicorn for a fiery bird,
And a foreign hero's life will end to save a crying maid.

The Eynlaean was on his way with the unicorn.

She would give him the firebird and let him leave—and then she would take Leo and Anika captive once more to lure him back.

She would buy vengeance at the cost of her soul.

38

$\mathcal{S}$omething was wrong with Gareth's mind, and that something had red hair and curves.

Anika was so fae-cursed *distracting*.

When Leo had guessed they were about an hour's ride from Callista's lair, they'd stopped for supper and to make camp. Across the fire from him, Anika was combing out and re-braiding her hair. He'd seen Raelyn braid her hair plenty of times. Raelyn had even taught him how to braid. There was no logical reason why watching Anika braid her hair, her fingers deftly flying through the red strands, should have him so captivated.

Part of the problem was he couldn't figure out if he wanted to touch her hair himself or if he wanted her to touch him. Gareth shook his head, as if that would dislodge the thoughts, and focused on his food.

Anika tossed her completed braid over her shoulder and stood. "I'll be back shortly. Send Leo if there's an emergency." She jogged off, disappearing into the bushes without waiting for a reply.

Sighing, Gareth leaned back on one hand, the other clasping a chunk of bread that was harder than he would have liked.

Leo looked up from the stewed vegetables he was eating and

licked his lips. "I'd like to ask you something."

Oh, good, a distraction. "Go ahead."

The fox tilted his head, as if considering how to phrase his question. "If you had to list your top three values, the things you believe in the most or think are the most important principles for a person or yourself to esteem, what would they be?"

Gareth eyed Leo warily. "Is this the start to some lengthy lecture and I'm going to regret entertaining this?"

"Just answer the question."

Gareth took another bite of dry bread while he considered. "Do I have to rank them one through three?"

"No, just top three. Exact order isn't important."

"Justice. Loyalty." He squinted, sorting through the values he held most dear. "Truth."

"Hm." Leo nodded slowly. "All right." He returned to eating.

Confused, Gareth straightened. "What do you mean, *all right*? Was that some kind of test?" And had he passed or failed?

After consuming his last bite, Leo peered over toward where Anika had disappeared into the bushes, his perky ears straining forward. He relaxed, apparently satisfied she hadn't returned yet. Turning toward Gareth, he didn't quite make eye contact.

"I…was wrong."

"Um…wrong?"

"It's all right." Leo turned his attention toward the fire. "That you like Anika. I thought I should tell you now. Just in case… I'm…I can feel myself losing my humanity. My first instincts are becoming more vulpine and less human. So if I lose the ability to speak…I give my permission."

Gareth lowered his bread to his lap and gaped, failing for a moment to find his voice. "What?"

"If you decide to court Anika." Leo traced a claw through the dirt. "I'd be all right with that. I think I could even handle you as my brother-in-law. If she wants you. Thought you should know, in case by the time you get up the nerve to ask her, I'm just a fox."

Leo giving his blessing to something Gareth had already reluctantly dismissed as an unrealistic possibility was more than he knew what to do with. Instead, he addressed the other part of his friend's admission.

"Stop that. You're not going to lose the ability to speak or stay a fox forever. I won't allow it."

"Really?" Leo deadpanned. "You won't *allow* it? Tell me, oh great enchanter, how do you propose to change me back?"

Gareth sputtered. "That—I—you! You said all curses have a way to break them."

"That doesn't mean every curse does, in fact, get broken. At least, not before death." Leo inspected one black-socked paw. "Death breaks all curses."

"No." Gareth's irritated energy propelled him to his feet. "No one is dying. This, this…fatalism is unacceptable."

"Oooh, *fatalism*. That's a fancy word for you, helm-head."

He pointed at the fox. "I am *not* taking that very obvious bait so you can distract me from the real problem and avoid this conversation."

Leo opened his mouth, then snapped it closed as his ears swiveled. Anika emerged from the bushes, a teasing smile on her face.

"What conversation are we avoiding? I'm intrigued to discover there's a topic Leo will refuse to discuss."

"Leo—"

A warning growl interrupted him. Leo glared at Gareth, his lips pulling back in a feral snarl. Then he blinked and smoothed his expression. "Idle speculation about who Callista is. You know I hate hypotheses that can't be tested and arguments that lack evidence."

Gareth gave Leo what he hoped was a *we aren't done with this* look, only to realize he was probably mimicking his father's expression, so he quickly stopped.

"So." Anika sat down with her back propped against a tree. "What's the plan for tomorrow?"

Gareth tapped his fingers on his knee. "I think I should go on my own."

Anika straightened. "I beg your pardon?"

"It's just…" He cleared his throat. "If you two aren't there, she can't threaten either of you. No leveraging our lives against each other. I'm hoping if Leo isn't close, she can't magically transport him to herself."

"What about Leo's curse? We need her to break it."

"Surely he doesn't need to be nearby for that to happen. Or perhaps I can get her to give her word she'll break the curse and not harm him, then Leo can go."

Leo huffed. "I don't know where you get your boundless self-confidence."

"I propose an ambush," Anika said.

"With two people and a fox?" Gareth lifted a brow. "Does that count as an ambush?"

"Now I'm unsure whether your self-confidence has faltered or if you simply don't believe in us," Leo grumbled.

Gareth scowled. "Callista swore she would let me go free after I bring her the unicorn, but she made no such promises for either of you, which makes your presence risky—"

"Don't I get a say in what risks *I* am willing to take for myself?"

The hurt in Anika's tone made him wince. He knew how it felt to have someone else take away his choices "for his own good."

"I'm not trying to speak for or control you," he said. "I wasn't trying to forbid it. Those are my thoughts, but the choice is yours."

"Good." Anika settled back against the tree trunk. "But I

suppose you're right. She did make a binding promise that she would let you go, and she didn't say anything about us." She tapped her forefinger on her chin. "Perhaps you should make the initial exchange, and then we can go together to steal the unicorn back."

"Agreed." Gareth scratched his cheek and frowned at the stubble that had already grown back since he'd shaved at Raylor Estate. If he wanted to be an itinerant knight, he might have to give up and embrace the bearded life. "Maybe the witch won't suspect it if I show up alone, exchange the unicorn for the firebird, and leave as if I don't dare oppose her."

Anika nodded. "We will remain here for now, then, so Leo hopefully won't be within the reach of her magic." Her eyes narrowed. "But only if you promise you'll come back for us before attempting to rescue Tempest."

Gareth placed a hand over his heart. "I swear it."

It would still be dangerous, but he'd seen her fight. She was as capable as he was. And if Leo was right, and there was a chance for Gareth to court Anika... She deserved someone who respected her right to make choices for herself.

39

The Eynlaean knight had come alone.

That wasn't what Callista had expected. Leo was close enough her magic could reach out and sense his cursed form, but he was far enough away that if she tried that summoning spell, it would drain her. That was fine. She'd find the twins later.

Callista stood in what used to be the courtyard of the castle, although now it was full of grass and wildflowers and moss-covered rubble. On the ground beside her rested the golden cage containing the dozing firebird.

The knight dismounted from his own buckskin stallion, sunlight winking on his armor and the pommel of the sword at his hip. He passed the crumbling wall and stalked toward her, leading a massive golden unicorn. She'd never seen one before, and it nearly took her breath away. When she opened her magical senses, she felt the glaringly bright, pure power contained within the creature. It made her want to hide herself and the dark magic use that had tainted her soul.

But Callista held herself firm and straight, keeping her impassive expression and a forbidding stare fixed in place. She willed her heart to be stone and refused to picture the lively young man with blood staining his shiny cuirass and the light dying from his eyes...

She clenched her jaw. Too much was at stake for her to waver now.

"I've brought a unicorn." The knight's eyes flashed as he held the reins out to her. "You won't harm her, right?"

Relief that she didn't need to do that or lie about it flooded her, but she didn't let it show. "No. I give my word."

She took the reins, and the unicorn snorted and tossed its head. A spike of fear shot through her. Did it sense her inner darkness? The pain and vengeance in her heart and the sins she'd committed to get to this point? Would it put that fearsome horn through her chest?

The knight patted the unicorn's neck and murmured that it was going to be all right, and the creature subsided. Sorrow showed in the Eynlaean's heavy expression, and his throat bobbed.

Odd. It seemed they shared some kind of bond.

He edged closer, and she stiffened, her magic leaping to her fingertips in a faint purple glow, but he only pointed at the firebird's cage.

"Is this still spelled, or can I take it?"

Callista let some of the tension ease from her shoulders. "Yes. Take it and go, and our deal will be complete. You may feel a sensation like something pulling out of your chest. That will be the binding spell dissipating and is not cause for alarm."

Why was she reassuring him? After she felt the spell break, she would take the next step in luring him to his death.

"What about Leo?" His knuckles whitened as he clenched the loop at the top of the cage. "Change him back."

"I will when his part is done," she returned levelly.

The knight's jaw ticked. "And will that be before or after he loses all traces of his humanity and becomes a literal fox?"

She stifled her surprise. That hadn't been an intended side effect of the transmogrification, but it had also been difficult to find information on that particular curse. "I give my word. Leo will be restored to his uncursed state soon—but not if you don't leave now."

The Eynlaean looked rather like he wished to argue, but he gave a stiff nod. After one last look at the unicorn, he marched out of the castle, fastened the firebird's cage to his warhorse, and rode away.

Callista stood there, holding the unicorn's reins, until she felt a sensation like a knife removed from her ribs—but the momentary discomfort gave way to relief.

Now what? She hadn't expected her quarry to not come to the castle. Of course now the twins would develop a sense of self-preservation.

She looked at the unicorn. "What am I supposed to do with you? Turn you loose?"

The prophecy didn't specify anything after the trades. Those complete, she wasn't entirely sure what to do next. So many decisions and so much uncertainty. She was so tired.

The unicorn sniffed at her hair. Fear gripped her again, locking her joints.

Then the unicorn stretched its neck forward and tucked its massive head over her shoulder. Its jaw knocked against her back, and she stumbled forward as it pinned her between its head and chest. She held her breath, every muscle tense.

Seconds ticked by, and still the unicorn held her, almost like...

A hug.

A sob tore from Callista's throat, and she threw her arms around the unicorn's thick neck and buried her face against its warm, soft shoulder. The unicorn gave a quiet whinny and tapped its chin against her back. Silent tears slipped down her cheeks into the unicorn's coat as her fingers clenched its mane.

She didn't understand why it was happening or what it meant, but she hadn't felt any affection or comfort in so, so long.

"Are you trying to tell me to stop?" Callista mumbled, still clutching the unicorn's neck. "Is this to convince me to let it go? Let them go?"

The unicorn lifted its head and pulled back, out of her arms, to regard her out of one eye.

"I can't," she whispered. "It's too late."

She'd already given too much, lost too much, sacrificed too much. Even the castle ruins around them shouted for the Faines to be punished. She was too close to succeeding to stop.

Wiping away her tears, Callista closed her heart back up. She removed the gold-stitched bridle and stepped back.

"Go, then. You don't belong here."

The unicorn shook its head, making its mane fly. It trotted out of the castle ruins, leaving her, once again, alone.

40

The faint stabbing sensation of the binding spell withdrawing was less painful than when it took effect, but its absence didn't bring Gareth any peace.

He'd done what that witch wanted, helping her accomplish whatever wicked scheme she was orchestrating. And he'd left an innocent unicorn in the care of a heartless villain.

Although, he reflected as Fury's hooves clomped over the forest floor, she'd almost seemed afraid of the unicorn. It was said unicorns carried incredibly pure magic—maybe someone who dabbled in dark magic had reason to be afraid. The possibility brought a satisfied smirk to his lips.

Maybe Tempest would end the witch and they wouldn't even need to steal her back.

When he arrived at their camp, Gareth looked around in confusion. Their supplies were still scattered about the banked fire, but neither Leo nor Anika was in sight.

He jumped down from Fury's back. "Anika? Leo?"

Strange. Perhaps they'd wandered off to gather firewood or hunt, but they'd had hours to do either. He'd have thought they'd be impatiently awaiting his return, to make sure he was all right and ask what the witch had said and prepare to storm the castle ruins.

"Hello?" Gareth removed the cage containing the firebird from the saddle and set it down, then tied Fury's reins to a branch. Only the ominous quiet of the forest answered him.

"Leo! Anika! I'm back!"

Nothing.

No yapping fox bark or sarcastic remark.

No boisterous laughter or flash of red hair.

He stepped further into his campsite, telling himself not to panic. Anika was a capable knight and Leo did have teeth and claws, after all. It couldn't have been bandits, because their supplies were still here. But then what had happened? The witch couldn't possibly have reached the camp *before* him, could she? There was that legend about Sir Roderick where a sorcerer used magic to move so quickly Roderick couldn't strike him with his sword…

Gareth's gaze caught on the glint of silvery metal beneath some nearby bushes. He raced over, sliding to a crouch as he reached forward—

And his fingers closed around the hilt of Anika's unsheathed sword.

No. No, no, no.

"Anika!" He shoved to his feet and spun in a circle. "Leo!"

This had to be a prank. A horrible prank that he would never forgive them for.

"Where are you?"

He scoured the campsite and found Anika's dagger on the ground also without its sheath, but the ground was too trampled to show any obvious signs of a fight or even which direction they'd gone. At last, he found a hint. He'd missed it at first, because it overlapped their trail from the previous day. Among the hoofprints heading toward their camp, a boot print headed the opposite direction. And there—a long groove, as if someone had stumbled or dragged their foot.

No, this couldn't be happening again. He couldn't have lost someone he cared about in unfamiliar forests with only a trail through underbrush as a clue *again*. His heart beat faster, his breath coming in short gasps as he followed the tracks after they diverged from the hoofprints.

The grass obscured the trail, but when he reached a muddy section near a stream, he was able to confirm—there were two sets of boot prints. No paw prints, though.

So where was Leo? Had his curse broken?

That didn't seem likely. One of the sets of footprints was heavier, as if the person kept digging in their heels, and sometimes there were scuffs and grooves. Gareth grimly recognized what that looked like.

He'd spent enough time getting dragged along as Tristan's prisoner to recognize the signs.

The question was, why was Anika stumbling so much? Was she injured? He hadn't seen any…

An invisible rock lodged in his throat as his gaze fell on the last thing he wanted to see.

Blood.

41

Anika's head pounded as Callista dragged her inexorably along. Blood congealed along the left side of her face from the wound near her temple. She tried to wipe the sticky liquid away from the side of her eye, but the firm grip Callista kept on the rope connected to her bound wrists didn't afford her enough slack.

They hadn't heard the witch approach. Leo scented her just before she appeared, but Anika had scarcely drawn her sword when Callista hit them both with a quick magical attack. Anika had gone limp, losing her grasp on her sword as she crumpled to the ground.

Without a word, Callista had stuffed Leo's sagging form into a large sack, then bound Anika's wrists in front of her and confiscated her dagger, leaving it on the forest floor. After lifting the spell so Anika could move, the witch had tossed the bag containing Leo over her shoulder and dragged Anika into the woods.

When Anika had tried to resist, a magical blast had knocked her into a tree, opening a gash on her forehead. The wound stung and made her skull ache.

"Where is Gareth?" Anika tried again. "What have you done with him?"

Callista didn't acknowledge her. She still held Leo in the sack slung over her shoulder, and only the occasional twitch and jerk in the bag reassured her that her brother was alive. A large leather pouch swung from the side of Callista's belt.

For such a skinny person, she was surprisingly strong, although Anika wasn't at her best at the moment. Still, had the witch used some kind of strength-enhancing spell? Anika had heard of those, although her tutors had dismissed them as not worth the effort, since they tended to have severe side effects when they wore off.

The brook they'd been walking beside met up with a larger river, about three paces across and burbling between rocks. They followed the river for a while, while the pounding in Anika's head made attempting any magic to fight Callista nearly impossible. Even if she felt more up to it, she wasn't sure she dared. She couldn't risk Callista further harming her twin.

Abruptly, the witch stopped and set down the sack that contained Leo. Her expression cryptically blank, she dragged Anika away from the river, looped the rope around a tree trunk, and securely knotted it.

"What do you want with us?" Anika pleaded. "Is Gareth alive? Please!"

Callista didn't even glance at her as she moved away, sat down on a boulder at the edge of the river, and…pulled food from the pouch on her hip. Dumbfounded, Anika stared while the witch devoured an entire meal.

In his sack, Leo hissed and thrashed. His claws put a small hole in the bag, but the witch kicked him through the burlap, and he went still.

"Are you going to say *anything*?" Anika demanded as Callista brushed crumbs off her hands. "Why don't you untie me, and we'll see how I fare in a fight against you when you don't cheat with surprise attacks and traps."

As stoic as ever, Callista ignored the taunt and rose to her feet. She gazed intently back the way they had come, as if watching for someone...

Anika straightened. Could it be Gareth? Was he all right and coming after them?

With Gareth's help, maybe they stood a chance. Gareth could draw Callista's attention long enough for Anika to cast a rending spell on the rope.

"I want you to know," Callista said, so softly Anika almost didn't realize she was speaking, "I wish there was another way. I'm truly sorry."

"If you don't want to do whatever it is you have planned, then don't!"

Callista shook her head. "This is unavoidable."

"Fae take you! Nothing is—"

A man's shout drew her attention. Further downstream, Gareth stalked toward them, his sword in hand and fury burning in his gaze. Her heart swelled, and she nearly wept. He was all right, and he had come for them.

Gareth stopped a few paces away from Callista, his rage-filled gaze sweeping over Anika before he raised his sword. "You shouldn't have hurt my friends. And where. Is. Leo!"

With the same emotionless calm she'd exhibited so far, Callista bent down and hefted the sack. Leo whined and tossed inside.

"Let them go, witch." Gareth bared his teeth in a challenging grin that Anika found strangely attractive. "And perhaps I'll make your death quick."

"So foolishly confident." Callista sighed. Then, in one fluid movement, she sidestepped into the river...

And shoved the sack containing Leo beneath the water.

42

"N o!" Gareth shouted at the same time as Anika released an earsplitting scream.

He stepped forward, but the witch raised her other hand, and a ball of purple flames flared over her palm.

She shoved the ball of magical fire toward him, and he barely batted it aside with his sword. The blade steamed and took on a reddish hue, and the ball of fire extinguished in the river with a sizzle. Callista already had another fireball hovering over her hand.

"Stop!" Anika tugged on the rope binding her, her horrified gaze fixed on the thrashing movement of Leo beneath the surface of the river. "Please!"

"Pull him up," Gareth snarled.

To his surprise, Callista obliged. Leo's choking gasps mingled with Anika's sobs while witch and knight stared each other down.

Wrath slid like molten steel through his veins. "Let him go and fight me instead of hiding behind him."

Holding Gareth's gaze in a way that unnerved him, the witch submerged Leo again, drawing another anguished cry from Anika.

"Stop this!" Gareth stepped forward, deflecting another fiery attack. His chest constricted as Leo struggled. "Why are you doing this? Haven't you hurt them enough?!"

For the briefest moment, Callista's expression contorted with something like shame.

"You can save them, knight." Her voice was as unyielding as steel. "Let me kill you."

"Let…" With a growl, he stepped forward only to be knocked onto his back by an arc of purple-tinted magic. His momentum as he hit the slippery bank carried him into the river. Sputtering and blinking water from his eyes, he shoved back to his feet.

Callista had pulled the sack back out of the river, and Leo whimpered between hacking breaths. Anika sobbed, and he glanced over at her.

His blood ran cold.

Anika knelt, bent forward as she strained toward the river, her braid hanging over her shoulder. A glowing shard of purple magic with a wickedly sharp tip pulsed over the back of her neck, dangerously close to descending and ending her life.

Fighting his own tears, Gareth hefted his sword and looked back to the witch. "Why are you—"

Callista plunged Leo back into the river, water splashing as his friend tried to escape. "Give me your sword and your life, foreign hero. Or all three of you will perish."

Bubbles rose from the sack, bursting along the surface of the river. Anika cried out in pain, and he jerked his head toward her. She'd gone still, folded over her knees as the magic blade pricked the back of her neck.

Gareth's mind raced through a dozen thoughts at once.

This wasn't what was supposed to happen.

Some knight he made.

It felt wrong to his core to give in to the demands of a villain, especially when he knew the potential consequences. Yet if knights were supposed to do anything, they were supposed to protect people. He didn't know with certainty whether his refusal or acceptance would prevent a violent prophecy, but he *did* know that surrender would save two lives. Did that mean he had to do something that went against every fiber of his being to save his friends?

Gareth had always known that if he became an itinerant knight, he'd risk his life every time he drew his sword. If he died in battle saving Anika and Leo, he'd say that was worth it—so why did surrender feel different?

Because surrender felt unheroic. It felt like failure.

Was his goal defeating Callista or saving his friends? *Saving my friends*, his heart cried.

This wasn't how he'd ever pictured doing that, but if caving to the witch's demands saved his friends, he wouldn't have failed. If his sacrifice was required, he was at peace with that. Afraid, but at peace.

And if his death activated the curse on the Faine line, the fault would lie with the murdering witch. He was not about to let two innocent people die on the *hope* he could halt the hand of fate.

"You promise if I surrender, you'll let them live and go free?" he asked quickly.

"I swear it." Callista gave him a solemn nod. There was no binding spell, but he'd have to trust that her word was as good as the gravity in her eyes suggested.

"Gareth," Anika said, her voice breaking. "Don't—"

He threw his sword into the river in Callista's general direction, careful that it wouldn't get too close to Leo. Maybe someone else would have made a different choice. But in that moment, relinquishing his weapon was the best way Gareth saw to live out his chivalric ideals.

The shard of magic vanished from above Anika. Callista withdrew Leo from the river and dropped him onto the bank.

But the sack didn't move. No sound came from it.

"Leo!" Gareth lurched forward, tripping out of the river and falling to his knees beside the sack. He tore apart the knot and shoved the bag open. Anika stumbled over to collapse at his side, her hands free of the rope, and her body shaking with sobs.

The soaked vulpine form lay there, limp and lifeless.

Grief and horror froze Gareth in place. The world tilted. Tears burned at Gareth's eyes. No. No, Leo was supposed to be saved even if Gareth died.

"Leo!" Anika wailed. Her trembling hands scooped him out of the bag. With the movement, Leo's body twitched, then he coughed.

Relief nearly made Gareth collapse as Anika set Leo down. The fox jolted and hacked out a lungful of water.

Cold, sharp steel slipped under Gareth's chin and pushed against his throat.

Callista loomed over him, his sword in her hands. "Stand up and move back."

While Anika stroked Leo as he gasped for breath, Gareth turned his glare on the witch that had caused all this suffering. He slowly rose to his feet and withdrew from the twins. She followed him, keeping the blade against his skin until his boot splashed into the edge of the river.

"That's far enough."

"I just want to know why," he said, his voice rough.

Callista's chin trembled. "Because I made a promise."

Then she sliced the sword across his throat.

43

The Eynlaean knight fell to the ground, clutching at his mortal wound. Callista spun away, unwilling to watch as he died.

Her gaze landed on the Raylor twins. Anika was still focused on her brother as he stopped coughing. At least Leo was alive. For a moment, she'd been terrified he was dead. Killing Leo had never been her plan, and two deaths at her hands would have been too much to bear.

The fox pushed up on shaky paws, water dripping from his drenched fur. "Gareth!" His teeth flashed as he growled at Callista. "I'll kill you—"

"You are no longer needed," she said. "I release you." The moment the words she had set as the curse-breaker left her lips, she sensed the enchantment snap.

Leo cried out in agony and collapsed. His pain would be temporary, but it still filled her with guilt.

"Leo!" Anika bent over her brother, but her furious gaze fixed on Callista. "What did you do?"

Callista couldn't find her voice, so she fled.

Her feet pounded the ground as she ran from the death and suffering she had wrought. Trees caught at her hair and clothes, but she didn't slow.

Anika's anguished wail when she'd thought her brother was dead and the fear in Gareth's eyes as he faced his death would haunt her forever. Perhaps Callista was more of a monster than she'd realized.

Angrily, she wiped at stray tears she had no right to shed and leaned against a tree. There was one final thing she needed to do.

She closed her eyes, found the bit of magic that had stolen memories of Leo, and snapped it. The magical effort stole more energy.

Her stomach panged with greedy hunger, twisting in on itself, and her growing dizziness wasn't only due to horror over what she'd done. She needed to get back to the castle before she starved.

A dark voice asked why it mattered. Perhaps starving to death was what she deserved.

But Callista hadn't felt anything to indicate that the fae curse had gone into effect. She had to stay alive long enough to hear word of whether the Faines had died. She needed to know everything she'd done hadn't been in vain, that she had succeeded in keeping her promise and achieving retribution.

So she kept going, kept pushing herself another step and another. Every minute stretched longer than the last. Why did the river have to be so far from the ruins? If only she had the energy to cast another speed enchantment. Staggering around a tree, she jolted to a halt and blinked.

The Eynlaean knight's buckskin destrier stared at her, its reins trailing on the ground. That would be faster… Guilt pricked her, but he wouldn't need a steed now.

Cautiously, she approached the horse. It shied away a step, but then let her take the reins and mount it. As she turned the horse toward the ruined castle, a golden gleam off to the side caught her attention.

A few paces away, the unicorn stood watching her. It nodded, then dashed away.

Had…the unicorn brought her the knight's horse?

Callista shook her head. She was delirious from lack of food.

"I'm sorry," she whispered to the horse. "I suspect he was a good man."

44

nika watched in shock as Callista disappeared into the forest. But then Leo whimpered, and she turned her back on the awful witch. She didn't dare touch her convulsing brother. Beyond him, Gareth knelt at the edge of the river, his eyes wide and frightened in his bone-white face. Blood trickled between his fingers where his hands clutched his throat. Panic coiled around Anika's chest, squeezing her until she couldn't breathe.

She wanted to save them both and didn't know if she actually could help either. Still, she had to try, but which one first? Her brother, or the man who had sacrificed himself to save her? Her twin or the man she was falling in love with?

Leo stilled, sprawled out on his side, but his chest still rose and fell, and he'd stopped crying.

A choked gurgling just audible above the splashing river tugged her attention back to Gareth. Still holding his throat, he collapsed onto his side, his body half in the river.

She didn't know what was wrong with Leo, and he was breathing. Gareth had seconds left, if that.

Tears clouding her vision, Anika rushed to Gareth, calling up her magic. Her hands shimmered with yellow-gold light as she pressed them over his hands against his neck.

The cut had severed a major artery. She'd never healed such a deadly wound before. All of the warm blood slicking her hands and the sensation of his life force flowing out made her nauseous, but she refused to let him die. Anika squeezed her eyes closed and concentrated on weaving the magic together to reconnect the artery and everything else to close the wound. The pounding in her skull built, aching behind her closed eyelids where white spots flashed.

Then the magic petered out, as if it had nothing left to do. An ache throbbed deep in her head from the expenditure of her magic. Slowly, fearfully, Anika opened her eyes.

Gareth lay still on the edge of the riverbank, his eyes closed. No visible breath moved his chest. When she withdrew her hands, his hands fell limply from his throat, one splashing into the water. There was too much blood covering his neck for her to see the results of her work.

"Gareth?" she whispered.

He didn't move.

A sob wracked Anika's chest.

Gareth had so much he wanted to do, dreams that at nineteen he should have had a lifetime to pursue. With his sense of honor, dedication to justice, and determination to help people, he deserved to have become a famous knight. Now he'd never save anyone else. He'd never find out if his father could truly see and understand him.

She'd always remember the moment he asked Callista to promise that if he surrendered, Anika and Leo would live. The look of acceptance in his eyes, the insistent but firm tone of his voice. The instant he threw down his sword, he'd chosen their lives over his own.

A prince impossibly out of her reach or not, Anika could have loved him.

Now he was dead, because she hadn't been vigilant and hadn't been strong enough to stop Callista.

"You were born to be a knight, Sir Gareth." Her voice warbled. "Selfless and brave to the last."

Tears clung to her eyelashes and dripped off her nose. She lifted her hand to wipe her face, and her stomach clenched at the sight of Gareth's blood staining her hands. She thrust her hands into the river and hurriedly scrubbed away the blood. Hopefully Gareth would rest in peace knowing his sacrifice had saved her life and Leo's—

A gasp tore from her throat. "Leo!"

He'd been breathing fine when she left him, but something had been wrong. Her twin had to be all right. Her head felt like someone had crushed it, and she didn't have any magic left to give if Leo needed it. If her brother never annoyed her again with his incessant philosophical prattling or believed in her when it felt like no one else did, she wouldn't be able to bear it. She leapt to her feet, spun around, and immediately froze.

Instead of finding a fox on the ground, her gaze moved from a pair of boots, up trousers and a shirt and embroidered vest, to Leo's tear-streaked, freckled face beneath red hair that was sticking out at all angles. She blinked once, hard, but Leo still stood there, fully human.

"Leo!" She crashed into him, squeezing his gangly frame as she buried her face against the top of his shoulder. "I was so afraid…"

"As if I'd let a stupid thing like drowning kill me and separate me from my sister," Leo said wryly as he returned her embrace.

"I didn't know what was happening to you, but you were breathing and had no obvious injury, and Gareth was…" Anika tightened her arms around her brother as tears burned her eyes. "I couldn't save him, Leo. I couldn't—" A hiccupping sob choked off her words.

He didn't say anything, but a tremble went through him as he leaned into her. His tears splashed onto the side of her neck. They held each other up while they mourned until their tears subsided enough Anika didn't feel like she'd collapse the moment she released Leo.

They eased apart from each other, both wiping their faces.

"I'm sorry I left you to help Gareth—"

"Why should you be sorry?" Leo shifted from foot to foot, his downcast eyes avoiding the direction of Gareth's body. "You thought I'd be all right, so you tried to help someone who was dying. That's why you'll make a great knight, Anika. You don't stop fighting to save anyone you can."

His words twisted her heart. She'd fought, yes, but she'd failed.

He motioned toward her temple. "Are you all right?"

"Hm?" Anika touched her face and dried blood flaked away. "Oh. Right. I think so. Head wounds always bleed like they're so much worse than they are." She returned to the river, far upstream from Gareth because she couldn't bear to go near his corpse again. She washed the dried blood off her temple, careful to leave the new scab in place.

When she returned to her brother, he was staring toward Gareth. Tears pooled along his lashes.

"Callista said I was 'no longer needed.' Gareth was right, in the end. I was turned into a fox and sent to lure him to his death." Leo's voice cracked, and he dropped to the ground. He turned his back to the river, tucked his knees up to his chest, and rocked back and forth.

"That witch will pay for this—" He wailed and buried his face against his knees.

Anika's head still hurt so badly that she was seeing flashes of light in her right eye. She wanted to see Callista punished, too, but she didn't know how they would do that. All she could do was mourn with Leo. She sat down, put her arm around his shoulders, and closed her eyes.

Another tremble went through Leo, his ribs shaking with each hiccupping breath. She tightened her grip on his shoulder and tried to remember Gareth's blue eyes crinkling with a smile instead of his pale, lifeless face.

The sun beat warmly on their backs, the river burbled merrily along, and somewhere, birds sang, oblivious to the sorrow rending her heart. Slowly, her headache eased to a dull pain in the background of her consciousness. She wasn't sure how long they'd been sitting there when Leo drew a deep breath.

"He deserved to live long enough to have legends written about him," Leo mumbled.

Anika opened her mouth, but words failed her.

Hoofbeats sounded behind them, in the direction of the river, and her breath caught in her lungs. *Please, not bandits.* Her magic hadn't recovered yet, and she didn't have the emotional energy to deal with a new threat.

A horse snorted.

They both twisted around to look, and Anika sucked in a breath.

Tempest stood over Gareth, eyeing them with what looked bizarrely like frustration. The unicorn snorted again and tossed her head. After backing up a couple of steps, she knelt by Gareth's back and lowered her head. The unicorn sniffed Gareth's blood-covered throat and sighed, but then looked right at the twins and gave what Anika swore was an approving nod.

Arching her neck as she lowered herself down, Tempest touched the tip of her shiny, golden horn to Gareth's breastplate. White light erupted from the base of the horn and traveled down to the tip, so blinding Anika and Leo had to shield their eyes. The light pulsed into Gareth, giving his skin a faint, silvery glow.

The light faded, and Tempest stood and released a trumpeting neigh.

45

With a sharp inhale that burned down his throat, Gareth jerked upright and blinked against the bright sunlight. His hands plunged into water as he steadied himself.

He was sitting at the edge of a river. His neck felt gross and sticky, his skin was oddly hot, and he was parched. Sorrowful resignation lingered in the back of his mind, but he couldn't remember why. What had happened?

Sunlight glared off the blade of Gareth's sword. Water flowed around the hilt, but on the muddy shore, dark red marked the sharp tip.

His own blood.

Dying. He'd been dying. Callista had killed him—

Something nudged the side of his head, and he looked over, coming face-to-face with Tempest's muzzle. The unicorn whinnied triumphantly and pranced before lipping at his hair.

"Hello to you, too." To his surprise, his voice came out fine, and not at all like he'd just had his throat sliced.

"Gareth!" Anika shouted, his name high-pitched and broken on her lips.

He turned from the unicorn as Anika barreled toward him. She slammed into him, and he would have fallen back into the river if not for her muscular arms pulling him close.

"You're alive." She trembled against him and hugged him tighter.

Gareth returned her embrace, squeezing her back as he buried his face in the hollow of her shoulder and neck. He'd just survived something that by all rights should have killed him, and he no longer cared if Anika was an Aedyllanian lord's daughter and he was an Eynlaean prince. He liked how she felt in his arms, and he wanted to hold her close.

"It's all right," he soothed, but then realized he didn't know that for sure—Leo had been alive last he knew, but was he still? Frantically, Gareth lifted his head from Anika's shoulder and cast about for the familiar coppery red of Leo's fur and stiffened when he saw something else instead.

Someone else.

A stranger stood a few steps away, watching them with a watery smile. The young man had no weapon, and his rumpled clothes were of fine make and looked more like what someone would wear to an afternoon tea than to rob someone. He was a bit gangly, and his head stuck forward slightly. The way he held himself reminded Gareth of one of his tutors.

The shape of his face and his freckles were oddly familiar, but it was the red hair that captured Gareth's attention. It was the same fiery copper as Anika's...

Gareth gasped and released Anika. "*Leo?*"

The young man grinned. "So you do recognize me when I'm not covered in fur." His voice sounded exactly the same as when he was a fox.

"What happened?" Gareth demanded. Remembering his conversation with Leo the day before about death breaking curses, his eyes widened. "You...you didn't die, too, did you? Or...was it because *I* died?"

Leo scoffed. "No. The witch changed me back. Didn't need a talking fox anymore, apparently."

Anika released her death grip on Gareth and stood. "And then she ran off."

Gareth nodded slowly. "So Callista broke Leo's curse, and then…" He gingerly touched his neck and traced his fingertips over a long scar. Drying blood painted his cuirass and flaked off his skin.

Memories overpowered him. Pain and fear flooded his mind, along with the sensation of struggling to breathe as he clutched his throat in a futile attempt to stop the blood pulsing between his fingers in time with his racing heart. And then, a recollection of Anika's panicked face as she reached for him with her hands glowing orange. The searing pain fading under her touch as black shrouded his vision and he lost consciousness.

With effort, Gareth drew in a slow breath. He was alive, against all expectations, and he wanted to forget the horror of dying.

"Then you saved me?" he asked in wonder.

Before Anika could say anything, Tempest's high-pitched neigh interrupted her. The unicorn bumped the back of his head with her muzzle.

"Ow!" He rubbed his head and frowned at the mare. "What was that for?"

"I did close the wound," Anika said quietly. "But it wasn't enough. You…died."

"Then how—"

"Tempest." Leo shook his head. "I knew unicorns had great power, but…I had no idea just *how* powerful they are. We've been keeping them in our stables like horses! It was incredible. This blinding white light and then you sat up!"

Tempest nickered with a proud toss of her mane, then lowered her head and slowly shook it back and forth.

Gareth wrinkled his eyebrows. "Why do I get the distinct impression that was 'I am very proud of myself, but we unicorns don't do that often'?"

"I'd call you out for overestimating your own importance again," Leo said as he tilted his head, "but that is what it looked like."

"I see." Gareth turned to the unicorn and bowed. "Thank you, Tempest."

She gave a satisfied snort, then motioned her head toward the water.

"And apparently she doesn't like blood," Anika said with a short laugh.

"I don't blame her." Gareth hurriedly removed his vambraces and cuirass, murmuring his thanks when Anika came to his aid. He pulled off his soiled tunic and undershirt, too, and set to work cleaning his hands, neck, shoulders, chest, and shirt.

When he finally finished, he straightened with a groan as his back protested the extended period spent crouched over. After laying out his dripping tunic atop a dry, sunbathed boulder, he turned to the Raylor twins. They'd both taken a seat nearby in the shade of an oak, but they stood and approached him.

Leo was almost as tall as Anika—in fact, if he spent less time curled over books and had better posture, they might be the same height.

"You're taller than I expected," he said without thinking.

Leo awarded him a narrow-eyed, annoyed look that was only missing flattened ears to match the one he'd given Gareth while in fox form. "I'm not usually two feet tall, thank you."

"Still red, though."

"Hilarious." Leo stepped closer to Gareth. His throat bobbed as he glanced away, then he bowed. "Thank you for sacrificing yourself to save us."

Taken aback by Leo's sudden turn toward formality, Gareth stared at him for a moment. Emotion squeezed his throat as he recalled watching Leo struggle in the sack beneath the river. A bit of wetness stung his eyes. He grabbed Leo's shoulder and tugged him into a crushing hug. "What are friends for? I'm glad you're both all right."

He was about to release Leo when his friend abruptly returned his embrace with surprising force.

"I'm so glad you're alive," Leo mumbled. He pushed away and lightly tapped his fist against Gareth's shoulder. "But don't do that again, Sir Reckless."

"Don't get captured again and I won't have to, fur-brains."

Anika cleared her throat. "What do we do now?"

His mood darkened. "I want that witch to pay for everything she's done and all the pain and suffering she's caused. We go after her before she has a chance to escape to a new hideout."

"I agree." Her expression took on a deadly edge. "She should face justice for torturing Leo and killing you. She expended a staggering amount of magic today, so she'll be weak. This might be the most vulnerable she'll ever be."

"And what, pray tell, will this justice look like?" Leo asked, his arms crossed as he squinted at them.

"I suppose we'll give her a chance to surrender. If she does, we'll turn her over to your courts to determine her just punishment for casting dark curses and committing murder." Gareth clenched his fists. "If she insists on fighting to her death, so be it."

Leo considered this for a moment before nodding. "That is acceptable. I will help."

"Er…" Gareth lifted a brow. "No offense, Leo, but I thought you were a scholar, not a warrior?"

Anika grinned. "Do you honestly think I'd allow *my* twin to be entirely defenseless? He can handle a dagger."

"I can also throw a decent punch. I just hate doing it. Makes my hand hurt and can split my knuckles. Have you ever tried to write with split knuckles? Not to mention then the other person punches you back and that's even worse." Leo waved a hand. "Besides, at the least, I can be very annoying and distracting, giving you two a better chance at subduing her."

Gareth couldn't help a teasing grin. "*You* can be annoying? You don't say."

"Almost as annoying as you," Leo quipped back, his expression at once haughty and serene. "Shall we return to camp for Anika's weapons and your horse, then?"

"Certainly."

Anika went over to the tree where she had been bound and used a bit of magic to undo the knot, then looped the rope around her waist. Meanwhile, Gareth pulled on his damp clothing with distaste, then frowned at his cuirass and vambraces. His garments would never dry underneath them, and Anika was already wearing her own armor.

Leo sighed heavily, as if someone had asked him to shovel manure. "I'll wear the darned things, so you don't have to put them over your shirt or tire your arms out."

"Wear…" Gareth hesitated, then held up the cuirass and vambraces. "This?"

With a look of extreme long-suffering, Leo nodded. Gareth's lips twitched toward a laugh, but he nodded and helped Leo don the armor. Once it was on, he stepped back and observed Leo, tilting his head back and forth as he took in Leo's rigid posture. Somehow, the armor didn't look right on him.

Anika snickered. "You don't look comfortable."

"I'm not," Leo intoned. Heaving another sigh, he started forward. "Let's go. We have a longer walk than I'd like."

With a snort, Tempest stepped directly into Leo's path,

blocking him. She pointed her nose toward her own back.

Gareth blinked. "You…want us to ride you?"

Tempest shook her head up and down in an exaggerated nod.

"All three of us?"

Another equine nod, emphasized with a neigh. The three of them looked at each other. Anika and Gareth shrugged, but Leo pursed his lips.

"I'm sure you two sword-swinging brutes can manage it, but, um… I have not personally perfected the art of mounting a large steed without a saddle and stirrups."

Gareth chuckled. "Not a problem." He stood at Tempest's side, bent down, and laced his fingers together. "Up you go."

A bit of red colored Leo's face as he stomped over. "Not. A. Single. Teasing. Word," he warned.

That made Gareth want to tease him, but he nodded and forced his expression into something more serious. He didn't want to actually hurt his friend's feelings. Besides, no sense in making Leo dislike him again after he'd said he wouldn't mind Gareth courting Anika. Although that had been when Leo was afraid that he might stay a fox forever.

As Leo placed his booted foot on Gareth's hands and grasped Tempest's mane, Gareth asked, "Does what you told me before, about approving, still stand?"

Leo frowned. "Yes, although strange time to ask."

"Just checking." Gareth boosted his friend up and onto the unicorn's back.

"Wait," Leo said. "If I'd said no, would you have thrown me right over Tempest's back?"

"Of *course* not." Gareth winked, enjoying the affronted expression on Leo's face, and turned to Anika. "Do you require any assistance, my lady?"

She gave him a confused look, then nodded. "Honestly, I

wouldn't mind. Tempest is tall, and I don't want to grab onto Leo and accidentally pull him down."

After relacing his fingers and helping Anika mount—glee rushed through him when she momentarily placed her hand on his shoulder to steady herself—Gareth prepared to mount. She held her hand out to him, and with a nod of thanks, they clasped each other's forearms. She tugged upward when he jumped, helping him get enough momentum to settle on behind her. There wasn't much room, so he had to press close against her back.

"This feels crowded," Leo complained.

"Says you." Anika squirmed. "I'm sandwiched."

Gareth blushed. "Sorry—"

"It's fine." She patted his thigh, nearly making him choke.

"As happy as I am not to be squished in the middle," Leo said, "this may have been a miscalculation. I'm unsure how to steer without r—" He cut off in a yelp as Tempest surged forward.

The unicorn raced through the woods, apparently sure in her sense of direction. It was all the rest of them could do to duck branches and hold on—which in Gareth's case meant his hands were firmly clasped around Anika's waist. Over her steel cuirass, unfortunately, but still. Racing through the forest on a unicorn's back while he held the most beautiful woman he'd ever known was enough to make his heart sing.

But when they reached the camp, his heart plummeted.

Their bags of supplies, the firebird in its gold cage, and Anika's sword and dagger were where he'd left them, but Fury was gone.

"Fury!" Gareth leapt down and spun in a circle, panic spiking. Internally, he apologized for every time he'd favored Tempest over his loyal steed. "Fury!"

Tempest nudged his shoulder with her muzzle, then lipped at his hair. He brushed her aside. "Fury!"

"It's all right, princeling. You'll see him again."

"It's not all right! And you don't know—" Gareth cut off abruptly. That hadn't sounded like Anika or Leo. It was a woman's voice, although it was deep and…strange, in a way he had difficulty articulating.

"Gather what you need to face your foe, and I will take you to Callista and your boring, non-magical horse."

Slowly, Gareth turned toward the unicorn. Leo stood nearby, looking sad, and Anika cast Gareth sympathetic glances as she sheathed her sword. "Did either of you say something?"

"Ah-ha!" Tempest pranced. *"You can hear me at last! I worried I'd done something amiss when I revived you. Usually unicorn-touched can understand us."*

Gareth gulped, wide-eyed as he pointed at Tempest. "The unicorn is speaking to me."

Leo tilted his head, much like he had as a fox. "Beg your pardon?"

"Tell him he was cuter as a fox."

"I'm not saying that." Gareth frowned. "Have you been talking this whole time—"

"But no one could hear me?" Tempest hung her head. *"Yes. Unicorns can understand each other, but I've been talking to myself this entire trip. It's worth it, though!"*

Anika looked between Gareth and Tempest. "She's really speaking to you?"

"Oh, tell her I know that when she was very little, she would get in trouble on purpose, so she'd be sent to shovel manure instead of study. Then she'd swing the pitchfork around like a sword."

Gareth laughed. "Sounds like me. Anika, would you really get in trouble on purpose because you'd rather shovel manure than study?"

"That isn't exactly what I said," Tempest protested.

Anika's entire face went red. "Um, yes."

"That's incredible!" Leo looked up at Tempest with awe. "I knew they were clever, but…amazing."

"*Yes, I'm very spectacular.*" Tempest tossed her head. "*But now is the time to confront Callista. She also has your ordinary horse.*"

"She *what?*" Gareth shouted. "That witch killed me and then stole my horse?!"

Anika gaped. "Callista took Fury?"

"*Calm yourself,*" Tempest said. "*Fury is perfectly safe with Callista.*"

Gareth stomped around the campsite, shoving things into saddlebags. "He better be."

46

The accursed rodents had gotten into her food.

Callista could have sworn she'd put the sack of food on the hook hanging from the ceiling as she always did, but it was on the floor with holes chewed through it. Most of the food was either gone or so nibbled on even she wasn't desperate enough to eat it.

She sank onto the floor beside the scattered crumbs and sorted through the mess until she found an untouched half of a loaf of bread wrapped in thick linen. The bread was insufficient, leaving her still hungry and dazed.

The silence of the castle ruins pressed in around her. She'd chosen this place because it wouldn't let her forget her purpose. It didn't matter that the king who had murdered the castle's inhabitants nearly half a century ago had died long before Callista was born. Every burnt stone was a reminder of the Faines' cruelty and how no one could stand against them. Still, it was so harsh and isolated. Even the rodents were quiet, doubtless scared off by her arrival and sluggish with their stomachs full of her food.

She wished she had her flute, to process her pain through a mournful song and fill the empty ruins. But she didn't. She had no one and nothing, not even the energy to find more food.

At long last, she let herself fall apart.

Doubling over with her arms crossed over her stomach, Callista let herself cry as she hadn't cried since Royce's death. Tears ran into her mouth and dripped off her chin as she struggled to breathe through her weeping. Her wails echoed off the burned stone, filling her ears with the sound of her brokenness.

Maybe that was why she didn't hear them approach.

When she finally slowed her gasps to normal breaths, wiped her eyes and dripping nose, and straightened, she drew in a sharp breath. The Raylor twins and the Eynlaean knight—who was alive against all logic—stood in her room, watching her with a mixture of suspicion and confusion. Anika and the knight pointed swords at her, while Leo held a dagger with a little less confidence.

Was this a nightmare conjured by her subconscious to torment her? Her tortured mind throwing at her an image of the lives she had ruined in her pursuit of vengeance?

"Um…" The knight took a step closer, his sword pointed directly at her throat. His boots made a dull thud on the rug-covered stone.

"You're alive?" she asked hoarsely.

A vicious sneer pulled at his upper lip. "Despite your efforts to the contrary, witch."

A new wave of horror and heartbreak washed over her. She had failed to kill the foreign hero. All of her work, all of her solitude and compromises, even Royce's death, all of it was for *nothing*. Her emotions faded to exhausted numbness.

She had failed, and there was no trying again.

The Faines would continue to get away with their abuses, people would continue to suffer, and her promise to her family would go unfulfilled…but at least it seemed she wouldn't be around to witness it.

"I see," she whispered. "Can you make it quick?" Staring at

the ground, she shook her head. As if the people she had used so horribly would be so kind.

I'm sorry, Royce. Father. Jacob. Mother. Kay. Anna.

She squeezed her eyes shut and waited, too cried out for even a single tear.

Hands grabbed her arms and pulled them behind her back. Her eyes flew open in surprise as rough rope bound her wrists. Leo had sheathed his dagger, and while the knight hadn't returned his sword to its scabbard, he had lowered it so its point rested on the ground. Both young men watched her, Leo with open curiosity, and the knight with a deeply furrowed brow and pinched frown.

Anika finished binding her wrists and stood. "I have doubts that this will hold her if she uses her magic again."

A bitter huff of a laugh escaped Callista. "I'd likely die if I attempted it. Rodents ate my food."

Anika went to stand beside the men again, her sword in its scabbard. "Is that how your magic taxes you? Hunger?"

She nodded.

The knight sighed. "I suppose we should give her some food, then, if we want her to be alive when we bring her in."

Callista almost asked what he meant, but she was too tired to find the energy to care.

"You stole my horse." The knight scowled at her.

It took her a moment to force herself to talk. "Found it wandering."

Another confused frown, then he muttered, "At least Tempest was right." She was too drained to care what that meant.

"Should we bring our supplies in here?" Leo asked.

Looking around Callista's room, the knight nodded. "Might as well. Anika can have the bed."

"I had a sleeping mat in my room," Anika said. "We can pull

that in as well."

"Leo can have it," the knight said as he turned to leave the room. "Reckon the firebird will be all right outside with Fury and Tempest?"

"I don't see why not," Leo said as they walked out together. "That's where she kept it, after all."

Their voices faded as they walked away, leaving Callista, still kneeling with her wrists bound, alone with Anika. She stared at a crumb on the floor, every muscle tense as she waited to see what Anika would do to pay her back for all the pain she had caused.

But her captors weren't out of surprises. Wordlessly, Anika swept past her and rummaged through the books and papers stacked on the desk. As it became apparent the redhead wasn't concerned with revenge at the moment, Callista eased onto her side. After a couple minutes of squirming, she gave up on finding a comfortable position. She shifted a little so she could see Anika's head over the top of the desk, absently curious what she was looking for.

A drawer slid open, and parchment rustled. Anika's eyes widened as she read something before she dropped heavily onto the stool behind the desk and Callista could no longer see her.

She'd found the prophecy then.

Time to find out if her captors decided that made her a worse monster or if that won her any sympathy.

47

The yellowed, wrinkled parchment crinkled in Anika's hands. A few smudges where it looked as if water had splashed on the scroll marred some of the thick handwriting, but she could still read every dire word.

The Fae Blessing and Curse of the Faines was real.

As they had feared, it was the reason for every cruel and strange thing Callista had done.

She didn't know how to feel about that. The witch's quiet, resigned words just before Gareth had found them earlier that day echoed in her mind.

"I wish there was another way. I'm truly sorry."

Raised voices sounded from the ruined hall outside, approaching the room.

"…just ride off!" Gareth protested.

"So you'll ride and drag her behind you like Tristan dragged you?" Leo challenged.

"*We* were innocent! She is guilty!"

"Tristan believed you and Alex and his friends were guilty."

"That's not the same," Gareth blustered as they carried their supplies into the room. "What then? Are you volunteering to ride with her after she *drowned you?*"

Leo's nose wrinkled. "Well, no…"

Anika approached them as they dumped their supplies on the floor. "Look at this."

Leo accepted the parchment, and Gareth peered over his shoulder to read it at the same time. As they scanned the lines, Leo's mouth fell into a small O and Gareth's eyebrows pushed up. The prince glanced at Callista, who had curled onto her side on the floor, looked back to the prophecy, then both men stared at Anika.

Gareth was the first to speak. "Was…I fated to come here by a two-hundred-year-old fae prophecy?"

"It hardly calls you by name, *Gareth*," Leo said dryly. "Calm your ego."

"Oh, come on!" Gareth threw his hands up. "I get sent to Tremblay weeks before this all starts and just happen to be the knight guarding the firebird the night Callista struck, and you're going to tell me this piece of paper didn't bear my destiny this entire time? All of our destinies?" He motioned to the three of them.

Anika shrugged. "I think if it hadn't been you, it would have been someone else. Same with Leo and me."

"Exactly," Leo said as he rolled up the scroll. "These *events* were fated. Like Callista told Anika, prophecies need to come true. We're the arrows an archer happened to grab. Of far greater urgency than existential and unanswerable questions of fate and destiny—what do we do now?"

Gareth crossed his arms. "What do you mean? This doesn't change anything."

Anika agreed. For some reason Callista appeared to believe she'd had no choice but to follow the prophecy and had seemed reluctant to hurt anyone. That didn't change that she had. They still needed to bring her in for trial for witchcraft and murder.

"It changes everything!" Leo said in exasperation. "If we take Callista to the palace for her trial, it will come out *why* she did what she did. Option one: This prophecy is fake. But King Silas isn't known for being rational, and if he learns we cooperated with her at all—like trading the unicorn—he might accuse us of being involved.

"Option two: It's real, but it didn't work and the Faines are still in power. The king might kill us just for knowing the contents of the prophecy to prevent us from telling anyone or trying again. Either way, he won't be impartial in judging Callista.

"Option three: The curse has already been activated, and if we go to the palace now, we might wander into the middle of a battle for the throne. If we survive that, who knows? Perhaps whoever wins the crown is so tickled that Callista made it possible he rewards her and has us executed for turning her in."

"You sure want to predict our execution," Gareth muttered.

Anika tapped her thumb on the pommel of her sword. This was out of her depth. She would suggest they go to Highrook in case there was a battle, because then at least she could feel useful, except she still didn't want to fight her fellow Aedyllanians.

A heavy sigh came from Callista, and they turned toward her as she sat upright. "I failed. The foreign hero lived." She motioned with her head toward Gareth, something in her eyes hollow and shattered.

"Not necessarily," Leo said. "Prophecies can be tricky. Gareth's life didn't permanently end, but I'm certain he *was* dead before Tempest revived him. Only unicorn magic could have brought him back."

The witch perked up, a bit of hope flickering in her gaze. "Truly?" She slumped back to the floor and closed her eyes, a tenuous smile on her face. "If that is true, if I did what I promised *and* no innocents were killed...I might die in peace."

Gareth's eyebrows lowered. "What do you mean by that? What you promised?"

Callista only shook her head, her thin form relaxing as if her last reserves of energy were spent.

"We should give her food," Leo noted glumly. He handed the prophecy back to Anika and crouched to rummage through their bags.

Anika folded the parchment into an easier to transport square while she sorted through her spinning thoughts. "I think," she said slowly, "we should go home. We can take her with us. Father will be informed if anything happened to the Faines, and he might have more insight into what should be done about Callista's crimes."

And whether they were crimes to be judged the same as any other if they were predestined, but she kept that musing to herself.

"I wonder if Father and Conrad will take up arms if it comes to that," Leo mused. He closed the bags and stood, holding a sack of dried fruit and a piece of dried, salted meat.

"Another reason for us to hurry home," Anika said.

Leo crouched in front of Callista. "Ahem." When she didn't open her eyes, he poked her shoulder. Once she finally looked at him, he said, "I'm going to untie you for a moment so I can tie your hands in front of you. All right?"

With a tiny nod, Callista sat up, scarcely moving as Leo adjusted her hands and bindings. The moment he stood, she snatched up the food and devoured it.

"I agree with Anika," Gareth said. He cupped his hand over the back of his neck. "With the fae curse involved, I shouldn't go near the castle, regardless of whether it was activated. Aedyllanian ambassadors and lords have visited our palace. If I'm recognized hanging around Highrook during a possible upheaval, it might drag my father into things. I've already nearly drawn him into one war."

Anika looked to Leo, who nodded his agreement. "That's settled then—"

"I'm sorry…" Callista's voice croaked, and she cleared her throat.

To Anika's surprise, Gareth fished a canteen from their bags, removed the stopper, and held the flask out to the witch.

Callista blinked at it. Her shoulders scrunching toward her ears, she accepted the canteen and took a long drink. Her throat worked as she dragged her gaze up to Gareth's face. "Who are you? I…I thought you were a knight."

"I am a knight. I'm also a prince."

Callista blanched. "Oh," she whispered.

"Would knowing that have changed anything?" Gareth asked, his tone too casual.

Her lips flattened, and Anika found herself leaning closer as she awaited the answer. "No," Callista said at last.

Gareth tilted his head. "Because you know a prince's life shouldn't matter more than a knight's?"

A prince's life did always matter more than a knight's, everyone knew that. But when Gareth said it, Anika was certain he genuinely didn't see himself as more important. The thought brought an unexpected warmth and zing of hope to her chest. If Gareth didn't see himself as intrinsically better than a knight…did that mean she might have a chance with him?

"It would have made me hesitate more, because an Eynlaean prince dying on Aedyllanian soil could risk war," Callista said quietly. "But as Leo Raylor said, I had no choice but to work with the arrows I found."

"You don't think what you've done risks war?" Leo asked.

Callista shrugged. "If the Blessing and Curse didn't exist, don't you think we would have had rebellion and war by now anyway?"

Her simple declaration startled Anika with its obvious truth.

"Hm." Gareth turned toward the door. "I'm going to go untack Fury."

Anika joined him. "I'll go with you."

When he smiled at her, that warm feeling grew.

*E*veryone was exhausted after the events of the previous day and slept hard. Despite feeling unsettled about sleeping in the same room as the woman who had killed him, Gareth had found he couldn't keep his eyes open. Next thing he knew, sunlight was streaming in through the cracks between the wood slats covering the window.

They were all slow to wake, their movements lethargic. Well, Callista hardly moved at all. She sat in a corner, staring into space while Gareth and the twins woke up and sorted through and re-packed their supplies. There was less food left than they'd realized, and what remained wouldn't last as long now that they had to feed Callista. They elected to save the packed food for the road and catch something else for breakfast.

They had to clap in the witch's face to get her attention.

"We need more food," Gareth said. "Can we trust you not to try anything stupid if Anika and I leave to hunt?"

Callista nodded, as if that were all she had the energy to do.

Leo patted Anika's dagger, which he'd attached to his own belt. "I'll be fine." He motioned to the desk. "I have a weapon and reading material. What else could a person need?"

A person might need to not be asked to spend time alone with someone who'd nearly killed them, but Gareth just nodded. "We'll be back as soon as we can."

Anika didn't look happy about leaving Leo alone with the witch either, but she'd offered to use her trapping spell. They walked through the quiet forest, the moss muffling their footsteps. Gareth watched with great interest as Anika used her magic to set a trap. Long grasses spun into rope and tied and positioned themselves on the forest floor. The yellow-orange glow of her enchantment faded and left the trap blending unobtrusively into the undergrowth.

"How do you lure something in?"

Her mouth pinched, and Gareth forced himself not to stare at her lips. He'd occasionally wondered about kissing—he wasn't immune to the beauty of women—but he'd never noticed a woman's lips or been so preoccupied with the idea of kissing a specific person before.

"There's probably a spell, but I don't know it." She reached into the pouch on her belt and carefully placed some dried fruit in the trap, then stood. "Now we leave the area and wait."

"Leave?"

"So we don't scare anything away. The trap springs whether we're here or not, and I'll sense when it does." She tucked her red hair behind her ear as she turned to him.

Gareth nodded, hoping he didn't look as hopelessly starstruck as he felt. "Is your head all right?"

"That's a fairly small spell. There's a hint of an ache"—she tapped her forehead—"but it's mostly ignorable and should fade quickly."

For a few minutes, they strolled through the peaceful forest. Dust motes danced in the slanted golden rays of the morning light filtering between the trees. The grass rustled lightly beneath their feet, insects buzzed, and birds sang in the distance. It was beautiful, and as he drifted closer until his arm was nearly brushing Anika's, he wondered if maybe it was a little romantic.

When they reached a more open area with a larger gap between the trees, he finally got up the courage to ask something he'd been wanting to for a while.

"So…how about that rematch?"

Anika stopped walking and spun toward him, her eyes widening in what looked like anticipation. But then her excitement dimmed. "Are you certain you're up for that?"

"My shoulder barely twinges anymore. It's fine."

"I meant…" Her gaze briefly darted to his throat. "After…"

"Please." He flexed his fingers, ignoring the urge to touch his scar. "If anything, I need to get my confidence back after dying on my own sword."

She winced, which wasn't what he'd intended.

"Come on. You promised me a rematch, my lady."

"Using *sharpened* swords, Your Highness?" she asked, her tone layered in melodramatic shock.

"We're both wearing armor." He grinned. "Besides, if knights of Aedyllan can handle it, why can't knights of Eynlae?"

Her expression softened as she searched his face. Had he said something strange? Insulted her in some way?

But then she smiled, the look a touch feral as she reached for her sword. Gareth took a step back, and they drew their swords at the same moment.

"I won't go easy on you," she warned.

He met her taunting grin with one of his own. "I was about to say the same thing to you." Without waiting, he lunged and aimed a thrust at her torso.

She neatly parried, knocking his blade aside and sweeping her sword up to aim a downward slice at his head. Gareth blocked, and when the force of her blow rattled his teeth, it energized him further, pulling a delighted laugh from him.

Anika blinked, and he took advantage of her momentary surprise to disentangle his sword and swing toward her legs. She parried, but he was already adjusting the trajectory of his sword to slice upward toward her midsection as he stepped closer, pressing her back.

They ranged back and forth, jabbing and swinging, parrying and blocking. He had to focus on his own form and footwork so he couldn't truly study hers, but her skill at least rivaled his own.

Anika blocked his swing toward her neck, and he shoved against their crossed blades. His greater strength knocked her back a couple of steps into a golden beam of sunlight, and her jaw pulsed in irritation, but her eyes were bright.

Wolf's teeth, she was gorgeous and everything he hadn't known he wanted in a partner.

She swung toward his side, and he moved to parry, but her attack was a feint. Quick as a striking serpent, she stabbed toward his unprotected thigh. Gareth dodged to the side, and then she was swinging toward his neck—but she'd miscalculated how far he'd moved, overextending herself.

Gareth batted her sword aside. Aiming for speed over strength, he whipped his sword up to her throat, stopping just as the steel came dangerously close to her pale skin. They both froze.

A triumphant grin split his face as he stood with his sword hovering next to her neck, his arm extended. "Yield, Lady Anika."

She smirked. "Draw." Her gaze flicked down, and something lightly poked at his torso.

Speed over strength had been an error. He hadn't knocked her sword far enough aside, and while he'd moved his blade to her neck, she'd stabbed toward his torso. The point of her sword tucked under the edge of his breastplate at an upward angle, one strong shove away from a serious wound.

"I might survive that," he pointed out.

She appeared unfazed by the sharp edge of his sword so near her throat. "But who is to say if, supposing we hadn't stopped ourselves, I might have struck first and you wouldn't have made it to my neck?"

"No proof I wouldn't have been faster, either." He made a show of looking thoughtful. "Very well—a draw. We'll have to try again some other time." Carefully, he moved his sword away from her neck and slid it into its scabbard.

"Sure you're brave enough to fight me again?" Anika teased as she sheathed her own weapon. "You won't be a mopey loser?"

"Only if you won't be intimidated when I win." He winked, chuckling when Anika made a face.

"Best two of three, then." She held out her hand to shake on it.

Gareth clasped it, but the second her warm skin pressed against his and her fingers curled around his hand, all he could think about was that point of contact, and how he wanted…more.

He tugged on their clasped hands, and she staggered forward, her other hand coming up to steady herself against his chest. Internally he cursed the metal of his cuirass for coming between them.

"Anika…"

Her fingers tightened on his hand as her eyelids lowered. "Yes?"

Gareth's other hand found her waist, settling on the subtle curve of the side of her cuirass as he leaned closer. "You're spectacular," he murmured.

Anika's lips parted, so tantalizingly close. His eyes drifted to half-closed as he leaned even closer but still watched her reaction—

"Oh!" She hopped back from him as red suffused her entire face.

Gareth quickly released her. His heart sank as heat crept into his own cheeks. "Sorry—"

"No, I—it—sorry—trap!" She rubbed the back of her head, her expression sheepish. "It's a twanging sensation in my head, like someone plucking the string of a lute. Sort of startled me."

"Ah."

Did that mean it wasn't a rejection? Was she interested in kissing him?

Too late. The moment was broken, and it would feel forced if he tried to go back to it now. And if she *wasn't* interested, and the trap activating was a convenient distraction, it'd be even more awkward if he tried to pick up where they'd been interrupted.

"I suppose we should go get that, then."

49

$\mathscr{A}$nika kept sneaking glances at Gareth as they collected a fat rabbit from her trap and walked back to the castle ruins. She was certain he had been about to kiss her, and the thought made butterflies swirl in her stomach.

She'd never been kissed. A squire had tried it once—in the middle of a hand-to-hand combat training session, when she didn't believe she'd done anything to indicate she wanted that, and while he had her pinned on the ground. She'd turned her head and gotten a rather wet kiss on her cheek. It had scared her, so after she shoved him off, she'd punched him right in the mouth. At first, she'd been glad she gave in to the impulse, because after that, none of the other squires or knights made any unwanted advances. Occasionally she'd regretted it, because no one who lived in or frequented Raylor Estate dared to so much as flirt with her.

That hadn't stopped men who didn't know her well from trying to get handsy without provocation, which hadn't enamored her with the idea of kissing.

But Gareth wasn't like those knights. He'd released her so quickly when the magic trap startled her, she was certain if she'd told him to stop, he would have immediately and without question or complaint. He hadn't done anything untoward when he'd sat behind her on Tempest's back, either.

In fact, Anika had started to worry he didn't see her as a woman—at least, not in a romantic sense. When he'd asked her to duel and she'd pointed out they'd be using sharp weapons, he'd called her a knight of Aedyllan. At first, it had pleased her. He hadn't downplayed her skill by saying if a weak woman could handle it, then he could. Instead, he'd put her on the same level as him. But then she'd wondered if he *only* saw her as a knight like any other.

If the smoldering look in his eyes when he'd tugged her toward him was any indication, that wasn't the case at all.

He was very much aware, and he wanted to kiss her.

She thought.

She *hoped*.

Unfortunately, she didn't have the faintest idea how to go about kissing him now that she'd ruined the perfect opportunity.

Another opportunity would surely come. Right?

Fate continued to oppose her, as no occasion for kissing arose while they cleaned, dressed, and cooked their catch and then ate a very late breakfast. By the time they had Fury and Tempest saddled and ready to leave, it was nearly midday.

At least they had Fury back. All three of them sitting on Tempest—which was even more uncomfortable after they put her saddle back on—while holding their bags of supplies and a disgruntled firebird in a large cage was not an experience she wished to repeat. And now they had a prisoner as well.

After some back and forth in which no one cherished the idea of sharing a mount with Callista—and the witch herself looked tiredly resigned—they agreed to take turns. Callista would ride Fury and they'd tie the firebird's cage to Fury as well. Someone would lead the buckskin stallion, and the other two would ride Tempest. It made their progress slower, and this time, they took the roads. It was a less direct route but was easier with one of them on foot. As they rode, they kept a sharp eye out for bandits.

Gareth volunteered to walk first. Leo agreed to take the next walking shift, which Anika appreciated, because it meant Gareth mounted Tempest behind her instead of the other way around.

"You can hold on to my waist," she said as they started out.

From his position walking Fury, Leo glanced up at her and made a gagging face. Gareth didn't seem to notice, because his right arm slipped around her middle, bringing him closer to her back. Unfortunately, it wasn't half as cozy as she'd hoped.

Curse their stupid, rigid armor. Sure, Gareth looked good in it, and she was rather proud of her own, but at that moment, she would have liked to rip it all off of him.

No wait, not like that*!* She blushed as hard as if she'd voiced the thought aloud and was thankful no one was looking at her.

The steel was unforgiving, but she sank back against him anyway. When his other arm encircled her middle, she smiled.

When it came time for her to switch places with Leo, Anika had to smother her disappointment.

They stopped for the night shortly before sunset. They were all tired and hungry, and the firebird had taken to loud, mournful squawking and flinging sparks everywhere in protest of its cage swinging against Fury's side. The magical embers were harmless, but they made Fury skittish. Even after setting the firebird on the ground and giving it some dried fruit, it kept cooing sadly. At Callista's suggestion, they fed the bird some of their dried venison. It gave a cheerful chirrup and tore into the meat with enthusiasm.

After supper they had a brief argument about whether to set watches in case of animals or bandits, but mostly to ensure Callista didn't try anything while they slept.

"If I were going to try anything," Callista said tiredly, "I would have already. You have my promise I won't harm any of you or attempt to escape, and I don't give my word lightly. If that isn't enough, know that if I wanted to escape, one of you would not be enough to stop me."

Begrudgingly, Anika admitted she had a point.

Gareth tilted his head, then sighed. "Tempest says to trust Callista, and also that we can all sleep. She'll sense if there's danger and alert us."

Despite that reassurance, none of them slept well. None of them admitted it, either. The prior night at the ruins, exhaustion had granted Anika a deep, dreamless slumber. Better rested and with some space to process, she struggled to sleep. Every time she closed her eyes, Leo's still fox body or Gareth's blood-drained face haunted her.

Once during the night, she heard Leo whimpering in his sleep and looked over to see him curled tightly into the fetal position. Later she'd been staring at the stars through the branches when Gareth bolted upright with a gasp, clutching his throat and breathing hard. He silently went for a walk. When she got up, thinking of following him to ensure he was all right, she found Callista also awake, sitting against a tree and staring after Gareth.

The witch looked at Anika. "I can make you all sleep." Clear hesitation marked her suggestion.

Leo snorted without so much as rolling over. "No thanks. I'm good with your magic never touching me again."

Anika decided not to go after Gareth and pretended not to notice when he returned. She didn't know what to say.

After another slow start the next morning, they resumed their trek with the same rhythm of switching out who led Fury and Callista. Anika wished they could progress at a faster pace. She wanted to hand Callista over to the courts as soon as possible—although Callista wasn't much trouble. She mostly stared into the distance in silence, her eyes unfocused. All of the determination and ruthlessness Anika had come to expect from the witch had vanished.

It was approaching nightfall when they noticed the smoke.

Leo was walking again, so Anika was snuggled back against Gareth as much as their armor would permit. When Gareth pointed out the multiple plumes of white smoke on the horizon, she straightened. He removed his arms from her waist, and she felt his tension as their bodies bumped against each other with Tempest's motion. As they rode closer, three things became apparent.

One, there were no animals nearby—no birds or otherwise. They'd all gone into hiding.

Two, there were a *lot* of fires, and a growing sound of indistinct cacophony.

Three, the fires were on the road, past a large bend, likely spreading out on either side of the thoroughfare.

"Leo," Gareth said, his voice low, "mount Fury behind the witch."

Callista, who had been lively as a rock all day, didn't even flinch. Leo sighed but nudged Callista's foot from the stirrup. After some struggle and kicking the firebird's cage, which made the creature squawk and its light flare brighter, he swung up behind her.

"Be ready to ride, hard and fast," Gareth said.

Tempest nickered and shook her head.

"Hm." Gareth's exhalation brushed against Anika's ear, somehow both itchy and pleasant. "Tempest says we don't need to fear them."

"What?" Callista finally spoke.

"He can hear the unicorn," Leo said as casually as if he were noting that Gareth was Eynlaean. "She talks to him. You hadn't noticed?"

"No…what does she say?" Callista eyed Tempest as if this information troubled her.

"Tempest says, 'Nothing that she need worry about.' Whatever that means."

"If we don't need to fear them, can I get down?" Leo whined. "I'm not eager to get cozy with her like you are with Anika." He held his arms out to the sides around their prisoner, trying to hold on to the reins and not touch her at the same time.

Callista leaned forward to afford a sliver more space between them.

"Since you're already mounted," Gareth said, "let's take advantage of it and hurry."

Tempest must have agreed, because she burst into a gallop that had Gareth wrapping his arms back around Anika to stay on. Fury kept pace as they raced down the road.

When they rounded the bend, the source of the smoke came into view. Far ahead of them, sprawling across the road and spilling into the fields and forest on both sides, was a huge encampment. Men milled around tents that ranged from sturdy pavilions to little more than worn fabric tossed over a few sticks. Late evening sunlight glinted on spearheads and armor.

Although Anika hadn't given any such command with the reins, Tempest turned off the road, crashing into the forest. She further relaxed the reins, letting the unicorn do what she wanted. As the creature was fully rational and articulate, it seemed odd to have reins at all, but the mare didn't seem to mind. Fury followed them into the trees, whether by Leo's command, following his companion, or because the unicorn had somehow given the regular horse an order, Anika had no idea.

"She says she doesn't want to deal with everyone ogling her or asking prying questions," Gareth said, his voice not loud enough to carry to Leo and Callista. It was probably only that he didn't want to shout, but something about his words being meant only for her made her giddy.

They trotted along, weaving through the trees not too far from the road, until Tempest stopped. Leo fumbled with pulling Fury to a halt beside them.

"How do you *know* that?" Gareth asked, and Anika realized he was talking to Tempest again.

"A hunch. Great. Let me guess, you were so insistent that I pick you also on a hunch?"

A brief pause as he listened, then Gareth laughed, and she felt him twist to the side to face Leo. "Ha! Tempest says she wanted me to take her because I was fate-marked."

"What in Miraveld does fate-marked mean?" Leo made a face. "And only you can hear her. You might be lying."

In response, Tempest neighed and stomped a forehoof.

"She says that's rude." Gareth sighed. "She also says we all were fate-marked, but only after Callista drew us into the prophecy. So you were right. The prophecy wasn't *specifically* about us..." He listened. "Until it was. So what, it both was and wasn't about us?" Another pause. "Ugh, destiny makes my head hurt. I don't like it."

Tempest gave an amused whinny.

"Anyway." Gareth released Anika and dismounted. "Tempest has a *hunch* that we should approach the army. Which sounds like madness to me." He planted his hands on his hips and glared at the unicorn. "Oh? Well why didn't you say that in the first place?" He tilted his head, listening, and then stepped forward and stroked Tempest's neck. "Yes, well, I spent the last several days with a talking fox. Talking magical creatures are becoming my new normal. You're still amazing and magical and impressive."

Tempest's flattered, proud-sounding neigh made Anika smile.

Gareth looked up at her. "She says since she's been in your family's care since she was born, she has a connection to you all. Your father and brother are somewhere in that camp."

Anika perked up and immediately dismounted. "Really?"

Leo also dismounted—if the way he got stuck squirming between Callista and the firebird's cage could be called dismounting. Gareth had to catch him and help him to the ground. By his grim expression, Leo was more anxious to get away from Callista than excited to see their father…who possibly still didn't know him. Anika whirled toward the witch.

"The memory erasure curse! You—"

"I already removed it." Callista didn't meet her eyes. "After I undid his curse. I'd always planned to do so."

"After you nearly drowned him," Gareth snapped.

She flinched. "That was an accident. When he almost died, I was horrified. I'd never have forgiven myself if—"

"Excuse me?" Leo said tightly. "Shoving me underwater felt very on purpose!"

"You read the fae curse." Callista's voice dropped to a soft whisper. "I'd only meant to make Anika cry because the prophecy said she'd be crying, and to give the…the prince further incentive to surrender quickly. I'm sorry."

Angry red spots mottled Leo's face as he pointedly turned his back on her. Anika clenched her fists, fighting the urge to lash out at the witch for her awful methods.

"So our father and brother will remember him?" Anika confirmed.

Callista nodded.

Grabbing her brother's hand, Anika started in the direction of the camp before faltering. "Wait… Gareth, I suppose you'll have to remain behind to guard her."

Gareth opened his mouth, paused, raised an eyebrow in Tempest's direction, then shrugged. "Tempest will watch her." He helped Callista dismount, then tied a rope between her bound hands and the stirrup of Tempest's saddle. He gave Callista a warning glare. "We'll be back soon."

50

As the foreign prince and the Raylor twins disappeared into the woods, Callista studied the unicorn. Tempest, apparently. She'd read once in some ancient scroll at the University that there were tales of unicorns speaking to people using a mind connection. She'd dismissed it as just that—tales. It was incredible to know it was true, and she had no doubt her professors would have been fascinated.

Was it too much to hope Tempest might speak to her?

Probably. Unicorns were pure and good, and she was…

Irrevocably tainted by the atrocities she'd committed.

Tempest turned her head to fix one eye on Callista. They regarded each other until the unicorn snorted and looked away. She had no idea what that meant, but clearly the unicorn was not going to speak to her.

The question was…should she attempt to escape?

Part of her was too worn down to care. The last two years had been dedicated to one goal, and now that she'd tried and wasn't certain whether she'd succeeded, she didn't know what to do with herself.

Wait.

Callista snapped her head back in the direction the others had gone.

She'd been too numb to heed what any of them were saying, but abruptly, their words clicked into sharp focus.

Army.

There was an army on the road. Two and a half days after she had killed Prince Gareth, the last condition of the prophecy, an army was gathering.

Tempest had also said she believed Lord Raylor and his heir were with them. What could prompt the Lord of the Unicorn Stables to leave his post and join an army—other than a major upheaval within Aedyllan?

In which direction had they been traveling? Callista tried to picture one of the rough maps of the roads in Aedyllan to determine where they might be. If they were where she supposed they were, the road they'd been traveling would cross with one that led to the palace…

Right around where the army was encamped.

A thrill of excitement and relief went through her.

Had King Silas and his wretched family received the retribution they deserved?

She couldn't flee now. It didn't matter that this might be her best chance. Hope had taken root in her soul, but it was tenuous, and she *needed* to know for certain.

The evening stretched on, punctuated by the occasional flapping of the firebird's wings or its squeaking chirp or the snuffling of the equines. Callista waited impatiently for the Raylors and Prince Gareth to return. The sun set and night approached, and finally, she heard movement in the trees.

She thrust to her feet, and her legs, which had been crossed for a while, protested the movement. Leaning forward, she caught sight of them returning.

51

erhaps we should have sent Gareth on his own," Leo muttered as they wove through the camp. "He wouldn't have drawn attention."

It was true. Gareth scowled and moved between Anika and a man whose bugging eyes trailed over her body as they walked past. With a female knight and a young man who wasn't wearing a lick of armor and looked out of place, the trio was attracting more attention than he was comfortable with.

After asking a couple of men, they were pointed in the direction of Lord Raylor's tent.

"Can't miss it," a gray-haired man said as he smoked a pipe. "Has a unicorn on the side."

Sure enough, they finally spied the teal tent with its white unicorn head emblem. Anika's steps quickened, and both Gareth and Leo increased their speed to keep up.

She made a beeline for the entrance, and a guard standing in front turned toward them, his hand going to his sword.

"Hold—Lady Anika?" The man gaped at them. "And young Master Leo! Is it really you?"

"Yes. Is my father inside?"

Before the guard could answer, the tent flap was swept aside and Lord Raylor emerged, his expression strained as he glanced around wildly until he saw his children.

"Anika! Leo!" Raylor charged forward, and Gareth stepped aside to give them space. Their father swept his children into his arms, smooshing them. Leo's teary face buried into his father's shoulder, and Anika's fist tightened on the fabric of his surcoat.

"My children," Raylor cried. "I'm so sorry. I'm so, so sorry." He pulled back, looking over them. "You're both all right? You're not hurt?" He placed a hand on Leo's cheek. "I'm so happy to see you, son."

Leo swiped the back of his hand over his eyes and grinned. "I missed you all so much."

Raylor looked to Anika. "I'm sorry I asked you to stay behind, even for a moment. You brought back your brother. Well done."

"Thank you, Father."

Gareth wondered if his own father would be so happy to see him—or ever apologize for doubting him.

"Come inside, come." Raylor grabbed his children's wrists and dragged them toward the tent.

"Sir Gareth is with us." Anika pointed toward him with her free hand, and Gareth inclined his head.

After a momentary frown, Raylor nodded. "Come along as well."

Once they were inside, Raylor urged them to sit on the cushions on the floor. Conrad had wandered off with some other lord's sons, he explained, but should be back later. He pulled out honey bread rolls for them, shoving them into their hands, including Gareth's, and set about pouring a cup of mead for each of them, then sat as well.

"I am so relieved to see you, Leo, whole and well! Both of you, but when we suddenly remembered Leo again, we wondered about the curse and if the next time we saw you, you would still be a fox. How did it occur?"

Leo stared down at his cup while Anika's face drained of color. Gareth grimaced and fiddled with the fringe on his cushion. Raylor looked between them with alarm.

"Is all well? Is Leo not permanently cured?"

"No, I am. I'm pretty sure." Leo's mouth twisted to the side. "The witch broke the spell."

"After nearly killing him," Gareth muttered.

Lord Raylor nearly dropped his mead. "What?" His gaze darted over his son again, searching for any sign of injury.

"I'm fine now." Leo shrugged, although it was jerky.

If Gareth wished he could scrub away the memory of Leo thrashing in that submerged sack, he couldn't imagine how horrifying the memory must be for his friend.

"More pressingly," Leo said, "what's going on here?"

"Did Callista succeed?" Anika retrieved the folded parchment from the pouch on her belt. "We found the Fae Blessing and Curse of the Faines. It seems likely the prophecy was fulfilled."

Raylor's lips pursed as he accepted the parchment. "It must have been. Two and a half days ago, there was a fire and an earthquake in Highrook Castle. Sections of the palace collapsed. The king, queen, the princes and their wives and children all perished."

The pronouncement hung heavily in the air. Gareth's shoulders slumped. As flattering as it was to be fated and play a role in something historical…he wished he hadn't.

"How many are dead?" he asked quietly.

Raylor cast him a quick glance as he unfolded the parchment. "By some miracle, very few servants or guards died, although many sustained injuries and last I heard, a couple are missing and presumed dead. At around the same time, various accidents, natural disasters, and other incidents resulted in the deaths of…well, everyone legitimately bearing the Faine name." Sorrow crossed his face. "At least forty casualties, all told."

Gareth's stomach roiled. So much death and suffering, and his actions had helped it happen.

"I admit," Leo said quietly, "thinking about the effects of the fae curse being activated and actually understanding the reality are not the same."

"And the war hasn't even started yet," Anika whispered.

Her father sighed. "No. The moment the king's death was confirmed, nobles at court in Highrook sent word by messenger birds and couriers. Armies started gathering. Reportedly, Lord Ackroyd has drawn support from the poor knights who support his recent proposals to diminish inequalities between the ranks of the nobility. However, most lords and their vassals are standing behind one of two likely contestants. Baron Shafer"—Raylor's expression contorted with disgust—"who is generally volatile and power-hungry but has a keen mind for warfare, and Duke Alimer, who, thank the stars above, was unaffected, despite being a descendant of the first Faine king's daughter."

Gareth tilted his head. "In the legends, fae words can be tricky and surprisingly literal. The prophecy says *no Faine* shall sit on the throne again. They may share some blood, but he claims the house of Alimer, not Faine."

Lord Raylor nodded. "Indeed, and it's a boon for Aedyllan. Although Duke Cassius Alimer is young and unfortunately unwed, he's a good man, well-educated, compassionate yet just, honorable, and honest. Alimer lands have had the fewest issues with bandits, thanks to Duke Cassius and the captain of his guard, whom he has already named as his general. I'll gladly fight under his banner." He turned his attention to the Fae Blessing and Curse in his hands.

Gareth rubbed the pommel of his sword. Aedyllan was looking at a possible three-way war, although it didn't sound as if Lord Ackroyd would be much of a contender, so perhaps only two sides. If Duke Cassius Alimer lost, though, and Raylor was right about

Baron Shafer…things would not be improved for Aedyllan over their last king, and worse, neighboring kingdoms might be threatened. The guard set at Tremblay Barony in Eynlae might no longer be mostly a formality, but a truly necessary—and dangerous—posting.

As much as Gareth longed to stay and help Anika and her father…no, the Aedyllanians. He wanted to help the Aedyllanians put a worthy king on their throne, one who wasn't interested in conquest, but a prince shouldn't get entangled in another kingdom's war. Yes, he wanted the opportunity to fight and to prove his worth as a knight. Yet a quiet voice whispered he couldn't wash away the blood of those who had already died by taking up his sword. More importantly, he wasn't needed in Aedyllan.

He needed to warn Baron Tremblay and his father that Aedyllan was about to be unstable and possibly become aggressive, and they needed to be prepared.

He really hated being a prince sometimes.

Raylor's head jerked up as he looked from the parchment to Gareth. "I don't understand. How did the curse activate? The prophecy was not fulfilled. You live. Or did you encounter someone else?"

"Oh. That." Gareth's fingers drifted to his neck of their own accord, feeling the scar left by Anika's healing spell. He cleared his throat and shoved away the haunting memory. "I was brought back. By Tempest."

Lord Raylor blinked. "I need to hear this story in full, starting from after you left my home."

Even though they kept their story brief, by the time they finished their tale, Lord Raylor looked like he wasn't sure if he wanted to be sick, kill someone, or faint, but the love and concern with which he looked at his children planted a spark of jealousy in Gareth.

"I feel like all this"—Anika motioned vaguely around them, indicating the entire encampment—"is partly my fault. Our fault."

Her father vehemently shook his head. "At worst, you were used against your will by Callista. I suspect this"—he waved the parchment bearing the Blessing and Curse—"was ready to happen with or without you specifically. This even says, 'Beware, for should your line no longer be of noble heart.' It was the Faines' wickedness that truly caused this, although I'm surprised the prophecy didn't occur years ago."

Raylor lowered his head. "I regret how much bloodshed this method has already caused and will yet cause. But I struggle to regret that the Faines' uncontested rule is at an end. The Faines once did great things for Aedyllan, but King Silas was self-serving and no longer worthy of receiving the benefits of the blessing."

How complicated life was outside of his books of legends, Gareth reflected glumly. Still, he didn't like knowing that forty people might still be alive if he hadn't surrendered to Callista. Possibly not *all* of them were as guilty as Silas Faine. At the same time, Anika and Leo *were* alive, and that was not insignificant. Not to him.

"I'd like to join Duke Alimer's forces." Anika lifted her chin, but Gareth could see the haunted look in her hazel eyes. She was as uncertain of the right thing to do as he was, which was strangely comforting.

"You barely know who you're fighting for," Leo muttered.

"Father believes he'd be a good ruler, and he certainly sounds better than Baron Shafer. I want to help Aedyllan, Father."

Lord Raylor slumped and gave a weary shake of his head. "You want to atone for what you are incorrectly taking responsibility for," he said gently. "You did not ask a fae woman for an impossible and irresponsible gift, like your line always holding power. You did not grant that blessing nor bestow the counterbalancing curse. Forcing the prophecy was not your doing. And you did not cause this division among our people that is preventing Duke Alimer—or anyone else—from peacefully ascending the throne."

"Still," Anika said, her voice strong. "I can fight."

"I know you can." Pain flashed across her father's face. "So don't take this as me doubting your abilities or resolve, my fierce daughter. You have enough demons from the things you've already endured. War is horrifying, Anika, and I would spare you more nightmares. Not to mention that should you be taken as a prisoner of war…you may be treated worse for your gender."

Raylor motioned to Leo. "The battlefield is also no place for your brother, and I suspect he needs you right now more than the duke needs one more knight."

Gareth shifted "I—"

"Don't even suggest it," Leo interrupted. "If you join the battle and any of those ambassadors or visiting lords that you mentioned recognize you, you will spark an inter-kingdom incident when someone concludes that Eynlae has officially backed Duke Alimer."

Gareth started to protest that wasn't what he was going to say, but Lord Raylor spoke first.

"I fail to see how a single Eynlaean knight could—"

"Father, Prince Gareth Argent." Leo waved between them, more of a careless flicking of his hand. "Prince Gareth, my father, Lord Braden Raylor."

Somehow, despite tales of killing gryphons and bandits, of curses and resurrection and talking unicorns, *that* seemed to have truly shocked Lord Raylor. He turned toward Gareth, his jaw falling open.

"Why are you here?" His eyes narrowed. "Are you spying—"

"No." Gareth groaned. "I really was serving as a knight at Tremblay Barony and entered Aedyllan to retrieve the firebird. I'm here as a mere knight."

"Ah." Lord Raylor's lips thinned. "But Leo is right. If anyone else learns of this, it may not be interpreted that way."

Gareth nodded wearily. "I understand. I *was* going to say I already decided I have to return home and warn my father to be alert in case…" He trailed off, not wanting to say *in case you lose.*

But Raylor clearly understood what he'd left unsaid, because he shifted uncomfortably. "I suppose it would be good for your kingdom to be aware. King Weston will not…try to take advantage of the situation?"

"No." Gareth shook his head emphatically. "He sacrificed his only daughter to avert a war. He won't seek a different conflict."

"Good." Raylor fixed his gaze on Gareth with startling intensity. "Take my twins with you."

"What?" Leo and Anika said simultaneously.

"Please, Prince Gareth. If you take them out of Aedyllan and give me your word as prince that you will protect and care for them, I will know they are out of harm's way. Once things have settled, I can send word that it is safe to return."

Take Anika to Eynlae? The idea sent a thrill through him.

"I…" He looked over at the twins. Leo appeared thoughtful, but Anika's expression was unreadable. "I won't ask them to accompany me if that is not their wish. If Lady Anika wishes to fight for her people, I won't attempt to dissuade her. Nor will I force Leo to leave."

"I'll go," Leo piped up. "No forcing necessary."

"Good." Raylor's posture eased. "Anika, the choice is yours. I want you far from this conflict, and I believe you will be of more use to your brother than here. You don't appear to have enjoyed your fight with those bandits, and war will be worse. But whatever you choose, to stay or to go…" He hesitated. "I will respect and support your decision."

Anika flushed. "I…can I think about it?"

"We don't have time for deliberation. Once Duke Alimer's main forces join us, we will be moving to engage Shafer's army within days. If one or both of you are leaving, I'd rather you leave at once." Her father frowned. "I'd also like the prince's word on the matter, and if you wait to decide, I might not have time to secure a promise from him."

"I will return to Eynlae, one way or the other." Gareth rubbed his thumb over the edge of his opposite vambrace, then met Raylor's eyes. "Should just Leo or Leo and Anika accompany me, I, Prince Gareth Argent of Eynlae, promise on my honor that they shall be under my protection, and I will take responsibility for their wellbeing while they remain in Eynlae."

Lord Raylor nodded. "Good enough. As a token of my gratitude, you may take Tempest with you. For now, you all should leave this camp. Anika and Leo because I don't want you getting caught up in this should we receive orders to move sooner than expected. Gareth because it's best if Eynlaean royalty doesn't spend time in the army's encampment."

Gareth agreed that was wise, but they had another problem. "What about the witch?"

"Oh." Raylor thrummed his fingers against his knee. "I'm unsure who would have the authority and time to sentence her… A trial is hardly the most pressing concern with a battle approaching. There's a reason courts are usually delayed during conflicts and there are predetermined punishments in place for incidents with soldiers. We can't worry about keeping her prisoner while we fight a war, but Duke Alimer ordering her execution without a trial is too reminiscent of the Faines. And it would be ridiculous for you to take her to Eynlae."

Gareth nodded. He refused to travel with Callista any further than necessary, and he preferred to get her far away from Leo and Anika. Surely there was *someone* available with the authority to hear their testimony and order her execution.

After a long, silent deliberation, Lord Raylor sighed and shook his head. "Do with her as you deem fit. Prince Gareth is actually the highest ranking noble in Aedyllan at the moment, and among us he is the most qualified and has the most authority for passing judgments."

Gareth barely suppressed a flinch. Lord Raylor's assumption made sense, but he didn't have any training in judicial proceedings—although some lessons he'd evaded or daydreamed through had likely touched on the matter. He'd never felt so guilty for evading his studies.

"Uh, I…" He floundered for something to say without admitting his self-imposed lack of education. "What if someone learns an Eynlaean royal took justice into his own hands in Aedyllan?"

"It is unlikely anyone will know," Raylor said. "If you decide she should be executed and somehow it is discovered, we can claim she attacked you and you had no choice."

"You mean, if *we* kill her?" Leo asked incredulously.

Raylor raised an eyebrow. "Suddenly less keen on capital punishment?"

Just then, the tent flap opened, and Conrad Raylor hurried in. "Fath—Anika? Leo!" He dove to his knees so he could drag his younger brother into a tight embrace. "Leo! You're—you're you! And you're here! You're *here*?! Leo, you idiot; an army is no place for a scholar—"

"I'm well aware, Conrad! I'm not here on purpose." Leo shoved his brother off of him and straightened his clothing as if he were indignant, but he wore a broad smile. "It's good to see you. Glad you missed me after you remembered me."

It lifted Gareth's spirits to see Leo happy with his family instead of crushed and lonely.

Conrad swiveled to face their father. "You're sending them away, right—oh, wait!" He scrambled to his feet. "General Vallyn Drake has arrived ahead of Duke Alimer. He called a meeting to get an idea of our forces and any information the lords have."

Lord Raylor nodded and stood. "Anika, Leo, be safe." He looked at Anika. "I hope you will go with them, but I understand if you insist on doing your duty as a knight. However, I think you may live to do far more good as a knight over a longer lifetime if you go to Eynlae."

"Eynlae?" Conrad glanced around the group. "They can't just run off to—"

"Sir Gareth has powerful connections in Eynlae," Lord Raylor said, his level gaze falling on Gareth. "And he has sworn to protect them if they accompany him home."

Leo rose to his feet and hugged his father. "You be safe, too." He looked at Conrad. "Both of you. I want to see you both when I return from Eynlae."

Conrad's too-wide smile seemed forced. "Obviously. Someone has to take over Raylor Estate after you two run off to fight monsters and read dusty old books."

Leo rolled his eyes as he pulled away from his father.

Anika rose to her feet more slowly, her expression troubled.

"Go with your twin," Raylor said as he wrapped Anika in a tight embrace. "Keep taking care of him."

She squeezed her eyes shut. "I haven't done a good job of that."

"I think the fault lies more with fate than you, dear daughter." Raylor pulled back, gripping her upper arms as he looked into her eyes. "What did your tutors tell you about retreat?"

"It is not always cowardice," Anika mumbled. "I'm still thinking about it. But in case I don't see you again until after things have settled, be safe and careful."

"We will." Raylor brushed a hand over the side of her head, then strode out of the tent.

After a moment's hesitation, Gareth ducked out after him. "Lord Raylor!"

The older man turned back. "Yes?"

Gareth stood close, and with a glance back to ensure Anika hadn't yet left the tent, he lowered his voice. "In case she does agree to accompany me…I'd like to ask for your permission to court Anika."

Raylor's eyes widened. "Erm…"

"To be clear, I'd *never* force myself on her, and I would behave chivalrously toward her. It would only be if she agrees, and I'll honor my vow to protect them both regardless of her answer. But if I spend any more time with her, I know I'll ask her to court me." He rubbed the back of his neck. "Leo approves."

The wrinkle between Raylor's eyebrows disappeared. "Very well. You have my blessing to *court* her only. Now, I must be going." He spun on his heel and strode away.

As Gareth turned back to the tent, Leo and Anika emerged.

"We were talking to Conrad," she said.

"He gave us some coin to purchase supplies," Leo added, tossing a small, jingling sack.

Anika peered at Gareth curiously. "Why'd you run out?"

A bit of a smile tugged at his lips as his heart swelled. Even more than before, he hoped Anika would agree to accompany them. "Just a quick question for your father."

Once they were out of the encampment, as they walked through the trees and the growing darkness back to where they'd left their mounts and the firebird—and Callista—Gareth looked over at Leo. "Why'd you agree so quickly to come with me to Eynlae?"

"To have access to your royal library, obviously." Leo gave him a saucy grin. "What, you didn't think it was because I enjoy your company so much, did you?" He held up a hand, palm down, near his head. "The ranking is royal library"—he moved his hand down to shoulder height—"a desire to get away from any more bloodshed and death"—again he moved his hand down to rib height—"respecting my father's wishes"—he lowered his hand to near his thigh—"and spending more time with my new friend."

Gareth opened his mouth to make a sarcastic remark back, then blinked. "Wait, we're truly friends now?"

Leo made a face. "If everything we've been through and the fact you saved my life twice doesn't make us friends, I'm very concerned about your standards of friendship."

With a laugh, Gareth threw his arm around Leo and pulled him down so he could knuckle his hair. "At *least* friends. Best friends! Not sure I've ever had a best friend, other than Raelyn. Complexities of being a prince."

"Ugh." Leo shoved him aside and attempted to tame the mess Gareth had made of his hair. "Maybe I'll take it back, you boisterous suit of armor."

"Too late!" He laughed at the unconvincing snarl Leo sent his way, then looked past him at Anika. She wasn't paying much attention to them, her forehead deeply furrowed as she stared at the ground ahead of her feet.

"I don't expect royal libraries are enticing to you, Anika?"

"Hm? Sorry. I wasn't listening." She bit her lower lip. "I was just…" A sigh heaved her chest. "I don't know what to do. So much death and turmoil, and I can't decide if we carry any blame."

Leo shook his head. "Father is right. We didn't cause any of this."

Gareth was still sorting through his own confused feelings on the subject, but he knew one thing. "But Callista did. On purpose.

And now we have to decide what to do with her."

They all fell silent.

It rankled. The complexity, that it fell on them, and that Gareth had neglected his princely training only for it to actually become relevant. And Lord Raylor's words echoed in his mind.

"King Silas was self-serving and no longer worthy of receiving the benefits of the blessing."

Did that mean Callista had done the right thing? How could all the terrible things she'd done be the right thing?

There was something else that still bothered him. Before they made any decisions, he had a question for Callista, and this time, he wanted an answer.

52

ell?" Callista asked, her eagerness a marked contrast to their morbidly serious expressions as they approached. "What is the news? Has the king fallen?"

The prince scowled at her, but she was too impatient for news to care about his judgment. "Yes," he said flatly. "Along with many others. Some bearing the Faine name, and a few servants or guards caught in the fallout. Forty people are dead, and more will die in the fighting that is approaching. Are you happy?"

Callista sank to the forest floor, so unburdened she felt only a distant sorrow for the innocent lives lost. King Silas had cost many innocents their lives over the years of his reign, and while it hurt to know more people may have lost innocent family members in the fallout, in the end, it was still the Faines' fault. Things wouldn't have ended this way if the kings had been noble.

All that mattered to her in that moment was that her promise had been kept—her family and friends were avenged. The Faines had received justice for their misdeeds and wouldn't hurt anyone else. If her captors killed her now, she could face Royce in the afterlife knowing that she had not failed him. A tear slipped down her cheek as a wobbly smile pulled at her lips.

"You are happy." Gareth didn't sound as disgusted as she

would have expected. "Why? Why did you do all of this? What made the curses and the murder and the pain you put us all through, all of the death and bloodshed you have caused, what made it worth it?" He knelt before her, his gaze burning into her. "What promise did you make?"

Callista bent her head. She owed this royal nothing.

After several heartbeats, Gareth gave a frustrated growl and stood. "You see! Witches are simply evil, Leo. She probably *wanted* to cause all this violence for the fun of it—"

"I wanted justice!" She jerked her head up. Let them judge her for her methods, but she would not sit quietly while some spoiled prince misjudged her reasons. "I wanted Silas Faine to pay for all of the hurt he and his family have caused. I wanted him to burn, like the people who died inside the castle his grandfather burned. I wanted to see the ridiculous fae magic that protected that despicable family end before anyone else lost people they loved to the Faines' callous selfishness!"

Gareth and the twins were silent for several long moments. Finally, it was Anika who spoke, her voice gentle.

"Who did you lose?"

"Everyone," Callista muttered. She drew her knees up to her chest and wrapped her arms around them, wincing a little when the ropes binding her wrists bit into her skin. "You want to know my tale of tragedy and suffering? Fine. Where shall I start? With a good friend I met at the Royal University, the daughter of a lesser noble, who was assaulted by one of the princes and the king had it covered up? She left the University, her heart and mind too wounded to continue facing the whispers. Those monsters ruined her life.

"Or maybe a friend of one of my brothers, who was mugged on the road after the king withdrew all of the highway guards, and died in agony from his wounds?

"Perhaps I should tell you about my mother, who worked as a servant in the castle and was forced to nurse the younger prince because the queen couldn't be bothered? Yet when she fell ill, not one member of the Faine family cared. They wouldn't *lend* us money for her treatment, nor to bury her when she died. Shall I tell you how the only reason I didn't end up as a maid in the palace like my mother was because I had enough magic that not only was I accepted into the Enchanters College, I was granted a full scholarship?"

Now that she'd started speaking, her wrath flowed out of her. She had undammed the festering wound in her heart, in her very soul, and even if they refused to understand, someone else in this fae-cursed world would know her pain.

"I can tell you about my father and brothers, who worked as royal guards. When that man tried to kill the king by burning down that inn, Silas Faine, who deserved to die, escaped, but my father and one of my brothers died! They burned alive for his sins!" She was crying now, but she didn't stop. She couldn't stop.

"And what did the king do? *Nothing.* He did nothing to honor them and didn't so much as offer condolences to me or my other brother. My brother had been on duty at the castle and watched the king and his retinue return without his father and brother. Silas Faine illegally seized lands and denied his subjects' complaints, so he was the target of a provoked attack for his misdeeds, but who suffered? Who paid the price? *My* family!"

Callista gulped down the sobs making her tremble and turned her teary, furious gaze on Prince Gareth. "So when my brother begged me to use my magic to break into the palace vault to steal the Fae Blessing and Curse of Mortimer Faine that was rumored to be kept there so we could force the reckoning the entire kingdom had been denied, I agreed. His fellow guards put an arrow through my brother's abdomen. He was bleeding out while I was too drained of magic to heal him, so when he begged me to swear to make the prophecy happen and end the Faines' blessing, I promised him I would."

She looked away. "We hadn't read it yet. I didn't know what it said. I didn't know that it would demand I cross lines I never thought I would cross and break oaths that will prevent me from ever setting foot in the Enchanters College again. But I'd promised Royce I would avenge our family and friends and him, and while I regret the methods I was forced to employ, I won't apologize for it. Silas and his wretched sons are dead, no longer protected from the consequences of their actions by a blessing they did nothing to deserve. Good riddance and may Aedyllan fare better without their taint."

Her ranting exhausted, Callista fell silent. The pale moonlight and stars and the strange, dim glow of the unicorn's golden horn gave the surrounding forest an eerie glow. She awkwardly dried her face with her bound hands. Even though she kept her gaze on the silver-limned trees, she felt her captors' stares.

The stillness dragged on until she couldn't take it anymore.

"If you are going to execute me, please get it over with. I don't regret enacting the prophecy and won't apologize for the curse's effects if that's what you're waiting for. I am sorry for how I used you to achieve it, but I won't ask for your forgiveness—I don't deserve it. I won't beg for my life. I have nothing and no one left in this world. No one who will miss me or who I need to stay for. Just the weight of missing everyone I've ever loved, and the relief of knowing I secured justice for them in the end, even if I polluted myself in the process."

Callista rested her forehead on her knees, utterly drained—emotionally, if not physically or magically. They'd fed her enough she could break the ropes binding her, knock down her captors, and flee with the prince's warhorse, but the twins and the prince didn't deserve that. She, on the other hand, deserved whatever they wanted to do to her. Closing her eyes, she waited for them to deliver their judgment.

53

*H*orror grew in Gareth's chest with every word Callista spoke. Horror and rage—but not toward her. Toward the royal family of Aedyllan. Witch she might be, a villain who had caused so much suffering…but the injustice and loss she had endured tore at his heart.

Kings were supposed to espouse justice and protect and serve their subjects. They held incredible power, and with that power, they were to be the leader of armies to defend their kingdom and the seat of law to see that the wicked were punished and victims were granted justice. Princes were as well.

The thought hit him like a slap.

Princes held power, too. Even non-heir princes had a duty to their subjects and the ability to do great good…or great harm, as the Faine princes had done. Ashamed, Gareth realized he'd never taken that duty or ability seriously. He'd been so focused on his dreams of knighthood that he hadn't believed his father and tutors when they suggested he could do good as a prince. If only he'd listened instead of always running off to read tales of sword-swinging heroes. Of course, he wouldn't be in Aedyllan at all if he hadn't filled his days with training and his mind with tales of adventure and chivalry.

Meanwhile, the Faine princes had not merely neglected their power as royals. The entire Faine royal family had selfishly and willfully abused their power to benefit themselves without a care for the suffering they left in their wake. It was a perversion of justice.

As Gareth watched Callista curl in on herself, her knees tucked up to her chest and her arms—still tied at the wrists—hugging her legs, she looked so thin and frail. Not at all like the powerful enchantress he knew her to be, but like everything she had experienced had settled on her bony shoulders like a weight she couldn't escape.

Her words still rang in his ears, burned forever into his mind. She had witnessed so much suffering and survived so much loss. He could not imagine the depth of her sorrow. He'd nearly broken when Raelyn went missing. If he'd watched Raelyn die before his eyes…

Callista had done terrible, harmful things that had painful consequences for all of them. He wouldn't deny that. But she showed remorse and an understanding of right and wrong that told him she wasn't beyond redemption.

More than that, he understood.

He hated King Silas for allowing the pain and injustice that had driven Callista to do the things she'd done. To sacrifice a scholarship and promising career at the Enchanters College. To isolate herself in a ruined castle while she mourned the loss of her family alone. To curse and kidnap and murder, even though he believed she truly did wish there had been another way, because she had no other recourse for restitution.

If King Silas wasn't already dead, Gareth would have been tempted to kill the man himself.

Leo was right. Witches weren't *always* evil.

The realization shook Gareth to his core.

Maybe Leo was right about many things.

Maybe Raelyn had made the choices she had in Rethalyon

because she'd mastered a lesson Gareth hadn't yet learned—that the duty of a prince or princess was to seek the greatest good. Not the perfect good. Not the greatest good only for themselves. But the greatest achievable good for the greatest number of innocent people. The good that did the least harm.

Raelyn had spoken in Alexander's defense despite the risks and also been willing to do her duty to prevent a war. In his narrow-minded focus on personal wrongs, Gareth hadn't recognized her reluctant compromise as selfless courage.

Rather like the desire to protect his friends had led Gareth to surrender his life.

Maybe, in his own way, Father had also been courageous when he agreed to betroth his infant daughter to an unknown child prince to secure a treaty that would benefit the kingdom. Maybe when Father had ended the search for Raelyn and sought another way to fulfill the treaty, he'd been doing what he thought was best for all of Eynlae rather than for himself. Perhaps Father really *had* wanted to keep Gareth safe when he forced him to stop searching, even if it had felt like giving up.

Sometimes life was messy and didn't have any good answers, and people did the best they could, and sometimes that meant sacrifices and difficult choices.

The desire to hasten back home thrummed through him. He needed to tell Father that while he might not completely agree with him, he understood.

And finally, as dismaying as it was to admit, Gareth had treated Tristan with contempt beyond what he deserved. He had seen only Tristan's wrongs and had closed his eyes and ears to anything else. He'd scoffed at the notion that Tristan had suffered, too. When Tristan had apologized, Gareth had dismissed Tristan's attempts to improve and overcome the lies he'd internalized as insufficient.

He returned his thoughts to the present.

Gareth wasn't certain he forgave Callista, exactly. But he understood her now, and if he knew anything, it was that she had already suffered enough. Her vengeance was accomplished, the people responsible for so much of her grief were dead and gone. Perhaps she deserved the chance to see who she was now that she was free of the shackles of injustice.

After all, not all witches were *evil*.

"Now you see, princeling." Tempest's voice in his mind sounded pleased. *"Now you understand the value of not only justice, but also of compassion. Only when you pair your passion for justice and righteousness with a heart of mercy and empathy will you be a knight and prince worthy of the title of hero."*

Gareth startled. *You can hear my thoughts?*

"When I choose to listen." The unicorn turned her head toward Callista's hunched form. *"There is good in her yet. I can sense it. She is not as corrupted as even she believes herself to be."*

"If we let you go," Gareth began, but his voice came out rough and like it was on the verge of breaking. He swallowed. "If we let you go, will you swear to never curse, kidnap, steal from, murder, or otherwise harm an innocent person or creature again?"

Leo and Anika spun toward him, gaping, but he ignored them.

Callista raised her head and searched his face. "What?"

"If we agree to let you go free," Gareth said, slower, "will you give your word that you will turn away from dark spells and not cause harm? Will you swear to only use your magic and your actions to help people?"

"Yes. Yes!" She scrambled to her feet, her jaw quavering. "I never wanted to use witchcraft or hurt or kill anyone who didn't deserve it. I'll gladly swear—no, I'll use dark magic one last time to do a binding spell—"

"No, thank you." Gareth held up his hands as he drew back

involuntarily. "I'd rather never feel that again."

"It also seems to me that using dark magic to swear you won't perform dark magic is incongruous," Leo said.

Callista shifted. "Then I simply give my word. I won't cast curses or use my magic to harm any innocents and won't kidnap, murder, or otherwise harm without my magic, either."

"Then there's only one thing left." Gareth turned to Anika and Leo. "She hurt you both. I won't release her if you don't both agree."

"I agree," Tempest said.

Gareth huffed. "Tempest agrees. I wasn't aware she had a vote."

"Of course I have a vote. I'm a powerful magical creature who is wiser than all of you combined and knows even more." Tempest tossed her head. *"Tell them what I said."*

"Apparently she gets a vote because she's magically wise," Gareth said drily.

"Not that part! About Callista!"

"How was I supposed to know that's what you meant?" He sent her an annoyed side-eye. "Tempest also says there's still good in Callista. That she isn't as corrupted as she believes herself to be."

Callista stared at the unicorn, and she looked like she might start crying again.

"I agree," Leo said easily, as if it weren't a staggering declaration to pardon the person who had cursed and nearly killed him. "I support what she was trying to accomplish, and the method it took wasn't her idea or her fault. I'm probably going to have nightmares about drowning for the rest of my life"—Callista flinched—"so I can't say that excuses her. But I also don't think she deserves any punishment beyond what she has already suffered."

Anika took a long, probing look at Gareth and Leo before speaking. "I was already trying to decide if I could suggest letting her go. She hurt both of you far worse than she hurt me. If you both can agree to release her…I also agree.”

A small sigh came from Callista, and she seemed to relax, as if a little of that invisible weight had slipped from her back. “Thank you for your mercy.” A slight quiver marked her words as she bowed low over her tied hands.

Drawing her dagger, Anika hurried forward. She sliced off the ropes. “Do you want to take any food?”

Callista lightly rubbed her freed wrists. “No, thank you. I couldn’t bear to take anything more from you.” She turned to go, and Gareth cleared his throat.

“Um…” He glanced around the dark forest. “You don’t *have* to go right this moment. You could leave in the morning when it’s light.”

She hesitated and glanced between them. “You…don’t mind me being around you? You aren’t worried?”

“We’re letting you go free on the presupposition that you will keep your oath.” Leo scowled. “If we can’t trust you to sleep the night in our vicinity without putting a knife through our chests or cursing us, then we shouldn’t release you. Either you intend to keep your word and we trust you, or you don’t and we do not. As you have made your promise and we have agreed to trust that you will keep it, there should be no harm in allowing you to share our fire for one final night. Don’t you agree?”

“Oh. I…yes.”

Gareth barely stifled a smirk. It was satisfying to see someone else bear the brunt of one of Leo’s logic tirades.

That settled, they went about gathering firewood and pulling out food for a late supper from their dwindling supplies. Callista lit the fire for them, and then tried to refuse the offered food, but after a stern look from Anika, she accepted her serving—and wolfed it down like she was half-starved. Eventually, Gareth, Anika, and Leo all settled in fairly close together, and Callista curled up on the opposite side of the fire.

When Gareth awoke to the golden light of early dawn glistening on the dew-covered forest, the enchantress was already gone.

It surprised him to realize, but he found that wherever she ended up, he wished her well—and hoped she would find some rest for her heavy heart.

54

When Gareth returned to their camp after relieving himself, Anika and Leo were awake and helping themselves to breakfast—although, by Anika's bleary eyes, *awake* might be generous.

"Didn't sleep well?" Gareth asked as he took some dried fruit and nuts for himself.

Anika blinked at him, as if it took her a moment to comprehend what he'd said. "Sorry." She shook her head. "Clearly, no."

"Sorry to hear that."

The firebird gave a sad chirrup as Gareth sat down not far from its cage. With a sigh, he sacrificed more of his dried fruit and meat to the troublesome thing, and it happily beat its wings in a shower of harmless sparks before digging in.

Anika plucked a blade of grass and spun it between her fingers. "I had nightmares."

"Were they about living off of nuts and dried fruit for all of eternity?" Leo asked, his nose wrinkling. "Because I had that one."

Gareth sent a chastising look Leo's way. A part of him still found it strange to look in the direction of Leo's voice and see an entire *person* with red hair and freckles like Anika's. Although, of course, Leo didn't have the scars his sister did, and he had paler skin and far fewer freckles.

"Do you want to talk about it?" Gareth asked.

Her throat bobbed. "Leo dying. You dying. Being on a battlefield and everyone around me is dying, but I can't move or do anything to stop it. Then this hulking knight swings toward me, and I still can't move to lift my sword or step back or anything."

She shuddered, and Gareth wished he'd sat down closer to her. Would it be strange if he moved over next to her, so he could put a comforting hand on her shoulder or something? Would that even help?

Leo narrowed his eyes at a dried cranberry pinched between his fingers. "I keep waking up feeling like my lungs are filling with water." He tossed the cranberry into his mouth like he was suspicious it might be poisoned but had no choice. "Please come with us, Anika." His voice was smaller and quieter than Gareth had ever heard from him before. "I…I don't want to be without you."

Anika crossed her arms over her stomach and rubbed her hands over her upper arms. "Honestly, it…sounds tempting. I'm not ready to leave you after almost losing you so many times, and I would like to see Eynlae." She lowered her head. "But I feel like a coward."

Sucking up his pride, Gareth dusted off his hands, stood, and moved to sit next to her. He didn't touch her yet, afraid of making her more uncomfortable rather than putting her at ease, but he didn't want to have to raise his voice to talk to her.

"You've said several times you don't want to fight your fellow Aedyllanians." He dared to lean a little closer. "It won't be like those bandits, where one opponent falls and you're done fighting and know the man you killed was a criminal who attacked you first. I don't think wanting to avoid a war against your own neighbors or supporting your brother when he needs you makes you a coward."

And two bodies were bad enough. Gareth's stomach felt

uneasy at the thought of a battlefield littered with the fallen. But he didn't voice that thought.

"Maybe that's what your dream was trying to tell you," Leo said. "That you'll struggle to raise your sword against people you know aren't truly your enemy. Most of the men you'd face will be fighting simply because they owe fealty to the wrong lord, and because a few noblemen were too stubborn to decide who should rule without slaughtering each other's subjects. Additionally, as happens on occasion, I agree with Gareth. Not wanting to partake in needless bloodshed doesn't make you a coward. Perhaps it means you're wise enough to know when a conflict isn't worth dirtying your hands over."

"You *do* always find a way to disagree or agree in the most long-winded fashion," Gareth teased.

Leo stuck his tongue out, and Gareth was so startled to find he did that even in human form that he barked a very undignified, rather high-pitched laugh, which seemed to amuse Leo.

"It'd also give us more time for that rematch," Gareth said, keeping his tone casual. "Or several rematches. While Leo buries himself in the royal library, Sir Christopher would love to compare notes on Eynlaean and Aedyllanian training styles and fighting techniques, I'm sure. And we could have some private training sessions."

Leo gave Gareth a flat look and then melodramatically rolled his eyes.

Blessedly, Anika had turned to look at Gareth and wasn't paying attention to her brother. "That does sound agreeable. I wouldn't mind spending more time with you."

"Would you court me?" Oh, wolf's teeth, had he just blabbed that? Just like that? When she hadn't officially agreed to come yet and he didn't even know if she was interested in a relationship? His entire face burned, and he quickly looked away from her in a panic.

"That is—you don't have to," he rushed to say. "It's not a condition or anything; we can still be friends, just friends—I like you as a friend; of course I like you as a friend. I also like you maybe as more than a friend, and well, Leo said he'd be fine with it, and I didn't even bring it up to him. Your father, too, although I did ask him. You don't have to answer right now. Or ever…oh why am I still talking!" He clutched his hands to the sides of his head and stared at the charred remains of the fire, wondering exactly when he'd lost his mind and why he had neglected to practice talking to girls other than Raelyn.

A chuckle turned into a loud laugh until Leo was wheezing for air between laughter that shook his entire body.

Gareth ducked down further. "It's not that funny," he muttered under his breath.

"Leo, stop acting like a wild animal," Anika chided. "You're human now."

"Laughter is very human," Leo said around a few lingering giggles.

"Gareth?" Anika asked.

A soft touch on his shoulder prompted Gareth to drop his hands from his head. With a deep, fortifying breath, he looked over at her and resisted the urge to cringe at his humiliating rambling.

"You…want to court me?"

He had to swallow before he could get his tongue to work. "I do. I know it hasn't been long, but I'm not asking you to marry me. Yet. I just…I'd like to court you. If you're interested in courting me; I mean, obviously not if you're not interested, that'd be—" He cut off with a groan. *Get it together, Gareth!*

An amused smile lightened Anika's expression and set her eyes dancing. "I'm interested," she murmured. "You even asked my father?"

He scratched the back of his head as his shoulders inched up toward his ears. "It seemed proper."

Her pleased smile wavered. "What about…your father?" This time, she looked away. "I'm…probably not really an appropriate bride for a—"

"You're the most appropriate!" Gareth frowned, trying to determine how to salvage that word choice.

Leo snorted. "You're good at this."

"Shut up," Gareth grumbled. "That is—I never thought much about marriage, partly because I didn't think I'd ever meet someone who understands me and who could truly be my equal partner in everything I want to do. Then I met you. All I'm asking is for the chance to court you and find out if I'm right. Let me worry about my father."

Slowly, Anika turned back to him, her glittering hazel eyes lifting to meet his. "I wasn't ever particularly interested in courting or marriage, either. I doubted I'd find a man who sees me as *both* a woman and a knight. And then…I met you. But you're a prince, and so far above my station—"

"That's ridiculous." He lifted a hand to her face and ran his thumb over her cheekbone, scarcely noticing the bumps of the scars as he gazed into her eyes. His voice dropped. "You're amazing, Anika. Everything about you is amazing, and you deserve all of Miraveld. If anything, I'm not good enough for you."

Another snort from Leo. "Obviously."

Gareth ignored him. "I won't ask anything of you that you don't want to give…" His gaze dropped to her lips without conscious thought. "But I'd be honored to court you, Lady Anika Raylor, Knight of Aedyllan."

She leaned toward his mouth, her pale eyelashes fluttering as her eyes drifted closed. He let his own eyes close—

"*Please* for the love of Miraveld don't kiss my sister in front of me!" Leo protested. Loudly.

Gareth was tempted to continue ignoring him, but Anika pulled back, and his hand fell from her cheek. Sighing, he opened his eyes.

Anika blushed as she angled away from him. "I don't really want my first kiss to be in front of my brother, either, honestly."

"First kiss?" Gareth nearly crumpled with relief. "Oh, thank the stars. I was worried it'd be obvious I don't know what I'm doing."

"If your declaration of intentions was any indication," Leo said, "it's *very* obvious."

Casting a glare Leo's way, Gareth replied, "It annoys me it no longer makes sense to threaten to turn you into a fur coat."

Leo pressed a hand to his chest in a way that was oddly reminiscent of how he would do the same thing as a fox. "To say such things after I almost *died*. I never would have guessed princes have such terrible manners."

"Almost? How tragic! I *did* die, but you don't see me mentioning it every hour, fluff-brains. Although I really need new insults for you now that you aren't a ball of fur." Gareth turned his attention back to Anika. "Can we, um…maybe forget about this conversation? Give me another chance later to do it better?"

She lifted an eyebrow. "I'd have to agree to go with you to Eynlae for that."

He fumbled, at a loss. Was she not going?

As if taking pity on him, she smiled. "We should pack up and head for Eynlae."

Gareth's heart swelled with the implicit promise in those words. "We should, yes."

There was something supremely satisfying about the looks on everyone's faces—the other knights, servants who stopped to gawk, Captain Plinworth, and Baron Tremblay, who looked rather like a beached fish—as Gareth rode into Tremblay Castle on a golden unicorn with a beautiful, sword-bearing redhead sitting behind him. The firebird's golden cage was tied to Fury's saddlebags behind Leo, who was getting much more comfortable handling the big warhorse.

They'd ridden as quickly and ceaselessly as they could, stopping only to sleep and, briefly that morning in a small town, to buy some food. It was already well past noon, which annoyed Gareth. He wanted to get much further into Eynlae before nightfall.

Anika leapt down as he reined in Tempest, and he dismounted after her. After retrieving the cage containing the firebird from Fury's back, he approached the baron and captain.

"Your Lordship." Gareth bowed deeply. "Captain." Another, smaller bow. "I have returned successfully." Bending forward in another bow, he held forth the golden cage.

The firebird ruffled its feathers, releasing a shower of glowing sparks, and cocked its head at the baron. It released a pleased-sounding chirp.

"Ember!" Tremblay snatched away the cage while Gareth suppressed his amusement at the unimaginative name.

As Gareth straightened, Captain Plinworth gawked at him. "You actually did it, Your H—Sir Gareth. I'd thought you'd be back within a few days, so we'd begun to fear the worst, but…you did it and brought along…" His gaze flicked past Gareth. "Interesting souvenirs."

"Yes." Tremblay cleared his throat. He called another knight to take Ember to the firebird's garden, then turned back to Gareth. "I had begun to worry I might have to explain your loss to your father." He wrung his hands and glanced at the captain before rather forcefully dropping his hands to his sides and throwing back his shoulders. "Where in Miraveld did you find Ember? And…what's all of this?" He motioned toward Gareth's friends.

"I found the firebird in Aedyllan, in the possession of a witch."

Plinworth's eyes widened, and Tremblay paled.

"A—a witch?" The baron's chin quivered. "We are fortunate and grateful you are all right then, Your…Sir Gareth." Another awkward clearing of his throat. "You must have quite the tale to tell. Do come inside—"

Gareth inclined his head. "Apologies, Your Lordship. I do have urgent news to tell you, but I don't have time to tarry. I must also beg leave to carry this news to the king at once."

Alarm showed in his cousin's eyes. "Urgent news? The king?"

"King Silas Faine and the Faine line have been overthrown," Gareth said without preamble. He did not wait for the baron and captain to process their obvious shock. "When we left, armies were gathering to determine who will rule Aedyllan. I humbly suggest instructing the guards to be more vigilant in case the unrest in Aedyllan affects the border. And I request leave to take this news to my father myself, so he can consult with his advisors and prepare for the incoming change of power in Aedyllan."

"Did you get yourself involved in a coup while in Aedyllan?!"

"No," Gareth reassured the baron. Technically, he sort of had, but not in the sense Tremblay was thinking. "Rest assured my presence in Aedyllan coinciding with these events will not affect Eynlae—except that I have the good fortune of knowing what has happened, so the news will not take our king by surprise once the dust has settled."

Tremblay and Plinworth exchanged a look, then the captain nodded and turned sharply away, barking orders for the guards to gather at once.

"I certainly grant you leave to bring this troubling news to the king yourself," Tremblay said, worry etching lines into his face. "Thank you for retrieving my prized firebird." His gaze flicked to the gash in Gareth's breastplate. "Please accept my apologies if the quest put you in unnecessary peril."

Gareth shrugged, a bit of a smile quirking his mouth. "It was my duty and my honor…and possibly my destiny."

"Leo is right," Tempest's amused voice said in Gareth's mind. *"You have an ego, princeling."*

It's not an ego if I'm really part of a legend, now is it?

Tempest's reply was an audible nicker.

"If you wish to return to serve at Tremblay in the future, you are welcome," the baron said. "But I shall leave that judgment up to your father."

"Thank you, Baron Tremblay."

Gareth then asked for some supplies, which the baron was happy to provide. Within the hour, they were back on the road, although Anika was in front of Gareth this time. He preferred that, because even though their armor wasn't cuddly, he still enjoyed wrapping his arm around her waist.

It was also the closest to romantic that he could get as they hurried across Eynlae, their pace preventing him from getting a moment alone with her to give his courtship proposal a second go—or get that kiss he was longing for.

At last, the Eynlaean royal castle appeared in the distance, its wall and crenellated turrets towering over the rolling green fields. The mountains that ran along the border between Eynlae and Rethalyon were blue bumps on the horizon beyond the castle.

Home. Unexpected warmth flooded Gareth, along with a rising mixture of nerves and impatience.

"Our estate suddenly seems very unimpressive," Anika said.

"I've heard the Aedyllanian castle is bigger," Gareth replied.

"We'll see if it still is when all is said and done back home." A note of heaviness marked Leo's tone, but then he shook his head and looked over at Gareth. "Ready to face your father?"

"Yes," he said quietly. "I think I am."

55

Sir Christopher was the first to greet them in the courtyard, his expression flickering between concern, awe, and confusion, then back to concern with a hint of what looked like an impending lecture.

"Sir Gareth." Sir Christopher's sharp eyes assessed them as Gareth dismounted from Tempest. "How…exceedingly unexpected. In multiple ways."

"Don't worry." Gareth flashed a grin. "Baron Tremblay granted me permission to return. I have urgent news for my father."

The concern in the knight's expression deepened to fear. "Has Aedyllan attacked?"

"No. I think they're preoccupied at the moment." Gareth motioned toward his companions. "I need to speak to my father at once, but Fury and Tempest need to be rubbed down and stabled, and Lady Anika and Master Leo Raylor of Aedyllan need guest rooms."

Still looking troubled, Sir Christopher nodded. "I'll see that it's done. I'm unsure what His Majesty is currently doing or whether he is otherwise occupied."

Gareth waved a hand, already headed toward the steps leading up to the massive double doors of the castle. "I'll hunt him down, and if he's doing something more important, perhaps I'll change my clothes." He hadn't changed clothing in days, but he'd rather speak to his father first.

Before he reached the doors, one creaked open, and someone burst onto the steps in a rush of blue and gold.

"Gareth!" Nathaniel paused as if to confirm it was him, then slammed into Gareth so hard they almost tumbled down the stairs. His arms clutched around Gareth's cuirass. "Why are you back already? Are you all right?"

He leaned back and gaped at the tear in the breastplate before peering up at Gareth's face. "What happened? We hadn't heard anything from you in so long we were worried something was wrong, and then Baron Tremblay didn't respond to Father's message asking about you. Now you show up here unexpectedly with a *rip* in your armor?"

Gareth couldn't help a laugh as he mussed Nate's hair. "Aw, I didn't realize you cared so much, little brother."

"It's been so *dull* with you gone," Nathaniel pouted, finally releasing him. He retreated up a stairstep. "And you're annoying, but still my brother, and I'm going to worry about…" His eyes bugged as he looked past Gareth's shoulder. "Is that a unicorn?"

"Indeed." Gareth glanced back to see a stablehand leading Tempest toward the stables. "That's Tempest. I'll introduce you later." He stepped around Nate. "Right now I need to see Fath—"

"Gareth!" Frederick emerged from the shadows in the doorway, his eyebrows low over his eyes and mouth twisting down.

Gareth barely stopped himself from groaning. "Hello, Fred."

His older brother's scowl deepened. "You aren't expected back."

"Great to see you, too," he muttered.

A servant woman murmured an apology as she led Anika and Leo past them into the castle. The twins cast him pitying looks before they went inside. Frederick glanced at them, his eyes narrowing further.

"Who are they?"

"Friends," Gareth grunted. "Where's Father? I need to speak to him at once."

"Reviewing reports on projected grain yields, I believe."

How thrilling that sounded. "Good. That sounds interruptible. *Where*, exactly?"

"In his study, but—"

Gareth sprinted past his brothers and down the hall, ignoring Frederick's demand that he stop.

The contrasting darkness after the sunshine outside forced him to slow down, and he blinked at the shadowy halls. Fastest route to his father's study…past the great hall, up the servants' staircase, down two more hallways, and…

There it was.

Gareth hesitated in front of the cherry wood door carved with a mountain range beyond ploughed fields. He started to check his clothes and hair, then decided that was a wasted effort. After taking a deep breath, he raised his hand and knocked.

There was no reply.

Either Frederick had told him incorrectly, or Father assumed anyone who was knocking could wait. Summoning his courage, Gareth gripped the handle and pushed the door open.

Father sat at a sprawling wood and marble desk before a gigantic lattice-work window. Scrolls, parchments, and ledgers cluttered the desk, and Father stooped over a stack of paper, a quill in hand and his hair mussed as if he'd been tugging on it. His crown rested atop a closed ledger, the gems inlaid in the gold winking in the sunlight streaming through the window.

"That was fast—" Father cut off abruptly as he lifted his head and their eyes met. "*Gareth?*"

"Let me start by saying Baron Tremblay did *not* send me back because I caused trouble." Gareth eased the door closed. He dragged his feet across the plush carpet, realizing belatedly he was rather dirt-coated for the king's pristine study. He stood beside an upholstered chair on the opposite side of the massive desk from his father and did not sit.

Father stared at him, then slowly placed his quill in an inkwell and settled back in his chair. His gaze traveled up and down Gareth, lingering on the jagged slit in his cuirass.

"What has happened?" Father asked at last, his voice heavy.

"Nothing affecting Eynlae," Gareth hurried to say. Some of the wariness in Father's eyes faded. "I do come bearing important news, but it can wait long enough for me to say something else first."

Now that it came to it, all the pretty speeches he'd been turning over in his mind during the last several days turned to smoke. Fear that Father's reaction would be a dismissive *finally, you fool; obviously I was right all along* tempted him to give up before trying. Shame heated his neck. He'd promised himself he would do this *without* assuming Father's thoughts.

The moments slipped by. His tongue stuck to the roof of his mouth as he searched for the right words. Well, he'd always said he wasn't an orator. Maybe simple was best.

"I'm sorry."

Father's entire body flinched. His mouth opened slightly, as if he weren't sure what to say.

"I've been pridefully narrow-minded." Gareth took a deep breath. "I insisted on believing there could only be *one* right choice, one correct way of dealing with problems, at the cost of ignoring the complexity of many situations. I have consistently failed to try to understand others' perspectives and reasoning. I wanted to believe the right thing to do was always whatever immediately felt right to my gut, which caused me to overlook nuances I shouldn't have, and worse, to assign cowardice or ill motives where there were none. I don't completely agree with everything you've done, but...I think I understand, and I believe that you did what you thought was best—and often what *was* best—for the most people, even if I couldn't see it."

He hung his head and winced at his grimy boots sinking into the maroon carpet. "I'm sorry for blaming you instead of listening. Sometimes there are no perfect choices. I see that now. We won't always agree on the best choice, and sometimes that hurts, but it was recklessly, stubbornly haughty of me to believe that compromise or even surrender are inherently wrong. It was worse of me to hate you for choices I refused to even attempt to understand. I'm sorry."

In the silence that followed, Gareth swore he could hear his own heart beating and the flow of blood in his ears. There was a creak and a shuffling sound, but he didn't raise his head as he waited for some response. Father's shiny boots appeared at the edge of his vision, and then a hand grabbed his upper arm. He braced himself—he wasn't sure what for. But then his father tugged him hard against his chest. The embrace was so tight, Gareth didn't know how his armor wasn't digging into Father's chest and arms.

He gulped, staring over his father's shoulder at an overstuffed bookshelf. "I'm really dirty—"

"I don't care." Somehow, Father's arms tightened further, and he leaned his head over Gareth's shoulder. "I always forgive you, my son. You are passionate and have a true core of justice, and yes, at times I have been frustrated with you, hurt by you. But you're also right that often there is no perfect choice. I won't claim I have never deserved your ire or have never doubted my own choices.

"And *I* am sorry. I'm sorry for my lack of patience with you. These weeks without you, after you seemed so pleased to leave and when you haven't written—it forced me to do some self-reflection, too, and I realized… Perhaps you were right, and I have been trying to force you to be someone you are not. I railed against your lack of comprehension without modeling equal courtesy in striving to understand and respect you. I never meant to drive you away, Gareth, and I'm sorry that I did."

Maybe it was everything that had happened over the last couple of weeks, or the exhaustion from their rapid travel across the kingdom, but Father's earnest words were more than Gareth could take. He had dared to entertain the possibility that he and his father could mend their torn and battered relationship, but it was more than he'd ever dreamed that Father would already be willing to acknowledge he *wasn't* perfect and even admit some blame.

With a strangled sob, Gareth returned the embrace and clutched fistfuls of the back of Father's soft tunic. His eyes squeezed shut as for the first time in what seemed like an eternity, he felt his father's love—or perhaps, he finally was willing to see and understand it.

The door creaked, and Gareth lifted his head and eased his grip on Father's tunic.

"Found it, Your Maj—oh." A clerk with a massive leather-bound ledger in his hands froze in place. "Um, I'll…" He set the book on the ground beside the door. "Excuse me, Your Majesty, Your Highness." The clerk bobbed a bow and scurried out of the study.

With a sigh, Father released Gareth, and they took a step back from each other. For a moment they regarded each other, both flicking away a few stray tears. Abruptly, Father tensed. He reached up and tilted Gareth's chin up and to the side, so more sunlight fell on his neck. He sucked in a gasp.

"What happened?" His words were jaggedly rough and demanding. Trembling fingertips brushed over the scar on Gareth's throat. "Who did this?"

"An Aedyllanian witch." He didn't quite succeed in keeping his tone casual and unbothered. "It's related to the other thing I need to tell you. The reason why Baron Tremblay gave me leave to return, even though I told him only a very minuscule part of it."

Father's expression turned stony. "Sit." He gripped the shoulders of Gareth's cuirass and guided him into a chair. "Clearly you have a story to tell, and I want to hear it from the beginning. In detail."

56

a, can't pull the same trick on me twice." Gareth grinned at Anika as he parried her swing, which had followed close behind an easily blocked thrust and a feinted cut from the other direction.

Anika adjusted her tactics, and Gareth had to fall silent again, focused on the fight and blinking sweat out of his eyes. This was their fourth duel of the day, and his arms and legs were beginning to burn with the exertion.

They'd moved from the knights' training field to a grassy lawn in the private gardens, as their sparring had drawn attention. It was only their third day at the Eynlaean palace and the first time they'd been able to get away from his family to spar, and it was awkward to have so many eyes following their every move. Observers weren't conducive to making a second attempt at romance, either.

Perhaps some would scoff at his idea of setting a romantic mood by spending time trying to hit each other with metal sticks and getting all sweaty while they were at it, but Gareth was having the time of his life. By the smoldering fire in Anika's eyes and occasional upward twist of her lips, so was she.

Her foot caught on some bindweed hiding in the grass, and sensing an opportunity, he pressed his advantage. His thrust was easily parried, but he'd hooked his foot behind Anika's ankle, and she fell backward with a panicked gasp and a sharp *oof.*

He followed her down, crouching above her as he placed the side of his blade—a dull one, at Sir Christopher's horrified insistence—against her neck. "Yield?"

"Yield," she sighed.

Grinning, he stood and offered her a hand.

She lifted an eyebrow and accepted his help to get back to her feet. "Don't look so smug. That just makes us tied again."

"Maybe I'm not counting anymore," he murmured as he tightened his grip on her hand and tugged her closer.

She stumbled toward him and dropped her training sword to catch herself against his chest. He let his own weapon fall to the grass and threaded his arm around her middle as their eyes locked.

Her hand on his sweat-soaked shirt drifted up to his neck, and her fingertips twined into the ends of his hair.

"Anika…" His voice came out in a low groan as her thumb stroked his skin beneath his ear. He gripped her waist, glad she was wearing a tunic and no rigid armor. When her lips parted and her breath brushed against his lips, he crumbled.

Gareth released Anika's hand, lightly grasped the back of her head, closed his eyes, and pressed his lips to hers. Her answering kiss drove all doubt from his mind…and all rational thought. As they deepened the kiss, he would have believed they'd drifted off the ground. There was no awkwardness or hesitancy left, just the warmth of the sun on their skin and the crackling heat of their kiss. It was delicious, and over too soon—any length of time would have been too soon.

But Anika pulled back, and Gareth reluctantly admitted he needed a moment to take deeper breaths. His eyes still closed, he leaned his head forward until their foreheads touched.

"I feel all tingly," Anika said, her voice breathy.

He chuckled softly. "I feel like I could walk through fire."

Her forehead left his, and he opened his eyes to see her shaking her head and grinning.

"I don't know what stories you've been reading, but kisses, even from an enchantress, do not make you invulnerable to fire."

"Have you tested that?"

"Obviously not."

He leaned closer. "Maybe we should test it." He mumbled against her lips, "For research."

"Mmm, yes, research…" Just as she started to kiss him again, a male voice intruded.

"What are we researching?"

Gareth pulled away from Anika with a loud groan. "*Leo!*"

Anika laughed as they both turned toward her twin—and Nathaniel, who was walking beside him. Just perfect.

"Looked to me like they were researching each other's mouths." Nate made a gagging face.

"Oh?" Leo blinked in feigned innocence and swung the large blanket-covered basket he carried. "Did she accept your courtship proposal?"

Gareth drew in a deep, exasperated breath through his nose. "No—"

"Good thing we brought dinner to interrupt this debauchery, then."

"Because you keep interrupting me before I have a chance to ask her again!" Gareth protested. "Ruining a perfectly romantic moment."

"You were just sparring." Leo set down the basket beside them. He sniffed. "And you smell like workhorses. Probably are starving like workhorses, too."

Running a hand through his hair, Gareth searched for a way to salvage this situation. Leo and Nathaniel nudged aside their practice blades and spread out the blanket. Anika laid a hand on his arm and motioned with her head away from their brothers.

They withdrew to the edge of the small meadow, into the shade of a sycamore tree.

"Did you have something to ask me?"

This wasn't how he'd pictured it, but maybe he could at least not bungle it up as badly this time. "Will you court me?" he asked softly. "With marriage in mind? Not that it's a promise or contract or anything, but I—I think I might love you. And I'd like to court you."

Anika smiled. "I didn't think I'd ever find someone who would ask me a question like that while I'm sweaty after practicing swordplay."

He grinned in return. "I never dreamed I'd find a woman who would train alongside me."

She reached out and clasped both of his hands, threading her fingers between his. "What about your father and court? I'm not a politically advantageous marriage."

"Thankfully, that's up to my father and not my brother or the court. Father, I think, will approve, or at least not forbid it. We're making progress." He pitched his voice lower. "But if he wants to disown me for choosing you, I'd happily let him."

To his surprise, she threw her head back and laughed. "Gareth, I think we both know you wouldn't be heartbroken to not be a prince, regardless."

His smile turned apologetic. "Actually…I don't mind the title as much as I used to. It does give me some power to do good that I wouldn't have otherwise. I keep thinking about everything Callista said. Had she and her family and friends and so many others had access to justice, if they'd had someone with influence who would have listened and fought for them not with a sword but in the court, Callista might never have stolen the prophecy. Maybe I can be that person. Someone who ensures no one in Eynlae is denied justice simply because they have no power. If there's a way for me to be a knight *and* a prince, that's what I really want. Would…that be all right with you? If we get married and I remain a prince, you'd be a princess, and that would mean sometimes we'd have to leave the armor behind and attend boring events."

Uncertainty and a bit of nervousness flickered in her expression.

"I'd help you learn everything you need to know," Gareth said quickly. "I'm kind of learning how to be a proper prince myself, anyway."

A short laugh escaped her.

He rubbed the back of her hand with his thumb. "We don't have to figure everything out right now. But I suspect, even more than I want to be a prince and knight, I want you. Will you court me?"

"You're not going to stop asking until I say yes, are you?" Anika teased, her eyes dancing.

"Or no. If you say no, I won't ask you again. I respect you too much for that."

Her expression softened. "I think I love you, too, my prince." She leaned forward and gently kissed his cheek, the feeling of her lips lingering long after she met his eyes again. "Yes. I want to court you. With marriage in mind. Whether you're a prince or a knight or both."

Someone cleared their throat, but the sound came from the direction of the castle, not the meadow where Leo and Nathaniel were chatting. Gareth turned his head toward the new intruder and nearly jumped out of his skin as a figure stepped out from behind the sycamore's trunk.

"Father!" He felt his entire face go red.

Anika dropped his hands so she could give an awkward bow,

as she wasn't wearing a skirt. "Your Majesty."

He tilted his head. "I suppose it is far too early in this court-ship for me to request you address me as *Father*."

Anika's mouth dropped open.

Gareth squinted. It wasn't the shadows of the foliage playing tricks on his mind. A playful smile graced Father's face.

"Then you approve?" Gareth asked, his optimism barely con-tained.

"Cautiously, based on what I know of her so far, yes." Father studied Anika for a moment before turning his attention to Gareth. "I can see you two value each other for who you already are." He tilted his head to the side to look past them, the move-ment somehow regal. "I was going to ask you to join me over din-ner to discuss something, but it seems you have other plans, so I won't draw you away."

A lump formed in Gareth's throat. "Discuss…something? Something serious?"

"Yes, but no need to look so nervous." Father smiled, but Gareth wasn't reassured. "Actually, overhearing you just now an-swered one of my questions."

"Questions?"

"Whether you still want to abandon your title."

"Oh." Gareth's shoulders fell, although he wasn't entirely sure why he felt so embarrassed and unsure of himself. As king, would Father accept Gareth's intention to be both knight and prince?

Anika shifted back a step. "I'm going to go see what our brothers brought. I'll see you soon, Gareth." She bowed again. "Your Majesty." Then she hastily withdrew.

Father watched her, then shook his head with a light chuckle. "She seems good for you."

"She's perfect."

"No one's perfect," Father said, his tone softly berating. "Don't put that pressure on her. But I see what you mean." He folded his arms, and Gareth mentally steeled himself. "Since I can see you're going to be distressed if I don't explain, I wanted to talk to you about retaining you as prince and keeping you in the line of succession, but pushing you down it. After Nathaniel. Which would make you third in line. Fourth if Angela has a boy in about five months."

Gareth whipped his head up. "Fred and Angela are finally having a baby?"

Father nodded. "The physician thinks all is going well, so they'll be announcing it officially next week. Even if this one is a girl, hopefully the next one will be a boy. They're young and have plenty of time. But with Nathaniel as second in line, even if they don't have sons, then Nathaniel and any sons he has would be crowned before you. It will also make your marriage to a young lady of low rank a non-issue, as she's unlikely to be a candidate for queen."

Numbly, Gareth nodded. He could still be a prince and not raise questions about his legitimacy by being struck from the succession entirely. "The lords will agree to this?"

Father snorted, an oddly undignified action for him. "I won't give them a choice, but I doubt they'll argue. As long as the succession is clear and secure, they don't care." His face fell. "As long as Eynlae isn't at risk of falling into war like Aedyllan."

"Thankfully," Gareth said with forced cheerfulness, "there aren't any prophecies about the downfall of our entire family." A sudden horror struck him. "Are there?"

"Goodness, no. Our ancestors were smarter than to make deals with or accept favors from the fae. Which I suppose you will have to be, too, if you're going to be traveling around Miraveld as a knight errant. Just because fae haven't been seen as much in recent centuries doesn't mean you won't run into one."

The air seemed knocked out of Gareth's lungs. "You'll let

me be a traveling knight?"

"On the condition you return often and are honorable in your princely duties." Father raised an imperious eyebrow. "And as your father and king, I'll have to insist you wed your lady knight first if you want to take her with you, so you may need to delay your travels for the duration of your courtship."

Gareth shook his head, smiling so wide his cheeks ached. "That's fine! I think I, uh, have some studying of princely duties to catch up on, anyway. I'd like to have a better understanding of the good I can do in both roles." He jabbed his thumb in the general direction of Leo. "And I have a new friend who will gladly lecture me endlessly on matters of ethics and philosophy and I'm sure would love to study any other topics with me."

Father's eyes appeared watery as he laid a hand on Gareth's shoulder. "That sounds wise, Gareth."

Winter had never been Gareth's favorite season. Typically, he was forced to spend more time indoors than he'd like.

Courtship was tempting him to reevaluate his attitude toward winter. Cold provided many opportunities for cuddling. A room illuminated by firelight, with the scent of pine pervading the air, was so cozy.

Even with Leo and Nathaniel acting as chaperones.

Currently, Gareth and Anika sat on a rug in front of a sitting room's massive fireplace while he braided her hair. Nathaniel sat in one of the big armchairs, fiddling with a puzzle box Raelyn had sent him. Stretched out on a couch, Leo had his nose buried in some academic book.

Gareth paused to examine his work. "I think I've finally got it down." Although Raelyn had taught him a simple three-strand braid, he'd been determined to learn the five-strand one after watching Anika do it.

A knock sounded on the door, and they all swiveled toward the entrance and shouted, "Come in!"

A servant entered with a bow. "Pardon the intrusion, Your Highnesses. An ambassador from Aedyllan just arrived, and he was carrying a letter for Master and Lady Raylor."

Anika leapt up with a gasp and rushed to the servant. Gareth watched with a mixture of defeat and amusement as the braid slowly unraveled. "Thank you!"

The servant bowed and departed.

Anika went to the couch and nudged Leo's legs. "Move."

Leo sat up and set aside his book, his expression more cautious than Anika's. Lord Raylor had written a few months ago to inform them that Cassius Alimer had been crowned, but the situation was still tense. They hadn't heard any news since.

Anika and Leo leaned together as they read the letter, and the smile on her face and the way Leo's expression relaxed eased Gareth's worries.

"They're all doing fine," Anika said. "The last of the dissenters have been dealt with. King Cassius even reopened the Royal University. Father says we can return home now—but only if the passage is safe." She frowned. "The date on this was nearly three weeks ago."

Leo sighed and flopped back. "The roads are becoming icy and probably slowed the ambassador. Which means travel home right now would not be safe."

"I agree." Gareth fiddled with a loose thread on the rug. "Is…staying here over the winter…objectionable?"

Another melodramatic sigh from Leo. "Depending on when we return, it might mean I won't be able to enroll in the Royal University as soon as I'd like. Otherwise, no. I'll happily stay in my massive room with access to your royal library."

Anika set the letter aside and returned to sit beside Gareth. "No, not objectionable, my prince. I'm disappointed that I'll have to wait another few months to see my family and friends, but I like living here with you. If I didn't, I'd have already broken off our courtship, silly." She planted a kiss on his cheek that made him blush.

Secretly, Gareth was also disappointed that he'd have to wait another few months to marry Anika. Lord Raylor had been clear he'd only granted permission for courtship, and Anika wanted to get married at her family's estate. Gareth had happily agreed, much to Mother's dismay. He didn't want an elaborate royal wedding.

Ah, well. A longer courtship with a woman he loved was far superior to an arranged marriage to a woman he'd never met.

White apple blossoms swirled across the field. The breeze played with the loose strands of red hair framing Anika's smiling face. Gareth fought tears as his breathtaking bride approached him in a pale-green dress with draping sleeves and a loose skirt that swayed with her movement.

The small gathering of her family and friends and the knights of Raylor Estate faded away until it seemed to Gareth it was just the two of them, holding hands and staring into each other's eyes. They repeated the vows the magistrate intoned and added their own promises—to always be each other's support and defense, to face their enemies together and remember when they disagreed that in marriage as in battle, they were a team and won or lost together.

When the magistrate declared Gareth could kiss his bride, he swept her into his arms, dipped her low, and kissed her while apple blossom petals showered over them.

Two days later, they saw Leo settled into the Philosophers

College dormitory at the Royal University. Leo insisted they tour all four colleges with him before they left—Philosophers, Mathematicians, Enchanters, and Linguists. The sprawling city at the base of the mountains and the imposing Highrook Castle perched above it were admittedly impressive. And as they toured the University, he thought he caught sight of a familiar tall, dark-haired woman—but she was seated with a small group outside a tea shop, smiling and laughing.

The next day, Gareth and Anika awoke at sunrise and donned the exquisite armor and weapons his father had gifted them before their departure for Aedyllan. They put their packs on Fury—Gareth might have snuck him a couple of apples as an apology while the other equines weren't looking—and mounted Graedyr and Tempest.

"Ready?" Anika asked with a twinkle in her eyes.

Gareth grinned. "I've been ready for months. Let's go on our honeymoon."

And by "honeymoon," they meant search for adventures to have, monsters to slay, and people to protect.

Epilogue

"You were right!" Anika shouted as she cut down another hissing cave serpent.

The gray-scaled creature, about as thick around as Anika and nearly as long as she was tall, writhed in the torchlight, its black blood sizzling where it sprayed over the rocks. Despite the steel armor they wore from helm to boots, they both sported burns.

"That this is Alexander's fault?" Gareth shouted back, his voice echoing above the hissing of the nest of serpents and the ear-grating scrape of scales against rock.

A serpent launched toward his face, its jaws unhinged as if the monster intended to swallow him whole. Considering they'd been investigating livestock that were disappearing around Mount Klainar without a trace, maybe swallowing him was a possibility. He kicked aside a smaller serpent and brought his sword down in a mighty arc, neatly cleaving a line down the middle of the attacking serpent. He turned his head, and most of the hot blood splattered against his helm, but a bit landed on his nose, which he quickly wiped away with his gloved hand.

Anika struggled against two small serpents twining around her legs and biting her greaves. With a low growl, Gareth seized the serpent on her right leg and pulled it back far enough to decapitate it. She sliced off the other one and darted back a couple of steps toward the entrance to the cave.

"Probably that too," Anika said, "but I meant when you said this would be an exciting detour, even if Raelyn is going to yell at us."

"Only if we tell her," Gareth said as he cut down two more snakes.

"We're going to arrive late. She'll know why."

There'd been a noticeable uptick in monster activity in the Forbidden Mountains since Alexander's curse had broken over two years prior, especially around Mount Klainar. Alexander had admitted he probably should have seen that coming. When he'd lived on Klainar, he'd blocked off passages in the mountain caves that reeked of monsters, but no one was repairing the blockades now. Many beasts probably had lain low to avoid his dragon form. Plus, Alex had confided to Gareth, after a chimera had killed Jasper's wife many years prior, he'd secretly spent a couple of angry nights slaying every monster he found.

But the curse was broken, so the dragon was gone. That was good for many reasons, except that the monsters had crawled back out of hiding.

Ah, well. Gareth now possessed a small collection of monster trophies, and he'd enjoyed the thrill of slaying a monster.

He was getting annoyed with cave serpents, though.

"Wolf's teeth, why are there so *many*?"

"I was just wondering the same thing!" Anika cut down another serpent. "Ugh, enough. Keep them off me."

Without waiting for a response, she set down her sword with a clatter and held her hands toward the torches they'd dropped on the ground behind them. Gareth moved in front of her as her palms glowed orange. The serpents' hissing intensified, and several flung themselves forward, as if they sensed what she was doing.

"The dragon's gone," Anika muttered. "But dragons aren't the only ones with fire."

Gareth recognized his cue and spun around behind her, just in time to avoid the torrent of flames his wife directed at the seething mass of gray scales, flicking tongues, and wicked fangs. The cave serpents screamed, and the heat pressed against Gareth even behind Anika.

All at once, the blinding flames died out, leaving only the sputtering torches, the stench of burnt snake, and dark spots dancing in Gareth's eyes. Anika tottered a bit, and he leapt back in front of her, ready to fend off any remaining serpents. Most of them were reduced to ashes, although a few writhed as they died, their scales smoking.

One final serpent that was larger than Gareth slithered out from the back of the cave, crushing its remaining brood. Patches of its scales smoldered, but it flashed long teeth before striking out at Gareth with terrifying speed.

"Drop!" Gareth leapt to the side, spun, and brought his sword down.

The serpent's large head darted past him and through empty air where Anika had been, as she'd dove to the ground at his shout. His blade bit into the creature's scales, and she rolled to the side, out of the path of its descending head. Gareth's swing followed the monster down, severing its spine as it crashed against the rocky floor. He braced a boot against its scaled side to tug his sword free before turning to check on his wife.

She was already up and collecting her sword, scowling at the dark blood covering the blade.

"How's your head?"

Anika winced. "Throbbing, but I'll be fine, especially after we get out of this cave."

The scent of burnt serpent was becoming overwhelming. "Agreed."

They wiped off their blades, then collected their torches, which were burning dangerously low, and followed the chalk markings they'd left on the tunnel walls.

"Well. That was exciting."

Anika laughed. "Never a dull moment with you, my love."

"I propose when we tell this story to our brothers, it was at least two hundred snakes."

"Oh, certainly, at *least*. Although Leo won't believe it."

Gareth heaved a dramatic sigh. "Neither will Fred, but he won't be able to prove it, so he won't say anything. Nate still believes anything I say, and Conrad is too proud of you to question it. But Leo, Leo, Leo…he hasn't even finished his university degree, but he thinks he knows everything."

"Considering the university has all but guaranteed him a professorship, his pride might be warranted," Anika noted. "Even if I wish he'd let me get away with a little embellishment in my own adventures."

"At least he'll back us up if we tell anyone else."

"Naturally. What are twins for but to call you out in private and swear to everything you say in public?" She laughed. "Raelyn, though…let's tell her it was fifty serpents."

As they stepped out of the cave into the blinding sunlight of midday, Gareth laughed. "Oh, definitely. Fifty at most, and it was easy. We're in for enough of a haranguing as it is. I don't know why she's so worried about us being *alive* to meet their twins. Obviously I'm going to live long enough to get to know my namesake." He scoffed.

"Your sister is sweet but has unrealistic expectations," Tempest said. *"And naming one of her boys after you has done nothing for your ego. How many of the foul snakes were there, truthfully?"*

"Hm." Anika lifted a hand to shield her eyes from the sunlight. Earlier that year, she'd expended too much magic in a fight against an ice hydra. Tempest had healed her, and ever since, she'd been able to hear the unicorn, too. "Around a hundred, probably."

Tempest shook her head. *I hate snakes.* She took a step closer. *Do you need any magic for your headache?*

"I'll be fine with some rest and water."

Anika patted her mare Graedyr on her way to Fury, who was carrying their supplies. Gareth frequently spoiled Fury in secret to make up for making him primarily a pack horse, but Tempest refused to carry their bags. Fury seemed ambivalent as long as he still received attention and was ridden regularly. And since Tempest would not participate in jousts, Fury was still Gareth's tourney mount.

Anika pulled off her helm and fished a canteen out of their bags. The sunlight set her copper braid ablaze and brought out the freckles on her cheeks and nose. Even the way the light accentuated her scars made her look fierce and awe-inspiring.

"You're beautiful."

Anika chuckled. "Even covered in cave serpent gore?"

"Hm." He frowned at the drying black blood on her armor and the burned patches on her exposed clothing. "Not my favorite look, to be sure, but even still."

"Oh? What's your favorite look?"

"A difficult choice…" Gareth gave her a wicked grin. "But I think you know."

"Scoundrel." Anika shook her head and took another long drink.

"You know you love me, my enchantress knight."

"That I do, my warrior prince."

The End

Want to know more about Marcus Alimer and Adriana Faine, daughter of Mortimer Faine?

The Crownless Prince

Releases December 1, 2023

A dreamer prince. A princess out of his reach. A second chance to keep their promises.

After four years of unjust imprisonment, a prince escapes to find his kingdom in ruins and his beloved princess engaged to a cruel man hiding his true nature in this gender-swapping retelling of Maid Maleen.

The Crownless Prince is a short novel set about two hundred years prior to *A Fated Quest*, and is part of Once Upon a Prince, a multi-author series of clean fairy tale retellings.

Also Available in The Miraveld Chronicles:

A Lonely Dance

A strong-willed crown princess cursed to spend her nights
at a ball she can't remember.
A lonely ambassador running from his past misdeeds.
Can Tristan dare to love the kind princess despite believing he's a villain unworthy of her affection? And can Ilara afford to love a man who doesn't trust himself?

A reimagining of *Twelve Dancing Princesses* about love and redemption. Book two in The Miraveld Chronicles (happens concurrently with *A Fated Quest*).

Acknowledgments

This book has been…interesting. First it was hard to find a fairy tale that felt like Gareth's story, then the plot ideas and characters came quickly. I knew from the beginning the book would deal with the insufficiency of strict black-and-white morality in a broken world that needs grace and mercy alongside justice, but the exact theme and Gareth's arc went through several iterations and tweaks. Then in writing—and especially in editing—this book swung several times between feeling like "this is easy!" and "this book is going to be the death of me." More than once I thought, "This is it—no more books after this." (However, my soul always ends up rebelling at the thought of quitting.)

So first of all, thank you to my family, friends, and the ladies in the Virtual Coffee group for your support, listening ear, sympathy on hard days, celebrations on good days, and encouragement. Thank you to my social media followers for your kind words and empathy on my vulnerable posts.

Thank you to everyone who read *A Thieving Curse* and loved Gareth and was excited for a Gareth book.

Thank you to my alpha and beta readers: Mom, Alexis, Becky, Kate, Laurel, Jessica, and Kelly. So many of your critiques and suggestions helped make this book stronger, and your laughter and positive feedback helped sustain me when I wanted to burn the manuscript. ;) Extra thanks to Mom for reading this several times and Kate for reading it twice.

Tatum Cito, thank you so much for the gorgeous cover illustration that is even more epic than I'd hoped it would be.

Finally, thank you to God, the only One capable of perfect

justice and perfect mercy, who has grace and compassion on me in my bad choices and messy attempts at right choices. I know I don't always properly honor the gift of the ability to write and publish that you have given me, but thank you for blessing my imperfect efforts anyway.

About the Author

Selina R. Gonzalez is a Colorado native with mountains in her blood and dreams that top 14,000 feet. She loves chocolate, fantasy, costumes, bread, history, superheroes, faux leather, things that sparkle, medieval Britain, snark, dogs, and Jesus—not in that order.

She loves to travel and has driven coast-to-coast in the US, visited Britain three times, and has a list of places to go as long as Pikes Peak is tall, but always comes back home to Colorado.

Make sure you don't miss any of Selina's future books by subscribing to her newsletter at:

SelinaRGonzalez.com/newsletter-subscription/

Reviews on Amazon, Goodreads, or the retailer or site of your choice are always greatly appreciated!